MUSIC
EDUCATION
HANDBOOK

Yehudi Menuhin with some of the pupils of the Yehudi Menuhin School. Right: Colin Carr (cello) with whom Menuhin performed Brahms's Double Concerto in Liverpool in November 1974. (Photo: Brecht-Einzig Ltd)

MUSIC EDUCATION HANDBOOK

A Directory of Music Education in Britain, with Reference Articles and Tables

Edited by
ARTHUR JACOBS

Consultant Editors:
Brian Trowell, King Edward Professor of Music,
University of London
Gordon Reynolds, Editor, 'Music in Education'

BOWKER
LONDON & NEW YORK

Published in the United Kingdom by Bowker Publishing Company

1976

© Bowker Publishing Company Limited, 1976

ISBN 0 85935 032 0

Printed and bound in Great Britain by
REDWOOD BURN LIMITED
Trowbridge and Esher

Contents

Foreword

Yehudi Menuhin

If my greatest sympathy and concern go out to the music teacher, it is because in my humble and amateur way I like to think of myself as one of them and, like them, know full well the eternal problem of reconciling one's exultant vision with the daily grind of endless routine. Yet we all realize that this vision must never falter; it must continually illuminate the routine. The most enlightened 'teaching' is that which manages ceaselessly to reshape the vision into more or less attainable form.

To teach is to convey, and to learn is to absorb: therefore it follows as the night the day that it is wrong to conceive of teaching as a one-way track. Rather is it an ebb and flow in which the teacher imparts a skill and an understanding and, as the results flow back to him or her on the tide, finds both the initiative and the rewards ideally and evenly distributed, receiving as much from the responsive pupil as he from the devoted teacher.

I think it of paramount importance that the young child be taught about the primary meaning and purpose of music to which certain oral musical traditions hold the key. For instance, I believe teaching means starting with the way in which various sounds made by the vocal cords carried deep tribal and spiritual significance on ritual occasions from time immemorial; progressing through the various simple woodwind instruments of the shepherd, the mountain calls from community to community, the emotional purpose of sound in festive dance, the hunt, burial or war; and arriving at the stage where such sounds turn into the co-ordination of formal music. Thus the child can be brought to see that our music too, although preserved in the dehydrated form of notation, is essentially a fossil record of some living moment of expression in its totality of thought, feeling and motion. Thus, by this very token, the purpose of playing is to resurrect forever the original moment of its creation in time and space, in all its depth and intensity. Music alone is able in its evocation of past experience, of emotion reflected in melody, to regenerate life.

We know in the full sense of sharing and recognizing, for instance, the reverence, exaltation, compassion and resignation of that early Protestant congregation in Leipzig when we listen to the St Matthew Passion of Bach. We can place it likewise in its exact period in history. We know it in a direct and magical way which no amount of historical study could possibly convey. Our hearts, our very bones are at one with that congregation and with Bach. In the same way we know our pastoral ancestry upon which respose our philosophies, our astronomy, and our meditative capacities; when we listen to a shepherd's flute on some remote Greek island, we understand why Hippocrates prescribed this haunting out-of-doors sound as conducive to convalescence. And when we listen to the drums of Africa, we realize how one's blood can be heated in preparation for the hunt. This miracle of sound become music: this transubstantiation should fascinate and galvanize child, student and teacher alike and carry them through the inevitable tedium and depression of effort which accompanies the learning of all techniques.

Whether music is actually taught as a part of the curriculum in schools or not, there should be to my mind an aural musical offering at the beginning of the school day, if only as part of a daily physical and mental hygiene. At my musical boarding school this is one of the moment which I most treasure: the children there, drawn from all quarters of the globe, gather at 8.45 a.m. and join in (and are joined by) music, singing, thought and silence. It is devotional and thoroughly non-denominational because it is so basic, so simple and so satisfying. The lungs are aired in measured cadence and pitch, the group is made one, their minds and hearts focus on the meaning of a short text, chosen from any one of the great philosophical or religious prophets and poets, and read by the Headmaster, and a minute of silence follows which enables inner voices to be heard. The communication with God — with the Universal in whichever form he appears to each and every child — thus ensures that the day is at least begun in the right spirit.

Music is for everybody — definitely not for professionals alone — from the healthy to the disabled, the handicapped and the sick. Teacher courses and institutions must, therefore, be based on every kind and level of musical activity from passive reaction and participation to the highest performance. Today especially, when music is recognized as the prime mover of personal and communal fulfilment, when fields of application range from therapy to electronics and from ethnology to technology, the teacher (or the team of teachers available in institutions) plays a cardinal role in preparing a future harmonious society, by which I mean one capable of resolving dissonances. For my part, at the Yehudi Menuhin School, I have from its inception stressed that our goal is as much to offer society a first generation of dedicated, professional teachers as it is to produce orchestral or virtuoso performers: the perfect result would be to prove that the two are indeed inseparable.

In line with the 1944 Education Act — which would seem to encourage a flexible approach, bringing each student the formation matching his aptitudes and talents — I wish to put in a word for the boarding school, not only in its traditional role as prep or public school, but as among the choices open to the child who, by nature of his background and his particular talent, cannot grow optimally without belonging to a small community. Such a child may, as well, be without home or family and may therefore need all the more that special atmosphere of a community dedicated to a musical, theological, military or scientific way of life around the clock.

Teachers are by far the most valuable members of society, which has not done nearly enough to encourage and elevate the calling. We have a long way to go before we reach the point of more or less knowing what it is we must give our younger people — what constitutes even a fraction of what they desperately need in order that they and we may do justice to a future and pay homage to a past. Teaching, however, is not only an isolated profession: it is really part of the daily existence of everyone from parent to infant, from professor to street-cleaner. Let us remember the benefit to the teacher, for we do not begin really to know what we think we know until we begin to teach; nor can we discover all we do not know until we try to teach, an experience both enriching and humbling. It behoves us, therefore, to be generous whilst hoping to hide our ignorance! Thus socially we renew and invigorate ourselves by sharing the curiosities, the feelings, the gratitude of our younger friends.

May I also make a plea that the actual performance of music should take a larger part in music teachers' training at a College of Education? And that more use should be made of practical performing musicians as teachers — who, though they may not have all the academic qualifications necessary in the pedagogical sense, can nevertheless bring the irreplaceable experience of performance to the student? If we make a comparison with the ballet, we must recognize that the training of young people in the most exacting of art-forms cannot be achieved without the vitality and presence of the skilled performer. Even at university level, as in the ethnological study of comparative forms of physical expression in dance and mime, we would still benefit from the living example.

And finally let us praise excellent ideas: I applaud the high standard and timelessness of the articles in this first *Music Education Handbook*. May it reach into every musician's heart as it does to the heart of the matter. Music has the extraordinary power of co-ordinating spirit and matter, thought, mind and heart. It is wonderful to see the spontaneous and voluntary discipline which it evokes in its own service. This contribution of self-discipline is perhaps more than ever important today when other disciplines have lost their hold. The value of music for the individual and for society cannot be too highly stressed, for cultural values are indeed rooted in natural instinct — and the summoning forth of such values creates the best in mankind. Nietzsche said: 'Perfect things teach hope', and the teaching of perfect things such as music likewise brings hope.

Editor's Introduction

'Down with school music! Up with music in schools!' I make no apology for quoting the final words of an article I wrote a dozen years ago (March 1964) in the *Musical Times*. The launching of the present *Music Education Handbook* springs from a conviction that music education is too much isolated from music in its other aspects — and perhaps also from education in the more fundamental sense of that word. Music as a career; music as a curriculum subject at school and college; music as professional training; music as recreation, as historical knowledge, even (as Yehudi Menuhin suggests in his Foreword) as providing direct insights of 'a philosophical nature — all these are inter-related, and all demand rigorous yet free-ranging discussion.

Some of the articles in this book attempt a direct contribution to that discussion; others are intended to guide the teacher and student more practically. The Directory section of the book defines the range of action by setting out — in more detail than ever before in a single volume — the institutions and personnel of British music education. Much of this tabulation has been taken from the larger, more expensive *British Music Yearbook*, now approaching its fourth (1976) edition. But all the material in the present book has been specifically selected, updated and revised for its purpose, and much is completely new.

The *British Music Yearbook* itself will continue to have a section devoted to education, but not in such detail as here. Other sections of the *British Music Yearbook*, for instance those on Music Libraries, Competitions and Festivals, will continue to be of special interest to teachers, students and educational administrators.

My editorial thanks are due to Mr Menuhin for his Foreword, to my distinguished consultant editors and contributors, and to many institutions which have responded fully and conscientiously to requests for detailed information; also to Ms Susan Clarke and Ms Meredith Sutcliffe for their unfailing help in the compilation of the work. Suggestions for the improvement of the work in future editions will be gratefully received by me at Erasmus House, High Street, Epping, Essex CM16 4BU.

ARTHUR JACOBS
London, autumn 1975

Section One

TEACHER AND STUDENT

Crisis and Opportunity in School Music

Brian Trowell
King Edward Professor of Music,
University of London

What crisis? Where's the fire? In an age when crises seem to boil up three times a week, many readers of this book — even if they are music teachers — may feel that they can excuse themselves from reading about yet another.

There are many music teachers, after all, who lead perfectly satisfying lives practising their art in congenial surroundings with good resources and a reasonable work-load. These are likely to be employed in a rather privileged kind of school, either a public school or one with highly selective entrance procedures; or they may teach in a university or college of music (though such institutions are now just beginning to feel a cold draught); or they may perhaps be private or peripatetic instrumental teachers, more concerned with the gifted individual pupil than with the musical culture of a whole school, let alone the country at large. Many other teachers, though, will certainly not need me to tell them that there is a crisis: if their reactions are sceptical or jaded, it will be because they are exhausted by long struggling and hope deferred, because they believe that the system is bound to defeat them, because they are giving it up to teach English or maths instead.

Nobody who is in any way responsible for the provision of good music-teaching in our schools can afford to stand aloof from what is happening. Head teachers and departmental heads in state schools (particularly primary and middle schools), music advisers to local authorities, music teachers in colleges of education, the school music inspectors of the Department of Education and Science — these are in the front line and know only too well the dangers that the immediate future holds. But the crisis must also affect anyone who cares about the nation's musical well-being: parents, students and potential music teachers, of course, and also careers advisers, librarians, municipal advisers and administrators, the Arts Council and its regional equivalents — who can fail to be concerned? At a time when music has never before been so freely available, when the nation has never before spent so much money on music and musical education, almost nobody wants to teach music in a state primary or middle school, and the supply of well-trained teachers in the senior school is also failing.

Sitting in your senior common room, or snatching a quick coffee in the staff club of a busy music college, you may well not have known about it; worse, you may have thought that it did not really affect you. But some university music departments must have noticed that they are not getting as many bright and well-prepared applicants for entry as they might have expected; and all music colleges continue to deplore the shortage of good violinists, who have to be identified well before the age of eleven. The indifference that many of my colleagues in both types of institution show (I have taught in both) is the strongest possible condemnation of the wasteful triplication of resources and the divisive class-system that we have allowed to develop in our institutions of higher musical education — the universities, the music colleges, and the colleges of education.

Some of the problems in our schools are, of course, social problems which may perhaps be eased, but rarely solved, by devoted teachers. In any case, the sensational horror-stories of inner city schools attract too much attention away from the wider problem of switched-on tellies and switched-off parents, which can affect the grammar school quite as much as the comprehensive. But I am no expert in these matters, and my purpose here is the limited one of pointing out some of the difficulties that bedevil school music. I take on the job with many misgivings, for I have never taught in a school. I did attend one, though; most of the students I have taught, whether at university or at music college, had come straight from school, and talked to me about their experiences. So, of course, did dozens of other aspiring students at interview; and many of my ex-students have returned to tell me of their experiences as schoolteachers or lecturers in colleges of education.

Through university responsibilities and through work with the Council for National Academic Awards, I have become fairly familiar with the music departments of many colleges of education, their staffs, resources and methods, and with various proposals for the B Ed in Music and other degrees that they are hoping to develop. Finally, I have become involved with the task of helping to re-structure A-level examinations in music. All this has thrown up many questions, some fairly fundamental, and a good number of facts which were new to me and may be to others. My intention here is simply to repeat some of the questions in the hope of starting some honest and informative discussion: I do not have the direct experience, nor have I undertaken the necessary research, to provide answers to them. All the same, I shall mention several positive opportunities which we appear to be neglecting at present.

Goals and boundaries

Education for what? For the appreciation, interpretation and perform-ance of music? — and if so, what music? — or for the deeper levels of creativity, originality, improvisation and composition? Redder blood than mine has been spilt in the battle between traditionalists and experimentalists. Of course it all depends on the teacher; but genius is rare, and the conservative and often too brief training that many teachers receive makes them prefer the path of routine and safe results. Can we blame them, when the prestigious high-culture music of our concert-halls and opera-houses (not to mention many universities and music colleges) is itself so conservative and backward-looking? All the same, we should be aware that live performances of this kind of music are attended by only about 3% of the population, the comparatively well-off and highly-educated, and that the whole expensive apparatus could collapse if the economic climate grows worse. Should we not train our performers to be more self-reliant and to question accepted values, and steer them towards their own local community rather than towards the bright lights of the profession? Why should everyone of serious pretensions feel obliged to head for the artifical Mecca of London, to lead a rootless, anonymous existence in an 'international' culture that has few real roots in the broader musical life of the country?

And what of the less gifted? Those who were born outside that well-off and highly-educated 3% will start with a tremendous disadvantage, certainly so far as academic music is concerned. Most 'high culture' music, too, rewarding as it is for the initiate, is wordless instrumental music, not obviously functional: the sonata, concerto and symphony developed very late in musical history, and their appreciation exacts a very high degree of sophistication from the listener. Opera is also an extraordinarily stylized form, and usually comes, like Bach cantatas and Byrd masses, with foreign words attached. In trying to share our own sophisticated enthusiasms with the naïf, we sometimes talk of 'building bridges'; should we not remember that from the other bank the bridge too often looks like a drawbridge leading into the rather forbidding ramparts of high culture? Why should our whole examination system (and insecure teachers prefer a centalized examining authority) lock out or alienate so many musical children because they have grown up in the present with little sense of the past? When we condemn the shortlived fashions of Pop culture as 'disposable', are we not forgetting that Handel's operas and Bach's Passions were in their time every bit as 'throw-away'? Even ritual medieval plainsong never froze solid as our classical tradition has, but continued to develop right into the 16th century; the stolid Lutheran chorale kept on slowly changing over 300 years.

On the other hand, someone will now mention babies and bathwater. And someone else will complain that there are no longer any standards by which to teach or judge original composition: a circular argument, since it has been the weight of conservative taste that has served to push many composers into an extreme position. You can do more or less anything with concrete. Some architects nevertheless manage to use concrete imaginatively enough for particular functions in particular contexts. Should we not put our weight behind the movement to get 'curriculum music' into a functional relationship with other performing arts, with language, drama, mime and dance? Hard to examine, of course, and much of the resulting composition, perhaps, would not stand up as self-sufficient music. But can a culture support a great composer without dozens of second-rank composers and hundreds of third-rank ones?

The primary and middle school

The shortage of specialist music teachers affects schools for all ages, and by no means only in the inner city areas, but its consequences are most serious for the primary and middle schools. My own daughters, during a (combined) seven years' attendance at a new state primary school in a middle-class neighbourhood, never once encountered a specialist music teacher; they were lucky for about three of those years to learn the recorder from a conscientious 'supportive' music teacher who could also splash through a hymn on the piano. But there was no specialist for this supportive teacher to support. When she left, the mums banded together and started a highly successful recorder class, out of school hours. What would have happened in a less privileged area?

Countless advertisements in the educational Press produce no applicants for what are called 'scaled music posts', for specialist music teachers. One LEA with good intentions and a previously good record for music has had to resort to the expedient of appointing 'area music teachers', each of whom is responsible for the specialist direction of music-teaching in no less than 13 primary schools. The same unlucky number recurs in a recent document in which 13 LEAs reported that their lack of music specialists was 'critical'. No wonder that the DES has declared that music is now a national 'shortage' area for teacher supply. Let us hope that the declaration has come soon enough to save some of the teacher-training places that were due to vanish in the re-organization of the colleges of education.

There are many schools today, particularly but not only in urban areas, where the children are receiving no planned or continuous musical experience or musical education of any substance. In some there is no provision at all. The most impressionable years are left fallow. Children arrive at middle school with no experience of organized music-making and little interest in it. Some five years ago, a survey of children at O-level age revealed that they found music the least enjoyable and least useful of all curriculum subjects — far below Religious Education and Latin. This area of acutest crisis and greatest opportunity, the primary and middle school, is staffed almost exclusively (where it is staffed at all) by music teachers and supportive teachers trained in Colleges of Education. Specialist teachers trained in university depart-ments and music colleges, whose studies are now topped up with a one-year course for the postgraduate certificate of education, make for the secondary schools — partly because they lack the special training for teaching younger children, and may have unhappy memories of how they themselves were taught at that age, but largely (one imagines) because they feel safer with a familiar examination structure and because there are better facilities for the more gifted children. Colleges of education also provide about half the teachers for the upper age-range.

At secondary level

In the secondary school timetable there are supposed to be periods of music for all classes until the point where children start to specialize in particular subjects to be taken in public examinations. Much can be achieved here by a lively teacher, even with children who have hitherto had little or no regular music; but in a 'difficult' school, the temptation to burke the general class teaching and concentrate on the few more gifted children must be great. Many children — probably most — now hold classical instruments in their hand for the first time. Piano, woodwind and brass can be started with some hope of success at the age of eleven; but for a string-player, since results are slower to appear on the violin and the physical problems of co-ordination are greater, eleven is a dangerously late age to begin (besides, the thing is sissy). After a couple of years, the teacher will have some idea which of his performers has a quick enough ear and intellect to attempt an O-level or CSE in music; there are also, of course, the Associated Board (or other) practical and theory examinations.

The child performer's work may, however, become dissociated from his curriculum studies. He may receive his individual instruction out of school hours, perhaps from a teacher unconnected with the school; or he may receive it during a period stolen from some other disciplines. This is apt to cause annoyance, and make music lessons into an embarrassment and a nuisance. The child may find that he cannot use his performing skill to the full to gain credit in the public examination system. This situation is now changing, but examining authorities tend to use Associated Board grades rather than set up their own practical examinations. Such an arrangement saves the authority time and money, but it leaves the child out of pocket; and the practical skills become regrettably divorced from the historical and theoretical side of the examination. Some CSE boards handle this side of things much better than the GCE authorities.

I have already suggested that O-levels and A-levels in music are often far too 'academic' and tradition-biased. If the performer is ever to gain the true academic respect that he deserves in school society, then the dignity, the self-discipline, the developed sensibility and the intellectual qualities inherent in excellent performance ought surely to be rewarded with a separate A-level examination. Not all performers have a turn for history or musical theory as it is currently taught, and those who play melody instruments or sing are sometimes at a considerable disadvantage in theoretical work as against a pianist or organist. But a respectable amount of well-motivated study of history, theory and ear-training could be built up around the child's interest in his instrument, around the pieces he plays, their form and expressive content, and related problems of interpretation and performance practice. Should not all responsible teachers be pestering the examining authorities for so sensible a reform?

While they are about it, they should also be asking for the ear-tests and theory at O- and A-level to be made simpler and more relevant to the musical experience of the child and his school community. These aspects of study, along with the history and formal analysis, should be centred on a much longer list of set works, most of which should be the kind of piece that the child might perform or at least have some chance of hearing 'live' in his locality. Much more than knowing a lot about music, the would-be professional musician needs to know a lot of music. As it is, universities have to spend at least two terms un-teaching their music students, trying to show them how historical studies, analysis and performance should go hand in hand and inform each other. Most A-level history papers at present are superficial studies in chronology, not history at all: they tend to cover far too wide a period and encourage the student to cram and regurgitate whole sheaves of parrotted notes, often dictated by the teacher. A serious music student needs to know where and how to find things out, not merely what tricks of memory to play. If all examining boards took the more sensible line that the Joint Matriculation Board is now moving towards, a good many more performers would be encouraged to take O- and A-levels; this in turn would help to make a minority subject more viable and would integrate performance studies with school work. There would have to be more Mode III (school-based) syllabuses — and why not?

There is also a crying need for a music examination that the non-professional might take. Years of tutoring in adult education have shown me what can be achieved in the way of intelligent commentary on music by students who cannot read notation. In point of fact, thanks to my diligently pushing operatic vocal scores in front of such students over a three-year period, several who could not read music eventually cottoned on and learned how to. They could have done this more easily at school age than in their forties and fifties. The technical requirements at O- and A-level are at present so fierce that, given the rival claims of different disciplines and the inevitable timetabling difficulties, the child who wants to develop an intelligent interest in music without any professional ambitions is simply advised to try another subject. Our thinking is excessively dominated by the printed page: you do not have to be able to read music in order to have a good ear or even to perform well, as the entire body of medieval minstrels, numbers of jazz virtuosi, and generations of opera-singers have proved.

The music teacher's career

The teachers could have transformed the public examinations by now if they had really wanted to. In fact, there is already a healthy wind of change blowing from the livelier state schools and generated by some of the new CSE syllabuses. The wonder is that it took a separate kind of examination to stir up some activity. The British sense of hierarchy remains amazingly strong. The old Oxbridge B Mus or Mus B, and the BA in music that was later modelled on it, were in their time perfectly sound and progressive solutions to the problem of furnishing cathedral organists and public school teachers with an academically respectable degree in music; but the kind of thinking that these original degrees represented has remained in force in the curriculum of most of our junior universities, and in the public examinations that prepare students for entry to them, long after the need for such training has shrunk: it now answers to only a tiny proportion of the musical needs of our society. Formidable indeed is the Voice of Authority from the bastions of High Culture.

Yet that is not the whole story. What music teacher in a state school has the time to think? — assuming he could stop the perpetual tunes-in-the-head that seem to prevent most musicians from thinking clearly at all except by fits and starts. Even discounting social problems and indiscipline, the music teacher has a much more demanding job than most of his colleagues. True, he may have less marking to get through, but the claims on his extra-curricular time are exceptionally heavy, and the tasks of rehearsing, conducting, practising, and arranging concerts constitute equally exceptional demands on his emotions and vital energy. The authorities could put this right by lessening his curricular teaching or putting him on a shift system, but will they? I doubt it, for that would give rise to similar demands from physical education and drama teachers, not to mention Mr X who looks after the Stamp-Collectors' Club. Nor, I suppose, would a teachers' trade union plead the musician's special case. All the same, I am convinced that this factor is an important discouragement to many useful musicians who might otherwise enter the schoolteaching profession; in the case of those already teaching, it combines with the ever-increasing shortage of new recruits to make the teacher's difficult life absolutely intolerable. A musician can perhaps get used to doing the work of two or three men — but not 13!

The training of music teachers

A further discouragement to those thinking of entering the profession is the nature of the training which a music teacher may receive in some Colleges of Education. Let me repeat that virtually all the music teachers in primary and middle schools in the state system, and about half those in secondary schools, have come up by this route. The courses such teachers have taken have included hefty dollops of Education with a capital E, and the thinking behind such courses is now being institutionalized in the new B Ed degrees that are currently extending their scope all round the country. Not all are identical, but the basic philosophy behind most of them is this: 'The degree is in Education, not in Arts or Science or Music, and therefore the greater part of the student's time must be spent on Education — its Theory, Philosophy, History and Psychology'. In other words, what ought to be the ancillary element has become the main content. One proposal for a B Ed (Ordinary), a three-year degree with teaching qualification, expects to unload specialist music teachers in our schools with as little as four terms' training in basic musical skills; a four-year B Ed (Honours) would have five terms' music. That would not be nearly enough even if music were only half the complex subject that it is, and if the students were twice as gifted as they usually are. Many are potentially very able late developers, but most have failed, or would fail, to get into a university or music college.

If I were a candidate for entry to such a degree course, I should want to read all the specifications of the course-units and syllabus very carefully indeed. I should wish to be assured of exactly how much *musical* training was offered, and how consistently it was pursued throughout the three or four years of the course (in some colleges you may well find that a whole year is devoted to Education studies, with precious little time for you to practise). It must have been a very brilliant Educationist indeed who first decided that the personal intellectual development of the B Ed student, the 'widening of his cognitive horizons' as the weird poetry runs, should be pursued through the study of the Theory, History, Philosophy and Psychology of Education, and not through the special love or skill that had actually led the student to take up teaching, and in which he wished to become an authoritative instructor.

Towards a theory of musical education

Many of the present problems in the training of music teachers would never have arisen if university music departments, who ought to be powerhouses of the theory of the art, had looked up a while from their concentration on such vital and absorbing matters as 16th-century polyphony or 18th-century fugue, to examine how music was faring in the social and cultural conditions of contemporary Britain. The university Institutes of Education up and down the country have usually been far too concerned with the 'Central Disciplines of Education' to found chairs and readerships concerned with the teaching of a particular skill such as music. There are a few distinguished musical educationists, and we badly need more — but they have more or less taught themselves, and are not to be found in university Faculties of Music.

There appears to be regrettably little source material published in the field of musical education, and very little co-ordinated research going on, except in the psycho-physiological and cognitive aspects of the subject. The DES must have gathered a great deal of useful information about school music, but they do not normally make it public. (They will however show it to a *bona fide* researcher.) Their inspectorate, unlike the officials of the ILEA, do not speak out at meetings or make public pronouncements. If they organize a conference, the proceedings are a state secret. This is surely to be regretted. If protocol forbids a change of policy, may I at least invite the DES to make funds available to start up an authoritative Journal of Research in Musical Education? There is at present no central forum in which music teachers from all kinds of institutions, in primary, secondary and tertiary education, can come together to share their views and experience. Could this perhaps be a function of the new UK Council for Music Education?

Meanwhile, this book for the first time brings together in one place a great deal of useful information about the institutions and people who are responsible for our musical education. Students and teachers alike — or those contemplating either role — should read it carefully and use it as a basis for questions. The persistent, intelligently inquiring individual will soon find his way to others of like mind, and will learn which doors to knock at. The present system grew as it did because particular persons and committees — which consist of particular persons — took particular decisions. Most administrative structures are run by benevolent, hard-working men and women who are only too glad when someone rings up or writes in to talk common sense to them or to give them the rare chance of learning how their decisions affect the outlying worker at the coal-face.

The Local Education Authority and the Gifted Young Performer

John Hosier
Staff Inspector for Music,
Inner London Education Authority

'Is it possible to give adequate training to the gifted musical performer within an ordinary educational system?' asked the *Guardian* in an article about the Full-Time Course for Young Musicians run by the Inner London Education Authority at Kingsway-Princeton College. The question was, in this instance, answered affirmatively.

A number of LEA colleges (technical, polytechnic, further education) are running specialized music courses in recognition of the special needs of talented young instrumentalists. These courses, together with the numerous Music Centres up and down the country that operate on Saturdays and in the evenings to develop instrumental skills, indicate the seriousness with which the public sector of education can assume its responsibility towards identifying and nuturing individual talent. This is not elitism. It is an acceptance of the implications behind the 1944 Education Act, which imposed on education authorities a duty to provide 'such variety of training as may be desirable for the different ages, abilities and aptitudes of pupils, including practical instruction'.

In the empirical, instinctive, haphazard, amateur way of a great deal of British education, this is our compromise between the methods of private enterprise of the West and the detailed methodological legislation of certain East European countries. In Hungary, for example, the state has taken on the responsibility of drawing up the detailed programmes and syllabuses to meet the needs of musically gifted children. These children begin their musical education in a music primary school. Then at 14, if they wish to become professional musicians, and if they show enough talent, they take an entrance examination to a conservatory, where they undergo an intensive and systematic training for four or five years, before going on to the Academy at Budapest, or a teachers' training college. Each conservatory is run in association with a secondary school where the children receive

The views expressed are those of the author and do not necessarily represent those of the Authority.

their non-musical education for 24 hours a week. At the conservatory they take their principal instrumental study (two hours' individual tuition a week), plus piano, aural, music theory (written skills, analysis, harmony etc.), music literature, orchestra or choir, and towards the end of the course, folk-music and chamber music. There are five such conservatories in a country with the same population as London!

It is totally impractical, of course, ever to imagine the possibility of a wide-scale musical training at such an intense level in Britain, where our philosophy of education, our attitude to 'culture', the status of music, the wide variety of musical influences working on children, and the training of teachers go against a systematic and consolidated musical education. We may claim, of course, that we have orchestras and ensembles that are amongst the best in the world. But this high standard has been developed in spite of our system rather than because of it. It is the result of a fight for survival in a highly competitive profession. The British orchestra's celebrated facility for sight-reading has probably grown out of desperation, because of the absurdly inadequate rehearsal time that is usually allotted to concerts.

Even for our own needs, old procedures have shown themselves inadequate. For some years we have faced a great shortage of good string-players. Teachers at our music colleges complain about the technical inadequacies of students when they arrive for full-time training. Their three years in a college are usually a fight against time, particularly with string-players. One of our most distinguished cello teachers, Joan Dickson, has told of her experience of going abroad for postgraduate studies, only to find herself an amateur compared with the Continental students, and having to get down to working at basic technique. This is an experience shared by many of our young instrumentalists who go to summer schools abroad.

This inadequacy in basic training is now compounded by a gradual erosion of bourgeois cultural values. Except where a special Russian-Jewish tradition in string playing exists, it has been on the whole from middle-class musical homes and with the encouragement of parents that the bulk of our young string players have come. In an egalitarian society, it is hard to have to admit that this is true, yet those of us who run youth orchestras, particularly in urban areas, can almost draw a map of where, socially speaking, the various kinds of instrumentalists come from. The decay in such recruitment is alarming.

It may be objected that the traditional orchestra, the 'penguin platform' and the opera house are dying. But it remains part of the function of musical education to produce those performers who will maintain our contact with the tradition of European post-Renaissance music and find fulfilment in it, performing for those comparative few who derive spiritual and emotional sustenance and exhilaration from it. A healthy culture needs the masterpieces of the past as a context for the present. Moreover, the developing of a skill through exercising it in the music of the past also produces those performers who will provide our society with the sort of music it demands — contemporary music, the instrumental backings to Pop, signature tunes, incidental music to TV westerns, jingles, and the means to a coaxing atmosphere in the supermarket.

Schools and Music Centres

The more the state takes over the responsibility for education, the more important becomes the role of the local authority in providing not merely for classwork, but for specialist instrumental training. The training of young instrumentalists must be the result of a sensible collaboration between the school and the education authority.

Musical talent needs to be identified and trained early; for string players in the primary school, if possible. The child must start with sound basic instruction and good technical habits. He will soon need the opportunities and disciplines of ensemble work to help his sight-reading and intonation, and to give him the satisfaction and challenges of making music with good, or better, players. Even where schools, with the participation of visiting teachers, can provide instrumental lessons, they are not usually in a position of giving ensemble opportunities at a high level for their most talented players; nor is there usually scope for giving the more gifted children intensive training in general musicianship. Primary schools are desperately short of musically experienced and confident teachers, and the role of the secondary school teacher has become more and more complex. The old, amorphous 'school music' is beginning to be transformed into a variety of 'musics' that happen in school.

To keep pace with this, the music teacher has to be conductor, composer, choir trainer, creative catalyst, manager, instrumentalist, ethnologist, historian, therapist, folk-singer, pop enthusiast, media operator, manipulator of traditional skills, and examination crammer. No three years of teacher-training or college of music course can possibly provide a thorough preparation for all of these. More and more, therefore, the local authority must provide facilities from its central resources to support those aspects of music in school where help is needed. Hence the importance of Music Centres serving a whole LEA area (and, in practice, functioning mainly in the evenings and on Saturdays). By pooling the available instrumental teaching talent, Music Centres can supply an essential for developing instrumental skills at a high level, providing ensemble opportunities worthy of the best young talents.

Often these Music Centres are the only available means of ensuring continuity in systematic training in general musicianship. They provide the necessary atmosphere for purposeful and concentrated work in music, which the committed young musician needs. A local authority which provides them may at the same time support the Junior Exhibition Schemes at the main music colleges, but these are useful only for those children living fairly near the colleges. Often, for financial reasons, the colleges themselves have not allocated their most experienced teaching staff to work with these younger students on Saturdays.

Music Centres, therefore, have a crucial role. They, like the youth orchestras, are not intended to cream off the talent from the school, but to feed back into it young players who will enrich its musical life by taking part in its activities with more technical assurance and musical maturity. The pressure of places in Music Centres does mean that only children who already show some instrumental aptitude can be given places, so that the initial responsibilities for starting children on instruments and giving them their basic training must usually take place in school. Teachers who have been trained to deal with general classroom situations are not always the best equipped to advise and train potentially gifted instrumentalists in the appropriate conditions. This usually takes professional expertise that is only found in the experienced performer. What a pity that, at present, we do our best to keep such practitioners out of our schools! (Most of the best instrumental teachers and ensemble directors are not deemed 'qualified' by the present regulations.)

The drawback of the Music Centres, with their limited hours of operation, is that they cannot provide for regular musical activities during the week or for supervised practice. But with the growth in comprehensive schools, there could be more experiments with music-biased courses within the school framework. Talented young instrumentalists would have systematic training in their first- and second-study instruments, timetabled and supervised practice, a variety of ensembles and orchestras, and general musicianship work in small groups. Young musicians would find this a stimulating musical environment, but they would also undertake general academic studies with other children as at a 'normal' school. Those children on the music-biased course who may lose their commitment (and this sometimes happens) can move over completely into the main school without the disruption that could happen if they were at private specialist music schools, where a failure to do well would mean a change of school at a critical age. Some of the results already obtained in this direction by the Pimlico School in London are very encouraging. Other schools listed on p.170 have instituted similar programmes.

The instrumentalist and GCE

By the age of 16, young instrumentalists should know the nature of their commitment to music. If they are specially talented, this is the right age to concentrate single-mindedly on preparing for a career in music. At this age it is still not too late to rectify bad physical habits in playing. It is more important to make full-time training available at this stage — approximately the two years between O- and A-level — than to add automatically another two years on to the end of course at a college of music. The Gulbenkian report* recommended making grants from the age of 16 to students seeking a career as performers. Local authorities with a pool of first-rate instrumental teachers to draw from can arrange this preliminary full-time training under the aegis of their Colleges of Further Education or Polytechnics. Several courses are already operating up and down the country. But basic approaches vary.

Unfortunately the task of preparing for O- and A-level often conflicts with the special training of the young performing musician. The high degree of technical perfection demanded by present-day standards drives him towards specialization as soon as possible. Young instrumentalists today, when they enter the profession, are called upon to play a wide range of music in an enormous variety of styles in a variety of performing situations from the Royal Festival Hall to a multi-track recording studio. Admittedly, there is a danger of premature overspecialization. It is claimed that the musician should be a well-rounded individual with broad intellectual and cultural horizons, and that better-educated persons make better musicians. Bruno Walter once wrote: 'A specialized musician is only half a musician'. On the other hand a technically incompetent, inadequately trained one is not even half a musician — he just does not survive professional life. What is more, he must be trained as a *soloist*, not only because any young player worth his salt believes that is what he will become, but because the modern orchestral repertory makes virtuoso demands on all players in an orchestra.

A good many of our best young players, because of the time they have spent on music, developing and co-ordinating those essential relationships between their visual, vestibular, acoustic and motor-kinaesthetic centres, may not necessarily have had time to prepare themselves adequately for GCE examinations. Indeed we all know young musicians whose only real communication with the rest of the world is through their playing. None the less, five O-levels or the equivalent are now demanded of an instrumentalist who may wish to train to teach his instrument. It is generally a good idea if even the most promising young player has his minimum GCE qualifications for any form of higher education behind him, should the two years of intensive training prove too much for him and he feels impelled to move his sights from a career mainly in performance to one mainly in teaching.

Reforming the A-level

'You can get an A-level for analysing a symphony or concerto, but damn-all for playing it,' as my predecessor with ILEA, Peter Fletcher,

---

Gulbenkian 1975 (Calouste Gulbenkian Foundation, Lisbon: United Kingdom and British Commonwealth Branch).

remarked (quoted in the *Music Yearbook*, 1973—4). Much could be done to help young musicians by reforming A-level requirements. Proposals have been made on several occasions in the past for two separate Mode III (school-based) examinations instead of the single music A-level (Mode I). These would not be a national replacement for Mode I, but drawn up for the special requirements of colleges with preliminary courses for potential gifted musicians.

The potential numbers for this scheme could now be well over 150 students annually. The first of the two Mode III A-level examinations would comprise a paper on harmony, counterpoint and composition, a paper on history based on study of set works, aural, *viva*, and the examination of a portfolio of compositions. The second examination would be centred on music performance, comprising a recital (equivalent, at least, to a good grade 8 of the Associated Board), sight-reading, aural tests, transpositions, score-reading, and a *viva voce* on the pieces performed at the recital — technique, interpretation, historical and social background.

These two examinations would give the practical musician some academic recognition at the end of a course, and the opportunity for two A-levels for those who may wish to apply to a university for one of the degree courses with a strong performing component. Although several Examining Boards have made some attempt to strengthen the practical element in the present A-level (the Oxford and Cambridge and the Joint Matriculation Boards, for instance), these do not go far enough to meet the needs of talented young performers.

Whether the present A-level or a reformed one lies ahead, the provision of the two-year course (after O-level) calls for careful planning. Here a local authority can help where a school may find it impractical to offer A-level tuition in music (because too few candidates are concerned, or teaching cannot be provided). A centalized institution for A-level music has certain advantages. As part of a College of Further Education it may offer other subjects for A-level too, those students who have opted for music simply coming together for this one subject. Additionally, for those students who are gifted performers and whose specialization is to lead to a career in music (probably via a subsequent period at a college of music or at a university), a full-time course in music may be offered, embracing the A-level syllabus but only incidentally so, in so far as certain aspects of that syllabus provide good grounding for any educated musician. The emphasis on the latter type of course is the preparation of skilled performers, with an entrance to a college of music, or in some cases to university, in mind.

The ILEA's full-time music course

The ILEA provides such a course at Kingsway-Princeton College of Further Education. The operation there is on two levels. There is the Full-time Course for the Young Musician, with its emphasis on training talented young performers. The auditions and interviews for this course are of critical importance, as only young players showing exceptional talent and commitment can be accepted. Because of the practical nature of the course, it happens that some students do not take A-level examinations at the end. It is therefore essential that such students are recognized from the outset as being of a calibre likely to gain admission to a performing course at a music college. Otherwise, the course would be held responsible for under-qualified 18-year-olds looking for a place in higher education.

The course ensures adequate time each day for practising, and all students are encouraged to take up a second instrument when necessary. There are a variety of ensemble opportunities at high level. The course is particularly suited to string players, who at this stage need as much scheduled practice time as possible. Wind-players, for obvious reasons, cannot usually take up all the practice time that is made available in this course, and additional ensemble opportunities are available in other parts of the Authority's activities. As the course is part of a College of Further Education, there are opportunities for students to take other O-levels (or, in certain cases, A-levels) where they need to make them up. Each student has a tailor-made timetable to suit his needs.

The other part of the musical operation at the College concerns those students who are of a lesser performing standard and are studying music on a less than full-time commitment. They take the A-level music course (common to both them and the full-time, specialist students) and receive up to 15 hours' teaching a week, which compares very favourably with what is usually offered in schools.

The balance between a college course and a school sixth form has to be judged very sensitively. A school cannot provide all the opportunities for a talented young player (particularly a string player) that the college can. On the other hand, a wind-player who may wish to go on to university to read music, and who comes from a school with an active music department and good sixth form teaching, should consider the possibility of staying on at school. It is rather hard on a school to have educated their musicians up to the sixth form, only to lose them at a time when they could be making their biggest contribution to the musical life of the school. But of course, it is the interest of the musician-in-training that must, in these circumstances, come first.

The success of any of these preliminary courses depends on the quality of the teaching which, to some extent, depends on the location of the course. With its proper ratio of students to teachers, its flexibility in timetabling, reasonable opportunities for taking up other options, and its body of highly motivated students, the course perhaps comes as near as a local authority can get to the syllabus provided in a Hungarian conservatory. There are implications in catering for this new breed of student that will have to be taken up by the colleges of music. As one distinguished string teacher at the Royal Academy pointed out: 'The 18-year-olds will arrive on the scene having mastered the basic skills, and used to performing with others. They won't have to spend

LOCAL AUTHORITY AND GIFTED YOUNG PERFORMER   19

their first couple of years learning to play scales properly in four octaves.'

Certainly those teachers who have worked on the full-time course at the Kingsway-Princeton College have remarked on the way the youngsters begin to think like professional musicians, work with dedication, and have their own will to practise.

Perhaps that's what it is all about.

Higher Education:
The Music Student's Choice

Peter Le Huray
Lecturer in Music, University of Cambridge

The young man or woman seeking a specialized higher education in music may find the choice of institution not a simple one. There has been a veritable explosion in academic music studies since the Second World War, particularly since the establishment of full-time BA courses in music at Cambridge in 1948 and Oxford in 1950.

Whereas in the early 1950s there were no more than a dozen music departments of university status in the British Isles, there are now 36 offering courses that allow considerable if not exclusive specialization in music. This in turn has influenced the pattern of studies at the traditional, old-established 'conservatories' (that is to say, the colleges of music at Birmingham, Glasgow, London and Manchester), where diploma courses of graduate status have been established to enable the gifted performer with wider interests to get to grips with non-practical problems of an analytical, historical and educational nature.

A similar revolution was going on at the same time in the field of higher education that catered for students who intended to go into primary and secondary teaching. 'Teacher Training Colleges', as they were called, now became 'Colleges of Education', offering broad yet vocationally oriented courses in which music played a substantial role. More recently still, courses in music, with diplomas that are open both to the full-time and to the part-time student, have begun to be offered by Colleges of Technology (I use this as a term of convenience to embrace also Colleges of Arts and Technology, Polytechnics, etc.). Now, most recently of all, music can be taken as part of an Open University degree. It has been argued that such explosive growth has not altogether been in music's best interests, and indeed a powerful case could be made out for a rationalization of facilities and for a clearer differentiation of functions. One fact, however, is unarguable: never has the prospective student been confronted with so bewildering and tempting an array of alternatives.

How then to choose between a College of Technology, a College of Education, a Conservatory or a University? It might be as well first to point out that the choice of one channel does not necessarily rule out another: suitably qualified students at the Colleges of Education have the chance, if they so wish, to take a university degree in Education; students at a College of Technology may in some cases read for a university degree; it is possible at some conservatories to read for a degree (the Royal Academy, Royal College and Trinity are 'recognized schools' of the University of London); and quite a few university students manage to spend some time at a conservatory either before or after taking their university qualifications.   Still, the four main streams of higher musical education maintain distinct identities.

Of these, the College of Education presents the prospective student with the clearest choice, since it is unashamedly vocational in its aims. Those who are planning to go into primary or secondary school teaching and who wish to develop general musicianship, and a competence in such practical skills as performance, conducting, harmonization at the keyboard, and instrumentation (geared especially to school situations) will find that this is the most appropriate stream for their needs. Students who do particularly well in their Certificate of Education courses have the opportunity, in many colleges, to go on to a Bachelor of Education course that is musically oriented.*

Such a B Ed course (or, under some new schemes, it may be a BA or Bachelor of General Studies course) is not offered everywhere. Students aiming at such a degree status, as distinct from the lower 'certificate' status which has lesser rank as a teaching qualification, will naturally place this consideration at the forefront when making a choice among colleges of education.   The situation is fluid, and it is advisable to keep an eye on such journals as the *Musical Times* for advertisements of new courses offered.   This apart, there is such a multiplicity of colleges that a rough-and-ready guide can hardly be given here.   The ratio in the college timetable between time for music and time taken by other studies is important, and so is location — not merely for reasons of personal or family convenience.   A college situated in a leading musical city will present the student with musical opportunities as performer and listener which he will miss in remoter (if sometimes more beautiful) surroundings.   Think, similarly, about the availability of practice-rooms and a good music library.

Technical colleges and polytechnics have undergone a growth, and an advancement in status, which is among the most remarkable recent features of British education.   It is not always realized that they now occupy a firm place in music, some even ranking in courses and facilities with the older colleges of music (see p.103).   The famous and old-established Birmingham School of Music is actually part of a polytechnic.   But whether or not the older 'conservatory' training and status is given, the technical college very often offers what is called a 'preparatory'

---

*See the *Handbook of Colleges and Departments of Education* (Lund Humphries; obtainable from the Country Press, Drummond Road, Bradford BD8 8DH) — especially Appendices 1 — 1C.

or 'foundation' course (i.e. between O- and A-level) and a 'diploma' course of two years which leads to an ensuing year at a college of education. Students who feel they do not, somehow, 'fit in' the usual pattern of development predicated in traditional music education may find that the technical college furnishes an answer — and indeed a variety of answers.

A career in performance

The choice is equally clear for those dedicated souls who are unshakably committed to the goal of a professional career in performance. They will make a bee-line for a Conservatory, but in the full realization, let us hope, that very few who choose this particular ladder ever manage to reach the top, whether as soloists or orchestral players. For others, the Conservatory training may turn out to be a qualification (or part of it) for a career in teaching.

Many prospective students, however, will have no very clear idea of what ultimately they intend to do. They may think about going into the higher levels of music education, or into music administration; they may hope to combine some practical activity with work of a more academic nature, or they may even be planning eventually to enter non-musical employment. (From the very rough figures that are available, some 10–20% seem to do this.) In hedging their bets, they will find that both universities and conservatories are strong runners. There is a glib saying that the universities are for those who have the mental capacity to know but who cannot do, whilst the conservatories are for those who can do but cannot comprehend. A glance through the later information in this book should serve to squash this one for good and all. It is none the less true that the *bias* of teaching in the university department will be on comprehension, whilst the bias of conservatory teaching will be on practical skills.

The conservatories most closely approximate the universities in the graduate-status diploma courses that they all offer (usually three years, but that of the Royal Northern College of Music takes four). Lectures and seminars are provided on general musicianship, the fundamentals of composition, history, analysis and on a wide range of specialized, 'academic' subjects. None the less, the greatest emphasis is still placed on practical work, students being required to take weekly individual instruction on a first instrument (or voice), and in most cases to have additional tuition on at least one other instrument. It is probably true to say therefore that conservatory, graduate-course students have made that choice because they are interested rather more in performance than in the all-round study of the pehnomenon of music.

Of course, it is also true that most university students are keenly, if not predominantly, interested in practical matters: the calendars of musical events published by university music departments show this very clearly. If, however, you were to ask a university lecturer how ideally he saw the role of the university in music education he would probably answer, with Professor Peter Evans of the University of Southampton, that 'music is studied in a university because it is there, a strange creation of the human spirit that calls for investigation, a repertory of powerful effects that must have explicable causes'.* The model university student might be someone with a boundless curiosity about everything in his subject, whether of a practical, historical, technical, scientific, aesthetic or philosophical nature.

The university music department

How exactly do the universities choose to cater for this inquisitiveness of mind?　An examination of syllabuses and prospectuses reveals a remarkable similarity of approach. The preliminary stages, understandably enough, lay most emphasis on what Professor Ivor Keys of the University of Birmingham has called the development of 'basic musical literacy': fluency in reading various kinds of musical notation (such as vocal scores, orchestral scores and figured bass); the stimulation of the musical imagination (through extempore harmonization and improvisation); and the sharpening of the ear (by means of musical dictation and aural analysis).　Such techniques, once mastered, provide an essential basis for the investigation of the 'repertory of powerful effects' in music (Professor Evans's expression) – an investigation that has no immediate objective beyond the deepening of musical understanding.

Obviously, an essential step in this process must be the broadening of experience, to cover a wide range of styles and periods. It is hardly surprising, then, that nearly every department syllabus stresses the value of a first-hand knowledge of music through live performance. From the chart on p.239 it will be seen that in no fewer than 15 universities, instrumental tuition of some kind or other is obligatory, whilst in most others students are 'encouraged' to take practical lessons. Moreover, in nearly all syllabuses, performance is allowed as an option in the degree examinations, candidates being expected to reach a conservatory 'diploma' standard. Great stress is generally laid, too, on active participation in university ensembles, orchestras and choirs, and although conducting is examined only in half-a-dozen departments, the study of conducting through seminars and practical classes is offered almost everywhere.

Performance, however, is only one step in the process of understanding.　Here historical studies and analysis come into their own: and likewise, in almost every university department, does 'style composition' – in which the student composes exercises in the successive musical styles of different historical periods. Opinions on the value of this discipline differ widely.　It has been objected that the process is artificial and that (which no one could dispute) the pupil cannot hope to emulate the

*'Music as a University Study'. *Musical Times*, February 1973: see also other articles in the series, March, April, May, June 1973, and February 1974.

master. On the other hand it has been argued that work of this kind provides a progressive framework within which the student's experience may be led from the easily imagined sonorities of late-Renaissance polyphony to the vertical and horizontal complexities of current idioms. It has been argued, too, that in such exercises the student is made to realize most forcibly where his own grasp of the problem is most wanting, and that he thus becomes more sensitive to the qualities that distinguish genius from mediocrity.

The value of analysis as an essential tool of investigation is not in dispute. (Indeed, style composition presupposes a good deal of preliminary analytical study.) Few students, by the time they reach a conservatory or university, have made use of analysis in more than a superficial way: as often taught in schools, it comprises little more than the pigeon-holing of masterpieces into preconceived frameworks. But truly imaginative analysis concerns not academic forms, but actual musical experience, and it requires perception and imagination of a high order: an ability to follow the composer through the very act of composition, realizing the options that were open to him at any given moment and studying specific solutions in the context of the possible alternatives. These alternatives will themselves depend on the stylistic conventions of the time, the function of the piece in question, and even the personality of the composer himself. The appreciation of such factors demands a broad historical knowledge and a familiarity with a good deal of music. While none of these studies is directly geared to a strictly vocational end, it is easy to see their value in almost every professional situation — as an aid to interpretation; as a springboard for critical evaluation; even as a stimulus to original composition.

Original composition enters into all streams of higher music education, though at the most advanced levels it is a conservatory and university study. In general the universities introduce original work gradually in the second- and third-year courses (including, in many cases, electronic music), but some half-dozen make provision for it from the very beginning, as do most of the conservatories. Some half-dozen universities, too, offer postgraduate degrees in composition, and at Durham there is even a three-year course in composition leading to PhD, a degree that in all other universities is reserved for musicological work of a predominantly historical and analytical kind.

Music and specialized study

Beyond this general pattern of study, practically every university music department offers some speciality of its own, whether on undergraduate or graduate level, sometimes by means of a link with another department. Aberdeen for instance advertises a particular interest in late-18th-century music, Birmingham and Bristol in opera; several, including Durham and London, run one-year research courses for graduates leading to a Master's degree; at the University of East Anglia the music department is closely linked with the School of Fine Arts; at Keele there is a newly established centre of American studies; the City University in London, and the University of Surrey, cater particularly for scientifically inclined musicians who are aiming at a technological career; Sheffield is the home of a television course; Royal Holloway College (University of London), St Andrews and Sheffield offer joint music-and-language courses requiring residence abroad for at least part of the course.

In one important respect, the university does differ markedly from the conservatory, for it offers the student the option of combining the study of music with another subject or subjects of his choice. In deciding whether to take a joint course or to specialize wholly in music, it is worth bearing in mind that some courses are run in parallel, and some in series. Although the voltage may not be as high in the parallel system, the required flow of information may demand a facility in handling new concepts that puts the slower and perhaps more pene-trating mind at a disadvantage. Courses in series involve a change after a period of one or two years from one specialization to another. At Cambridge, for instance, the change is normally made at the end of the second year, a further two years being taken in whatever other subject is chosen, provided that the student is potentially suited to the course. The range of options is indeed vast and only by reading each prospectus can the intending student hope to inform himself fully. Also highly useful (in conjunction with the chart on p.239) is the most recent available edition of *Music (including Drama) Degree Course Guide*, by B. Blackwood (Careers Research and Advisory Centre, Bateman Street, Cambridge CB2 1LZ).

Other factors too are bound to influence the particular choice of college, university or conservatory — including the interests and qualifica-tions of the teaching staff. Full marks to the Royal Northern College of Music, and the Universities of Lancaster, Leeds and Sheffield for the information that their prospectuses provide — most university depart-ments are bad at this! Also relevant are library and reading-room facilities, and the ready availability of pianos, soundproofed practice-rooms, and playback equipment for records and tapes. These are indispensable adjuncts of a well-planned course, without which the student cannot begin to hope to turn his 'unbounded curiosity' to good effect. Being curious, too, about everything to do with music, the student will wish to know the range of practical musical activities that go on, not only within the department but also within the college or university and its environs — what choirs and orchestras there are; who conducts and plays in them; what kinds of music they perform; what chances there are for the students to gain experience in concert organization and direction; and what connections the department may have with professional groups and individuals outside.

Some consideration should be given, too, to differences in teaching and examination methods. Do the examinations, for instance, all take place in the final year, or are they spread over a period of two or three years? Do they take the form exclusively of written, limited-time papers (three hours seems to be the most popular length), or are there other methods of evaluation as well, such as continuous assessment, prepared dissertations and compositions? What is the balance between formal lectures and seminars? What provisions are made for individual teaching on a regular basis, i.e. once weekly or more? (This point is particularly important, since so much in music-teaching ideally requires a one-to-one relationship.) Is attendance at lectures in any way obligatory? What opportunities does the course offer for the exploration of individual interests? Only by asking questions of this kind can the student hope to find the solution that most nearly meets his needs, and to get the most out of the course when he has embarked upon it. A prospectus will probably not answer all the questions, and a prospective student should not hesitate to pursue inquiries by letter or by pre-arranged visit.

Bed, board, and travel

In making the final choice, the student will also have other, less academic questions in mind. One of the more important of these is the question of residential accommodation. He will wish to know what proportion of the students are housed in college or university accommodation, whether this accommodation is merely residential or whether it is organized on the kind of collegiate basis which provides for a wide range of extra-curricular interests and activities. He will need to know how costly such residence is, how far away it is from the university and departmental buildings, what the meals arrangements are like, what chances there are of securing an individual bed-sitter, whether he is allowed a piano in his rooms, what noise restrictions there are, which (if any) years he will have to live 'out' in digs, and whether first-year students are given priority in university accommodation. Time spent in travel is time wasted — and travel also happens to be increasingly expensive, even if you have an NUS concessionary ticket.

But, apart from the problems of choice, the prospective student also faces the problem of gaining admission to the institution — and that means the acquisition of certain preliminary qualifications. Broadly speaking the conservatories seem less concerned with 'academic' competence than with practical distinction, and a candidate *may* (at any rate if he is not eventually seeking a teachers' qualification) get in without A-levels, with only five O-levels and a Grade 8 in (at least) his first instrument. There is no one standard requirement for entry into a College of Technology, where a student may possibly be accepted for a diploma course with just five O-levels and a good practical interview (although one A-level would be reckoned desirable). Among Colleges of Education, an increasing number insist on two A-levels (one being in music), plus a high practical grade, and at least three additional O-levels. Others set less rigorous standards.

Most university departments stipulate at least two A-levels, plus three other subjects at O, together with a practical study to grade 7 or 8, and some keyboard experience. Many, however, will make special provisions for first-year students who have no skill at the keyboard. By no means all, incidentally, insist on A-level music, taking the view that a fair picture of a candidate's background and musicality can be obtained during interview.

It would be rash to attempt a summary of everything that is being tested during interview, for every examiner has his own strengths and weaknesses. Few would disagree, however, with the proposition that an interview is there to reveal something of the candidate's innate musicality, his intellectual curiosity and his powers of perception; to these three some might add, since music is a social art, personality. Musicianship is revealed in many different ways that range from the performance of prepared pieces to the negotiation of all kinds of aural tests and to an intuitive grasp of extempore harmony and improvisation. The breadth of a candidate's musical interests and his knowledge of music will reveal a good deal about his curiosity, and his grasp of aural and visual analysis will show something of his powers of perception.

So, from interview to entrance to course, the new and probably crucial step towards a musical career begins. In later life the professional is often asked how it was that he or she came to take up such a career. The answer almost invariably involves some remark to the effect that nothing else seemed quite so worth while.

On Being a Music Teacher

Gordon Reynolds
Editor, 'Music in Education'

I haven't heard the phrase 'a born teacher' for some time. It was the sort of accolade bestowed by grateful parents, who might well have been able to count a number of satisfied customers among the assorted, even unpromising, heads in their own families. One sees a vision of a sage and avuncular Mr Chips — or a serene and imperturbable Miss Fish. Yet even in novels, skills and wisdom in teaching develop out of long experience, and it is to be expected that Chapter I will be full of misunderstanding and frustration. That may satisfy the public, but few students contemplating a career will be attracted to a future which begins with classroom riots, includes an ill-fated romance and reaches fulfilment just in time for the white whiskers and the pension-book. There must be a few guide-lines which will see one through the first two-thirds of a career without too much disillusionment.

Still, it is worth noting that the teacher in the novel only gradually acquires a personal interest in pupils — and even then, sheer weight of numbers tends to make it only a semi-personal interest. It is in fact necessary to develop and maintain a professional attitude, nothing to do with clinical coldness, which ensures that the pupil derives the maximum benefit from lessons. It would be possible to be so very sympathetic as to be drawn wholly into the pupil's way of thinking. Carried to absurd conclusions, this would lead to the teacher developing an affection for awkward fingering, misplaced accidentals and childish articulation. Schoolboy howlers, once so popular, are only funny to those who know the right answers. Near-misses are endearing only if one hastens to correct them. It would be misplaced zeal to educate only laterally, with primitive vocabulary and expression. So, naturally, one expects a teacher to be in a position to open doors, widen horizons, point out avenues, remembering that all these tiresome clichés are only means of narrowing-down and rationalizing the ancient *inspiration*. Right-minded young teachers tend not to boast about inspiring their pupils. If they find that they have this gift, they keep quiet about it and let the pupils have the credit.

But there is nothing wrong with doing one's best. Having something to offer and having faith in that commodity, whether it be a knowledge or a skill or a burning enthusiasm, must be a good prelude to a teaching career. It would be altogether too much to expect that this must necessarily go hand-in-hand with experience of human beings or even of any avowed interest in them. Fate is kind to some ex-students in this respect. They arrive in their first teaching situations having already held positions of responsibility in school and in college. Others, slower to mature, or perhaps just less gregarious so far, meet this kind of responsibility for the first time. It takes all kinds to make a profession. There are plenty of pupils to go round, and some of them will respond warmly to the quiet and modest beginner. Not everyone reacts kindly to the extrovert salesman.

Be prepared

What matters more than personal magnetism (which, as in Mr Chips's case, will attract more as time goes on) is a capacity for organization. There is no more valuable time in the whole of a career than the gap between being appointed and the first day of one's first term. All the established teachers reading this will realize with a pang that this period of blessed innocence will never return. This is when one can look forward to some first-class lessons with no discouragement. Here is the golden opportunity to sort out in peace and quiet some useful material for various stages of pupils' development. Now is the time to make sure that it is known inside-out. Whether your future lies with children or adults, singly or in large numbers, there are certain aspects of professional expertise which you now have a little leisure to polish.

Some skills are requirements for almost all teachers. For example, a singing teacher or an instrumental teacher, of single pupils or groups, will need to be able to transpose. (Not everything under the sun, and not at sight – from now on, the teacher takes the decisions.) A selection of party pieces and exercises turned to perfection will last a long time. Class teachers will require files of material progressing through three terms, multiplied by the number of age-ranges to be taught. Teachers of individuals will be sorting out their bundles of pieces, with plenty of alternatives for each grade, to suit different tastes. Teachers of harmony and history will marshal their examples, ready to illuminate what they have to say.

It may be objected that such preparation may be quite invalidated on first meeting the pupils or on taking stock of the equipment available. But unless a considerable amount of preliminary thought has gone into stocking up one's personal armoury, the first year will seem a very long haul indeed. Such gaps as there are between contacts with pupils are likely to be sufficient for keeping pace with day-to-day requirements. The Christmas and Easter breaks pass all too quickly – and there are very many pupils to be kept on their toes meantime. However deficient the new teacher may be in experience of human beings, the first year could provide either a booster dose or what might seem like a knock-out blow. Nothing can save a teacher from the pressing needs of humanity in the mass except a sense of purpose, which can only be gained by slow and careful preparations. The best apparent improvisers, such people as widely differing in their talent as Tony Hancock and Winston Churchill, achieved their results by agonies of self-preparation. Like the comedian and the politician, the teacher needs a lot up his sleeve. Every accident brings surprises to the doctor as well as to the patient, but we all rely on the medical man having a fair idea of how the body works. We would derive little comfort from his having a desperate rummage among his textbooks.

If teaching offers little time for study, it will afford just as little for the clerical side of the job. However much or little the employer may require in the way of syllabuses and records, the teacher who even attempts to rely solely on his memory is embarking upon professional suicide. All professional workers have to keep their books in order, not to satisfy someone else, but to be able to look back and temper or goad their ambitions. A clear record of what it has actually proved possible to achieve in a given time is the best basis for concocting next session's scheme.

It is surprising how a little ardent concentration on mechanics and material can bring rewards in terms of improved relations with pupils. 'Pastoral' care is not enough. Some of the most hilariously inept student-teachers I have had to supervise at training college pleaded with increasing vehemence, as the final grading approached, how dearly they loved children. Some others, who had much to learn about sympathy and understanding, became in a short time favourites with pupils who deserved a little more warmth, because their professional integrity shone very bright.   ·

The world outside

It seems a little hard, having expounded at some length about the arduous nature of a teacher's life, to raise a complaint which is frequently made in the world of music, that the music teacher lives a life of unreal isolation. The teacher must recall that a musician is a musician, whether he earns his living by performing or teaching, and music is an art which can only be kept alive by practice. And not only practising — by listening to music, by reading about it and discussing it with one's fellows. This is why orchestral players and members of ensembles and choirs make noticeably good companions and, when called on to do a certain amount of teaching, lose no opportunity of throwing their pupils together in groups, of borrowing pupils to make up ensembles, of giving little concerts which are also social events eagerly looked forward to. They tend to treat their young pupils as miniature professionals. In short, the last word you could apply to them would be 'academic'. You cannot have a theoretical oboe player in an orchestra, so it stands to reason that an orchestral player's teaching will be of a highly practical nature.

The opposite, I am sorry to say, is often thought of the teacher who spends his normal working hours in school. Despite strenuous attempts by many members of the teaching profession, 'school music' ranks a little lower than 'music'. The blame for this sad situation must be variously apportioned. In the case of primary schools, there are not enough teachers adequately trained to cope with music among other subjects. Colleges of Education have so reduced the time alloted to music in the curriculum that only a small proportion of the students passing through can possibly have any idea of how to teach it. This has been going on for so long that many heads of primary schools despair of capturing even a pianist, let alone a music teacher. To teach the reading of music at primary level is a task which can hardly be said to be taken seriously, except where the school has been fortunate enough to attract a teacher who has had some musical training. And yet, perhaps because of this situation, the best response to in-service music courses comes from primary teachers.

Some excellent work has been done in primary schools, yet the musical profession tends to overlook them, treating the secondary level as being more interesting, because more adult. The music teacher in a secondary school is regarded as a musician of some weight, not least by other musicians thinking of their own children's education. He must have been trained in a professional environment if he is going to teach singing in parts, train orchestras and coach for O- and A-levels, as well as supervise instrumental teachers. He will take his place on the school platform with those other exalted beings who influence everyone's teenage years. He is much concerned with the world of examinations, the hurdles which most have to face and which few would care to face without expert guidance. Few people outside the circle of those who feel this particular call would care to take on so much responsibility in so many directions at once, working with age-groups known even to parents as difficult.

So any professional reserve shown by other musicians towards secondary school music has nothing to do with the nature of the job itself, nor does it signify any lack of admiration for those who tackle it. Nor has it arisen as a consequence of reorganization of secondary education. Similar feelings were abroad in the days of the old grammar schools. Then, as now, the teacher responsible for a school's music was recognized as a real musician, and necessarily a musician of some breadth. He might or might not be a first-class executant — but then your skilled orchestral player might not be able to turn his hand to adding three parts above a given bass.

Why is it, then, that in local communities the secondary music teacher is not always counted in among the musical worthies? Sometimes the answer is that he is rarely present to be counted — rarely seen outside school, that is. The formidable hours spent not only teaching but also preparing and marking might seem to make their own apology for absence. Yet there are enough teachers who do manage to mix in with outside activities to indicate that this may be a matter of individual organization. Unfortunately, the non-mixer who fails to join in after many invitations is often written off as indifferent.

There is everything to be said for regarding school as part of a larger community. From the start, the music teacher should get to know other musicians and bring them into his field as frequently as possible. Local meetings of the Incorporated Society of Musicians can provide opportunities for meeting instrumentalists, singers and teachers, adjudicators, speakers at society meetings, singing coaches for soloists, or indeed vocal and instrumental soloists themselves. They are not only willing to come — they are glad to be asked. What goes on in school is of great interest to them all, and their comments and advice are likely to be stimulating. Once the outsiders are brought in, mere school music as such begins to disappear and what goes on becomes part of the whole world of local music. Moreover, the musician outside the gates may have much to offer the pupils — opportunities for performance or practice, visits to concerts or rehearsals, or even just friendly conversation which will add another dimension to some aspect of study.

The teacher himself also needs at least one avenue of refreshment outside school. Membership of a choir, orchestra or ensemble which meets regularly will help to brush away classroom atmosphere. This is especially important to a young teacher who needs to be made aware of his own deficiencies in repertory or technique — and who doesn't? If further study would be beneficial, but the thought of examinations is anathema for the time being, an evening class, whether LEA, WEA or university extension, could provide a painless and profitable pastime. The fact that these are unlikely to be at professional level is an advantage. It is sometimes a mistake to reject offerings which look as though they might be inferior to what one remembers of college. Any opportunity to hear and discuss music is better than none, and the standard of discussion in such classes is sometimes shame-makingly well-informed. There is also the pleasure of being, for a change, a mere cog-in-a-wheel, free to pay critical attention or not.

Sharing enthusiasms

A teacher, moreover, needs to share his pupils' interests, which are influenced by what goes on at home, what goes on locally — and what goes on the screen. This is no mere duty — it is one of the perks which goes with the job, the most enjoyable perk of all. The local pub, the terraces of the football ground, the youth club, the parish hall — these are places where it is easy to share enthusiasms with neighbours. Every locality has its characteristics which can only be appreciated by those ready to become involved. The local flavour will not yield all its charm to the casual taster. The teacher for whom all this is a foreign world is, from the pupil's point of view, only half alive. So is the teacher who shares nothing of what the children see and hear on television and radio.

Blessed is he who is one step ahead, who can relate the humour of last night's screen situation to the present moment in the classroom, who can recall at the piano the pop tune of the moment and the signature-tune from the series everyone is watching. Blessed is he whose tastes are classless but whose critical faculties remain sharp in all situations, able to point out poverty or excellence of invention and workmanship wherever it is found — in pop music as elsewhere. The shortest way into a pupil's heart is to be able to quote to him something he knows and loves: he knows then that he and the teacher have something in common. The customers in each class represent the world in microcosm with all its variety of tastes and interests, which may be enriched, extended, intensified, modified perhaps — but not, surely, eradicated. Any missionary who feels himself being consumed by his own specialized real would do well to put his message in his pocket for a while and set about getting to know the natives. Any teacher who has no use for pop is denying himself access to a lot of creative material — and must find himself peering at his pupil through a gate which ought to be opened.

The secondary teacher sometimes feels very isolated. He may be the only person in charge of music in quite a large school and the nearest neighbour doing the same sort of thing may be miles away. It is difficult to get hold of new ideas in a notoriously tricky field. Very little stimulating advice has appeared in print, at least on the real mechanics of such teaching. Two people who should be informed when such a need is felt are the LEA adviser or organizer and the nearest music HMI. It is unfair to expect the traffic to move in only one direction. Courses can be arranged if the demand is there. There have been many complaints about courses for secondary teachers being under-subscribed — but if teachers became more vocal and specific about their requirements (first making sure that they had read the circulars about sessions already planned), provision could be more easily put where it is needed.

One local contact which should not be neglected is the church, of whatever denomination. Even if it is musically bleak, it is likely to have an organ, and singing with organ accompaniment is an experience children would enjoy now and then. It is more than likely that the church acoustics would be more favourable to a choral and orchestral concert than the average contemporary school hall, which seems better designed for emphasizing the least pleasant partials of musical sound. There may also be opportunities for placing pupils or staff in the choir. If the church is musical, the benefits to the school will soon be apparent. If not, more than one church has *become* musical through a sudden invasion of enthusiasts from school. Any doubt about the welcome will never be dispelled without a try, though the teacher will of course assess how far the church is or is not a 'natural' contact for the community in which he works.

Private teaching

As a small boy, I was amazed to hear my piano teacher say: 'Three pupils were away ill yesterday afternoon, so I went to the pictures'. For a brief moment I had an insight into a glorious world where teachers could, if they felt like it, pack up for the day and enjoy what was then six penn'orth of dark. The snag, which I could hardly be expected to appreciate at the time, was that the chances of a private teacher in those days having a sixpence to spare were remote. My teacher did nothing else for a living but welcome a stream of young people into her studio one at a time, day after day, starting them from scratch and seeing them through their grades and then through their diploma, if they stayed long enough and were up to it. It seemed to me a wonderful thing to have a studio (it was above a dentist's surgery, and one felt so much better in health than all the other callers) — a huge room containing nothing but a piano, a music cabinet, a desk and a few chairs. Music was greatly enhanced in such an atmosphere, but at the same time there was a businesslike air which seemed to frown upon time-wasting.

To have a private music teacher, who stoutly maintained total ignorance of anything that happened in schools ('What is all this *doh ray me* business? It sounds double-dutch to me!') was a bit like having a favourite aunt who, without a word of criticism, gave the impression that the family horizons were a bit limited, and that the boy could do with a few larky experiences. Here was the only person in the world who not only sympathized with my desire to play by ear but showed me how to get better at it. We spent quite a lot of time changing places at the keyboard to demonstrate to each other recaptured bits of film music, trying it in various keys and sometimes arguing about its content. (No one could possibly complain about this, so long as I passed examinations!) The teacher and I also exchanged views on life in general. Such conversations can only have been brief, as there was usually another pupil waiting, but they were memorable — such vivid little statements of hers as 'I don't go to church. I like choirs and I like organs, but I don't like sermons and I won't sing hymns!'

With this might come casual remarks relating the music to a whole world of experience belonging to over the hills and far away. Friends have told me of interests their private teachers have awakened in them which seem a long way from music — at random I quote Dickens, railway engines, the sound of German poetry well read, typography and the economics of home cookery. No one could survive the teacher's life without a breadth of human interest far beyond the momentary technical problem. Survival also means having a shrewd business sense, as well as a high degree of personal organization. The expertise involved covers more than the ability to correct common errors in *Für Elise*. There must be an inbuilt resistance to any sense of staleness or routine, and a sense of purpose which can convey itself to the pupil.

Some freelance teachers are able to vary their lives considerably by having more than one centre of interest. The church organist, whose work as a choirmaster has a close affinity with class teaching, may divide his time between his church duties and coaching of one kind or another. He is expected to be able to help not only with instrumental and vocal performance, but also with harmony and counterpoint and the day-to-day mysteries of his own trade such as scorereading and transposition. He needs also a considerable literary sense, having to spend a great part of his life dealing with the subtle interpretation of words, and a flair for historical associations and the juxtaposition of works from different historical periods.

There are other 'community' roles available. Several teachers are currently combining giving lessons with writing criticisms for the local press. There is usually no shortage of events to be covered, and an account of a concert might well be sent to the editor as a sample. Interest and conciseness are, of course, necessary — but not nearly so necessary as punctuality and doing precisely what was promised. It is perhaps unnecessary to point out that adult education offers a further field. Many classes run by LEAs and the Workers' Educational Association are taught by freelance music teachers, who find the challenge of group work a welcome change from dealing with individuals.

Retrospect and recommendation

Looking back, I believe I am fortunate in having been a teacher all my life. Even before I was old enough to go to school I taught anyone unwise enough to stray within earshot. When those had fled, I was left with a class of assorted dolls and animals, few of whom looked very hopeful cases. If my own years as a pupil were less successful than they might have been, it was perhaps because of my worm's-eye preoccupation with the act of teaching itself. Many future teachers may indeed absorb *as pupils* not only content but also the idea of orderly presentation.

My short teaching career in grammar schools (surely the ideal atmosphere for a music teacher, but fast disappearing) taught me many things, not least that one's best pupils so readily form an apostolic succession. I learnt that music flourishes best in a sociable environment, that the fight for time-table time is as nothing compared with the fight for out-of-school time, and that the only way to cope with the work and enjoy it at the same time is to stay at school as long as possible and spend most evenings working too. But there was one sad thing about the job. The first form entered the school almost as innocent of music as the bottom class in a primary school. What was happening in the primary schools? The opportunity to find out came too soon for my liking, but jobs in Schools Broadcasting crop up rarely. So, feeling like a traitor and a fool at the same time, I abandoned my assured happy future and pushed open the door of Broadcasting House.

Teachers always seem pleased to see the man from the BBC (even if they *do* sometimes think he's come to mend the set). He is not there to inspect, nor even to advise unless asked to (which he always is), least of all to teach (but this he nearly always manages to do). I learnt enough to plan and broadcast a new kind of teaching programme for infants. It has survived 25 years, and is now, of course, an old method. Though the job involved many kinds of production and performance — choral, orchestral and dramatic work providing many thrills and anxieties — the lifeline which made it all worth while was the chance of going into schools all over the United Kingdom.

My next post, at a college of education, was fun, a lot of it — and hell's delight as well. Fun because students are only too willing to be inspired by what you have to offer. Hell's delight because the college authorities do their best by a variety of devices and excuses to make a continuous course of instruction impossible. Later it seemed to me necessary to breathe the fresh air of direct teaching again. It has taken two forms — musicianship classes at Trinity College of Music (a final brush-up for third year students) and harmony and aural training at the Royal Military School of Music. This involves teaching student-bandmasters to rethink at a rather advanced age anything they may know about these subjects. It says much for their determination that they manage to reach a pretty high standard in two years. Now that my formal teaching is entirely with adults, my Chapel Royal boys at Hampton Court Palace restore a balance, for I have never been happy unless children came somewhere into my professional activities.

I love to recommend teaching as a career, because I have been very happy doing it. If you feel that you are a teacher, you will find yourself teaching people, whether paid for it or not. How lovely to be paid for doing what you like doing best!

Section Two

TECHNICAL ADVICE

Educational Use of Copyright Music and Records

M. J. Freegard
General Manager, Performing Right Society Ltd.

Copyright is a confusing concept to many people, and not least to many of those who rely upon it for their livelihood! For some educators it is, frankly, a bugbear, to be lived with uneasily and — so far as use of copyright material in schools and colleges is concerned — to be ignored as far as it is safe to do so. Others in the teaching profession — especially those who themselves create original artistic, literary or musical works — appreciate that, nuisance though it may appear to the administrator, copyright is an essential bulwark in the edifice of culture and civilization, and that without it the creation and dissemination of tomorrow's classics, as well as today's 'pops', would be fatally undermined.

The advent of new technological media such as communications satellites, audio-visual cassettes and computer 'software' has raised many complex legal and practical questions about copyright protection, in schools as elsewhere — questions with which it is beyond the scope of this article to deal. The United Kingdom Copyright Act of 1956 is currently under review by a Government Committee which, having heard evidence from copyright-owning and using interests (including educational users) will doubtless propose changes in the law, possibly of a far-reaching nature. But in the meantime it is the Act of 1956 which regulates matters: and it is with the practical implications of that Act, so far as music in schools and colleges is concerned, that this article will attempt to deal. What follows should not however be taken as an exhaustive statement of the law of copyright as it applies to educational use, but it is hoped that it will be helpful as a practical guide to the problems most commonly encountered in this field. More detailed information can be obtained from the Council for Educational Technology which in 1972 published a comprehensive guide to the subject entitled *Copyright and Education*.

Subject to certain limitations, the Act confers on authors and composers of musical, literary and dramatic works the right to control the publication, public performance, broadcasting, diffusion by wire, reproduction in any form (e.g. recording or photocopying) and adaptation (e.g. arranging or translating) of their works. Similar, *and quite separate* (though more limited) rights are conferred on the makers of *sound recordings* and *films* in respect of those products, and (subject to even greater limitations) to broadcasting organizations in respect of their *radio and television broadcasts.* It will be obvious from the foregoing that the use (in a manner restricted by the Copyright Act) of, say, a gramophone record of a musical work, or a film on whose soundtrack music has been 'synchronized', may involve simultaneous obligations to the composer of the music (or to his assignee, e.g. a publisher) on the one hand, and to the record-manufacturer or film producer on the other. The rights in a musical work subsist throughout the composer's lifetime and for 50 years from the end of the year of his death (or, if posthumously published, for 50 years from the date either of publication or of any of the other acts listed in Section 2(3) of the Act), and those in recordings, films and broadcasts for 50 years from the end of the year in which they were first published or transmitted. It should be noted that the term 'musical work' includes any words associated therewith, and also that copyright subsists in an *arrangement* of a musical work, even if the original work has fallen into the public domain through expiry of the 50-year period or is otherwise without copyright protection.

The most frequent uses of copyright musical material in schools and other educational establishments fall into three categories, namely (a) performance; (b) recording; (c) photocopying.

Performance

Only *public* performances are subject to the copyright owner's control, but the Copyright Act does not define what constitutes a 'public' performance. However, it has become clear over the years from judicial decisions that, subject to a few specific exceptions provided for in the Act itself, virtually all performances outside the domestic circle are to be regarded as 'public'. One of these exceptions, set out in Section 41(3) and (4) of the Act, is that where a musical work

(a)   is performed in class, or otherwise in the presence of an audience, and
(b)   is so performed in the course of the activities of a school, by a person who is a teacher in, or a pupil in attendance at, the school

the performance shall not be taken for the purposes of the Act to be a performance in public if the audience is limited to persons who are teachers in, or pupils in attendance at, the school, or are otherwise directly connected with the activities of the school. (It is to be noted that, for this purpose, the Act stipulates that a person shall not be taken to be directly connected with the activities of a school by reason only that he is a parent or guardian of a pupil in attendance at the school.)

This statutory education is limited to 'schools' as defined by the Education Act, 1944 and the Education (Scotland) Act, 1946. It covers, in effect, only primary and secondary schools, so does not apply to universities, polytechnics or other institutions for further education. However, in practice, the exemption is much more widely available because the Performing Right Society Ltd, usually known as PRS — which administers the performing right (and some other rights) on behalf of virtually all composers and music publishers (foreign as well as British) whose works are publicly used — has voluntarily abstained from charging for the use of copyright music *for any purposes forming part of the educational curriculum* at *all* recognized educational establishments.

Of course, not all performances of music in schools and colleges fall within the scope of this voluntary exemption, wide though it is. For example, a speech-day concert or a dance or film show given outside school hours would normally involve performances for which the PRS would make a charge. These matters are greatly simplified in practice, however, because it is the policy of the PRS to issue blanket licences to Local Education Authorities, on terms which have been negotiated with the Association of County Councils and the Association of Metropolitan Authorities. These licences cover all performances in buildings which are under the control of the Education Authority for educational purposes, *except:*

(a)   performances in *voluntary* schools which do not arise directly from their educational use (e.g. lettings of school halls to outside bodies);

(b)   performances at voluntary youth clubs and by community associations not given in school premises;

all of which need to be separately licensed by the PRS, as of course do entertainments at universities, etc., organized by Students' Unions or other bodies, e.g. pop concerts and dances for which professional musicians are often engaged at considerable cost.

Similar arrangements (negotiated with the Incorporated Association of Headmasters, the Association of Headmistresses and the Music Masters' Association of the Incorporated Society of Musicians) have been made by the PRS to cover non-exempted performances at independent schools, and also at independent colleges. These licences cover all the normal school activities — including parents' days, school concerts, dances and film shows — but do not extend to entertainments which are clearly outside the ambit of the schools' activities, such as a series of subscription concerts, or dances organized by an outside body. Performances of copyright music given at such entertainments should be licensed separately.

In order to be able to distribute the royalties collected under these licences to the composers and publishers whose works are performed, the PRS normally requires 'programme returns' listing the items performed, but in order to keep to a minimum the administrative work undertaken by teachers and local authority officers, the Society has agreed that these returns need be made by Education Authorities only in respect of performances to which there is an admission charge.

As regards the use of commercial gramophone records for performances in schools, etc. (e.g. for incidental music in school plays or for 'disco' type dances) a 'blanket' licence can usually be obtained from Phonographic Performance Ltd (PPL) which represents virtually all producers of sound-recordings for the purpose of licensing the performing rights in their recordings (whether those recordings be in the form of discs, tapes, cassettes or cartridges). So far as the use of records for curricular purposes is concerned, PPL follows a similar policy to that of PRS, i.e. it voluntarily extends exemption from charge well beyond the statutory limits (which are in any case rather wider than is the case with copyright music) so as to allow free use of copyright recordings at any recognized educational institution, except where records are used at functions at which members of the public are present.

It will be apparent from the foregoing that anyone responsible for putting on any form of entertainment or other activity involving the use of copyright music in an educational institution should first satisfy himself or herself that the proposed use is covered by a licence issued by the PRS, and if records or pre-recorded tapes are to be used, that a licence from PPL is also obtained. If in any doubt it is best to check the position with each or either body.

Recording

By virtue of Section 41(1) of the Copyright Act, the recording of a copyright musical work by a teacher or pupil *in the course of instruction* is permitted, but this facility does not apply to the copyright in commercial gramophone records or tapes, nor does it override the provisions of the Performers' Protection Acts which require that the prior permission of performers must be obtained before their performances are recorded or re-recorded. Apart from this, the recording of a copyright musical work (or of a substantial part of such a work) without the permission of the copyright owner is generally an infringement of the composer's rights, even if it is made by a private individual in his own home for his personal use. One exception to this, however, is where such a recording is made for genuine purposes of research or private study.

The unauthorized re-recording of a record or tape is similarly an infringement of the rights of the maker of the original recording (and is not even subject to the exceptions which apply to the recording of music as such). Moreover, recording 'off the air' from radio or TV programmes (even though this is permitted, as such, for private purposes) will nevertheless almost certainly involve infringement of rights in copyright material included in such programmes, including both musical works and recordings used for the purpose of the broadcast. Infringement of this kind (usually in all innocence) is unfortunately widespread, but there is no need for music teachers to be a party to it as simple procedures are available to schools and colleges whereby all the rights they are required to clear are available through blanket licences issued on behalf of musical copyright owners, record manufacturers and broadcasting authorities, at minimal cost.

Blanket licences permitting the copying of both copyright music and commercial gramophone records for curricular purposes are now available to educational institutions through the Mechanical Copyright Protection Society Ltd (MCPS) which, like the PRS in the fields of performance and broadcasting, acts for virtually all musical copyright owners (composers and publishers) in the matter of the recording right, and which by special arrangement with the British Phonographic Industry Copyright Association is empowered to act for this limited purpose for the makers of sound-recordings as well. These licences extend the statutory right to record copyright music 'in the course of instruction' to *all* recordings made for curricular purpose, and additionally they cover the re-recording of almost all commercially produced discs and tapes. They are granted for a minimal fee, but are subject to some necessarily strict conditions, for example, about the uses of which the recordings made under them may be put. (Moreover, quite apart from such conditions, it would in any case be illegal, under the Performers' Protection Acts, for such recordings to be offered for sale or otherwise made available to the public.)

Additionally, it is now possible under agreements made by the BBC and by the Independent Television Companies Association (ITCA) with the record industry and with certain performers' unions and other bodies, for BBC and ITV educational broadcasts (excluding Open University broadcasts) to be recorded 'off the air' by a teacher or pupil in the course of instruction — provided that the recordings thus made are used only for instructional purposes in class and that they are destroyed within a specified period. These facilities are available without formality as far as BBC educational broadcasts are concerned, but for the right to record ITV broadcasts prior application should be made to the ITCA. Open University programmes may be recorded on application to the Open University.

Photocopying

The legal principles governing photocopying are the same as those governing recording, since both acts fall under the general heading of 'reproduction'. Accordingly, the limited exemptions allowed by Section

41(1) of the Copyright Act apply to photocopying, and of course to all other forms of visual reproduction, in the same way as they do to recording. (It should be noted that the authority given by this Section of the Act to teachers and pupils to make reproductions *in the course of instruction* specifically excludes the right to do so by means of a 'duplicating' process — defined as 'any process involving the use of an appliance for producing multiple copies'.) It follows that the statutory right of an individual to make a recording for purposes of private study or research, referred to in parenthesis in paragraph on *Recording* above, applies equally to a photocopy (Section 6(1) of the Act.) Moreover the Act permits the copying of a musical work for purposes of criticism or review, provided such use is accompanied by sufficient acknowledgment (Section 6(2)), and under Regulations issued by the Department of Trade under Section 7 of the Act, in certain closely defined circumstances it is permitted for the library of a school, university or other educational establishment to make *single* photocopies of extracts from copyright works. However, such copies are only available for purposes of private study or research, and librarians are required to obtain written undertakings from those for whom the copies are made that this is the case.

It is perhaps not surprising that the ready accessibility of multiple-copying devices, combined with the pressures of inflation on the educational budget, has resulted in strong temptation to engage in the illicit production of multiple copies of musical scores for the use of school choirs and orchestras, thereby avoiding the need to hire or purchase copies from the publisher — a temptation which has proved too strong for some teachers in recent years. Such temptations should be sternly resisted by everyone in the educational world because, quite apart from the real risk of legal action against the teachers and institutions concerned, such activities, if allowed to proliferate, would make it completely uneconomic for music to be published at all.

The printing of sheet music, especially of choral and orchestral material, has become enormously expensive and unless publishers are assured of a reasonable return for themselves and for their composers from sales and hire fees they will not be willing to undertake it. This in turn will discourage new composition, to the great detriment of the educational world as well as of musical life generally. The income derived by composers and publishers from *performances* in educational institutions is minimal by reason of the statutory exceptions and of the extent to which performing rights are granted (through the PRS) at minimal rates of charge, so it is all the more important that teachers should scrupulously avoid the illicit production of multiple copies which is, in effect, stealing. Permission to make such copies must *always* be sought from the copyright-owner — normally the publisher. Music publishers' addresses, if not shown on the score which it is proposed to copy, can usually be obtained through the Music Publishers' Association (MPA). There is also an exhaustive listing in the *British Music Yearbook*.

Hi-fi in the Classroom

B. J. Webb
formerly Adviser for Audio, Leicestershire
Local Education Authority

The term *Hi-Fi* is a convenient and relative (although adjectivally inaccurate) abbreviation of *High fidelity sound reproduction*, and the reproduction of sound is an important educational factor from nursery school to university as well as in the home. The development of television in recent years has tended to shift emphasis in the visual direction, quite understandably, but it is not to be supposed that it is no longer necessary to give serious attention to quality of sound in the classroom on the grounds that 'sound only' presentations are on the way out. This is quite untrue, especially in the sphere of music. The quality of sound from television is generally poor (due to limitations in the sets rather than in the transmissions) but becomes more or less acceptable through the predominance of the visual image, particularly when it is in colour. In music, however, the visual image is obviously less important than in a number of other subjects, and faithful reproduction of the sound in the listening environment, whatever it may be, lies at the heart of the matter.

The object of this article is to provide practical observations, based on some 25 years of experience, on the provision of high quality sound in classrooms, and to indicate the possibilities of improvement of existing systems and arrangements. The subject is not an easy one to treat in general terms, and depends very largely on informed assessment of each particular situation. The advice given here is chiefly directed to the primary and secondary school. In universities, colleges and teachers' centres much more complex and expensive installations may be considered, including the provision of fully-equipped recording studios, and are indeed essential if teachers are to be capable of exploiting fully the potential of the more limited facilities which they will find in schools, and of spending to the best advantage the limited sums of money available for replacement, extension or improvement of these facilities. The provision of more short courses devoted to the understanding and practice of the simpler technology of hi-fi might well be considered by local education authorities and by the Department of Education and Science.

Classroom acoustics

Classrooms generally offer very poor listening conditions because of their acoustic characteristics, which present difficult problems. The only sound-absorbing objects found in them usually are the bodies of the occupants; no soft furnishings, carpets or curtains adorn them; they are usually regular in shape and full of hard reflecting surfaces arranged in parallel lines. Sound emitted in such conditions bounces to and fro between the parallel surfaces and takes so long to die away that muddle is inevitable, together with coloration of the sound. The situation is daunting, but there is no need to go on building unsuitable classrooms, given architects with some knowledge of acoustics.

Nor is the position in such rooms as those described beyond improvement, and although some expenditure must be involved, the cost need not be great. One possible improvement scheme is shown on p.53. This can be applied in varying degrees or stages, according to necessity, money available and the number of rooms to be treated. Curtains, which may be drawn across windows and reflecting walls when required, or acoustic tiles which remain permanently in position, or a combination of both may be used in order to reduce the 'liveliness' or reverberation time. A simple, fairly heavy curtain across the far end of a room can cut this time by half, producing notable improvement. I have seen old blankets, brought by pupils and cut, joined and dyed in the school used in this way with excellent effect, visual and audible, at negligible cost.

Although many remarks to follow will refer to mobile equipment and to *ad hoc* classroom arrangement, it is highly desirable that at least one room in a school or college should be specially equipped for music reproduction and also for live music-making and recording. The installation in such a music room should if possible remain there permanently, and not be moved around from one room to another. Such an installation might well consist, apart from the speakers, of a good receiver (tuner-amplifier) of not less than 20 watts per channel output, or a separate amplifier of similar capability with matching radio (FM) tuner, a disc player with a magnetic cartridge, together with a good open-reel tape recorder operating at 9.5 and 19 cm/sec (3¾ and 7½ inches per second) complete with a suitable microphone. All, with the possible exception of the microphone, should be stereo units, and twin microphones for stereo would be a real advantage if serious recording is to be attempted. Such a room as we envisage should receive acoustic treatment on the lines suggested above.

It must be understood that a room becomes part of any loudspeaker(s) used in it. The inevitable variations in the units of equipment themselves, and in the size and shape of the rooms, present a series of situations in which the basic rules are few, and in which the most satisfactory solutions can be found only by trial and error. Some guidance in the choice and use of audio equipment follows, which may enable more satisfactory results to be obtained. The complexity of an installation will necessarily depend upon its scope. In large school halls, with acoustic difficulties which cannot be corrected without extensive and prohibitively expensive treatment, it may be necessary to use loudspeakers of special type, and in such conditions the services of an audio consultant should be enlisted.

The choice of equipment: tape-recorders

The variety of equipment available today is immense, but much of it is quite unsuitable for application to classroom situations. Most education authorities can provide a service of information and advice on the choice of suitable audio-visual apparatus. Such services should always be employed when the need for new or additional equipment arises or the improvement of an existing system is being considered, in order to ensure that the best value for money is obtained and that anything added will match up with what is there already.

Choice of equipment must always be made in close relationship to the purposes for which it is intended to be used, and in conjunction with expert advice. It is not satisfactory to browse through catalogues, nor to choose on a cost basis or from specifications or consumer reports. Compatibility is a consideration of first importance. The term covers a wide range: the suitability of pick-ups for the amplifiers or tape recorders with which they are intended to be used, and vice-versa; the matching of radio and tuner outputs to amplifier inputs (and similar considerations in respect of tape recorders); the impedance of loudspeakers, their power-handling capacities and suitability for their intended locations and for the kinds of sound which they will be required to reproduce, etc. These matters, with such frustrating points as the correct termination of connecting leads from one piece of equipment to another, call for expert advice and usually for investigation in the actual room where the equipment will be used.

There is no doubt that the most versatile and useful single piece of equipment for classroom use is the tape-recorder. We are witnessing the rapid spread of the small, easily portable cassette machine, which has many valuable qualities, particularly in the hands of individuals or small groups, but which is also subject to inherent limitations. These machines are almost foolproof in operation, but the commercially recorded cassettes available are not the equivalent in quality of good records, nor are the machines satisfactory for the reproduction of sound for the benefit of everyone in a classroom, except in alliance with a suitable external amplifier and loudspeakers. Further, since we are consdering high-quality reproduction, whether of commercial or self-made tapes, from such a machine, a built-in noise-reduction system

— usually and preferably Dolby — is necessary, and this both adds to complexity and increases cost. It is also extremely difficult to edit tapes made on cassette machines except by transfer to open reels. Nevertheless, cassette machines are very handy tools because they can be used for purposes and in situations which preclude the employment of larger and heavier machines. This is especially true of those cassette recorders which operate from internal batteries or a.c. mains at will.

The open-reel recorder, in conjunction with a radio set and/or record player, can meet more requirements. Machines may be obtained which incorporate amplifiers of decent quality giving outputs of around 10 watts, which will drive an external speaker comfortably. It is necessary to ensure that such a machine has an input socket (usually marked 'phono' or 'gram') suitable for a record-player — and, moreover, that the input is technically suitable to the use of a magnetic pick-up. Most tape-recorders can accommodate only a crystal or ceramic pick-up, which is inferior to magnetic in quality of recorded sound.

Loudspeakers

Where possible, it is always desirable to use two loudspeakers rather than one. Stereo is now the hi-fi norm (in radio broadcasts as well as with records), and it is, of course, impossible with a single speaker. Even in playing mono recordings, the use of two speakers has the apparent effect of taking the sound 'out of the box' and putting it *between* the speakers. There is also some gain in efficiency (that is, in sound output for a given input level to the loudspeakers), while troubles due to standing waves and eigentones (room resonances produced by parallel walls) are reduced. It must be mentioned, with reference to our diagram, that only those seated roughly within the triangular area marked will receive full stereo effects; to those outside it, reproduction may appear predominantly right- or left-biased.

As for quadraphonic (four-channelled) sound, this is still at a provisional stage of technical development and marketing. It is at least doubtful whether, for serious listening, any true quadraphonic system has real advantages over the much less costly 'Surround Sound' or 'Ambiophonic' system, which requires only an additional pair of speakers and an inexpensive, passive device known usually as a 'resolver' or '4-channel adaptor'. Such a system may be used to replay both stereo and quadraphonic discs with greater realism for the benefit of a relatively small group seated in the central area of a music room, but it is not useful for ordinary classroom applications.

Loudspeakers need careful disposition. In an ordinary classroom, whether one or two are used, they are generally best placed in corners, on the short side of an oblong room, facing the diagonally opposite corners and raised about 5 ft from the floor. In a music room, where there will be a piano, the speakers should be placed as far from it as possible; and since they will, or should, be larger, heavier models specially designed for high quality music reproduction, they should rest either on the floor itself or be raised not more than 12 to 18 in. above it, on stands which allow clear space under the bases, so that the tops of the speakers are at roughly the height of the heads of the seated listeners.

Where the basic classroom installation consists of extension speakers fed from a central source, it is essential that the speakers are fitted with volume controls, and that they can be immediately detached from the sockets and used in conjunction with a tape-recorder or other equipment in temporary use in the room. When operating from the central source, it is a common error to turn up the amplifier volume control too far and to operate with the loudspeaker controls well down. The reverse procedure should be followed, with the loudspeaker controls at maximum and the source control no higher than is necessary for comfortable listening.

Loudspeakers should always be separate from the other units — otherwise we have the old radiogram or stereogram, which is quite unsuitable for classroom use, cannot provide decent stereo, and is not easily transportable. However, there are now available at reasonable cost some excellent transportable units (without speakers) which combine amplifier, FM tuner and record player with inputs and outputs for tape machines, enabling taped performances to be reproduced on them, or the reproduced sound itself to be transferred to tape. Such units are usually referred to as 'combination units' or 'audio units'. The combination unit can be connected to external loudspeakers, which need not be those made or offered by the maker of the unit, but which should be of the recommended impedance. Some instruments incorporate cassette decks in place of, or in addition to the record-player, but this reduces the field of use of the cassette machine, which is always better as a separate (transportable) unit.

Radio and record-playing equipment

The radio component in a classroom system must be capable of receiving FM (frequency-modulation) broadcasts (also known as VHF or Very High Frequency). Only these provide a really high quality of music reproduction. An efficient and suitable aerial is essential for good radio reception, particularly for stereo, and should be professionally installed with the aid of a signal strength meter. It may be combined with a television aerial.

The terms *tuner, amplifier,* and combined *tuner-amplifier* (also called 'receiver') will be encountered. An amplifier (divided into pre-amplifier and power amplifier) is a device to increase the level of a signal and provide the power necessary to drive loudspeakers. Various sound sources may be fed to it — radio, disc, tape and in some cases, microphone. There should also be a 'tape out' facility so that radio or disc material can be fed to a tape-recorder.

A tuner is a circuit unit designed to receive radio transmissions and convert them to a form and level suitable for feeding an amplifier input. It will not work by itself. A tuner-amplifier (or receiver) is a combination of these two units. It offers some advantages in space, economy, avoidance of extra connecting leads, and price. The amplifier lies at the heart of any audio system, and a great many factors have to be taken into account in making a choice: facilities, compatibility with any existing equipment, power output, reliability, ease of service, etc. Unless the person saddled with the task of making the choice has considerable audio experience, it is essential to call in expert advice and to provide *full details* of the requirements, because limitations of the amplifier or receiver will inevitably limit the whole system.

In operation, care should be taken not to short-circuit the speaker outputs of an amplifier, or to operate the amplifier on 'open circuit', i.e. with no speakers connected. If, for any reason, one channel only of a stereo amplifier is used, the other speaker output terminals should be connected together via a resistor of 5 to 15 ohms value and 15 watts minimum rating.

The term 'record player' can be misleading. In common use it describes a self-contained portable unit *with its own inbuilt amplifier and loudspeaker(s)* without pretensions to high quality reproduction, and not intended to feed external equipment. Such instruments have some applications in education, especially in the provision of musical stimulus or accompaniment to physical activities in the open air, when the only addition needed is an extension lead to the nearest mains socket; they are, however, really outside the field covered by this article. The units used for feeding external equipment (i.e. separate amplifier and loudspeakers) are usually called 'record decks'. They consist simply of a turntable and pick-up arm to which a pick-up *cartridge* (which carries the stylus) is fitted. A wide variety of such units is available, and they may be classified in various ways, the most important being speeds and mode of operation (manual or auto-change). Some of these are described as 'transcription' decks, a term which is intended to denote high quality, but which really has very little meaning.

Automatic record-changers should be avoided, or used only in the single-play mode. Not only is the more complex mechanism of the auto-changer more likely to give trouble, but sooner or later — probably sooner — the stacking of discs for auto-changing will cause damage to them. In these days when a complete symphony may take only one side of a disc, it is difficult to see why anyone should want the auto-change facility, particularly in a teaching situation. *Semi-automatic* operation, which lowers the pick-up gently on to the disc at any chosen point, and automatically raises it, returns it to the rest and stops the motor at the end of a disc, does have advantages, and more and more record decks now have this facility.

The quality of the record deck, and more particularly the mass and freedom of movement of the pick-up arm, will impose restrictions on the choice of pick-up cartridge. The manufacturer or supplier, or the technical service of the leading audio journals can offer informed and reliable advice on this and other matters concerning the choice and operation of audio components. It is always better to seek advice as early as possible, before items of doubtful compatibility have been acquired.

Most models today are two-speed, giving a choice only of 33 and 45 revolutions per minute, playing microgroove (vinyl) discs, whether mono or stereo. It should be noted that a stereo record requires a stereo pick-up with a special type of stylus (needle), which may also be conveniently used when playing mono records. But the converse does not apply: a pick-up and stylus designed only for mono records must *not* be used on stereo records, or fatal damage to the surface may result. A few record decks (and record-players) will also provide 78rpm speed for the older (shellac) type of discs which are still found in some school and college libraries: such records require a different type of stylus, which can be put in place in a few seconds (and which must not be used with microgroove records, whether mono or stereo).

Microphones, television

There are several different types of microphones, named according to their operating principles, or sometimes according to their reception patterns or polar diagrams. As in the case of pick-ups and amplifiers, not every microphone will work with every tape-recorder. The safe plan is to use a microphone recommended by the manufacturer of the tape-recorder, but the polar diagram must be selected according to the purpose for which the instrument will mainly be used. The cardioid is probably the most useful for music recording and for most school applications. Expert advice is highly desirable when making a choice.

The television receiver, though increasingly used in schools and colleges, does not properly come within the scope of this article. It is perhaps sufficient to note that the sound obtained on a standard television receiver is not of 'hi-fi' quality (nor is it stereo) but that an increasing number of BBC transmissions of important musical events are being made in simultaneous television and (VHF stereo) sound. On no account should an attempt be made to connect an external loudspeaker to a television set without expert advice. The result of such an attempt could be lethal.

Use and maintenance

Audio apparatus is frequently supplied with mains leads of insufficient length for classroom use. In such cases a mains plug should be fitted and a properly made-up extension lead used to reach the wall socket. Wiring mains plugs is a simple operation but the colour coding must be strictly observed. Speakers are best connected by means of non-reversible plugs and sockets or colour coded terminals and flex of heavy (23/.0076) gauge, plastic covered. A request for heavy twin-core flex, plastic covered, will produce the right article. Alternatively, three-core flex, as used for irons or fires, can be used, the yellow/green striped conductor (earth) being cut back and not used, and the brown lead connected to the amplifier and speaker terminals marked + (plus) and the blue to that marked − (minus) in each channel. This will ensure correct phasing of loudspeakers.

Installation and the initial checking of function will normally be carried out by the supplier or technician, but this is only half the battle, and it does not absolve the users of the equipment from their duty to read carefully the instruction booklets which accompany every piece of audio apparatus, and to do so with the equipment in front of

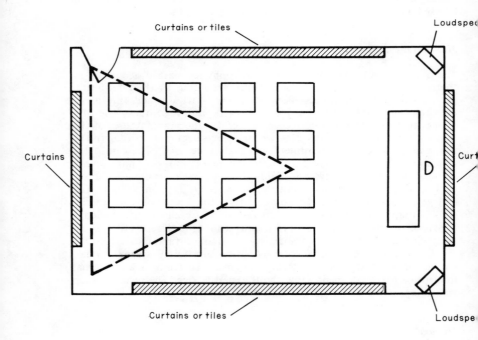

Basic classroom arrangement, with acoustic treatment. Curtains or tiles on side walls may not be necessary, if curtains across back and between speakers are adequate. Even a heavy curtain across back of room (wall at opposite end from loudspeakers) only will improve results.

them. Failure to do this is responsible for more poor results and unnecessary service-calls than any other single factor.

Maintenance of equipment by the user should consist simply of careful cleaning of tape machines according to instructions, the de-magnetizing of tape heads, regular cleaning of the pick-up stylus with a stylus brush, and an occasional check on the tracking weight of the pick-up, which should be set at the maker's recommended *maximum* for the particular cartridge in use. Once a year, during the summer holiday, all the equipment except the loudspeakers should be taken away by a competent and well-established audio engineer, completely checked over, and delivered at the beginning of the following term. When equipment is first installed or returned from service, and periodically during use, it is necessary to check that it is correctly set up and functioning properly. A test disc such as HMV SEOM 6, 'The Enjoyment of Stereo', is essential for this operation.

Tapes and discs should be stored in a cupboard or cabinet in a dry place away from any source of heat, such as radiators or direct sun. Gramophone records should be kept upright under slight pressure, not in stacks one on top of another, or leaning sideways. They should be cleaned before use with one of the many devices available for this purpose, bearing in mind that cloths, whether impregnated or not, are useless because they can remove only surface dust. The use of a 'dust bug', which traverses the surface while the disc is being played, is recommended.

A number of useful pamphlets may be obtained at low cost from The Educational Foundation for Visual Aids, 33 Queen Anne St, London W1M 9FB t 01-636 5742. List with prices on request. The following books currently (1975) in print give valuable technical advice:

Borwick, John. *Living with Hi-Fi.* General Gramophone Publications Ltd
Crabbe, John. *Hi-fi in the Home.* Blandford Press
Paul, Norman. *You and Your Tape Recorder.* W. & G. Foyle Ltd
Sharp, Peter E.M. *Sound and Vision.* MacDonald and Jane's
Weston, John. *Tape-recorder in the Classroom.* National Committee for Audio-Visual Aids in Education

A first-interest book for children 12 to 14 years is *Records, Tapes and Cassettes* by H.R. Schatter (Lutterworth Press).

In addition to purely technical journals, a number of publications which aim to guide the listener in the choice of records also provide technical news, reviews of new equipment, etc. — particularly *The Gramophone* and *Hi-Fi News and Record Review.* See full list of periodicals on p.228.

Section Three

INTERLUDE

The Pop Debate

The proper place of popular or light music in the process of music education is not a new subject. Gordon Reynolds in his article *On Being a Music Teacher* refers to the illicit pleasure which he and his teacher took long ago in introducing such music into the supposedly orthodox hour of piano lessons.

But the new pervasiveness of pop music, and in particular its commercial hold over the young, have reinforced the necessity for further discussion. Is it debased art, belonging to a kind of sub-culture — or is it part of a counter-culture? Or can it after all be reconciled with the classical mainstream, as might be suggested by the recognition which a composer like Leonard Bernstein and a critic like William Mann gave to the Beatles?

In spring 1975 a display-exhibition called *Pop Music in Education*, organized by Tony Attwood, was held by the Inner London Education Authority at its Teachers' Centre for Music. A sympathetic article by Keith Swanwick from which we quote below appeared in *The Times Educational Supplement* on 13 June 1975. No less strongly, Ruth Gipps in the spring 1975 issue of *Composer* (the journal of the Composers' Guild of Great Britain) expressed the opposite view that pop is a commercialization and a betrayal. Ruth Gipps is a conductor and composer and on the staff of the Royal College of Music; Dr Swanwick is a Senior Lecturer in the Music Department of the Institute of Education, London University.

The first extract is reproduced by permission of Dr Gipps; the second is reproduced from *The Times Educational Supplement* by permission.

Ruth Gipps

Ranging from the super-intellectual to the wildest and woolliest lunatic fringe, we have for years been given performances of worthless nonsense, while real composers have been labelled backward-looking, unenterprising, or 'unwilling to experiment'. The extremes of the avant-garde eventually meet the extremes of amplified 'pop', which leads young people through sheer volume and physical excitement of an unhealthy kind first to total selfishness — not minding disturbing others with the noise — and then to dirty living, drug addiction and crimes of violence. 'Pop' is no joke. It is a commercial product with the sole purpose of making money and, where good music uplifts, 'pop' debases. It was no coincidence that a particular organisation promoting both avant-garde and 'pop' was directed by a nihilist. It is time some of us came into the open and said what we know to be true — that, quite apart from the actual physical deafness it is causing, amplified 'pop' is evil and injures those who participate in it. The National Association of Schoolmasters has issued a statement (*Daily Telegraph* 31 Oct 1974) giving 'Pop Culture' as one of the reasons for indiscipline in schools. Every music teacher should instil into pupils the truth that it is harmful and incidentally stupid. In no circumstances should it be used as an 'introduction' to music — one might as well start a course on literature by teaching children to write rude words on lavatory walls.

'Pop' is not music. But then, nor are a lot of the nonsenses evolved under the heading of some gimmick or other, and presented — broadcast if their perpetrators can arrange it — with the sole motive of raking in the performing rights. (Good wangles are very long sustained notes clocking up, or *aleatoric music* which saves a lot of labour except for the unfortunate performers!) As for the use of 'pop' or 'beat' with amplified guitars to present the story of Christ — thereby implying that the greatest mind of all time had no vestige of artistic taste — it is an ugly blasphemy, both religious and aesthetic.

Keith Swanwick

Some music teachers have insisted that it is their business to give the children bread, even though they ask for Stones. Pop is still to many just 'bad music' which 'leads nowhere', and to have any truck with it in schools is a betrayal of both the young and our cultural heritage. More sensitively, though, it is possible to see pop as 'sacred ground', which can only be profaned if subjected to the coarse, institutionalized behaviour of teachers in schools.

But in any case it would be naive to assume that pop is always and merely a group-enforcing ritual. In a similar way, we are forced to differentiate a variety of pop music, rather than a single category. All pop may sound the same to the untutored adult ear, blasted by an unprovoked assault from Radio 1, just as all classical music can sound the same to the uninitiated. But a closer examination will reveal the different styles of reggae, soul, rock, perhaps progressive rock, possibly folk music rural and urban, as well as the intellectual offerings of performers like Steeleye Span or Simon and Garfunkel.

The effort required to develop aurally an understanding and discriminating attitude to pop seems particularly rewarding when the social environment of any school is such that pop is the basic tradition the youngsters have assimilated. But we ought not to feel that pop is only a last resort when a school has its back to the wall. It does often function as the folk music of our time, whether it is called that or not, and as such it has the power to influence the way we feel in fairly simple and direct ways. Recently I overheard a boy in a grammar school comment to a friend during a class rehearsal of 'The Streets of London': 'Every time I hear this song I want to cry.' And why not?

Section Four

NEWS

People and Posts

Appointments, etc., listed here were announced in the twelve months before 1 August 1975.

Arnold, Malcolm: hon Member, Royal Academy of Music
Bach, Erik: Forman Fellowship in composition, Edinburgh University
Baker, Janet: hon D Mus, London University; hon M Mus, Hull University; hon D Mus, Oxford University
Barenboim, Daniel: hon Member, Royal Academy of Music
Barker, Noelle: hon Member, Guildhall School of Music
Bate (John) Choir: first prize, large choir class, National Choral Competition 1975
Bent, Ian D.: Professor of Music, Nottingham University
Berkeley, Sir Lennox: president, Performing Right Society
Bernstein, Leonard: hon D Litt, Warwick University
Bolton, Christine: joint winner, Maggie Teyte Prize 1974
Bonington, Ian W. G.: lecturer, School of Fine Arts and Music, University of East Anglia
Bosanko, C. (head of music, Oakmead School, Bournemouth): MBE
Bowles, Anthony: hon Member, Guildhall School of Music
Brand, Geoffrey: director, Rural Music Schools Association
Brewer, Michael: director of music, Chetham's Hospital School, Manchester
Briggs, David: first prize, BBC Major Minor junior piano competition, Midlands 1975
Britten, Benjamin: hon D Litt, Warwick University
Burgess, Russell: MBE
Burton, Humphrey: head of arts and music programmes, BBC Television
Butterworth, Arthur: music adviser, National Youth Brass Band of Great Britain
Byrne, Andrew W. A.: senior lecturer in music, Reading University
Cain, David: composer in residence, Cumberland County
Campbell, David (clarinet): joint winner, Southern Musicians Scheme 1975

Cooke, John: northern commissioner, Royal School of
    Church Music
Cranmer, Philip: secretary, Associated Board of the
    Royal Schools of Music
Cudworth, Charles: hon doctorate, Open University
Dankworth, John: hon MA, Open University
Davenport, Glyn (bass-baritone): joint winner,
    Southern Musicians Scheme 1975
Davison, Arthur: hon M Mus, University of Wales
Deane, Basil: professor of music, Manchester
    University
Dick, W. M. (head janitor, Royal Scottish Academy of
    Music): BEM
Donington, Robert: hon Member, Royal Academy of
    Music
East, Leslie: director of music, Guildhall School
    of Music and Drama
Fermoy, Rt Hon Lady (founder and chairman, King's
    Lynn Festival): hon D Mus, University of East
    Anglia
Fischer, Karl von: hon Member, Royal Musical
    Association
Fitzwilliam String Quartet: quartet in residence,
    Warwick University
Francescatti, Zino: hon Member, Royal Academy of
    Music
Frank, Alan: chairman, Performing Right Society
Gibson, Patrick (chairman, Arts Council): life peer
Goehr, Alexander: professor of music, Cambridge
    University (from September 1976)
Groves, Sir Charles: hon Member, Guildhall School
    of Music
Grumiaux, Arthur: hon Member, Royal Academy of Music
Hague, Pauline: principal, Belfast Academy of Music
    and Dramatic Arts
Henze, Hans Werner: hon Member, Royal Academy of
    Music
Holliger, Heinz: hon Member, Royal Academy of Music
Holst, Imogen: CBE
Hunt, Donald: hon D Mus, Leeds University; organist
    and choirmaster, Worcester Cathedral
Ireland, Patrick (viola, Allegri String Quartet):
    hon M Mus, Hull University
Jones, Philip: head, School of Wind and Percussion,
    Royal Northern College of Music
Kenny, Yvonne (soprano): Kathleen Ferrier Memorial
    Scholarship 1975
Laine, Cleo: hon MA, Open University
Lampard, Ann: joint winner, Maggie Teyte Prize 1974
Langford, William (pianist): Gulbenkian Music Fellow-
    ship 1975
Leatherby, Carol (soprano): joint winner, Southern

Musicians Scheme 1975
Leggate, Robin (tenor):   Richard Tauber Memorial
   Prize, Anglo-Austrian Music Society 1975
Lutoslawski, Witold: hon D Mus, Lancaster University
McCredie, Andrew: Dent Medal for musical scholarship
   (International Musicological Society) 1975
McKendrick, J. E. (lately principal music teacher,
   Hillhead High School, Glasgow):   MBE
Magill, Ronan (piano):   joint best performer, Young
   Musicians 75, Greater London Arts Association
Maguire, Hugh
   M Mus, Hull University
Maidment, W. R. (director of libraries and arts,
   Camden):   OBE
Mann, Manfred: musician in residence, Goldsmiths'
   College, London University
Matthews, Colin: Ian Whyte Award for composition 1975
Matthews, Denis: CBE
May, Marius (violoncello):   Gulbenkian Music Fellow-
   ship 1975
Medici String Quartet: resident string quartet, York
   University
Meikle, R. B.:   director, School of Music, Leicester
   University
Menuhin, Yehudi: hon Fellow, Manchester Polytechnic
Minton, Yvonne: hon Member, Royal Academy of Music
Mitchell, John: lecturer, School of Fine Arts and
   Music, University of East Anglia
Morgan, Geoffrey: first prize, London Organ Week 1975
Muldowney, Dominic: composer in residence, Southern
   Arts Association
Munster, Countess of: hon Fellow, Royal Academy of
   Music
Murray, Ann (mezzo-soprano):   Gulbenkian Music Fellow-
   ship 1975
Nevens, David: first prize, Wangford Festival
   Composers' Competition 1975
Nichols, R. D. E.:   research fellow in music,
   Birmingham University
Oliver, Stephen: composition prize, Greater London
   Arts Association Young Musicians' Scheme 1975
Palmer, Jane: composition prize, Society of Women
   Musicians 1975
Parker-Smith, Jane: first prize, National Organ
   Competition, Holy Trinity Church, Southport 1974
Parsons, Geoffrey: hon Member, Royal Academy of Music
Parsons, James: Rushworth Trust Memorial Prize for
   improvisation, National Organ Competition, Holy
   Trinity Church, Southport 1974
Penderecki, Krzysztof: hon Member, Royal Academy of
   Music

Reeser, Eduard: hon Member, Royal Musical
  Association
Renshaw, Peter: head, Yehudi Menuhin School
Robinson, Michael F.: senior lecturer in music,
  Cardiff University
Rose, Bernard: president, Royal College of Organists
Roth, David (second violin, Allegri String Quartet):
  hon M Mus, University of Hull
Rushworth, James: hon MA, Liverpool University
Sampson, Dr Peggie: visiting research fellow in music,
  Edinburgh University
Schrecker, Bruno (violoncello, Allegri String
  Quartet): hon M Mus, Hull University
Schwarzkopf, Elisabeth: hon Member, Royal Academy
  of Music
Seeger, Charles: hon Member, Royal Musical
  Association
Soul, Betty Jean: director, National Operatic and
  Dramatic Association
Spink, Ian W. A.: professor of music, Royal Holloway
  College, London
Sudbury, Graham: director of music, University
  Church of Great St Mary, Cambridge
Sutherland, Joan: hon D Mus, Liverpool University
Sutton, Ivan: hon Member, Guildhall School of Music
Swayne, Giles: Lancaster University Composition
  Prize 1974
Thoday, Gillian (violoncello): joint best performer,
  Young Musicians 75, Greater London Arts Association
Tillett, Emmie: hon Fellow, Royal Academy of Music.
Tilmouth, Professor M.: dean of the Faculty of
  Music, Edinburgh University
Tippett, Sir Michael: hon D Litt, Warwick University;
  hon D Mus, London University
Toad Choir, Greenock: first prize, small choir class,
  National Choral Competition 1975
Tortelier, Paul: hon D Mus, Oxford University
Trowell, Brian: King Edward Chair of Music, King's
  College, London
Tureck, Rosalyn: Fellow, Wolfson College, Oxford
Wales, Roy: director of music, Warwick University
Watkins, Michael Blake: Menuhin Prize for composition
Westrup, Sir Jack (died April 1975): hon D Mus,
  Durham University, January 1975
Williams, G. L.: lecturer, Department of Music,
  University College of North Wales, Bangor
Williams, Jonathan (violoncello): Gulbenkian Music
  Fellowship 1975
Wood, Avril: hon Member, Guildhall School of Music

New Music, New Books

Pat Williams

MUSIC

The following selection of music published in the UK
between January 1974 and July 1975 is directed to
those involved in primary and secondary music education and also in the training of music teachers.
For comprehensive lists of new music, see the reviews
of music and lists of new publications in the *Musical
Times* each month.

Appleby, B. W. and F. Fowler. *The School Recorder
  Assembly Book*. Arnold 45p (music for assembly for
  voices, recorders and piano)
Arch, Gwyn and Pat Rooke. *That's the Spirit*.
  British & Continental 60p (musical play)
Arch, Gwyn. *The Discontented Man*. British &
  Continental 60p (musical play)
Beaumont, Geoffrey. *Hymn Tunes*. Weinberger 50p
  (unison voices)
Bell, Sybil (arr). *Six Christmas Carols from Europe*.
  Ricordi £1 (unison voices, recorders and percussion)
Bergmann, Walter. *When the Saints go Marching in*.
  Universal £1.15 (unison voices, recorders, Orff
  instruments and piano)
Bizet, arr. David Stone. *Carillon from L'Arlésienne
  Suite no. 1*. Boosey £1.50 (school orchestra)
Blom, Michael and Michael Hurd. *Hip-Hip Horatio*.
  Novello 90p (an 'oratorio' for narrator, chorus
  and piano)
Blyton, C. and P. Porter. *Konrad of the Mountains*.
  Belwin-Mills 60p (instrumental pieces, songs and
  poems for 9-10 year olds)
Burnett, Michael. *Songs for Naomi*. Ricordi £1
  (unison voices, recorders, percussion and piano)
Coombes, Douglas. *Songs for Singing Together*. BBC
  £1.25 (50 songs from the BBC programme)
Cruft, Adrian. *Suite for Strings, no. 3*. Chappell £2
Dodgson, Stephen. *Idyll for Strings*. Chappell £2
Dolmetsch, Carl. *The School Recorder Book 3*.
  Arnold 50p
Foster, A. *Jonah and the Whale*. OUP £1.59 (enter-
  tainment for junior choirs and audience with piano
  and optional instruments)

Fraser, S. *Full Fathom Five.* Thames 75p (song
cycle for SAB)
Gavall, John. *A First Book of Guitar Solos.* OUP £1
Gilbert, W. S. and A. Sullivan. *The Mikado.*
Cramer £1.20 (school edition by C. le Fleming)
Harrap, Beatrice. *Apusskidu.* A. & C. Black £1.75
(songs for children with instrumental accompaniment)
Hudson, Hazel. *The Shepherds.* Ashdown 40p (carol
sequence for voices and instruments)
Kelly, Bryan. *Half-a-fortnight.* Novello £1.60 (7
unison songs for group music making)
Lewin, O. *Brown Gal in de Ring.* OUP 40p (12
Jamaican folk songs)
Liadov, arr. David Stone. *Eight Russian Folksongs
Set 1.* Boosey £1.50
Lipkin, Malcolm. *The White Crane.* J. & W. Chester
£1.32 (musical play)
Lord, J. E. *Nonsongs.* Universal 60p (6 songs for
voices, descant recorders, percussion and piano)
McCabe, J. *Suite: The Lion, the Witch and the
Wardrobe.* Novello £3.50 (school orchestra)
Mahler, G. *Bruder Martin.* Bosworth 50p (school
orchestra)
Mathias, William. *Celtic Dances.* OUP £3.50 (school
orchestra)
Maughan, J. (arr). *Tommy Thumb.* OUP 65p (unison
voices and instruments)
Maxwell-Timmins, D. *Morning has Broken.* Schofield
& Sims, pupils' edition 55p; piano edition £1.75
(hymns)
Mendoza, Anne. *A Festival for Autumn.* Novello 50p
(voices, percussion, recorders, guitar/cello)
Mossman, Sheila. *Lyra Songbook.* Rahter/Schauer, 2
vols. 60p each
Muhr, Nessy. *Ding dong sing a song.* Ricordi £1.50
(6 canons for children)
New hymns for young people. Weinberger 60p
Panufnik, A. *Thames Pageant.* Boosey £1.50 (cantata
for young players and singers)
Parry, W.H. *St. Jerome and the Lion.* Keith Prowse
Music 75p (religious cantata for voices and
instruments)
Pavey, S. *Clog Dance.* Bosworth 50p (school
orchestra)
Windmills. Bosworth 50p (school orchestra)
Pehkonen, Elis. *Fafnir and the Knights.* Lengnick
£1.25 (cantata for treble voices and piano duet)
Platts, Kenneth. *Three Bird Songs.* Ashdown 30p
(voices and instruments)
Portnoff, L. *Concertino, op. 13.* Bosworth 75p
Rivers, Patrick (arr). *Novello Band Book.* Novello
£2 (studies and pieces for wind/brass band)

Reynolds, Gordon. *Praise with Instruments*. Novello
75p (instrumental pieces for informal acts of worship with primary children)
Rowen, Jon (arr). *Turpin Hero*. OUP £1.60 (30 folk
songs for voices and guitar)
Russell-Smith, G. and M. *A Box of Toys*. Novello 50p
(entertainment for speech and percussion)
Sargent, Brian. *Minstrels*. CUP 80p (medieval music
to sing and play)
Troubadours. CUP 85p (medieval music to sing and
play)
Shaw, Francis. *The Selfish Giant*. J. & W. Chester
£2.75 (opera for young people)
Sound in the Round. National Federation of Women's
Institutes 15p (20 rounds for primary and secondary
schools)
Stoker, Richard, *Chorale for String Orchestra*.
Breitkopf & Hartel 60p
Little Symphony. Boosey £1.50 (school orchestra)
Tchaikovsky, arr. Anthony Carter. *1812 Overture*.
Bosworth £1.50 (school orchestra)
Walton, William, arr. Bram Wiggins. *Miniatures*.
OUP, set 1 £2.50; set 2 £3.00 (wind band)
Warlock, Peter. *Candlelight*. Thames 90p (12 nursery
jingles)
Wesley, Samuel. *Symphony no. 5*. OUP £3.50 (school
orchestra)
Williamson, Malcolm. *The Glitter Gang*. Weinberger
70p (cassation for audience and orchestra or piano)
Wind Band Book. OUP £2.75 (seven pieces)
Withams, E. L. *The Horse of Wood*. Universal £1.35
(pop-style cantata)

BOOKS

The following list of books published in the UK
between January 1974 and July 1975 is specifically
directed to those involved in primary and secondary
music education and in the training of music teachers.
For a comprehensive list covering the whole range of
music and music education, see the BRITISH MUSIC
YEARBOOK

Alvin, Juliette. *Music Therapy*. (revised edition).
Hutchinson £4.25
Bessom, M., A. Tatarunis and S. Forcucci. *Teaching
Music in Today's Secondary Schools*. Holt, Rinehart
& Winston £5.20
Bontinck, Irmgard (ed). *New Patterns of Musical*

Behaviour: a survey of youth activities in eighteen countries. Universal £4.50

Burgan, A. *Basic String Repairs: A guide for string class teachers.* OUP £1.75

Chacksfield, K. M., P. A. Binns and V. M. Robins. *Music and language with young children.* Blackwell £4.50

Choksy, Lois. *The Kodaly Method: comprehensive music education from infant to adult.* Prentice-Hall £2.60

Cook, C. A. *Essays of a String Teacher.* Bosworth £3.50

Creative Music Making and the Young School Leaver. Blackie £1.40

Dobbs, J., R. Fiske and M. Lane. *Ears and Eyes.* OUP, Pupils' Books 1 & 2, 35p each; Teacher's Book £2.20 (music course for 7-9 year olds with word cards, tape or cassette)

Dwyer, Terence. *Making Electronic Music.* OUP, Pupils' Books 1 & 2, £1.50 each; Teacher's Manual, £1.90; sound material available

Enoch, Yvonne. *Group Piano Teaching.* OUP £2.30

Glynne Jones, M. L. *Music.* Macmillan £2.60 (middle school music)

Hart, Muriel. *Music.* Heinemann Educational 80p (primary school music)

Hinson, M. *The Piano Teacher's Sourcebook: an annotated bibliography of books related to the piano and piano music.* Belwin-Mills £2

Horsfall, Jean. *Teaching the Cello to Groups.* OUP £2.75

Ingley, W. Stevens and Hilda Hunter. *Music for Today's Children.* H. Hunter, 63 Highfield Road, Rowley Regis, Warley, West Midlands £1.50 (teaching method)

John, Malcolm. *Music Drama in Schools* (re-issue). OUP £1.50

Keetman, G. *Elementaria: first acquaintance with Orff-Schulwerk.* Schott £4.50

Kliewer, V. L. *Aural Training: a comprehensive approach.* Prentice-Hall £4.15

Lawrence, Ian. *Music and the Teacher.* Pitman £2

Morrish, D. L. *Basic Goals in Music* (new edition). McGraw-Hill, book 1 £1.10; book 2 £1.20 (ideas for junior music)

Paynter, E. and J. *The Dance and the Drum.* Universal £2 (integrated projects in music, dance and drama for schools)

Priestley, M. *Music Therapy in Action.* Constable £4

Schafer, M. *Readings in Music Education.* Collier-Macmillan £2.95

Steinitz, P. and S. Sterman. *Harmony in Context.* Belwin-Mills £2

Szony, E. *Kodaly's Principles in Practice: an
    approach to music education through the Kodaly
    Method.* Boosey £2.95
Thomson, J. M. *Your Book of the Recorder.*   Faber
    £1.25
Vajda, C. *The Kodaly Way to Music.* Boosey £3.75
Warburton, A. O. *Analyses of Musical Classics, book
    4.* Longman £1.75
Witham, June. *Music Workshop.* Macmillan £4.75
    (word-card approach for top infants and lower
    juniors)
Witkin, R. W. *The Intelligence of Feeling.* Heine-
    mann Educational £3.75 (creative arts in the context
    of education)

Section Five

DIRECTORY

1   Government Offices

Department of Education and Science, Elizabeth Ho,
York Rd, London SE1 7PH t 01-928 9222 tg aristides
Secretary of State Rt Hon Fred Mulley MP
Staff Inspector (Music) W. H. Parry

The Department has responsibility for education at
all levels in England and for further and higher
education in Wales, where primary and secondary
education is the responsibility of the Secretary
of State for Wales. HM Inspectorate works in close
association with the Schools Council, 160 Gt Portland St, London W1N 6LL t 01-580 0352, has access
to all institutions except the universities and
related bodies, and reports to both the Secretary
of State for Education and Science and the
Secretary of State for Wales.

Welsh Education Office, 31 Cathedral Rd, Cardiff CF1
9UJ t Cardiff 42661. *HM Inspector (Music)*
K. M. Evans

Scottish Education Department, St Andrew's Ho, Edinburgh EH1 3DB t 031-556 8501. *Chief Inspector
(Music)* J. Rankin

Department of Education in Northern Ireland, Rathgael
Ho, Balloo Rd, Bangor, Co Down BT19 2PR t Bangor
66311. *Chief Inspector (Music)* R. Simpson

2   H.M. Schools Inspectors of Music

The School Inspectorate includes a number of
inspectors specially for music. They are:

ENGLAND

Staff Inspector (Music): W. H. Parry, Dept of Education and Science, Turret Ho, Epsom Rd, Guildford,
Surrey GU1 3PH t Guildford 75159/76059

Eastern Division. M. G. C. Channon, Dept of Education and Science, 38 Museum St, Ipswich, Suffolk IP1 1JG; D. J. Wells, Dept of Education and Science, Caldicott School, Highbury Rd, Hitchin, Herts SG4 9RP

London and South Midlands. Mrs E. V. de Bray, Dept of Education and Science, 296-304 High St, London W3 9BJ

Midland Division. Mrs B. Rees-Davies, Dept of Education and Science, Calthorpe Ho, Hagley Rd, Birmingham B16 8QS

North Midland Division. W. H. Parry, Dept of Education and Science, Turret Ho, Epsom Rd, Guildford, Surrey GU1 3PH

Northern Division. R. Nicholls and T. N. Tunnard, Dept of Education and Science, 44-60 Richardshaw La, Pudsey, W. Yorks LS28 7OD

North-Western Division. I. P. Salisbury, Dept of Education and Science, 86 Northgate St, Chester CH1 2HT

Southern Division. J. W. Stephens, Dept of Education and Science, 42-8 St George's St, Winchester, Hants SO23 8BE; G. E. Trodd, Dept of Education and Science, 14c Lonsdale Gdns, Tunbridge Wells, Kent TN1 1PB

South-Western Division. W. Drabble, Dept of Education and Science, 115 Armada Way, Plymouth, Devon PL1 1HS; E. F. A. Suttle, Dept of Education and Science, 1 Wolseley Terr, Cheltenham, Glos GL50 1TH; B. M. Lane, Dept of Education and Science, Kingsmead Ho, James St West, Bath BA1 2DH

WALES

North Wales. H. W. Davies, 93 Penrhos Rd, Bangor, Gwynedd LL57 2BQ t Bangor 2714

South Wales. K. M. Evans, 18 Ael-y-Bryn, Energlyn, Caerphilly, Mid Glamorgan CF8 2QX t Caerphilly 883868

SCOTLAND

Eastern Division. J. A. Sloggie, 21 Blinkbonny Cres, Edinburgh EH4 3NB t 031-332 4443

Northern Division. C. Cleall, 29 Cotthill Circle, Miutimber, Aberdeen AB1 OEH t Aberdeen 732606

Western Division. R. S. Weir, 131 West Nile St, Glasgow G1 2RX t 041-332 0141

NORTHERN IRELAND

Chief Inspector (Music): G. B. Trory, Dept of
Education, Rathgael Ho, Balloo Rd, Bangor, Co
Down BT19 2PR t Bangor 66311

3   Associations and National Institutions

The following list includes bodies of particular
relevance to music in education. Many more music
organizations are listed in the current edition of
the *British Music Yearbook*.

Accordion Teachers' Guild, Somerset Ho, Guildford
Rd, Cranleigh, Surrey GU6 8QZ t Cranleigh 3554
Advisory Centre for Education, 32 Trumpington St,
Cambridge CB2 1QY t Cambridge 51456
Arts Council of Great Britain, 105 Piccadilly,
London W1V OAU t 01-629 9495
Arts Council of Northern Ireland, Bedford Ho, Bed-
ford St, Belfast BT2 7SZ t Belfast 41073
Assistant Masters Association, 29 Gordon Sq, London
WC1H OPT t 01-388 0551
Associated Board of the Royal Schools of Music, 14
Bedford Sq, London WC1B 3JG t 01-636 4478/9085
Association for Adult Education, 28 Greenhayes Av,
Banstead, Surrey SM7 2JE t Burgh Heath 53738
Association for Cultural Exchange, 9 Emmanuel Rd,
Cambridge CB1 1JW t Cambridge 65030
Association for Liberal Education, Stuart Ho, Mill
La, Cambridge CB2 1RY
Association of Assistant Mistresses, 29 Gordon Sq,
London WC1H OPX t 01-387 5674
Association of Headmistresses, 29 Gordon Sq, London
WC1H OPU t 01-387 1361
Association of Headmistresses of Preparatory Schools,
Meadow Brook, Abbott's Dr, Virginia Water, Surrey
t Wentworth 3258
Association of Heads of Girls' Boarding Schools,
Headington School, Oxford OX3 7TD t Oxford 62711
Association of Heads of Recognized Independent
Schools, Stower Cottage, Wavering La, Gillingham,
Dorset SP8 4NX t Gillingham 2261
Association of Head Teachers in Secondary Schools,
Ballynahinch County Secondary School, 103 Belfast
Rd, Ballynahinch, Co Down BT24 8EH t Ballynahinch
2424

Association of Higher Academic Staff in Colleges of
    Education in Scotland, Hamilton College of Educa-
    tion, Bothwell Rd, Hamilton ML3 OBD t Hamilton
    23241
Association of Polytechnic Teachers. 11 Queen's Keep,
    Clarence Pde, Southsea, Hants PO5 3NX t Portsmouth
    818625
Association of Teachers in Colleges and Departments
    of Education, 3 Crawford Pl, London W1H 2BN t
    01-402 6364
Association of Teachers in Technical Institutions,
    Hamilton Ho, Mabledon Pl, London WC1H 9BH t
    01-387 6806
Association of Teaching Religious, 41 Cromwell Rd,
    London SW7 2DH t 01-584 7494
Association of Tutors in Adult Education, 9 Norfolk
    Walk, Springfield Pk, Sandiacre, Nottingham NG10 5NW
Association of University Teachers, 1 Pembridge Rd,
    London W11 3HJ t 01-727 1458
Association of University Teachers (Scotland), Dept
    of Botany, The University, Glasgow G12 8QQ t
    041-339 8855
Association of Workers for Maladjusted Children, New
    Barns School, Church La, Toddington, Glos GL54 5DH
    t Toddington 200
British Arts Festivals Association, 33 Rufford Rd,
    Sherwood, Nottingham NG5 2NQ t Nottingham 61979
British Association of Early Childhood Education,
    Montgomery Hall, Kennington Oval, London SE11 5EW
British Broadcasting Corporation, Broadcasting Ho,
    London W1A 1AA t 01-580 4468
British Copyright Council, 29 Berners St, London W1P
    3DB t 01-580 5544
British Copyright Protection Association Ltd, 29-33
    Berners St, London W1P 3DB t 01-636 1491
British Council, 65 Davies St, London W1Y 2AA t
    01-499 8011
British Federation of Brass Bands, 47 Hull Rd, York
    YO1 3JP t York 59783
British Federation of Music Festivals, 106 Gloucester
    Pl, London W1H 3DB t 01-935 6371
British Institute of Recorded Sound, 29 Exhibition
    Rd, London SW7 2AS t 01-589 6603
British Jazz Society, 10 Southfield Gdns, Twickenham,
    Middx TW1 4SZ t 01-892 0133
British Phonographic Industry Copyright Association,
    International Copyright, EMI Ltd, 20 Manchester Sq,
    London W1A 1ES t 01-486 4488
British Society for Electronic Music, 49 Deodor Rd,
    London SW15 2NU t 01-870 4774
British Society for Music Therapy, 48 Lanchester Rd,
    London M6 4TA t 01-883 1331

British Standards Institution, 2 Park St, London
  WlA 2BS t 01-629 9000
Careers Research and Advisory Centre, Bateman St,
  Cambridge CB2 lLZ t Cambridge 54445
Cathedral Organists' Association, Royal School of
  Church Music, Addington Palace, Croydon CR9 5AD
  t 01-654 7676
Catholic Teachers' Federation, Edenvale, Stone Rd,
  Tittensor, Stoke-on-Trent ST12 9HR t Stoke-on-Trent
  659104
Central Bureau for Educational Visits and Exchanges,
  43 Dorset St, London WlH 3FN t 01-486 5101;   3
  Bruntsfield Cres, Edinburgh EHlO 4HD t 031-447 8024
Central Film Library, Government Bldg, Bromyard Av,
  London W3 7JB t 01-743 5555
Choir Schools Association, Cathedral Choir School,
  Whitecliffe La, Ripon, Yorks HG4 2LA t Ripon 2134
Church Music Association, Addington Palace, Croydon
  CR9 5AD t 01-656 4380
Composers' Guild of Great Britain, lO Stratford Pl,
  London WlN 9AE t 01-499 8567
Council for Educational Technology, 160 Gt Portland
  St, London WlN 5TB t 01-580 7553/4
Dalcroze Society Inc, 16 Heathcroft, Hampstead Way,
  London NWll 7HH t 01-455 1268
Department of Education and Science, Elizabeth Ho,
  York Rd, London SEl 7PH t 01-928 9222
Department of Education for Northern Ireland, Rathgael
  Ho, Balloo Rd, Bangor, Co Down BT19 2PR t Bangor
  66311
Dolmetsch Foundation, 14 Chestnut Way, Godalming,
  Surrey GU7 lTS t Godalming 7725
Educational Centres Association, Friends' Hall, Green-
  leaf Rd, London El7 6QN t 01-520 2867
Educational Development Association, 8 Windmill Gdns,
  Enfield, Middx EN2 7DU
Educational Interchange Council Inc, 43 Russel Sq,
  London WClB 5DA t 01-580 9137;   01-637 4695
English Folk Dance and Song Society, 2 Regent's Pk
  Rd, London NWl 7AY t 01-485 2206
European String Teachers' Association, 5 Neville Av,
  New Malden, Surrey KT3 4SN t 01-942 8191
Galpin Society, Rose Cottage, Bois La, Chesham Bois,
  Amersham, Bucks t Amersham 7580
Greater London Arts Association, 27 Southampton St,
  London WC2E 7JL t 01-836 5225
Gulbenkian (Calouste) Foundation, 98 Portland Pl,
  London WlN 4ET t 01-636 5313-7
Headmasters' Association, 29 Gordon Sq, London WClH
  OPS t 01-388 1765/6
Headteachers' Association of Scotland. I. R. Fraser,
  Inverness Royal Academy, Inverness IV2 3NG

Incorporated Society of Musicians, 48 Gloucester Pl,
London W1H 3HJ t 01-935 9791

Independent Broadcasting Authority, 70 Brompton Rd,
London SW3 1EY t 01-584 7011

Independent Schools Information Service, 47 Victoria
St, London SW1H OEQ t 01-222 7274

Independent Television Companies Association Ltd,
52-66 Mortimer St, London W1N 8AN t 01-636 6866

Inner London Teachers' Association, 19 Round Hill,
London SE26 4RF t 01-699 4872

Institute of Contemporary Arts, 12 Carlton House Terr,
London SW1Y 5AH t 01-930 0493

Institute of Musical Instrument Technology, 20
Disraeli Rd, London W5 5HP

International Association of Music Libraries, Music
Library, 269 Bowes Rd, London N11 1BD t 01-361 0047

International Liszt Centre for 19th-Century Music Ltd.
Head Office: 53 Priory Rd, London NW6 3NE t
01-624 4912

International Society for Contemporary Music, 105
Piccadilly, London W1V OAU t 01-629 9495

London Head Teachers' Association, 6 Brook Rd, Brentwood, Essex CM14 4PT t Brentwood 222989

London Schoolmasters' Association, 8 Welbeck Rd,
London E6 3EU t 01-472 6968

Mechanical Copyright Protection Society Ltd, 380
Streatham High Rd, London SW16 6HR t 01-769 3181

Music Advisers' National Association. P. L. Isherwood, Coventry School of Music, Percy St, Coventry
CV1 3BY t Coventry 23803

Music Masters' Association, Orchard Ho, Benefield Rd,
Oundle, Peterborough PE8 4EU t Oundle 3266

Music Publishers' Association Ltd, 73-5 Mortimer St,
London W1N 7TB t 01-636 6027; 01-580 3399

Music Teachers' Association, 106 Gloucester Pl,
London W1H 3DB t 01-935 6371

Musical Education of the Under Twelves, 55 Farm Close,
Seaford, Sussex BN25 3RY t Seaford 894188

Musicians' Union, 29 Catherine Pl, Buckingham Gate,
London SW1E 6EH t 01-834 1348

National Association for Gifted Children, 27 John
Adam St, London WC2N 6HX t 01-839 1861/2

National Association of Brass Band Conductors, 10a
Kathleen Rd, London SW11 2JS t 01-223 1796

National Association of Head Teachers, 41-3 Boltro
Rd, Haywards Heath, Sussex RH16 1BJ t Haywards
Heath 53291/2

National Association of Music Students' Unions.
Victoria Keir, SRC Office, Edinburgh University,
Edinburgh EH8 9YL t 031-667 1011

National Association of Schoolmasters, Swan Ct, Waterhouse St, Hemel Hempstead, Herts HP1 1DT t Hemel
Hempstead 2971

National Association of Youth Orchestras, 30 Park
    Dr, Grimsby, Lincs DN32 OEG t Grimsby 78002
National Federation of Gramophone Societies, 31
    Lynwood Gro, Orpington, Kent BR6 OBD t Orpington
    21801
National Federation of Music Societies, 29 Exhibition
    Rd, London SW7 2AD t 01-584 5797
National Festival of Music for Youth, 23a Kings Rd,
    London SW3 4RP t 01-730 2628
National Music Council of Great Britain, 35 Morpeth
    Mansions, London SW1P 1EU t 01-935 3777
National Operatic and Dramatic Association, 1 Crest-
    field St, London WC1H 8AU t 01-837 5655
National School Brass Band Association, 2 Gray's Clo,
    Barton-le-Clay, Bedford MK45 4PH t Luton 88560
National Union of Students, 3 Endsleigh St, London
    WC1H ODU t 01-387 1277
National Union of Teachers, Hamilton Ho, Mabledon Pl,
    London WC1H 9BB t 01-387 2442-6
Orff-Schulwerk Society, 31 Roedean Cres, London SW15
    5JX t 01-876 1944
Performing Right Society Ltd, 29-33 Berners St, London
    W1P 4AA t 01-580 5544
Phonographic Performance Ltd, 62 Oxford St, London
    W1N OAN t 01-636 1472-5
Pro Corda (National Association for Young String
    Players), Silver Birches, Crossfield Pl, Weybridge,
    Surrey KT13 ORG t Weybridge 42591
Professional Association of Teachers, 24 The Strand,
    Derby DE1 1BE t Derby 48672
Royal College of Organists, Kensington Gore, London
    SW7 2QS t 01-589 1765
Royal Musical Association. British Museum, London
    WC1B 3DG t 01-636 1555
Royal Philharmonic Society, 29 Exhibition Rd, London
    SW7 2AS t 01-584 5751 (mornings)
Royal Society of Musicians of Great Britain, 10
    Stratford Pl, London W1N 9AE t 01-629 6137
Rural Music Schools Association, Little Benslow Hills,
    Hitchin, Herts SG4 9RD t Hitchin 3446
Saltire Society (Scottish musical culture), 483 Lawn-
    market, Edinburgh EH1 2NT t 031-225 7780
School Broadcasting Council for the United Kingdom
    (30/BC), BBC, The Langham, Portland Pl, London W1A
    1AA t 01-935 2801
Schools Council for Curriculum and Examinations, 160
    Gt Portland St, London W1N 6LL t 01-580 0352
Schools Music Association, 4 Newman Rd, Bromley,
    Kent BR1 1RJ t 01-460 4043
Scottish Arts Council, 19 Charlotte Sq, Edinburgh EH2
    4DF t 031-226 6051

Scottish Education Dept, St Andrew's Ho, Edinburgh
EH1 3DB t 031-556 8501
Scottish Schoolmasters' Association, 41 York Pl,
Edinburgh EH1 3HP t 031-556 8825
Scottish Secondary Teachers' Association, 15 Dundas
St, Edinburgh EH3 6QG t 031-556 5919
Society for the Promotion of New Music, 10 Stratford
Pl, London W1N 9AE t 01-499 0573
Society for Research in the Psychology of Music and
Music Education, 19 Hansler Gro, East Molesey,
Surrey KT8 9JN t 01-979 6403
Society of Assistants Teaching in Preparatory Schools
(Music Group), Top-y-Pentre, Abercegir, Machynlleth,
Powys SY20 8NR (London telephone: 01-868 9311)
Society of Headmasters of Independent Schools, 8
Gwarnick Rd, Truro, Cornwall TR1 2LF t Truro 2735
Society of Schoolmasters, 308 Galpins Rd, Thornton
Heath, Surrey CR4 6EH t 01-689 7019
Songwriters' Guild of Great Britain Ltd, 52-3 Dean
St, London W1V 5HJ t 01-437 1439/1554
Standing Conference for Amateur Music, 26 Bedford Sq,
London WC1B 3HU t 01-636 4066
United Kingdom Council for Music Education.
J. P. B. Dobbs, Dartington College of Arts, Totnes,
Devon TQ9 6EJ t Totnes 862224
Universities Central Council on Admissions, PO Box
28, Cheltenham GL50 1HY t Cheltenham 59091
Welsh Arts Council, 9 Museum Pl, Cardiff CF1 3NX
t Cardiff 394711
Welsh Education Office, 31 Cathedral Rd, Cardiff.
CF1 9UJ t Cardiff 42661
Workers' Educational Association, 9 Upper Berkeley St,
London W1H 8BY t 01-402 5608
Workers' Music Association Ltd, 236 Westbourne Pk Rd,
London W11 1EL t 01-727 7005
Youth & Music, 22 Blomfield St, London EC2M 7AP
t 01-588 4714

4   Music Degrees and Diplomas

The following are generally recognized music qualifications. It is to be noted that some pertain to
institutions no longer active - in particular, the
Royal Manchester College of Music and the Northern
School of Music, both of which have now been absorbed
into the Royal Northern College of Music.

UNIVERSITY DEGREES

BA	*bachelor of arts*
B Mus	*bachelor of music*
B Phil	*bachelor of philosophy*
D Mus	*doctor of music*
D Phil	*doctor of philosophy*
MA	*master of arts*
M Ed	*master of education*
M Litt	*master of letters*
M Mus	*master of music*
M Phil	*master of philosophy*
Mus B	*bachelor of music*
Mus Bac	*bachelor of music*
Mus D	*doctor of music*
Mus Doc	*doctor of music*
Mus M	*master of music*
PhD	*doctor of philosophy*

GRADUATE-EQUIVALENT DIPLOMAS

Dip Mus Ed (RSAM)	*diploma in musical education of the Royal Scottish Academy of Music and Drama*
FRCO	*fellow of the Royal College of Organists*
GBSM	*graduate of the Birmingham School of Music*
GGSM	*graduate of the Guildhall School of Music and Drama*
GLCM	*graduate of the London College of Music*
GNSM	*graduate of the (former) Northern School of Music*
GRNCM	*graduate of the Royal Northern College of Music*
GRSM	*graduate of the Royal Schools of Music*
GTCL	*graduate of Trinity College of Music*
M Mus RCM	*master in music of the Royal College of Music*

OTHER DIPLOMAS

These are usually awarded for either performing or teaching, and cover a wide range of subjects and instruments. Special qualifications may be additionally designated e.g. TD for 'teaching diploma'.

ABCA	*associate of the British College of Accordionists*
ABSM	*associate of the Birmingham School of Music*
ADCM	*Archbishop's Diploma in Church Music*
AGSM	*associate of the Guildhall School of Music and Drama*
ALCM	*associate of the London College of Music*
A Mus LCM	*associate in general musicianship of the London College of Music*
A Mus TCL	*associate in general musicianship of Trinity College of Music*
A Mus TS	*associate in general musicianship of the Tonic Sol-Fa College of Music*
ANSM	*associate of the (former) Northern School of Music*
ARAM	*associate of the Royal Academy of Music*
ARCM	*associate of the Royal College of Music*
ARCO	*associate of the Royal College of Organists*
ARCO (CHM)	*associate of the Royal College of Organists, choirmaster's diploma*
ARMCM	*associate of the (former) Royal Manchester College of Music*
ARNCM	*associate of the Royal Northern College of Music*
ATCL	*associate of Trinity College of Music*
ATSC	*associate of the Tonic Sol-Fa College of Music*
Dip Ed	*diploma in education (various institutions)*
Dip Mus Ed	*diploma in musical education (various institutions)*
DPLM	*diploma of Proficiency in Light Music of the City of Leeds College of Music*
DRSAM	*diploma in music of the Royal Scottish Academy of Music and Drama*
FLCM	*fellow of the London College of Music*
FRCO (CHM)	*fellow of the Royal College of Organists, choirmaster's diploma*
FRMCM	*fellow of the (former) Royal Manchester College of Music*
FTCL	*fellow of Trinity College of Music*
FTSC	*fellow of the Tonic Sol-Fa College of Music*
LBCA	*licentiate of the British College of Accordionists*
LGSM	*licentiate of the Guildhall School of Music and Drama*
LLCM	*licentiate of the London College of Music*
L Mus TCL	*licentiate in general musicianship of Trinity College of Music*

L Mus TSC	*licentiate in general musicianship of the Tonic Sol-Fa College of Music*
LRAM	*licentiate of the Royal Academy of Music*
LTCL	*licentiate of Trinity College of Music*
LTSC	*licentiate of the Tonic Sol-Fa College of Music*
Music Teacher's Cert	*of the London University Institute of Education*

HONORARY AWARDS

In addition to certain university degrees as above:

ARSCM	*associate of the Royal School of Church Music*
D Mus (Cantuar)	*doctor of music, awarded by the Archbishop of Canterbury*
FBSM	*fellow of the Birmingham School of Music*
FGSM	*fellow of the Guildhall School of Music and Drama*
FNSM	*fellow of the (former) Northern School of Music*
FRAM	*fellow of the Royal Academy of Music*
FRCM	*fellow of the Royal College of Music*
FRNCM	*fellow of the Royal Northern College of Music*
FRSAMD	*fellow of the Royal Scottish Academy of Music and Drama*
FRSCM	*fellow of the Royal School of Church Music*
Hon ARAM	*honorary associate of the Royal Academy of Music*
Hon ARCM	*honorary associate of the Royal College of Music*
Hon FGSM	*honorary fellow of the Guildhall School of Music and Drama*
Hon FRAM	*honorary fellow of the Royal Academy of Music*
Hon FTCL	*honorary fellow of Trinity College of Music*
Hon FTSC	*honorary fellow of the Tonic Sol-Fa College of Music*
Hon GSM	*honorary member of the Guildhall School of Music and Drama*
Hon LCM	*honorary member of the London College of Music*
Hon RAM	*honorary member of the Royal Academy of Music*

Hon RCM	*honorary member of the Royal College of Music*
Hon RSCM	*honorary member of the Royal School of Church Music*
Hon TSC	*honorary member of the Tonic Sol-Fa College of Music*

5   University Music Departments

At the following universities, degrees in music (or in music combined with one or more other subjects) can be taken. There is usually, but not always, a separate Department of Music. The address of the department or school concerned is given, together with the name of its head and a listing of teaching staff. Differences in the mode of listing correspond to differences in the prospectuses of the institutions. See also the tabulation on p. 239 Institutions are listed in alphabetical order of names (all parts of the University of London and University of Wales being grouped under London and Wales respectively), except that the Queen's University, Belfast, is listed under Belfast.

UNIVERSITY OF ABERDEEN, Department of Music

Reader: R. Barrett-Ayres B Mus

Powis Gate, College Bounds, Old Aberdeen AB9 2UG t Aberdeen 40241 ext 376. Courses, facilities, etc.: see p. 240

Senior Lecturer
Raymond H. Dodd MA, B Mus

Lecturers
Geoffrey A. Chew B Mus, MA, Mus B, PhD, FRCO
Peter H. Inness B Mus, PhD
Roger Jacob B Mus
Colin J. Lawson BA, MA

Research Officer
Barry A. R. Cooper MA, FRCO, PhD

QUEEN'S UNIVERSITY OF BELFAST, Department of Music

Professor David Greer MA

Belfast BT7 1NN t Belfast 45133 ext 397. Courses,
facilities, etc.: see p. 240

Senior Lecturer
E. B. John BA, M Mus, FRCO

Lecturers
A. F. Carver B Mus
Mrs. Jennifer Perl B Mus
A. T. Thomas B Mus, MA

*UNIVERSITY OF BIRMINGHAM, Barber Institute of Fine
Arts*

Professor Ivor C. B. Keys MA, D Mus, Hon D Mus, FRCO

Barber Institute of Fine Arts, Birmingham B15 2TS t
021-472 0622. Courses, facilities, etc.: see p. 240

Readers
N. C. Fortune BA, PhD
J. Joubert B Mus, FRAM

Lecturers
J. A. Casken B Mus, MA
J. D. Drummond PhD, BA, BMus
C. R. Timms MA, M Mus
E. J. Whenham B Mus, MA

Part-time Lecturer
J. M. Harper BA

Part-time Instructors
Kathrin Michaelis LRAM, ARCM
L. G. Ullmann LRAM

Instruction in Early Keyboard Instruments
N. A. Dyson MA, PhD, LRAM

Part-time Haywood Fellow
R. D. E. Nichols BA, FRCO

UNIVERSITY OF BRISTOL, Department of Music

Professor Raymond Warren MA, Mus D

Royal Fort House, Tyndall Avenue, Bristol BS8 1UJ t Bristol 24161. Courses, facilities, etc.: see p. 241

Senior Lecturers
N. St. J. Davison MA, D Mus, FRCO
K. W. Mobbs MA, Mus B, FRCO, LRAM

Lecturers
A. Beaumont BA, D Mus, ARCM
D. D. Bourgeois MA, Mus D
H. Byard MA
R. Green MA
W. H. Thomas MA, ARCO

Special Lecturer in Acoustics
D. F. Gibbs MBE, BSc

UNIVERSITY OF CAMBRIDGE, University Music School

Professor Robin Orr CBE, MA, Mus D, Hon D Mus, FRCM, Hon RAM (from 1976-7: Alexander Goehr)

Downing Pl, Cambridge CB2 3EL t Cambridge 53322. Courses, facilities, etc.: see p. 241

Lecturers
G. H. Guest MA, Mus B
I. M. Kemp MA
P. G. Le Huray MA, PhD, Mus B
P. S. Ledger MA, Mus B
R. K. Marlow MA, PhD, Mus B
J. G. Rushton MA, D Phil
N. J. Shackleton MA, PhD, *physics and music*
J. E. Stevens MA, PhD, *reader in English and music lecturer*
P. A. Tranchell MA, Mus B

Assistant Lecturers
S. H. Boorman MA
R. J. Holloway MA, PhD

CITY UNIVERSITY, Department of General Studies

Senior Lecturer
Malcolm Troup D Phil, FGSM, ARCT

St John Street, London EC1V 4PB t 01-253 4399.
Courses, facilities, etc.: see p. 241

Don Finlay MSc (Eng), C Eng, MIEE
Charles Padgham MSc, PhD, DIC, ARCS, F Inst P
Adrian Seville MA, PhD

UNIVERSITY OF DURHAM, Music School

Professor Eric Taylor MA, D Mus, ARCO, Hon ARAM

Palace Green, Durham DH1 3RL t Durham 3489.   Courses,
facilities, etc.: see p. 241

James Murray Brown D Mus, Hon FTCL, LRAM
Richard Hey Lloyd MA, FRCO
David Lumsdaine BA
Peter David Manning BA
Brian Alfred Sidney Primmer MA, Mus B, ARCM, LTCL
Jerome Laurence Alexander Roche MA, Mus B, PhD, ARCO
Eric Robert Taylor MA, D Mus, Hon ARAM, ARCO
Alan John Thurlow BA, FRCO (CHM)

*UNIVERSITY OF EAST ANGLIA, School of Fine Arts and
Music*

Professor Peter G. Aston D Phil, GBSM, FTCL, ARCM

Earlham Hall, Norwich NR4 7TJ t Norwich 56161.
Courses, facilities, etc.: see p. 241

Senior Lecturer
Julian B. Webb MA, B Mus

Lecturers
D. F. L. Chadd MA
D. P. Charlton BA, PhD

EDINBURGH UNIVERSITY, Faculty of Music

Professor Kenneth Leighton MA, B Mus, D Mus, LRAM
Professor Michael Tilmouth MA, PhD

Alison House, Nicolson Sq, Edinburgh EH8 9BH t
031-667 1011.   Courses, facilities, etc.: see p. 241

Leon Coates MA, LRAM, ARCO
Edward Harper BA, B Mus, LRAM, ARCO
David Kimbell MA, D Phil, LRAM

Colin Kingsley B Mus, D Mus, ARCM
Margaret McAllister B Mus, PhD, LRAM, ARCM
Raymond Monelle MA, B Mus, ARCM
Peter Williams MA, B Mus, PhD

UNIVERSITY OF EXETER, Department of Music

Professor P. M. Doe MA

Knightley, Streatham Dr, Exeter EX4 4PD t Exeter
77911. Courses, facilities, etc.: see p. 241

Senior Lecturer
D. M. Cawthra MA

Lecturers
P. C. Allsop B Mus
D. W. James MA, FRCO
T. J. Samson B Mus, M Mus, PhD
N. J. Sandon B Mus

Part-time teachers
Michael Evans, *violoncello* (Dartington String Quartet)
Miss Margaret Gulley LRAM, ARCM, *piano*
Malcolm Latchem, *violin* (Dartington String Quartet)
Keith Lovell, *viola* (Dartington String Quartet)
Nicholas Maw, *composition*
Paul Morgan MA, FRCO
Colin Sauer, *violin* (Dartington String Quartet)

Eight other instrumental teachers

UNIVERSITY OF GLASGOW, Department of Music

Professor Frederick Rimmer MA, B Mus, FRCO

14 University Gdns, Glasgow G12 8QH t 041-339 8855.
Courses, facilities, etc.: see p. 241

Senior Lecturer
Kenneth Elliott MA, Mus B, PhD

Lecturers
Stephen Arnold MA
James Stuart Campbell MA, B Mus, FRCO, ARCM
Warwick A. Edwards MA, Mus B, PhD
Marjorie E. Soutar MA, PhD

Cramb Research Fellow in Composition
George Newson LRAM

UNIVERSITY OF HULL, Department of Music

R. B. Marchant MA, Mus B

Cottingham Road, Hull HU6 7RX t Hull 46311 ext. 7604.
Courses, facilities, etc.: see p. 241

Senior Lecturer
A. J. Hedges MA, B Mus

Lecturers
G. E. Beechey BA, Mus B, PhD
A. D. Ford B Mus
A. G. Sadler B Mus

UNIVERSITY OF KEELE, Department of Music

Professor Peter Dickinson MA, FRCO, LRAM, ARCM

Keele, Newcastle, Staffs ST5 5BG t Keele Park 371
ext 119. Courses, facilities, etc.: see p. 241

Senior Lecturer
G. M. Pratt B Mus, MA, ARCO

Lecturers
D. W. Galloway B Mus
N. A. Josephs B Mus, MA

UNIVERSITY OF LANCASTER, Music Department

Denis McCaldin PhD, BSc, B Mus

Bailrigg, Lancaster LA1 4YW t Lancaster 65201.
Courses, facilities, etc.: see p. 242

E. Cowie B Mus
I. C. Hare B Mus
R. Langham Smith BA

Also resident ensemble and part-time staff

UNIVERSITY OF LEEDS, Department of Music

Professor Alexander Goehr (to mid-1976)

14 Cromer Terr, Leeds LS2 9JR t Leeds 31751. Courses,
facilities, etc.: see p. 242

Senior Lecturers
James C. Brown MA, Mus B, FRCO
Frank S. Mumby BA, B Mus

Lecturers
Brian Newbould MA, B Mus
G. Richard Rastall MA, Mus B, PhD
Philip Wilby BA, B Mus, ARCM

Honorary Member of Department *(responsible for music
in Department of Education)*
Jack Pilgrim

Instrumental Teachers
John Barrow, *flute* (West Riding Wind Quintet)
Eta Cohen ARCM, *violin*
Frank Cooper, *violoncello* (West Riding String Quartet)
Robert A. Crinall ARCM, Hon ARSCM, *organ*
John Digney, *oboe*
Jon C. Earnshaw ARMCM, GRSM, LRAM, *piano, harpsichord*
Gerald Gentry, *conducting*
Alan Haydock, *clarinet* (West Riding Wind Quintet)
Eric Hill, *guitar*
Francis Jackson D Mus, FRCO, *organ*
Edmund Jones, *violin* (West Riding String Quartet)
Arthur Levick, *violin* (West Riding String Quartet)
Mavis Nicholls LRAM, ARCM, LGSM, *piano*
Enid D. Oughtibridge LRAM, *piano*
Honor Shepherd FRMCM, *singing*
Geoffrey Walker, *bassoon* (West Riding Wind Quintet)
Fanny Waterman OBE, MA, FRCM, *piano*
William Wesling, *viola* (West Riding String Quartet)
David Wise, *horn* (West Riding Wind Quintet)

UNIVERSITY OF LEICESTER, School of Music

R. B. Meikle MA, B Mus, PhD

University Road, Leicester LE1 7RH t Leicester 50000
ext 52. Courses, facilities, etc.: see p. 242

Lecturer
A. G. Wilson-Dickson MA, Mus B, D Phil, LRAM, ARCO

Part-time Lecturer
D. Munrow BA

UNIVERSITY OF LIVERPOOL, Department of Music

Professor Basil Smallman MA, B Mus, ARCO

PO Box 147, Liverpool L69 3BX t 051-709 6022. Courses, facilities, etc.: see p. 243

Judith H. Blezzard BA, B Mus, PhD, LRAM
R. F. N. Orledge MA, PhD, ARCO
M. O. Talbot Mus B, MA, PhD, ARCM
J. G. Williamson MA
H. B. Wood BA, ARCM

UNIVERSITY OF LONDON, GOLDSMITHS' COLLEGE, Department of Music

Head of Department: Stanley Glasser MA, B Com

Lewisham Way, London SE14 6NW t 01-692 0211. Courses, facilities, etc.: see p. 243

Miss A. M. Ayliffe FTCL, LRAM
M. Barry M Mus
I. J. Bartlett MA, M Mus, LRAM, ARCM
Mrs M. H. Bent MA, Mus B, PhD
Miss M. Carmichael LRAM, ARCM
H. Davies BA
F. Dobbins MA, D Phil
G. Kinnear LRAM, AGSM, FRSA
A. Milner D Mus, FRCM
P. J. N. Moorse GTCL, FTCL, FRCO (CHM)
M. Musgrave M Mus, FRCO, GRSM, ARCM
J. Dale-Roberts B Mus
P. Steinitz D Mus, FRAM, FRCO
Miss S. Sterman MA, Mus B, ARCM
Miss N. M. Webber B Mus, LRAM, ARCM

UNIVERSITY OF LONDON, KING'S COLLEGE, Music Department

Professor Brian L. Trowell MA, PhD

Strand, London WC2R 2LS t 01-836 5454. Courses, facilities, etc.: see p. 243

Visiting Professor
Geoffrey Bush MA, D Mus

Reader
Arnold Whittall MA, Ph D, ATCL, ARCO

Lecturers
Pierluigi Petrobelli, Dottore in Lettere; MFA
Thomas Walker AB
Peter Wishart B Mus, FGSM

UNIVERSITY OF LONDON, ROYAL HOLLOWAY COLLEGE, Music Department

Professor Ian W. A. Spink MA, B Mus, FTCL, ARCM

Egham Hill, Egham, Surrey TW20 OEX t Egham 4455.
Courses, facilities, etc.: see p. 243

Lecturers
J. F. Dack BA, B Mus
B. J. C. Dennis ARCM
E. W. Levi BA, B Phil
Mrs. R. McGuinness BA, MA, MA, D Phil
I. R. Parker BA
L. J. Pike MA, D Phil, B Mus, FRCO, ARCM

Jubilee Research Fellow
P. Hill BA

Visiting Teachers
P. Battine, *clarinet, guitar*
Miss A. Bentley, *bassoon*
Mrs. B. L. Black B Mus (New Zealand), FRCO, ARCM, *organ, piano*
Mrs. R. Conry ARAM, *piano*
D. J. Daniels, *oboe*
J. Dawson-Lyell BA, ARCM, *piano*
Miss M. Edes, *violoncello, double bass*
Miss A. Fahrni BA, M Mus, *viol*
Miss J. Gray GRSM, LRAM, ARCM, *singing*
Mrs. C. de Grey ARCM, *flute*
N. Griffiths, *trumpet*
Miss T. Lees ARMCM, *singing*
Mrs. M. Mitchell LRAM, *violin, viola*
M. Parry MA, *harpsichord*
A. Ross BA, FRCO, *organ*
Miss M. Valentine LRAM, ARCM, *piano*
M. Weaver, *horn*

UNIVERSITY OF LONDON, SCHOOL OF ORIENTAL AND AFRICAN STUDIES

Convenor of the Music Panel: A. V. King B Mus, PhD

Malet St, London WC1E 7HP t 01-637 2388. Courses,

facilities, etc.: see p. 243

Lecturers
Mrs. R. Datta BA, MA
J. R. Marr BA, PhD
D. K. Rycroft BA
O. Wright PhD

UNIVERSITY OF MANCHESTER, Faculty of Music

Professor Basil Deane BA, B Mus, M Mus, PhD

Denmark Road, Manchester M15 6FY t 061-273 3333 ext
356/7. Courses, facilities, etc.: see p. 243

Reader
Maurice Aitchison MA, Mus B, LRAM

Senior Lecturers
Ben Horsfall B Mus, Mus D, FRMCM
P. B. Smith MA, Mus B, MSc

Lecturers
R. W. Bray MA, D Phil
D. K. Elcombe MA, Mus B, FRCO, LRAM
A. C. Howie B Mus, PhD
P. T. Northway B Mus, M Mus

Assistants (part-time)
Paul Cropper FRMCM
Charles Meert
B. W. D. Griffiths ARMCM
P. A. Cosham ARMCM

UNIVERSITY OF NEWCASTLE UPON TYNE, Department of Music

Professor Denis Matthews CBE, FRAM, MA, D Mus, Hon FTCL

Armstrong Building, The University, Newcastle upon
Tyne NE1 7RU t Newcastle upon Tyne 28511. Courses,
facilities, etc.: see p. 243

Reader
Frederick Hudson D Mus, FRCO

Senior Lecturer
vacancy

Lecturers
Percy Lovell MA, Mus B, LRAM
Benedict Sarnaker M Mus

UNIVERSITY OF NOTTINGHAM, Department of Music

Professor Ian Bent MA, B Mus, PhD

Lenton Grove, Beeston Lane, Nottingham NG7 2QN t
Nottingham 56101. Courses, facilities, etc.:
see p. 243

Senior Lecturer
S. Metheringham Laming B Mus, ARCM

Lecturers
Jennifer E. Baker B Mus
J. M. Morehen MA, PhD, FRCO
R. J. Pascall MA, D Phil, FRCO, ARCM

OPEN UNIVERSITY

See p. 164

UNIVERSITY OF OXFORD, Faculty of Music

Professor Denis Arnold MA, B Mus, ARCM, Hon RAM

32 Holywell, Oxford OX1 3SL t Oxford 47069. Courses,
facilities, etc.: see p. 243

A. C. Baines MA
J. A. Caldwell B Mus, MA, D Phil, FRCO
H. J. M. Dalton MA, FRCO, ARCM
D. J. Lumsden MA, D Phil, Mus B
H. J. Macdonald MA, D Phil
D. E. Olleson MA, D Phil
S. J. Preston MA, Mus B, FRAM, ARCM
B. W. G. Rose MA, D Mus, FRCO
R. Sherlaw Johnson D Mus, MA, B Mus, BA, ARAM, ARCM
F. W. Sternfeld MA, PhD
A. W. Tyson MA, MB, BS
Mrs. S. L. F. Wollenberg MA, D Phil
D. Wulstan MA

UNIVERSITY OF READING, Department of Music

Professor Ronald Woodham BA, D Mus, FRCO, ARCM

35 Upper Redlands Rd, Reading RG1 5JE t Reading 83583.
Courses, facilities, etc.: see p. 244

Senior Lecturers
Andrew Byrne D Mus, FRAM, LRAM
H. Diack Johnstone MA, D Phil, Mus B, FRCO, FTCL, ARCM

Lecturers
Bojan Bujic D Phil
Christopher Wintle BA, B Mus

Lecturer (part-time)
John Barstow ARCM

School of Music
Martin Bochmann, *violoncello, chamber music*
Michael Freyhan MA, LRAM, *piano*
Suzanne Green Mus B, LRSM, FTCL, *singing*
Sean Greenwood LRAM, *oboe*
Philip Hattey ARAM, ARCM, *singing*
Cecily M. Haussmann BA, LRAM, *flute*
Belinda Heather LRAM, *piano*
Walter Hillsman MA, B Mus, FRCO, *organ*
Anthony Lunt, *guitar*
Brien Stait ARMCM, *violin, viola*
Martha Kingdon Ward, *clarinet*
Yu Chun Yee LRSM, ARCM, *piano*

UNIVERSITY OF ST ANDREWS, Faculty of Arts

Professor C. Thorpe Davie OBE, Hon LL D, FRAM, ARCM

North St, St Andrews, Fife KY16 9AL t St Andrews 4411.
Courses, facilities, etc.: see p. 244

Lecturers
Christopher David Steadman Field MA, D Phil, ARCM
Mrs. Elizabeth Ann Frame Dip Mus Ed, RSAM, LRAM

UNIVERSITY OF SALFORD, Music Department

Director: Herbert W. Winterbottom MSc, FNSM, LRAM,
LTCL, ARCM

Crescent, Salford M5 4WT t 061-736 5843. Courses,
facilities, etc.: see p. 244

Full-Time Staff Lecturers
Michael P. Allen BA, M Phil, LTCL
Michael A. Almond Mus B, ARMCM
Harvey Marsden BA, LRAM

Regular Visiting Tutors
Randolph Colville LTCL
George Fisher B Mus, FRCO, FLCM
Teresa Huxham
Gladys Kallenberg GNSM
Martin Roberts
Stuart Roebuck BBCM
David Sumbler GNSM

UNIVERSITY OF SHEFFIELD, Department of Music

Professor Edward J. C. Garden D Mus, FRCO

Western Bank, Sheffield S1O 2TN t Sheffield 78555/
667234. Courses, facilities, etc.: see p. 245

Musicologists and Performers
A. M. Brown MA, Mus B, PhD, LRAM, FRCO
R. S. T. Bullivant MA, B Mus, D Phil
G. M. Philippa Drummond MA, B Mus, D Phil

Composer and Musicologist
D. H. Cox B Mus, MA

Lindsay String Quartet
Peter Cropper, *violin*.
Ronald Birks, *violin*
Roger Bigley, *viola*
Bernard Gregor-Smith, *violoncello*

Convocation Pianist in Residence
Danielle Salamon GRSM

UNIVERSITY OF SOUTHAMPTON, Department of Music

Professor P. A. Evans MA, D Mus, FRCO

Southampton SO9 5NH t Southampton 559122. Courses,
facilities, etc.: see p. 245

Senior Lecturers
D. C. Brown MA, B Mus, PhD, LTCL
J. D. Harvey MA, PhD, Mus D

Lecturers
R. G. Bowman M Mus, AKC, FRCO, ARCM
E. H. Graebner MA, D Phil, ARCO

Resident Pianist
Rosemarie Wright ARAM

UNIVERSITY OF SURREY, Department of Music

Professor R. Smith Brindle D Mus, DiplAcSCec (Rome)

Guildford, Surrey GU2 5XH t Guildford 71281. Courses, facilities, etc.: see p. 245

Musical Director
Brian Brockless B Mus, ARCM, ARCO, Hon ARAM

Senior Lecturer in Recording Techniques
J. N. Borwick BSc

Lecturers
Hans Heimler DrPhil, DipKmstr (Vienna)
S. Forbes Mus B, MA, ARCO, LRAM, ARCM
N. D. C. Conran B Mus, ARCM

UNIVERSITY OF SUSSEX, Music Department

Professor Donald Mitchell MA

Arts Building, Falmer, Brighton, Sussex BN1 9ON t Brighton 66755. Courses, facilities, etc.: see p. 245

Lecturers
Anne Boyd BA, D Phil
David Osmond-Smith MA
David Lloyd Roberts Mus B, ARMCM

Staff Tutor in Music (Centre for Continuing Education)
Michael Hall BA

Visiting Lecturer
John Birch MA, FRCO, LRAM, ARCM

Visiting Fellow
Raymond Leppard MA

UNIVERSITY OF WALES, UNIVERSITY COLLEGE OF WALES,
Aberystwyth, Department of Music

Professor Ian Parrott MA, D Mus, FTCL, ARCO

Old College, King Street, Aberystwyth, Dyfed SY23 2AX
t Aberystwyth 2711. Courses, facilities, etc.:
see p. 245

Senior Lecturer
David Harries D Mus

Lecturer
J. G. Evans BA, MA, Mus B, ARCM

Executants and Teachers include
Roderick Jones FRAM, LRAM, *singing and voice production*
Thomas Noble MBE, ARCM, *wind instruments*
Robert Jacoby FLCM, LRAM, ARCM, *violin*
Leonard James, LRAM, AGSM, *violin*
Peter Kingswood ARCM, *viola*
Geraint John Dip Mus, *violoncello*
Geoffrey Buckley ARMCM, LRAM, *piano*

Honorary Professorial Fellow
Mansel Thomas OBE, B Mus, FRAM

UNIVERSITY OF WALES, UNIVERSITY COLLEGE OF NORTH WALES,
Bangor, Department of Music

Professor William Mathias D Mus, FRAM, LRAM

College Rd, Bangor, Gwynedd LL57 2DG t Bangor 51151.
Courses, facilities, etc.: see p. 245

Senior Lecturer
Robert Smith D Mus, FTCL, LGSM

Lecturers
John Hywel M Mus, ARCO
Jeffrey Lewis M Mus, ARCM
Thomas Messenger B Mus, ARCM, ARCO
Gwyn Williams M Mus, ARCM

Eric Morris BA, *violin*
Frank Thomas GRSM, LRAM, *piano*

Part-time staff
Andrew Goodwin BA, MA, FRCO, *organ*
Yvonne Mathias LRAM, *singing*
Shirley Ratcliff GRSM, ARCM, *piano*

Jean Thomas LRAM, *piano*

Also teachers of orchestral instruments

UNIVERSITY OF WALES, UNIVERSITY COLLEGE, Cardiff,
Department of Music

Professor Alun Hoddinott D Mus, Hon RAM

PO Box 78, Cathays Pk, Cardiff CF1 1XL t Cardiff
44211. Courses, facilities, etc.: see p. 245

Honorary Professorial Fellows
Morris J. Beachy BM, MM, DMA
H. C. Robbins Landon B Mus, Hon D Mus

Senior Lecturer and Assistant Director of Studies
I. M. Bruce MA, Mus Bac

Lecturers
Robert Bruce Mus Bac
Denis N. Harbinson B Mus, PhD
Michael F. Robinson BA, B Mus, D Phil
Richard Elfyn Jones BA, M Mus, FRCO
C. Malcolm Boyd B Mus, MA, ARCO
David Wyn Jones B Mus, MA

Temporary Lecturer
David Wynne D Mus

Assistant Director of Practical Studies
George Isaac

Ensemble in residence
Alfredo Wang, Laureat SAM, *violin*
James Barton LGSM, *violin*
H. Stephen Broadbent LRAM, *viola*
George Isaac, *violoncello*
Martin Jones LRAM, ARCM, ARCO, ARAM, *piano*

Piano Teachers
Stephen Price B Mus, LRAM, LTCL
Richard McMahon B Mus, LRAM, ARCM
Arnold Draper B Mus, LRAM, ARCM, FTCL, LGSM

Senior Tutor (Singing)
Clifford Bunford BA, LRAM

Senior Experimental Officer
Peter van Biene

Tutorial Fellow
Richard D. P. Jones BA

Tutors (Part-time)
David G. Bibby ARMCM, *percussion*
Beryl Boyd BA, *piano*
Anne Bunford BA, *singing, piano*
Colin Casson, *trumpet*
William Davis, *horn*
Helena Evans LTCL, *piano*
Glenys Gordon Fleet ARCM, *harp*
David Hannaby, *trombone*
Gordon Hunt, *oboe*
Rowland Jones, *singing*
Clifford Lewis LRAM, *piano*
Charles Roberts LTCL, *guitar, lute*
Martin Ronchetti ARAM, LRAM, *clarinet*
David Rowsell, *tuba*
Michael Smith D Mus MA, B Mus, FRCO, ADCM, LRAM,
LTCM, *organ*
Ronald Smith, *double-bass*
George Tofield, *bassoon*
Douglas Townshend, *flute*

UNIVERSITY OF YORK, Department of Music

Professor Wilfrid Mellers MA, D Mus

Heslington, York YO1 5DD t York 59861.   Courses,
facilities, etc.:   see p. 245

Senior Lecturers
D. L. Blake MA
J. F. Paynter D Phil, GTCL

Lecturers
D. Kershaw MA
R. Orton MA, Mus B
B. Rands M Mus
N. F. I. Sorrell MA
G. Treacher FRAM

University Organist and Visiting Lecturer in Organ
Studies
N. Danby ARCM, LRAM

6 Principal Colleges of Music

The curricula of the following institutions include courses of full-time study leading to music degrees from universities as specified or from the Council for National Academic Awards (CNAA), or to internal diplomas with recognized graduate-equivalent status. Courses for performers, with less 'academic' work, are also offered. The address of the institution is given, together with the name of its head and a listing of teaching staff. Differences in the mode of listing correspond to differences in the prospectuses of the institutions. See also the tabulation on p. 247 Institutions are listed in alphabetical order of name.

BIRMINGHAM SCHOOL OF MUSIC

Head: Louis Carus LRAM

City of Birmingham Polytechnic, Paradise Circus, Birmingham B3 3HG t 021-235 4355/6. Courses, facilities, etc.: see p. 248, 250

Orchestral Director
Harold Gray FBSM

Singing
Bernard Dickerson
Freda Hart ARAM, GRSM, LRAM
Barbara McGuire ABSM
Johanna Peters, *producer*
Frederick Sharp, Hon ARCM
Linda Vaughan LRAM, ARCM

Keyboard
Marjorie Bates LRAM, ABSM
Coris Cartwright
Marjorie Hazlehurst LRAM
Renna Kellaway LRSM, ARCM, UPLM
George Miles FRCO, Hon ABSM
Christine Smye LRAM, ABSM, MRST
Paul Venn GRSM, ABSM
Joseph Weingarten FTCL
Frank Wibaut ARCM
Janice Williams LRAM, ARCM
Malcolm Wilson GBSM, ARCM

Strings
Antonia Butler
Sylvia Cleaver ARAM
Ernest Element Hon ABSM
Barbara Seely LRAM
Christopher Staunton

Wind
David Cowsill Hon ABSM, ARCM
Roy Curran
Alan Davis BA, ARCM
Arthur Doyle
David Haines FTCL
Timothy Harmon
Rachel Herbert ARCM
Angela Malsbury LRAM, ARCM
Anthony Miller
Colin Parr
Reginald Reid
Delia Ruhm

Gordon Rutherford GBSM, ARCM, ABSM
John Schroder
Frederick Walsh
Alan Whitehead
Muriel Wiley LRAM, ARCM

Harp
Muriel Liddle ARMCM

Guitar
Brian Whitehouse

Percussion
Norman Parker

Lecturers
David Brock MA, B Mus, FTCL, LRAM, ARCM, ARCO
Anthony Cross MA, B Mus, LTCL
Keith Darlington MA
Stephen Daw MA, *careers adviser*
Frank Downes Hon ABSM
Geoffrey Duggan ARCM, AGSM, A Mus TCL
Ruth Gerald Mus B, LRAM, ARCM
Barrie Grayson LRAM, LRSM
Richard Greening MA, B Mus, FRCO, Hon ABSM
Peter James B Mus, PhD
Maxwell Menzies MA, B Mus, FRCO (CHM), ADCM
Anthony Pither B Mus
Norman Price B Mus, LRAM, LTCL
Richard Silk MA, Mus B, FRCO

DARTINGTON COLLEGE OF ARTS

Director of Musical Studies: Jack P. B. Dobbs BA,
M Ed, M Phil, LRAM, LTCL, Dip Ed

Totnes, Devon TQ9 6EJ t Totnes 862224.   Courses,
facilities, etc.:   see p. 248,250

Composition
Helen Glatz ARCM
Richard Hames B Mus

Singing
George Dinneen FTCL, LRAM

Keyboard
Jean Churchill LRAM, ARCM, *piano*
Helen Glatz ARCM, *piano*
Roger Smith GTCL, LTCL, *piano*
John Wellingham ARCO, *harpsichord, organ*
Valerie Wood ARCM, ABSM, Cert Ed, *piano*

Strings
Michael Evans LRAM, AGSM, *violoncello* (Dartington
String Quartet)
Malcolm Latchem ARCM, *violin* (Dartington String
Quartet)
Keith Lovell ARCM, *viola* (Dartington String Quartet)
Colin Sauer LRAM, LTCL, ARCM, FTCL, ARAM, FRAM,
violin (Dartington String Quartet)

Wind
Anne Kimber ARCM, Cert Ed, *flute*
Roger Smith GTCL, LTCL, *brass*
John Wellingham ARCO, *recorder*
Lorna Westren LRAM, ARCM, *clarinet*
Heather Williams, *oboe*
Alexandra Woolner ARCM, *bassoon, oboe*

Guitar
Ruby Godwin

Tutors
Alastair Dick BA, *Indian music*
Robert Hanson BA, ARCO, *twentieth-century music*
Geoffrey Kinder Cert Ed, *music in education*
Michael Lane B Mus, ARCM, ARCO, *music in education*
Roy Truby D Mus, GRSM, ARCM, LRAM

GUILDHALL SCHOOL OF MUSIC AND DRAMA

Principal: Allen Percival CBE, Mus B, Hon FGSM, FRCM,
Hon RAM, Hon FTCL
Director of Music: Leslie East M Mus

John Carpenter St, Victoria Embankment, London EC4Y
OAR t 01-353 7774 tg euphonium. Courses, facilities,
etc.: see p. 248, 250

Composition
Carey Blyton B Mus, FTCL
Alfred Nieman FGSM, FRAM
Buxton Orr FGSM
Edmund Rubbra CBE, MA, D Mus, LLD, FGSM, Hon RAM
Patric Standford FGSM
Barclay Wilson FGSM

Choral and Orchestral Conductors, Coaches
John Alldis MA, FGSM, ARCO
Harold Dexter MA, Mus B, FGSM, FRSCM, FRCO, ARCM
Yona Ettlinger FGSM
John Georgiadis
George Hurst, *guest conductor*
Wilfrid Kealey FGSM, ARCM
J. Edward Merrett Hon RCM
André Previn Hon GSM, *guest conductor*
Rudolph Schwarz Hon GSM, *guest conductor*
Christopher Seaman FGSM, *guest conductor*
Vilem Tausky FGSM
Adrian Thorne BA
Denis Wick FGSM, LRAM
Howard Williams M Mus
Barclay Wilson FGSM

Opera
Ailsa Berk, *movement*
Ernest Berk, *movement*
Gisella Birke, *make-up*
Jane Gibson, *movement*
Fraser Goulding BA, ARCO, *music coach*
Gerald Kitching FGSM, *designer*
Dennis Maunder FGSM, Hon ARAM, *head of production*
Leslie Murchie FGSM, LRAM, *music coach*
Vilem Tausky FGSM, *head of music*
Patricia Watts, *acting*
Arlan Wendland, *movement*

Singing
Fabian Smith FGSM, *head of department*

Jean Allister FRAM, Hon RAM

Marjorie Avis ARCM
Noelle Barker MA
Celia Bizony FGSM
Robin Bowman M Mus, FRCO, ARCM
Peter A. Bucknell ARCA, FGSM, FRSA
Bryan Drake BA, LRSM
Walther Gruner FGSM
Elizabeth Hawes
Esther Hulbert FGSM, ARAM
Llewelyn John
Anthony Rolfe Johnson AGSM
Rowland Jones
Ellis Keeler FGSM
William McAlpine FGSM
Mary Makower Hon ARAM
Joyce Newton FGSM
William Parsons
Rudolf Piernay
Michael Pilkington MA, LGSM, LRAM
Arthur Reckless FGSM, LRAM
Dorothy Richardson LRAM, ARCM
Duncan Robertson LRAM, Dip RSAM
Laura Sarti
Geoffrey Shaw
Richard Standen FGSM
Dorothy Stanton ARAM
Pamela Woolmore FGSM

Coaches
Cecil Belcher FGSM, LRAM, ARCM
Anna Berenska
Frances Collins ARCM
Cyril Gell FGSM, ARAM, ARCO
Leslie Murchie FGSM, LRAM
Michael Pilkington MA, LGSM, LRAM

Languages
Tina Ruta, *Italian*
Hélène Tasartey L és L, *French*
Richard Wigmore BA, *German*

Keyboard
James Gibb FGSM, *piano, head of department*

Neil Van Allen FGSM, L Mus, *piano*
Norman Anderson FGSM, ARCM, *piano*
Terence Beckles FGSM, ARAM, *piano*
Cecil Belcher FGSM, LRAM, ARCM, *piano*
Celia Bizony FGSM, *harpsichord*
Robert Collet BA, Mus B, LRAM, *piano*

Nicholas Danby LRAM, ARCM, *organ*
Harold Dexter MA, Mus B, FGSM, FRSCM, FRCO, ARCM, *organ*
Bernard Foster FGSM, ARCM, *piano*
Laurence Gerrish MBE, BA, B Mus, *piano*
Carola Grindea, *piano*
Meriel Jefferson GRSM, ARCM, LRAM, *piano*
Christopher Kite BA, ARCM, *harpsichord*
Cimbro Martin FGSM, ARAM, *piano*
Leslie Murchie FGSM, LRAM, *piano*
Alfred Nieman FGSM, FRAM, *piano*
Bernard Oram B Mus, FRCO, L Mus TCL, *organ*
Geraldine Peppin, *piano*
Mary Peppin, *piano*
Emile Philippe FGSM, *piano*
Michael Pilkington MA, LGSM, LRAM, *piano*
Howard Riley MA, M Mus, D Phil, *jazz*
Robert Smith B Mus, FRCO, FTCL, DSCM, *organ*
Ruth Stewart BA, LRAM, Dalcroze Cert, *piano*
Mary Verney LRAM, *harpsichord*
Edith Vogel ARCM, *piano*
Amanda Warren BA, LGSM, LRAM, ARCM, *piano*
Brigitte Wild, *piano*

Strings
Yfrah Neaman FGSM, *violin, head of department*

Joan Broadley, *violoncello*
Geoffrey Clark, *double-bass*
John Georgiadis, *violin*
John Glickman, *violin*
Eli Goren FGSM, *violin*
Perry Hart, *violin*
Kenneth Heath FGSM, *violoncello*
Patrick Ireland ARCM, *viola*
Nannie Jamieson FGSM, ARCM, *viola*
Sharon McKinley, *violoncello*
J. Edward Merrett Hon RCM, *double-bass*
Max Morgan FGSM, *violin*
Reginald Morley FGSM, ARCM, *violin*
Anthony Pleeth AGSM, *violoncello, baroque violoncello*
William Pleeth FGSM, *violoncello*
Bernard Richards FGSM, *violoncello*
Suzanne Rozsa, *violin*
Jane Ryan, *viols*
Joan Spencer FGSM, *violin*
Leonard Stehn B Sc, *violoncello*

Wind
Wilfrid Kealey FGSM, ARCM, *clarinet, head of wind and
percussion department*

James Anderson, *tuba*
Horace Barker, *trumpet*
William Bennett, *flute*
Roger Birnstingl ARCM, *bassoon*
Francis Bradley FGSM, *horn*
Bernard Brown BA, FGSM, FRAM, *trumpet*
Jeffrey Bryant, *horn*
Anthony Camden ARCM, *oboe, baroque oboe*
Anthony Chidell, *horn*
Yona Ettlinger FGSM, *clarinet*
Peter Gane ARMCM, *trombone*
Martin Gatt ARCM, *bassoon*
Tony Halstead FRMCM, *horn*
Bernard Hazelgrove LTCL, *cornet, brass band arranging*
Colin Hinchliff ARCM, *horn*
Simon Hunt, *flute*
Hans Jurg Lange, *baroque bassoon*
Kathryn Lukas M Mus, *flute*
James MacGillivray, *oboe*
Neville MacKinder AGSM, *bassoon*
Paul Nieman AGSM, *sackbut, tenor cornet*
Donald Osgood, *brass band arranging*
Philip Pickett AGSM, *recorder, renaissance instruments*
Stephen Preston AGSM, *baroque flute*
Rainer Schuelein AGSM, *flute, recorder*
Edward Selwyn, *oboe*
Victor Slaymark, *clarinet*
Richard Taylor, *flute*
Stephen Trier, *bass clarinet, saxophone*
Denis Wick FGSM, LRAM, *trombone*
Averil Williams ARCM, *flute*
Trevor Wye LRSM, *flute*

Harp
Sidonie Goossens MBE, FGSM

Guitar, Lute, Sitar
Antonio Albanes AGSM, *guitar*
Viram Jasani MA, *sitar*
Blanche Munro AGSM, *guitar*
Hector Quine Hon ARAM, *guitar*
Anthony Rooley, *lute*

Percussion
David Arnold
Kurt Goedicke
Robert Howes

Academic
Harold Dexter MA, Mus B, FGSM, FRSCM, FRCO, ARCM,
head of department

Neil Van Allen FGSM, L Mus
Malcolm Barry M Mus
Adrian Cruft Hon ARCM
Kyla Greenbaum Hon ARAM, FRAM
Kathryn Lukas M Mus
Edward Moar BA
Alfred Nieman FGSM, FRAM
Philip Pickett AGSM
Patric Standford FGSM
Adrian Thorne BA

Practice Techniques
Paul Collins

Music Therapy
Juliette Alvin MT, FGSM, *head of department*

Ernest Berk FGSM
Alfred Nieman FGSM, FRAM
Margaret Pickett LGSMT
Fred Turner AGSM
Janet Weiner

HUDDERSFIELD SCHOOL OF MUSIC

Head: P. G. Forbes MA, ARCO

Huddersfield Polytechnic and Technical College,
Queensgate, Huddersfield HD1 3DH t Huddersfield
30501. Courses, facilities, etc.: see p. 248, 251

Conductors
Patrick Forbes MA, ARCO
John Gulley LlB
Prabhu Singh B Mus, ARAM, LRAM, FRCO
Donald Webster B Mus, FRCO, ADCM, FTCL, LRAM, ARCM

Singing
Patricia Hamilton ARCM
John Highcock
Shirley Leah ARMCM
David Lennox BA, PCE, LRAM
Rita McKerrow
Victoria Molteno GRSM, LRAM, ARCM
Owen Wynne ARMCM

Keyboard
Eileen Bass GRSM, ARCM, *piano*
Peter Clare BA, LRAM, *piano*
Winifred Coppell, *piano*
Graham Cummings MA, B Mus, *piano, harpsichord, organ*
Neil Garland MA, *piano*
Geoffrey Hamilton BA, LRAM, *piano*
Gladys Horner FTCL, LRAM, *piano*
Keith Jarvis MA, FRCO, LRAM, ARCM, *organ*
Michael Kruszynski Ph D, *piano*
Heather Lawson ARCM, GRSM, *piano*
Heath Lees MA, B Mus, ARCM, *piano*
Priscilla Minton ARMCM, GRSM, *piano*
Juliet Moorhouse ARMCM, *piano*
Kathleen Mountain LRAM, *piano*
Ronald Newton ARMCM, *piano, harpsichord*
Ruth Ramsden GRSM, LRAM, ARCM, *piano*
Joan Sheard FTCL, LRAM, ARCM, *piano*
Eleanor Singh GRSM, LRAM, ARCM, ARCO, *piano*
Prabhu Singh B Mus, ARAM, LRAM, FRCO, *piano*
Winifred Smith B Mus, FRCO, LRAM, *organ*
Keith Swallow M Mus, ARMCM, LTCL, *piano*
Harold Truscott ARCM, *piano*
Donald Webster B Mus, FRCO, ADCM, FTCL, LRAM, ARCM,
organ

Strings
Jean Brier ARMCM, *violin*

George Brown ARCM, *violin*
Michael Davis, *violin*
Pauline Dunn BA, LRAM, ARCM, *violoncello*
Ronald Gould LRAM, ARCM, *viola*
Peter Leah, *double-bass*
Kathleen Mountain LRAM, *violoncello*
Kenneth Rafferty LRAM, ARCM, *violin*
Richard Steinitz MA, *violoncello*
Herbert Whone B Mus, ARCM, *violin*

Wind
Maurice Ashworth, *bassoon*
Thomas Atkinson, *tuba*
John Barrow ARMCM, *flute*
Eileen Bass GRSM, ARCM, *oboe*
Rodney Bass ARMCM, *saxophone*
Adrian Baxter ARCM, *flute*
Judith Clare B Mus, ARCM, *clarinet*
Stuart Coldwell ARMCM, *flute*
Ian Coull DRSAM, *trumpet*
Neil Garland MA, *clarinet*
John Gulley LlB, *horn, trumpet*
Julian Hall LRAM, LGSM, *clarinet*
Allan Haydock, *clarinet*
Valerie Lockwood ARCM, *oboe*
Michael McKenna LGSM, ARCM, *oboe*
Maurice Murphy, *trumpet*
Colin Sutcliffe ARMCM, *flute*
Robert Ward, *flute*
Barrie Webb BA, *trombone*

Harp
Honor Wright ARMCM

Guitar
David Taplin Cert Ed

Percussion
Eric Wooliscroft

Full-Time Staff
Arthur Butterworth ARCM
Peter Clare BA, LRAM
Graham Cummings BA, B Mus
Neil Garland MA
John Gulley LlB
Geoffrey Hamilton BA, LRAM
Patricia Hamilton ARCM
Michael Holloway B Mus, ARCM
Harry Sterndale Hurst B Mus, FRCO, ARMCM
Keith Jarvis MA, FRCO, LRAM, ARCM

Michael Kruszynski PhD
Peter Lawson BA, B Mus
Heath Lees MA, B Mus, ARCM
David Lennox BA, PCE, LRAM
George Maskell ARAM, GRSM, LRAM
Kathleen Mountain LRAM
Ronald Newton ARMCM
Stephen Oliver BA, B Mus
Prabhu Singh B Mus, ARAM, LRAM, FRCO
Winifred Smith B Mus, FRCO, LRAM
Richard Steinitz MA
David Taplin Cert Ed
Harold Truscott ARCM
Barrie Webb BA
Donald Webster B Mus, FRCO, ADCM, FTCL, LRAM, ARCM
Herbert Whone B Mus, ARCM

LONDON COLLEGE OF MUSIC

Director: W. S. Lloyd Webber D Mus, FRCM, FRCO, FLCM,
Hon RAM

47 Great Marlborough St, London WlV 2AS t 01-437 6120
tg supertonic. Courses, facilities, etc.: see p. 249, 251

Singing
John Chapman Hon FLCM, LRAM
Ivor Evans ARCM
Joan Gray GRSM, LRAM, ARCM
Vere Laurie FLCM
George Prangnell LRAM

Keyboard
David Campbell LLCM (TD), *piano*
J. Laurence Clarke FRCO, FLCM, ARCM, *piano, organ*
Charles Collins FRCO, ARCM, *piano, organ*
Denys Darlow FRCO, Hon RCM, *organ*
Christopher Fry ARCM, *piano*
John Gredley LLCM (TD), ARCM, LRAM, ATCL, *piano*
Eric Hope FLCM, ARCM, *piano*
Philip Jenkins ARAM, *piano*
Raymond Leetham LRAM, LLCM (TD), *piano*
Maureen McAllister FRCO, ARCM, LRAM, LTCL, A Mus TCL,
organ
Andrew Morris GRSM, LRAM, ARCO, *piano*
June Ross Oliver ARCM, *piano*
Antony Peebles Mus B, LRAM, *piano*
Gordon Phillips FRCO, FLCM, ARCM, *organ, harpsichord*
Doreen Stanfield LRAM, *piano*
Robin Stone FLCM, LLCM (TD), FRSAMD, *piano*
Raphael Terroni GLCM, ARCM, *piano*
John Vallier FLCM, *piano*

Strings
Joan Bucknall LGSM, *viola*
Rose Roth, *violin*
Jack Silvester, *double-bass*
Rodney Stewart LRAM, *double-bass*
Harald Strub ARCM, *violoncello*
Peter Turton ARCM, *violin, viola*
Dora Zafransky FTCL, LRAM, *violin*

Wind
Bernard Bean ARCM, *tuba*
Edward Blakeman GLCM, LLCM (TD), *flute*
Adrian Brett ARCM, *flute*
Wilfred Goddard ARCM, *clarinet*
Stefan de Haan, *bassoon*
Wilfrid Kealey ARCM, *clarinet*

Maureen McAllister FRCO, ARCM, LRAM, LTCL, A Mus TCL, *recorder*
J. Anthony Parsons ARAM, *trombone*
Stephen Pierce GLCM, LLCM (TD), *clarinet*
Edgar Riches ARCM, *trumpet*
Rainer Schuelein AGSM, *flute*
Derek Taylor, *horn*
John Wolfe, *oboe*
Denis Wood, *oboe*

Guitar
Oliver Hunt B Mus, LGSM
George Zarb FLCM, LLCM (TD)

Professors Responsible for Classes, Lectures, Ensembles
W. R. Pasfield D Mus, BA, FRCO, FLCM, LRAM, *head*

Gerald Barnes FRCO, GRSM, ARCM
Alan Bullard MA, B Mus, ARCM
John Burn FLCM
David Christie GLCM
Christopher Fry ARCM
Errol Girdlestone BA (Hons), ARCO
Bernard Harman Hon RCM
Joan Kemp-Potter ARCM
Raymond Leetham LRAM, LLCM (TD)
Maureen McAllister FRCO, ARCM, LRAM, LTCL, A Mus TCL
Andrew Morris GRSM, LRAM, ARCO
Ronald Rappoport GGSM
Eleanor Richards B Mus
Robin Stone FLCM, LLCM (TD), FRSA
Paul Sturman GRSM, LRAM, ARCM
Reginald Thompson ARCM, LRAM, ARCO
Brian Trueman B Mus, FRCO, FTCL, LRAM, ARCM
Francis B. Westbrook D Mus, BA, FRSCM

NEWTON PARK COLLEGE

Head of Music Department: W. J. Richards BA, Mus B, Dip Ed

Bath BA2 9BN t Saltford 2681. Courses, facilities, etc.: see p. 249, 251

Singing
Cynthia Glover
Richard Graves

Keyboard
Peter Blackwood, *piano*
Jane Dawkins, *piano*
Joan Taylor, *piano*

Strings
Michael Brittain, *double-bass*
Michael Evans LRAM, AGSM, *violoncello* (Dartington String Quartet)
Malcolm Latchem ARCM, *violin* (Dartington String Quartet)
Keith Lovell ARCM, *viola* (Dartington String Quartet)
Colin Sauer LRAM, LTCL, ARCM, FTCL, ARAM, FRAM, *violin* (Dartington String Quartet)
Vivienne Thomas, *violin, viola*
Daphne Webb, *violoncello*

Wind
John Berry, *trombone, tuba*
Ann Boothroyd, *flute*
Deborah Brittain, *clarinet*
Wilfred Goddard ARCM, *clarinet*
John Jones, *horn*
David Mason, *trumpet*
Stephen Nye, *oboe*
Michael Oliver, *recorder*

Percussion
Denis Blyth

Lecturers
Dudley Holroyd Mus B, FRCO (CHM), ARCM, ADCM
Ken James M Mus, BA, LGSM
George Odam B Mus, BA
Jennifer Paterson GGSM, ARCM
Eric Roseberry BA, B Mus
Peter Salt FNSM, LRAM, LGSM, ATCL

NORTH EAST ESSEX TECHNICAL COLLEGE AND SCHOOL OF ART

Head of Department of Music: Donald J. Hughes D Mus, BSc (Econ), FRCO, LRAM, FTCL

Sheepen Rd, Colchester, Essex CO3 3LL t Colchester 70271. Courses, facilities, etc.: see p. 249, 251

Composition, Harmony
Richard Arnell Hon FTCL
Peter Jacobs GRSM, ARCO, ARCM, LRAM
Lyndon Marguerie D Mus, FRCO

Singing
April Cantelo ARCM
Nancy Evans
Eileen Poulter FTCL
Lesley Tremethick LRAM

Keyboard
Ann Barbanell LRAM, ARCM, *piano*
Robert Bell LRAM, AGSM, *piano*
Harold East GRSM, ARCM, *piano*
Ruth Harte FRAM, *piano*
Barbara Hewison LRAM, ARCM, *piano*
Graeme Humphrey LRAM, *piano*
Ronald Lumsden ARCM, LRAM, *piano*
Hilary Macnamara ARCM, LRSM, *piano*
J. Harrison Oxley MA, B Mus, FRCO, ARCM, *organ*
Harold Parker LRAM, ARCM, *piano*
Roy Teed ARAM, LRAM, *piano*

Strings
Tessa Robbins ARCM, *violin*
John Wingham ARCM, *violoncello*

Wind
Ray Allen, *trumpet, trombone*
George Churchill LGSM, *trumpet, trombone*
Duke Dobing BA, LRAM, ARCM, FTCL, *flute*
Vernon Elliott, *bassoon*
Angela Fussell GRSM, LRAM, ARCM, *clarinet*
Simon Hunt, *flute*
Ifor James Hon ARAM, *horn*
Valerie James GRSM, ARCM, LTCL, *recorder*
William Newton, *trumpet, trombone*
Stephen Waters ARCM, Hon RAM, *clarinet*
Rosemary Wells, *oboe*

Guitar
Thomas Hartman BA, LRAM, ARCM
Valerie James GRSM, ARCM, LTCL

Percussion
Celia Dudley

Full-Time Staff
William Tamblyn BA, *principal lecturer*

Bryan Barnes MA, LRAM
Noel Britton AGSM, ARCM
Michael Clack B Mus, GLCM, FTCL, LRAM, ARCO
John Cooper M Mus, FRCO, ARCM
Percy Crozier ARCM
David Cutforth B Mus, BA, LRAM, ARAM
Donald Goodall B Mus, ARMCM
Allan Granville BA, ARCM
Peter Holman M Mus
Ronald James B Mus, LRAM, ARCM, LGSM
Pamela Jenkins LTCL, LRAM
Christopher Phelps FRCO, GRSM, ARCM, LRAM
Ian Ray FRCO, LRAM, ARCM
Eric Stanley GTCL, LTCL
Norman Tattersall ARAM, LRAM
John Wolton GRSM, ARCM

Staff Accompanist and Coach
S. Wainwright Morgan B Mus, LRSM

ROYAL ACADEMY OF MUSIC

Principal: Sir Anthony Lewis CBE, MA, Mus B, Hon
Mus D, Hon RAM, FRCM, Hon FTCL, Hon GSM

Marylebone Rd, London NW1 5HT t 01-935 5461. Courses,
facilities, etc.: see p. 249, 251

Composition, Harmony
Timothy Baxter ARAM
Edgar Brice MA, D Mus, Hon ARAM, FRCO
Brian Brockless B Mus, Hon ARAM
Christopher Brown
Gavin Brown MA, B Mus, Hon ARAM, FRCO
Alan Bush D Mus, Hon D Mus, FRAM
Cornelius Cardew FRAM
R. H. Clifford-Smith MA, D Mus, FRAM, Hon RCM, FRCO
M. E. Gwen Dodds Mus B, Hon RAM
Eric Fenby OBE, Hon RAM
Norman Fulton FRAM
John Gardner B Mus, Hon RAM
Derek Gaye MA, Hon RAM, Hon RCM, ARCO
Simon Harris MA, B Mus, Hon ARAM
Margaret Hubicki FRAM
James Iliff B Mus, FRAM
Malcolm Macdonald MA, Mus B, Hon RAM
Hugh Marchant FRAM, ARCO
Geoffrey Pratley B Mus, ARAM
Arthur J. Pritchard D Mus, Hon RAM, FRCO, FTCL
Stephen Rhys B Mus, ARAM
David Robinson B Mus, ARAM, FRCO
Paul Steinitz D Mus, FRAM, FRCO
Richard Stoker FRAM
Alwyn Surplice Mus D, B Mus, FRCO
Roy Teed ARAM
Philip Tomblings Hon ARAM, FRCO
Sven Weber B Mus, ARAM
Arthur Wills D Mus, Hon RAM, FRCO
Georgina Zellan-Smith B Mus, ARAM

Orchestration
Leighton Lucas Hon RAM

Conductors and Teachers for Orchestras, Choirs and
Chamber Music
John Davies FRAM
Meredith Davies MA, B Mus, Hon RAM, FRCO
Norman Del Mar CBE, Hon RAM
Gwynne Edwards FRAM, Hon RCM
John Gardner B Mus, Hon RAM
Sidney Griller CBE, FRAM

Maurice Handford FRAM
Douglas Hopkins D Mus, FRAM, FRCO, FGSM
Sir Anthony Lewis CBE, MA, Mus B, Hon Mus D, Hon RAM,
FRCM, Hon FTCL, Hon GSM
Maurice Miles FRAM
Wilfrid Parry Hon RAM, FTCL

Opera Class
John Streets FRAM, *director*

Steuart Bedford BA, FRAM, FRCO, *principal conductor*
Tom Hammond Hon RAM
Mary Nash ARAM
Anna Sweeny

Singing
Kenneth Bowen MA, Mus B, BA, Hon RAM
Henry Cummings FRAM
Jean Austin Dobson ARAM
Raimund Herincx Hon RAM
Mary Jarred Hon RAM
Mary Makower Hon ARAM
Joy Mammen Hon ARAM
Flora Nielsen Hon RAM
Constance Shacklock OBE, FRAM
Marjorie Thomas Hon RAM, FRMCM

Languages
Lella Alberg Hon ARAM, *Italian*
Jean Parzy Hon ARAM, *French*

Keyboard
Jean Anderson ARAM, *piano*
Sybil Barlow FRAM, *piano*
Else Cross Hon ARAM, *piano*
Ivey Dickson FRAM, *piano*
Christopher Elton ARAM, *piano*
Gordon Green Hon MA, Hon RAM, FRMCM, *piano*
Kyla Greenbaum FRAM, *piano*
Sidney Harrison Hon RAM, FGSM, *piano*
Ruth Harte FRAM, *piano*
Alan Harverson ARAM, *organ*
Jean Harvey FRAM, *piano*
Douglas Hawkridge FRAM, FRCO, *organ*
Michael Head FRAM, *piano*
Eric Hope Hon ARAM, Hon FLCM, *piano*
Douglas Hopkins D Mus, FRAM, FRCO, FGSM, *organ*
Philip Jenkins ARAM, *piano*
Geraint Jones FRAM, *organ, harpsichord*
Guy Jonson FRAM, *piano*
Alexander Kelly FRAM, *piano*

Joan Last Hon **ARAM**, *piano*
Mildred Litherland FRAM, *piano*
Hamish Milne ARAM, *piano*
Dennis Murdoch FRAM, *piano*
John Palmer FRAM, *piano*
Lois Phillips ARAM, *piano*
Geoffrey Pratley B Mus, ARAM, *piano accompaniment*
Alan Richardson FRAM, *piano*
George Rogers Hon ARAM, *piano*
Martindale Sidwell FRAM, FRCO, *organ*
Rex Stephens FRAM, *piano accompaniment*
John Streets FRAM, *piano accompaniment*
Peter Uppard, *piano*
Madeleine Windsor FRAM, *piano, piano accompaniment*
Georgina Zellan-Smith B Mus, ARAM, *piano*

Strings
Lionel Bentley Hon RAM, *violin*
Joan Bonner FRAM, *violoncello*
Derek Collier FRAM, *violin*
Winifred Copperwheat FRAM, *viola*
Gwynne Edwards FRAM, Hon RCM, *viola*
Max Gilbert FRAM, *viola*
John Gray ARAM, *double-bass*
Sidney Griller CBE, FRAM, *violin*
Frederick Grinke FRAM, *violin*
Jean Harvey FRAM, *violin*
Ralph Holmes FRAM, *violin*
Florence Hooton FRAM, *violoncello*
Emanuel Hurwitz FRAM, *violin*
Vivian Joseph FRAM, Hon FTCL, *violoncello*
Marjorie Lavers FRAM, *violin*
Jack McDougal Hon ARAM, *violin*
Hugh Maguire FRAM, *violin*
David Martin FRAM, *violin*
Clarence Myerscough ARAM, *violin*
Dennis Nesbitt, *viola da gamba, violone*
Manoug Parikian Hon RAM, FTCL, *violin*
Lilly Phillips FRAM, *violoncello*
Rosemary Rapaport FRAM, *violin*
Stephen Shingles FRAM, *viola*
Derek Simpson Hon MA, FRAM, *violoncello*
John Walton FRAM, *double-bass*
Trevor Williams FRAM, *violin*

Wind
Evelyn Rothwell Barbirolli Hon RAM, *oboe*
Gwydion Brooke FRAM, *bassoon*
James Brown OBE, Hon RAM, *horn*

Janet Craxton FRAM, *oboe*
John Dankworth CBE, FRAM, *saxophone*
John Davies FRAM, *clarinet*
Georgina Dobrée ARAM, *clarinet*
Michael Dobson FRAM, *oboe*
Sidney Ellison FRAM, *trumpet*
John Fletcher Hon ARAM, *tuba*
Alan Hacker FRAM, *clarinet*
Derek Honner FRAM, *flute*
Ifor James FRAM, *horn*
Anthony Judd ARAM, *bassoon*
Norman Knight FRAM, *flute*
Sidney F. Langston Hon RAM, *trombone*
Betty Mills ARAM, *flute*
Gareth Morris FRAM, *flute*
Harold Nash ARAM, *trombone*
William J. Overton Hon RAM, *trumpet*
Christopher Taylor, *recorder*
Barry Tuckwell OBE, Hon RAM, *horn*
Ronald Waller ARAM, *bassoon*
Keith Whitmore Hon ARAM, *horn*

Harp
Osian Ellis CBE, Hon D Mus, FRAM
Enid Quiney ARAM

Guitar
Hector Quine Hon RAM

Percussion
Reginald Barker Hon ARAM
Susan Bixley
James Blades OBE, Hon RAM

History, Analysis, Repertoire
George Biddlecombe MA, GRSM, LRAM, ARCM
John Gardner B Mus, Hon RAM
Simon Harris MA, B Mus, Hon ARAM
Jean Harvey FRAM
Peter Holman M Mus
Arthur Jacobs MA, Hon RAM
Geoffrey Pratley B Mus, ARAM

Early Music Classes
Peter Holman M Mus

Contemporary Music Classes
John Carewe
Paul Patterson ARAM

Jazz Study Group
John Dankworth CBE, FRAM

ROYAL COLLEGE OF MUSIC

Director: David V. Willcocks CBE, MC, MA, Mus B,
FRCM, FRCO, Hon RAM

Prince Consort Rd, London SW7 2BS t 01-589 3643 tg
initiative. Courses, facilities, etc.: see p. 249,
                                                    251
Composition, Theory, Keyboard Harmony
Robert Ashfield D Mus, FRCO, Hon ARCM
Philip Cannon FRCM
Lawrence Casserley B Mus, Hon ARCM
Justin Connolly ARCM
Adrian Cruft Hon ARCM
Jeremy Dale-Roberts B Mus, Hon RCM
Denys Darlow FRCO, Hon RCM
Stephen Dodgson FRCO, ARCM
Ruth Gipps D Mus, Hon RAM, FRCM
Douglas Guest CVO, MA, Mus B, FRCM, Hon FRCO, Hon RAM
Joseph Horovitz MA, B Mus, Hon ARCM
Herbert Howells CH, CBE, D Mus, FRCM, FRCO, Hon RAM
Kenneth V. Jones Hon ARCM, ARCO
Bryan Kelly ARCM
John Lambert LRAM, ARCM, ARCO
Richard Latham FRCM, FRCO
Anthony Milner D Mus, FRCM
Alan Ridout ARCM
Edwin Roxburgh BA, B Mus, ARCM, LRAM
Timothy Salter MA, LRAM, ARCO, MTC
Humphrey Searle CBE, MA, FRCM
Christopher Slater FTCL, ARCM
Gerald Smith MA, ARCM
John Somers-Cocks Mus B, ARCM
Bernard Stevens MA, Mus D, FRCM
Derek Stevens FRCO, LRAM, ARCM, LGSM
Gordon Stewart MA, B Mus, LRAM, ARCM
W. S. Lloyd Webber D Mus, FRCM, FRCO, FLCM, Hon RAM
Philip Wilkinson D Mus, M Mus RCM, FRCM, LRAM
John R. Williams MA, Mus B, FRCO, Hon RCM
John W. Wilson MA, Mus B, FRCO, ARCM

Conductors
Richard Austin FRCM
Philip Cannon FRCM
Denys Darlow FRCO, Hon RCM
Norman Del Mar CBE, FGSM, Hon RAM, ARCM
Michael Lankester GRSM, ARCM
John McCarthy Hon RCM
Harvey Phillips FRCM
David Willcocks CBE, MC, MA, Mus B, FRCM, FRCO (CHM),
Hon RAM

Opera and Drama
Richard Austin FRCM
Helen Barker GRSM, ARCM
Catherine Lambert Hon RCM
Margaret Rubel Hon RCM
Joseph Sorbello Hon ARCM
Marion Studholme ARCM
Joyce Wodeman Hon RCM

Singing
Hervey Alan OBE, FRCM, Hon RAM
Margaret Bissett Hon ARCM
Margaret Cable ARCM
Gordon Clinton FRCM, Hon RAM, FBSM
Gerald English ARCM
Paul Esswood ARCM
Veronica Mansfield FRCM, LTCL
Ruth Packer FRCM
Mark Raphael Hon RCM
Meriel St Clair FRCM
Frederick Sharp Hon ARCM
Marion Studholme ARCM
Robert Tear MA
Lyndon van der Pump ARCM

Languages
Lella Alberg Hon ARAM, *Italian*
Bertha Taylor Hon RCM, *German*

Keyboard
John Barstow ARCM, *piano*
John Birch Hon MA, FRCO (CHM), LRAM, ARCM, *organ*
Herrick Bunney MVO, B Mus, FRCO, ARCM, *organ*
Nicholas Danby LRAM, ARCM, *organ*
Denys Darlow FRCO, Hon RCM, *organ*
Oliver Davies ARCM, *piano*
Hubert Dawkes B Mus, FRCM, FRCO, *piano, harpsichord*
Maria Donska Hon ARCM, *piano*
Ralph Downes CBE, MA, B Mus, FRCM, Hon FRCO, Hon RAM, *organ*
Ruth Dyson ARCM, *piano, harpsichord*
Peter Element ARCM, *piano*
Raymond Fischer LRAM, LTCL, *piano*
Ruth Gerald Mus B, LRAM, ARCM, *piano*
Alasdair Graham B Mus, Hon RCM, Diplomé Vienna State Academy, LRAM, *piano*
Douglas Guest CVO, MA, Mus B, FRCM, Hon FRCO, Hon RAM, *organ*
Barbara Hill GRSM, ARCM, *piano*
Colin Horsley OBE, FRCM, *piano*
Ian Lake ARCM, *piano*
Richard Latham FRCM, FRCO, *organ*

John Lill FRCM, Hon FTCL, FLCM, *piano*
Michael Gough Matthews FRCM, LRAM, ARCO, *piano*
Angus Morrison FRCM, *piano*
David Parkhouse FRCM, *piano*
Harry Platts LRAM, ARCM, *piano*
Margaret Plummer GRSM, ARCM, ARCO, *piano*
Richard Popplewell FRCO, ARCM, *organ*
Eileen Reynolds FRAM, Hon RCM, *piano*
Bernard Roberts ARCM, *piano*
Alan Rowlands MA, LRAM, ARCM, *piano*
John Russell BA, LRAM, ARCM, *piano*
Stephen Savage LRAM, ARCM, *piano*
Phyllis Sellick OBE, FRAM, Hon RCM, *piano*
Millicent Silver ARCM, *piano, harpsichord*
Gordon Stewart MA, B Mus, LRAM, ARCM, *piano*
E. Kendall Taylor FRCM, *piano*
Joan Trimble BA, Mus B, LRAM, Hon ARCM, *piano*
Roger Vignoles, *piano*
Peter Wallfisch, *piano*
David Ward LRAM, ARCM, *piano*
Yu Chun Yee, ARCM, LRSM, *piano*

Strings
Francis Baines Hon RCM, *viols*
Hugh Bean CBE, FRCM, *violin*
Roger Best ARMCM, *viola*
Eileen Croxford ARCM, *violoncello*
Joan Dickson FRCM, LRAM, *violoncello*
John Yewe Dyer B Mus, FRAM, Hon RCM, *viola*
Jose Luis Garcia Hon ARCM, *violin*
Brian Hawkins ARCM, *viola*
Leonard Hirsch FRCM, Hon FRMCM, *violin*
Helen Just FRCM, *violoncello*
Felix Kok ARAM, LRAM, Hon RCM, *violin*
Maria Lidka Hon RCM, *violin*
John Ludlow Hon ARCM, *violin*
Margaret Major Hon MA, ARCM, *viola*
Keith Marjoram ARCM, *double-bass*
Frances Mason ARCM, *violin*
Ralph Nicholson ARCM, *violin*
Harvey Phillips FRCM, *violoncello*
Anthony Pini FRCM, *violoncello*
Carl Pini, *violin*
Kenneth Piper ARCM, *violin*
Frederick Riddle FRCM, *viola*
Tessa Robbins ARCM, *violin*
Sylvia Rosenberg Hon RCM, *violin*
Bernard Shore CBE, FRCM, FTCL, Hon RAM, *viola*
Anna Shuttleworth ARCM, *violoncello*
Rodney Slatford, *double-bass*
Jack Steadman FRCM, *violin*

Bertha Stevens LRAM, Hon RCM, *violin*
Charles Taylor OBE, FRMCM, Hon RCM, *violin*
Jaroslav Vanecek Hon RCM, *violin, viola*

Wind
Julian Baker, *horn*
Sebastian Bell, *flute*
Colin Bradbury ARCM, *clarinet*
James Brown Hon RCM, *oboe*
John Burness, *double bassoon*
Kerrison Camden ARCM, *bassoon*
Alan Civil Hon RCM, *horn*
Sidney Fell FRCM, *clarinet*
John Francis FRCM, FGSM, *flute*
Sarah Francis ARCM, *oboe*
Geoffrey Gambold Hon RCM, *bassoon*
Peter Graeme Hon ARCM, *oboe*
Christopher Hyde-Smith Hon ARCM, *flute*
John Iveson B Mus, LRAM, ARCM, *tenor trombone*
Natalie James Hon RCM, *oboe*
John Jenkins, *tuba*
Thea King FRCM, *clarinet*
John McCaw ARCM, *clarinet*
Andrew McCullough ARCM, *clarinet*
Terence MacDonagh BEM, FRAM, FRCM, *oboe*
Gerald McElhone, *bass trombone*
David Mason ARCM, *trumpet*
Graham Mayger ARCM, *flute*
Douglas Moore FRCM, ALAM, *horn*
Elisabeth Page ARCM, *recorder*
Sydney Sutcliffe Hon ARCM, *oboe*
Stephen Trier Hon ARCM, *bass clarinet, saxophone*
Basil Tschaikov Hon ARCM, *clarinet*
Richard Walton FRCM, *trumpet*
Arthur Wilson Hon RCM, *tenor trombone*
Michael Winfield Hon RCM, *oboe*

Harp
Fiona Hibbert GRSM, ARCM
Marisa Robles Hon RCM
Renata Scheffel-Stein

Guitar, Lute
Patrick Bashford AGSM, *guitar*
Carlos Bonell, *guitar*
Michael Jessett Hon RCM, *guitar*
Diana Poulton Hon RCM, *lute*

Percussion
Alan Cumberland Hon ARCM
Bernard Harman Hon RCM
Michael Skinner

Professors Responsible for Classes, Study Groups,
Repertoire, Ensembles
Richard Austin FRCM
Philip Cannon FRCM
Jeremy Dale-Roberts B Mus, Hon RCM
Denys Darlow FRCO, Hon RCM
Hubert Dawkes B Mus, FRCM, FRCO
Ruth Dyson ARCM
Peter Element ARCM
Raymond Fischer LRAM, LTCL
John Francis FRCM, FGSM
Ruth Gipps D Mus, FRCM, Hon RAM
Alasdair Graham B Mus, Hon RCM, Diplomé Vienna State
Academy, LRAM
Christopher Grier MA, Mus B, Hon RCM
Joseph Horovitz MA, B Mus, Hon ARCM
Adrian Jack LRAM, ARCM, ARCO
John Lambert LRAM, ARCM, ARCO
Richard Latham FRCM, **FRCO**
Else Mayer-Lismann Hon RCM
Anthony Milner D Mus, FRCM
Harvey Phillips FRCM
Richard Popplewell FRCO, ARCM
Mary Remnant MA, D Phil, GRSM, ARCM
John Russell BA, LRAM, ARCM
Bernard Stevens MA, Mus D, FRCM
Gordon Stewart MA, B Mus, LRAM, ARCM
Elizabeth Vanderspar LRAM, Dalcroze Cert (Lond),
 Dalcroze Cert (Geneva), Hon RCM
Roger Vignoles
Yvonne Wells Hon RCM
Philip Wilkinson D Mus, M Mus RCM, FRCM, LRAM
John R. Williams MA, B Mus, FRCO, Hon RCM
John W. Wilson MA, B Mus, FRCO, ARCM

ROYAL NORTHERN COLLEGE OF MUSIC

Principal: John Manduell FRAM, Hon FTCL

124 Oxford Rd, Manchester M13 9RD t 061-273 6283.
Courses, facilities, etc.: see p. 249, 251

School of Composition and Performance
John Manduell FRAM, Hon FTCL, *head of department*
Terence Greaves MA, B Mus, Hon ABSM, ARCM, *associate head of department*

Sir William Glock CBE, Hon Mus D, BA, ARCO, *tutor laureatus*

Composition
Peter Maxwell Davies
Anthony Gilbert

Performance (Music)
Isobel Flinn GRSM, *répétiteur*
Martin Holland GRSM, *répétiteur*
Brian Hughes BA, LRAM, *répétiteur*
Colin Jones GRSM, *opera chorus director*
David Jordan FRMCM, *staff conductor*
Rosemary Walton Mus B, *répétiteur*
Stephen Wilkinson MA, *motet choir director*
John Wilson FNSM, ARCM, LRAM, *head of opera music staff*

Performance (Drama)
Malcolm Fraser, *lecturer in opera and drama*
Sheila Barlow, *intendant*
Elaine Bevis Dip NCSD, LRSM, *diction, dialogue*
Mary Forey Ass ISTD, Dip LCDD, *movement*
Geza Partos Dip Acad Drama, *stagecraft*
Brenda Urion LRAM, *mime*

Singing
Alexander Young, *head of department*
Joseph Ward FRMCM, *assistant head of department*

Betty Bannerman
Frederic Cox OBE, MA, Hon RMCM
Caroline Crawshaw ARMCM
Albert Haskayne FNSM, LRAM
Thomas Hemsley MA
Sylvia Jacobs ARMCM
Colin Jones GRSM
Ellis Keeler FGSM
Dianne Matthews ARMCM
Patrick McGuigan ARMCM

Ena Mitchell
Maryrose Moorhouse FTCL, ARMCM, LRAM
Nicholas Powell ARMCM
Delcie Tetsill LRAM
Irene Wilde FNSM, LRAM
Maimie Woods ARCM, ARMCM, LRAM
Owen Wynne ARMCM

Languages
Josephine Barber BA, *German*
Robert Hall BA, LRAM, *English*
Hannah Hickman BA, *German*
Margarethe Müller Dip Philos (Vienna), *German*
Ernesta Partilora LRAM, *Italian*
Hélène Pax, Grad Brussels Conservatoire, *French*
Cecilia Wardlaw ARMCM, *Italian*

Keyboard
Clifton Helliwell FRMCM, *piano, head of department*

Krystyna Adams GRSM, ARMCM, *accompanist*
Sulamita Aronovsky, Dip of Distinction (Vilnius), MA
 (Moscow Conservatory), *piano*
Ryszard Bakst, Order of Polonia Restituta, MA (Moscow
 Conservatory), *piano*
Geoffrey Barber FMCA, FRMCM, Hon RSCM, *church music*
Shirley Blakey ARMCM, LRAM, *piano*
Una Bradbury ARMCM, *piano*
Michael Callaghan ARCO, LRAM, ARCM, LTCL, *organ*
Eileen Chadwick FNSM, LRAM, *piano*
Eric Chadwick FRCO, FRMCM, *organ*
Marjorie Clementi ARMCM, *piano*
Robert Elliott FRMCM, *harpsichord*
Doris Euerby FNSM, LRAM, *piano*
Ronald Frost B Mus, FRCO, FRMCM, Hon RSCM, *organ*
David Garforth FRCO, GRSM, ARMCM, LRAM, *organ*
Anthony Goldstone GRSM, *piano*
Manola Grecul GRSM, *piano*
Donald Greed ARMCM, *piano*
Gordon Green Hon MA, Hon RAM, FRMCM, *piano*
George Hadjinikos, Dip Athens Conservatory, Dip
 Salzburg Mozarteum, *piano*
Michael Hancock GNSM, LRAM, *accompanist*
Robert Hayes BA, ARMCM, LGSM, *accompanist*
Richard Holloway GRSM, *accompanist*
Marjorie Hopwood LRAM, *piano*
Colin Horsley OBE, Hon ARCM, *piano*
Constance Kay FNSM, LRAM, *piano*
David Lloyd ARMCM, *piano*
Kathleen McGrath ARMCM, *piano*
Marjorie Proudlove FNSM, LRAM, *piano*
Stephen Reynolds GRSM, ARMCM, *accompanist*

Heather Slade GRSM, *accompanist*
David Smith LRAM, ARCM, *piano*
Hedwig Stein, *piano*
Terence Taylor FNSM, LRAM, *piano*
Eva Warren ARMCM, *piano*
Herbert Winterbottom M Sc, FNSM, LRAM, ARCM, LTCL, *organ*
Maimie Woods ARCM, ARMCM, LRAM, *accompanist*
Rosemarie Wright, Dip Vienna State Academy, ARAM, *piano*
Derrick Wyndham, *piano*

Strings
Cecil Aronowitz FRCM, Hon ARCM, *viola, head of department*

Adrian Beers Hon ARCM, *double-bass*
Rudolf Botta, *violin*
Oliver Brookes LGSM, *viola da gamba*
Maurice Clare, *violin*
Sydney Errington, *viola*
Sylvie Gazeau, Dip Paris Conservatoire, *violin*
Bronislaw Gimpel, Grad Hochschule für Musik (Berlin), *violin*
Kathryn Hardman GRSM, *violin*
Walter Jorysz LLCM, *violin*
Clifford Knowles FRMCM, *violin*
Peter Mark BA, M Sc, *viola*
Mark Marshall GNSM, ARCM, *violoncello*
Ludmila Navratil ARMCM, *viola*
Ian Rudge LRAM, *violoncello*
Bernard Shore CBE, FRCM, FTCL, Hon RAM, *viola*
Raphael Sommer, *violoncello*
David Usher LRAM, *violin*
Oliver Vella FRAM, *violoncello*
Paul Ward ARCM, *violoncello*
Terence Weil ARAM, *violoncello*
Yossi Zivoni, Grad Israeli Academy of Music, *violin*

Wind
Sydney Coulston FRMCM, *horn, senior tutor in brass*
Sidney Fell FRCM, FRMCM, *clarinet, senior tutor in woodwind*

Cecil Cox Hon RCM, *flute*
Stanley Cox, *trombone*
Charles Cracknell, *bassoon*
Neville Duckworth ARCM, LTCL, *clarinet*
Leonard Foster ARCM, ARMCM, *clarinet.*
Martin Hardy GRSM, *bassoon*
Philip Jones, *oboe*

Philip Jones ARCM, *trumpet*
Cecil Kidd ARCM, *trumpet*
Alan Lockwood ARCM, *flute*
Norman McDonald, *clarinet*
Kenneth Monks, *horn*
Patricia Morris GRSM, *flute*
Terence Nagle ARMCM, *trombone*
Bernard O'Keefe, *oboe*
Thomas Ratter ARCM, *oboe*
Stuart Roebuck, *tuba*
Roger Rostron, *flute*
Anthony Walker ARAM, *flute*
William Waterhouse ARCM, *bassoon*
Dominic Weir, *reed making*
Sonia Wrangham ARMCM, *oboe*
Trevor Wye, *flute*

Harp
Jean Bell

Guitar
John Arran ARMCM
Gordon Crosskey B Sc, ARCM
John Williams

Percussion
Gilbert Webster FGSM, *senior tutor in percussion*

Jack Gledhill
Henry Massey

Theory and Humanities
John Wray MA, D Mus, FRCO, FTCL, Hon RMCM, *head of department*
Percy Welton Mus B, GNSM, LRAM, ARCM, *assistant head of department*

John Bertalot MA, FRCO
Keith Bond MA, Mus B, FRCO, ARMCM
Michel Brandt, Dip Paris Conservatoire
John Brooke MA PhD
Derrick Cantrell MA, B Mus, FRCO
Leslie Clifton FRCO, ARMCM
Paul Crunden-White B Mus
Robert Elliott FRMCM
Enid Ferguson GRSM
Ronald Frost B Mus, FRCO, FRMCM, Hon RSCM
Margaret Gowland GRSM
John Howarth B Mus, FRCO, LTCL
Geoffrey Jackson Mus B, GRSM
Delyth Jones Mus B, GRSM, ARMCM

Martyn Lloyd Mus B, GRSM, ARCO
Donald Mearns FRCO, ARMCM
Michael Mullett BA, M Litt
Stephen Pilkington GRSM
Dorothy Pilling FNSM, LRAM
Marjorie Proudlove FNSM, LRAM
Keith Rhodes B Mus, FRCO, Hon RSCM
Bertram Seton MA, B Mus
Joseph Shennan BA, PhD, FR Hist S
Nicholas Smith GNSM
Julia Wallace GRSM
Thomas Walsh GRSM

ROYAL SCOTTISH ACADEMY OF MUSIC AND DRAMA

Director, School of Music: David E. Stone B Mus, ARAM, LRAM

St George's Place, Glasgow G2 1BS t 041-332 4101.
Courses, facilities, etc.: see p. 249, 251

Conductors
Roderick Brydon
James Durrant
George McPhee
Bryden Thomson

Opera
John Hauxvell
Elizabeth Henderson ARAD
Jack Keaney DRSAM
David Kelly FRAM
Mairi Pirie ARAM

Singing
David Kelly FRAM, *head of department*

Marjorie Blakeston Dip Mus Ed, SNAM, Dip Class
  Singing SNAM
Winifred Busfield FRMCM, LRAM
Margaret Dick
Muriel Dickson
John Hauxvell
Lilian Liddell LRAM
Neilson Taylor BA, LRAM

Keyboard
Wight Henderson FRSAMD, *piano, head of department*

Kathleen Belford MA, *piano*
Miles Coverdale, *piano*
Hester Dickson Mus Bac, LRAM, *piano*
John Dobbie LRAM, ARCM, *piano*
Margaret Evans LRAM, ARCM, FTCL, *piano*
Catherine Fearns Dip Mus Ed, RSAM, LRAM, ARCM, *piano*
Pearl Gelfer LRAM, ARCM, *piano*
Lawrence Glover FRMCM, *piano*
Jack Keaney DRSAM, *piano*
John Langdon BA, Mus B, FRCO, *organ*
George McPhee B Mus, FRCO, Dip Mus Ed (RSAM), *organ*
Raymond O'Connell, *piano*
Michael Redshaw B Mus, ARCM, *piano*
Béla Simandi ARCM, *piano*
Annabell Thomson LRAM, ATCL, *piano*

Stanley Thomson Dip Mus Ed (RSAM), LRAM, LTCL, *piano*
John R. Turner MA, Mus B, FRCO, *organ*
Geoffrey Walker B Mus, *piano*
Phyllis Walker B Mus, LRAM, ARCM, *piano*
Janet B. Wilson Dip Mus Ed, RSAM, ARCM, ALCM, *piano*

Strings
Peter Mountain FRAM, *violin, head of department*

Joan Dickson FRCM, FRSAMD, LRAM, ARCM, *violoncello*
James Durrant, *viola*
John Gwilt, *violoncello*
William Hoare, *double-bass*
Audrey Hughes, *violoncello*
Peter Hunt DRSAM, *violoncello*
Warren Jacobs, *violin*
Peter Moore, *double-bass*
Roger Raphael, *violin*
Stephen Shakeshaft, *viola*
John Tunnell, *violin*
Thirza Whysall, *violin*

Wind
Edgar Williams, *bassoon, head of department*

Marion Ayre, *oboe, cor anglais*
Jennifer Caws, *oboe, cor anglais*
Percy Cook, *trombone*
Shona Gidney DRSAM, *flute, piccolo*
Sheena Gordon DRSAM, *flute, piccolo*
Christopher Griffiths, *horn*
Janet Hilton, *clarinet*
Esther Hollister DRSAM, *oboe, cor anglais*
Enoch Jackson LGSM, ARCM, *trumpet*
David James, *trumpet*
Robert Jenner, *trumpet*
Harry Johnstone DRSAM, *horn*
Harry Macanespie, *trumpet*
Henry Morrison, *clarinet*
David Nicholson LGSM, *flute, piccolo*
Keith Pearson, *clarinet*
Anthony Swainson, *tuba*
Maurice Temple, *horn*
John Wiggins, *flute, piccolo*
Thomas Young, *clarinet*

Harp, Clarsach
Sanchia Pielou ARCM

Percussion
Glyn **Bragg** MA, Dip Ed
Leslie Newland

Academic
Frank Spedding D Mus, ARCM, *head*

Robin Barr MA, B Mus, ATCL
Janet E. Beat MA, B Mus
James Binnie MA, B Mus
Catherine Fearns Dip Mus Ed, RSAM, LRAM, ARCM
Robert D. Inglis B Mus, Dip Mus Ed, RSAM
Jack Keaney DRSAM
John Langdon BA, Mus B, FRCO
George McPhee B Mus, FRCO, Dip Mus Ed (RSAM)
Eric W. Rice B Mus, Dip Mus Ed (RSAM)
Margaret M. Spence LRAM, ARCM
George G. Taylor B Mus, DRSAM, ARCM
Annabell Thomson LRAM, ATCL
Stanley Thomson Dip Mus Ed (RSAM), LRAM, LTCL
Dennis Townhill Mus B, FRCO (CHM), LRAM, ADCM, Hon
RSCM
John R. Turner MA, Mus B, FRCO
John Weeks B Mus, FRCO, LRAM, ARCM

TRINITY COLLEGE OF MUSIC LONDON

Principal: Myers Foggin CBE, Hon FTCL, FRAM, FRCM,
Hon GSM

11 Mandeville Place, London W1M 6AQ t 01-935 5773.
Courses, facilities, etc.: see p. 249, 251

Conductors
James Gaddarn Hon FTCL, GTCL, LRAM, ARCM
Bernard Keeffe BA, Hon FTCL
Charles Proctor Hon FTCL, FRAM, FRCO, ARCM, FRSA
Leonard Smith FTCL

Opera
Myers Foggin CBE, Hon FTCL, FRAM, FRCM, Hon GSM, *head*

Christopher Fry ARCM
Errol Girdlestone BA, ARCO
Pauline Stuart Hon ARAM, LUDDA, CSD

Singing
Frederic Cox OBE, MA, Hon FTCL, Hon RAM, Hon RCM,
head of department

Irene Bell Hon FTCL, ARCM
Iris Bourne
Valerie Cardnell FTCL, LRAM
John Huw Davies GTCL
James Gaddarn Hon FTCL, GTCL, LRAM, ARCM
Gwendoline Hanson FTCL, LRAM, ARCM
Elizabeth Hawes LRAM, Hon FTCL
Adrian de Peyer MA
Robert Stuart Hon FTCL, LTCL
Ilse Wolf Hon FTCL

Coaches
Anna Berenska LRAM
Christina Ward LRAM, ARCM

Languages
Friederike Kautzsch, *German*
Tina Ruta, *Italian*

Speech, Drama, Acting
Doreen Fischer Hon FTCL, LRAM, RAM Dip
Raymond Roberts

Keyboard
Valda Aveling Hon FTCL, *piano, harpsichord*
Audrey Ayliffe FTCL, LRAM, *piano*

Vera Ayton Hon FTCL, LRAM, LGSM, *piano*
Joan Barker FTCL, *piano, harpsichord*
Eva Bernathova Hon FTCL, *piano*
John Bingham Hon FTCL, *piano*
Maria Boxall FTCL, *harpsichord*
Peggi Brock FTCL, *piano*
Hannah Brooke FTCL, LRAM, ARCM, *piano*
Harry Gabb CVO, Mus D, Hon FTCL, FRCO, ARCM, *organ*
John Evison Hon FTCL, LTCL, LRAM, ARCM, *piano*
Geoffrey Hanson Hon FTCL, GTCL, *organ*
Gwendoline Hanson FTCL, LRAM, ARCM, *piano*
Walter Hillsman MA, FRCO, *organ*
Wanda Jeziorska Hon FTCL, LTCL, *piano*
Jacob Kaletsky BL, MA, Hon FTCL, *piano*
George Kinnear Hon FTCL, LRAM, AGSM, *piano*
Alfred Kitchin Hon FTCL, *piano*
Irene Kohler Mus B, Hon FTCL, *piano*
John Lill Hon FTCL, *piano master classes*
Antony Lindsay Hon FTCL, *piano*
Alan MacKenzie Mus B, Hon FTCL, ARCO, *piano*
Jean Merlow FTCL, LRAM, *piano*
Frank Merrick M Mus, Hon FTCL, FRCM, *piano*
Rucky van Mill Hon FTCL, *piano*
Charles Proctor Hon FTCL, FRAM, FRCO, ARCM, FRSA, *piano*
Gladys Puttick Hon FTCL, *piano*
Charles Sealey FTCL, FRCO, LRAM, *piano, organ*
Herbert A. Shead LRAM, *piano*
John Simons Mus B, Hon FTCL, *piano*
Richard Stangroom B Mus, FTCL, FRCO, *organ*
Lettice Stuart Hon FTCL, *piano*
Cecil Turner Hon FTCL, LRAM, *piano*
Joseph Weingarten Hon FTCL, *piano*
Jacqueline Williams FTCL, LRAM, A Mus TCL, *piano*
Janet Wyatt GTCL, *piano*
Felicity Young Mus B, Hon FTCL, GTCL, LRAM, *piano*

Strings
Henriette Canter Hon FTCL, *violin*
Maryse Chomé Hon FTCL, LRAM, ARCM, *violoncello*
Montagu Cleeve Hon FTCL, LRAM, LGSM, *viola, viola d'amore*
Keith Cummings Hon FTCL, *viola*
Denis East Hon FTCL, ARCM, *violin*
Gwyneth George Hon FTCL, ARCM, *violoncello*
Thomas Geradine FTCL, *violin*
Vivian Joseph Hon FTCL, FRAM, *violoncello*
Vera Kantrovitch Hon FTCL, *violin*
Béla Katona Hon FTCL, *violin, violin master classes*
Samuel Kutcher Hon FTCL, *violin*
Alison Milne Hon FTCL, ARCM, *viola*
Yvonne Morris Hon FTCL, ARAM, *violoncello*

Nicholas Roth Hon FTCL, *violin*
Rohan de Saram, *violoncello*
Jack Silvester Hon FTCL, *double-bass*
Leonard Smith FTCL, *violin*
Bernard Vocadlo ARAM, *violoncello*
Frederic Wigston, *double-bass*
Dora Zafransky FTCL, LRAM, *violin*

Wind
William Barlett ARCM, LRAM, *flute, piccolo*
Maria Boxall FTCL, *recorder*
John Burden Hon FTCL, *horn*
Norman Burgess Hon FTCL, LTCL, *trumpet, cornet*
John Candor FTCL, *clarinet*
Harold Clarke Hon FTCL, LRAM, *flute, piccolo*
Tamara Coates LRAM, *oboe, cor anglais*
John Denman, *clarinet*
Vernon Elliott Hon FTCL, *bassoon, double bassoon*
Paul Harvey LRAM, ARCM, *clarinet*
Roger Hellyer PhD, MA, GRSM, FRCO, *bassoon, double
bassoon*
Edgar Hunt FTCL, LRAM, *flute, piccolo, recorder*
Walter Lear Hon FTCL, *saxophone*
Geoffrey Lindon Hon FTCL, *trombone*
C. F. Luxon, *tuba*
George Maxted FTCL, *trombone*
Stephen Nagy Hon FTCL, LTCL, ARCM, *oboe, cor anglais*
Keith Puddy ARAM, *clarinet*
Lowry Sanders ARCM, *flute, piccolo*
Clare Shanks MA, ARCM, *baroque oboe*

Guitar
William Grandison AGSM
Hector Quine Hon FTCL

Academic Work, Composition, General Musicianship
Richard Arnell Hon FTCL
Vera Ayton Hon FTCL, LRAM, LGSM
Mary Baddeley FTCL, LRAM, ARCM
John Bate MA, B Mus, GTCL, FRCO
Brian Blackwood PhD, MA, B Mus, ARCO
Hannah Brooke FTCL, LRAM, ARCM
Jane Scott Butler FTCL, ARCO
Peter Chase GTCL, ARCO, ARCM
Arnold Cooke BA, Mus D, Hon FTCL
Derek Fraser B Mus, LTCL, LRSM
Errol Girdlestone BA, ARCO
Peter Groome ARCM
Antony Haynes MA
Roger Hellyer PhD, MA, GRSM, FRCO
Jack Hindmarsh FRCO

Brian Hughes MA, Mus B, LRAM, ARCM, ARCO
Harold Jones MA, FTCL
George Kinnear Hon FTCL, LRAM, AGSM
Enid Langley Hon FTCL, LRAM, ARCM
Davitt Moroney M Mus
Peter Murray MA, FTCL
Madge Musgrave B Mus, ARCM
David Newbold MA, Hon FTCL
David Palmer GRSM, ARCM
Charles Proctor Hon FTCL, FRAM, FRCO, ARCM, FRSA
Charles Sealey FTCL, FRCO, LRAM
Lettice Stuart Hon FTCL
John Tavener Hon FTCL
Christopher Toon B Mus, Hon FTCL, GTCL
Cecil Turner Hon FTCL, LRAM
Jacqueline Williams FTCL, LRAM, A Mus TCL
Felicity Young Mus B, Hon FTCL, GTCL, LRAM

*WELSH COLLEGE OF MUSIC AND DRAMA/COLEG CERDD A DRAMA
CYMRU*

Principal: Raymond Edwards FTCL, FLCM, Hon GSM
Head of Music: Gerallt Evans BA, Dip Ed

Castle Grounds, Cathays Pk, Cardiff CF1 3ER t Cardiff
42854. Courses, facilities, etc.: see p. 249, 251

Singing
Leslie Jones ARAM, Gold Medal RAM, *lecturer in charge
of vocal studies*

Zoe Cresswell ALCM
Gerald Davies
Avril M. Harding B Mus, GTCL, LRAM, LTCL, A Mus TCL
Julia Hilger, Master Dip Vienna State Academy of Music
John Samuel
Margaret Tann Williams, Gold Medal GSM
Della Windsor

Languages
Jeanette Massocchi LRAM, ARCM, LTCL

Keyboard
Zbigniew Grzybowski, Gold Medal Warsaw Chopin Academy,
senior lecturer in charge of piano studies

Donald W. Bate FRCO, LRAM, LTCL, *organ*
Jennie C. Cuthbert BA, Dip Ed, LRAM, *piano*
Horace Field FTCL, LRAM, ARCM, ARCO, *piano*
Beate Popperwell MA, *piano*
Mary Rees LRAM, *piano*
John Samuel, *piano*
John Tilbury ARCM, *piano*
Emlyn Williams LRAM, *piano*

Strings
Walter Gerhardt, *lecturer in charge of string studies*

John Cullis, *violoncello*
Ernest C. Haigh, *double-bass*
Francis Howard ARCM, *violin, viola*
Philip Kent, *violoncello*
David Llewellyn ARAM, *violin, viola*
Gordon N. Mutter ARAM, LRAM, *violin, viola*
Glanmor Spiller, *violin, viola*

Wind
Frank Kelleher B Mus, FTCL, LTCL, LRAM, A Mus TCL,
lecturer in charge of wind studies

Colin Casson, *trumpet*
Robert Codd B Mus, LRAM, *bassoon*
D. W. Cronin, *bassoon*
John Crouch ARCM, *oboe, recorder*
William E. Davis, *horn*
Lesley Dunstan B Mus, LRAM, ARCM, *clarinet*
Stanley Gleave, *flute*
Daniel Hannaby, *trombone*
Gordon Hunt, *oboe*
T. Procter ARCM, *trumpet*
Michael Saxton, *clarinet*
Douglas Townshend, *flute*

Harp
Ann Griffiths BA, Premier Prix (Paris Conservatoire)
Meinir Heulyn

Guitar
Rhisiart Arwel ARMCM, Dip Ed
Ernest C. Haigh
Brian Noyes L Mus TCL, LTCL, LWCMD
John Vousden BA, LTCL

Percussion
David Bibby ARMCM
Clifton Prior

Lecturers
V. Anthony Lewis B Mus, *principal lecturer*

Roger A. Butler M Mus
Anthony R. Carter LRAM, ARCM
Jennie C. Cuthbert BA, Dip Ed, LRAM
Avril M. Harding B Mus, GTCL, LRAM, LTCL, A Mus TCL
Robert Joyce MA, Mus B, FRCO (CHM), ARCM, ADCM
Frank Kelleher B Mus, FTCL, LTCL, LRAM, A Mus TCL
Jeanette Massocchi LRAM, ARCM, LTCL
David H. Nevens M Mus
Christopher Powell BA, LRAM, FRCO
Cecilia Vajda, Dip Budapest Liszt Academy
Thomas Walsh LRAM, GRSM

7   Other Colleges of Music

Most of the following are independent institutions.
For music instruction in Colleges of Further and
Higher Education, under the control of local
authorities, see p.158. Institutions in London are
listed first, then others in alphabetical order by
towns.

LONDON
Actors Studio for Opera Singers, 87 Bensham Manor
   Rd, Thornton Heath, Surrey CR4 7AF t 01-684 8835
   mus dir Sandra Gelson LRAM, ARCM
Bharatiya Vidhya Bhavan School of Indian Music, 37
   New Oxford St, London WC1A 1BH t 01-836 0808;
   01-240 0815 *dir* Clem Alford
Blackheath Conservatoire of Music, 19 Lee Rd, London
   SE3 9RQ t 01-852 0234 *prin* Robert Munns LRAM, ARCM,
   ARCO (CHM), L Mus TCL
Cantica Voice Studio, 55 Hayes Rd, Bromley, Kent BR2
   9AE t 01-460 6239 *dir* Audrey Langford ARCM
Centre for Musical Interpretation, 30 Arkwright Rd,
   London NW3 6BH t 01-435 1610 *prin* Gerald Gover
Croydon and Purley Academy of Music, 4 Kendall Av,
   South Croydon, Surrey CR2 ONH t 01-660 4940 *prin*
   Howard Fletcher MA, Mus B (Cantab), FRCO
Dalcroze Society Inc, 16 Heathcroft, Hampstead Way,
   London NW11 7HH t 01-455 1268 *prin* Mrs A. Heron
Harrow School of Music, 54 Sheepcote Rd, Harrow,
   Middx HA1 2JF t 01-427 2760 *prin* Bloye Gilbert LRAM
Leschetizky School of Pianoforte Playing, 66 Parkhill
   Rd, London NW3 2YT t 01-485 3379 *dir* Sylvia Leeson
   ARCM, LRAM, ATCM (Toronto)
London Opera Centre for Advanced Training and
   Development Ltd, 490 Commercial Rd, London E1 OHX
   t 01-790 4468 *dir* James Robertson CBE, Hon RAM,
   Hon FTCL, Hon GSM, MA, FRCM
London School of Singing, 12 Earls Court Sq, London
   SW5 9BY t 01-373 5706 *prin* Arnold Rose
Marchesi Singing Academy, 15 Farmer St, London W8 7SN
   t 01-727 8804 *dir* Frances Gorick
Matthers' College of Music, 136 Brigstock Rd, Thornton
   Heath, Surrey CR4 7JB t 01-684 2586 *prin* Bernard
   Matthers LRAM, ARCM

Mayer-Lismann Opera Workshop, 61 Kings Rd, London
    SW3 5EQ t 01-352 1732 *dir* Else Mayer-Lismann Hon
    RCM
National College of Music, 20c Westbourne Terr,
    London W2 3UP t 01-289 1889 *prin* V. I. Moss FNCM,
    LRAM
Polunin (Tanya) School of Pianoforte Playing, 46
    Clarendon Rd, London W11 2HH t 01-229 2816 *prin*
    Tanya Polunin
Royal School of Church Music, Addington Palace,
    Croydon CR9 5AD t 01-654 7676 *tg* cantoris *dir*
    Lionel Dakers Mus B, FRAM, FRCO (CHM), ADCM,
    FRSCM, FWCC
Schwiller (Elisabeth) School of Singing and Opera,
    19 Canfield Gdns, London NW6 3JP t 01-624 6735 *dir*
    Elisabeth Schwiller
Southern Music Training Centre, Thanet Lodge, 16
    Holwood Rd, Bromley, Kent BR1 3EB t 01-460 8600
    prin Reginald Jevons ARCM
Spanish Guitar Centre (London), 36 Cranbourn St,
    London WC2H 7AD t 01-240 0754 *prin* Alan Gubbay MA
Spanish Guitar Studio, 72 Newman St, London W1P 3LA
    t 01-580 8094 *prin* Lock Aitken
Sufi Cultural Centre, 53 West Ham La, London E15 4PH
    t 01-534 6539 *dir* F. Inayat-Khan
Victoria College of Music, 8 Staple Inn, London WC1V
    7QH t 01-405 6483 *prin* Sam B. Wood Mus Bac, FTSC,
    FRSA

BELFAST
Belfast Academy of Music and Dramatic Art, 36
    Cromwell Rd, Belfast BT7 1JW t Belfast 29327 *prin*
    Mary O'Malley
Belfast (City of) School of Music, 99 Donegall Pass,
    Belfast BT7 1DR t Belfast 22435 *prin* Leonard Pugh
    B Mus, FRCO (CHM), LRAM
Ulster College of Music, 45 Windsor Av, Belfast BT9
    6EJ t Belfast 668141 *hon dir* Daphne M. Bell LRAM,
    LTCL
BOURNEMOUTH. Bournemouth Guitar Studio, 73 Alma Rd,
    Bournemouth BH9 1AD t Bournemouth 56453 *dir* Tony
    Alton
BRIGHTON. Brighton Guitar Studios, 34a Waterloo St,
    Hove, Sussex BN1 1AN t Brighton 70197 *dir* John
    Thackeray LGSM, LTCL
BRISTOL. Spanish Guitar Centre (Bristol), 2 Elton
    Rd, Bishopston, Bristol BS7 8DA t Bristol 47256
    prin Michael Watson
CHELTENHAM. Cheltenham Music Centre, Regent Ho, 3
    Queens Rd, Cheltenham, Glos GL50 2LR t Cheltenham
    35405 *prin* Alexander Kok ARAM, ARCM

CHESTER. Spanish Guitar Studio, 4 Upper Northgate
St, Chester CH1 4EE t 051-334 4379 *dirs* John Arran
ARMCM, John Harper
COVENTRY. Coventry School of Music, Percy St,
Coventry CV1 3BY t Coventry 23803 *dir of mus* Peter
Isherwood MA
DARLINGTON. Darlington Spanish Guitar School, 2 The
Mead, Darlington DL1 1EX t Darlington 2170 *prin*
John W. Reay LTCL
DUNFERMLINE. Carnegie Music Institute, Benachie,
Dunfermline, Fife KY12 7QQ t Dunfermline 23796 *sec*
Fred Mann
DUNS. International Cello Centre, Edrom Ho, Duns,
Berwickshire TD11 3PX t Chirnside 471 *dirs* Jane
Cowan and John Gwilt
EPSOM. Fitznells School of Music, Chessington Rd,
Epsom, Surrey KT17 1TF t 01-393 1577 *prin* Anthony
Carter B Mus, FLCM, LGSM, L Mus TCL, ARCM
GUILDFORD. County School of Music, St Nicholas Hall,
Millmead Terr, Guildford, Surrey GU2 5AT t Guildford
4335 *dir* Dorothy Owen MBE, LRAM
HARPENDEN. Williams School of Church Music, 20
Salisbury Av, Harpenden, Herts AL5 2QG t Harpenden
3048 *prin* Francis B. Westbrook BA, Mus D, Hon FRSCM
HARTLEPOOL. North-Eastern School of Music, 130
Grange Rd, Hartlepool, Cleveland TS26 8JJ t
Hartlepool 3850 *dir* T. I. Phizacklea LRAM, ARCM,
LTCL
HIGH WYCOMBE. Bucks School of Music, 14-15 High St,
High Wycombe, Bucks HP11 2BE t High Wycombe 26535
prin G. Frederick Bailey LRAM, MRST
LEEDS
City of Leeds College of Music, Cookridge St, Leeds
LS2 8BH t Leeds 452069 *dir* Joseph Stones ARMCM
Yorkshire College of Music and Drama, 19 Shire Oak
Rd, Leeds LS6 2DD t Leeds 51232 *prin* Audrey Cooke
LRAM
LEICESTER. British College of Accordionists, 5
University Rd, Leicester LE1 7RA t Leicester 23345
prin Leslie G. Law ARCM, ABCA (TD), LBCA
MANCHESTER. Manchester School of Music, 16 Albert Sq,
Manchester M2 5PF t 061-834 4654 *dir* John Grierson
LGSM
NEWCASTLE UPON TYNE. Spanish Guitar Centre, 10 North
Av, Newcastle upon Tyne NE3 4DT t Newcastle upon
Tyne 855046 *hon consultant* Malcolm Weller MA
NOTTINGHAM.
Nottingham College of Music, 67 Clifford Av, Beeston,
Nottingham NG9 2PX t Nottingham 254148 *prin*
M. S. Sholl ARCM
Spanish Guitar Centre (Midlands Area), 64 Clarendon

St, Nottingham NG1 5JD t Nottingham 48325 *prin*
Robin J. Pearson
PETERSFIELD. Petersfield School of Music and Drama,
72 Station Rd, Petersfield, Hants GU32 4AH t
Petersfield 3040 *prin* Kathleen Chappelle LRAM
SHREWSBURY. Royal Normal College & Academy of Music
for the Blind, Albrighton Hall, Broad Oak, Shrews-
bury SY4 3AQ t Bowmere Heath 279; Rowton Castle,
nr Shrewsbury SY5 9EP t Halfway House 427 *mus dir*
J. D. James FRCO, ARCM, LRAM
SOUTHEND. Essex Accordion and Guitar Centre, 19
Colchester Rd, Southend-on-Sea, Essex SS2 6HW t
Southend-on-Sea 40909 *prin* Jerry Mayes ABCA (TD),
LBCA
STEVENAGE. Hertfordshire County Music School,
Stevenage Music Centre, Six Hills Way, Stevenage
SG2 0QA t Stevenage 51138 *dir* David J. Wells MA,
ARCO
WATFORD
Hertfordshire Guitar Academy, 15 St John's Rd, Watford
WD1 1PU t Watford 34616 *prin* Ronald Taylor
Watford School of Music, Nascot Wood Rd, Watford WD1
3RS t Watford 25531 *prin* Kenneth Leaper BA

8   Teacher Training Institutions

Training in music teaching is offered by Colleges of
Education and university Departments of Education
(all of which admit both men and women, unless otherwise stated). The basic course, leading to a Certificate or Diploma of Education, normally takes
three years, but this may be shortened at some
Colleges for older students with above-average music
and academic qualifications. Students may remain at
certain Colleges for an extra year to take a B Ed
(or, exceptionally, a BA) degree. Some Colleges
also operate special training for peripatetic teachers,
and other specialized courses.
   For general entry to all courses in England and
Wales, apply to the Central Register and Clearing
House Ltd, 3 Crawford Pl, London W1H 2BN (no telephone
inquiries). Inquiries for prospectuses should be
made to individual Colleges. Each prospectus will
include an inquiry card; one card should be completed
and returned by the applicant to the Central Register
and Clearing House after mid-September in the year
before proposed entry.
   Colleges admitting GRSM and B Mus holders to one-

year Certificate of Education or Music Teacher's
Certificate courses are indicated by an asterisk; a
dagger indicates Colleges admitting LRAM and ARCM
holders to these courses. GRSM and B Mus holders
should write for a prospectus to the College of their
choice *as well as* requesting an application form from
the Graduate Teacher Training Registry, 3 Crawford
Pl, London WlH 2BN. LRAM and ARCM holders should
write for a prospectus and application forms to the
College of their choice, then apply through the
Central Register and Clearing House (see above).
     For entry to courses in Scotland, write to the
Admissions Secretary of the individual institution.
For entry to courses in Northern Ireland, write to
the Academic Registrar of the individual institution.
     For details of courses, see the *Handbook of Colleges
and Departments of Education* (Lund Humphries/Associa-
tion of Teachers in Colleges and Departments of
Education). Subject charts from this Handbook are
reproduced in the *Summary of Teacher Training Courses
at Colleges and Departments of Education*, available
at 45p post-free from the Central Register and Clearing House.

                            *

After the address and telephone number, the head of
music is named. Institutions in London are listed
first, then others in alphabetical order by towns.

LONDON
All Saints (College of), White Hart La, London N17
     8HR t 01-808 2842. Miss D. C. Holliday ARCM,
     Mrs M. Walker LRAM, ARCM
†*Avery Hill College of Education, Bexley Rd, London
     SE9 2PQ t 01-850 0081/6. Also at Mile End Annexe,
     English St, London E3 4TA t 01-980 2206.
     J. A. Fidler D Mus
Battersea College of Education, Manresa Ho, Holy-
     bourne Av, London SW15 4JF t 01-788 7771. Keith
     Stent B Mus, ARCM, GTCL
Borough Road College, Borough Rd, Isleworth, Middx
     TW7 5DU t 01-560 5991
Coloma College of Education, Wickham Ct, West Wickham,
     Kent BR4 9HH t 01-777 8321/4. Miss A. M. Cirket
     LRAM. Annexe at Tavistock Rd, Croydon, Surrey t
     01-688 8758
Furzedown College of Education, Welham Rd, London SW17
     9BU t 01-672 0131. Gordon F. Hughes B Mus, ARCO
†*Gipsy Hill College, Kingston Hill, Kingston-upon-
     Thames, Surrey KT2 7NB t 01-549 1141. Outpost at

34-8 Portsmouth Rd, Guildford GU2 5DJ t 0483 65006.
Bernarr Rainbow M Ed, FTCL, ARCM, LRAM, LGSM
*Goldsmiths' College, New Cross, London SE14 6NW t
01-692 0211. Stanley Glasser MA, B Comm
Maria Assumpta College, 23 Kensington Sq, London W8
5HN t 01-937 6434. Wilfred E. Smith MA, FRCO (CHM),
ARAM
*Maria Grey College, 300 St Margaret's Rd, Twickenham,
Middx TW1 1PT t 01-892 0121. G. R. Richardson GRSM,
LRAM, ARCM, ATCL
† Middlesex Polytechnic at Trent Park, Cockfosters, nr
Barnet, Herts EN4 0PS t 01-449 9691. Philip Pfaff
MA, Mus B
† Philippa Fawcett College, Leigham Court Rd, London
SW16 2QD t 01-677 9641. Mrs P. Turner LRAM
Rachel McMillan College of Education, Creek Rd,
London SE8 3BU t 01-692 7454/6. Annexe at 83 New
Kent Rd, London SE1 6RA
Roehampton Institute of Higher Education
Digby Stuart College, Roehampton La, London SW15 5PH
t 01-876 8273. C. G. Chapman MA, Mus B, Cert Ed
Froebel Institute, College of Education, Grove Ho,
Roehampton La, London SW15 5PJ t 01-876 2242
Southlands College of Education, Wimbledon Parkside,
London SW19 5NN t 01-946 2234. M. Burnett MA, FRCO
Whitelands College, West Hill, London SW15 3SN t
01-788 8268
Outpost at Teachers' Centre, Westcroft Rd, Carshal-
ton, Surrey t 01-669 2624
St Gabriel's College, Cormont Rd, London SE5 9RG t
01-735 3721
St Mary's College, Strawberry Hill, Twickenham, Middx
TW1 4SX t 01-892 0051. Donald Ray BA, FRCO, LRAM,
ARCM. Org schol £80 p.a.
Sidney Webb College, 9-12 Barrett St, London W1M 6DE
t 01-486 4771
*Stockwell College of Education, Old Palace, Rochester
Av, Bromley, Kent BR1 3DH t 01-460 9944
*University of London Institute of Education, Malet
St, London WC1E 7HS t 01-636 1500

ABERDEEN. Aberdeen College of Education, Hilton Pl,
Aberdeen AB9 1FA t Aberdeen 42341. Tom Johnston
BA, B Mus, LRAM
*ABERYSTWYTH. University College of Wales, Department
of Education, Cambrian Chambers, Cambrian Pl,
Aberystwyth, Dyfed ST23 1NU t Aberystwyth 2711
ABINGDON. Culham College of Education, Abingdon,
Oxon OX14 3BP t Abingdon 458. Ronald Burrow BA,
LRAM. Org/chor £50 schol comp
ALNWICK. Alnwick College of Education, The Castle,

Alnwick, Northumb NE66 1NH t Alnwick 2761/2
AYR.   Craigie College of Education, Ayr KA8 OSR t
   Ayr 60321/4
BANGOR
Normal College, Bangor, Gwynedd LL58 2DE t Bangor
   2122/2779
St Mary's College, Bangor, Gwynedd LL57 1DZ t Bangor
   2533 (women only)
University College of North Wales Department of
   Education, Bangor, Gwynedd LL57 2DG t Bangor 51151
BARNSLEY.   Wentworth Castle College of Education,
   Stainborough, Barnsley, Yorks S75 3ET t Barnsley
   5161 (women only)
BARRY.   Glamorgan College of Education, Buttrills Rd,
   Barry, Glam CF6 6SE t Barry 3101/3. R. G. Reynolds
   BA
†*BATH.   Bath College of Higher Education, Newton Park,
   Newton St Loe, Bath BA2 9BN t Saltford 2681
BEDFORD.   Bedford College of Education, Polhill Av,
   Bedford MK41 9EA t Bedford 51671. H. P. Kneale
   B Mus, LRAM, ATCL
BELFAST
St Joseph's College of Education, Trench Ho, Belfast
   BT19 9GA t Belfast 612144 (men only)
St Mary's College of Education, 191 Falls Rd, Belfast
   BT12 6FE t Belfast 27678 (women only)
Stranmillis College, Stranmillis Rd, Belfast BT9 5DY
   t Belfast 665271
BINGLEY.   Bingley College of Education, Bingley,
   Yorks BD16 4AR t Bingley 2375. Lyndon H. Jones
   BA, M Ed
BIRMINGHAM
 *Birmingham University School of Education, PO Box 363,
   Birmingham B15 2TT t 021-472 1301. J. B. Brockle-
   hurst MA, D Mus
†*City of Birmingham College of Education, Westbourne
   Rd, Birmingham B15 3TN t 021-454 5106. V. W. Payne
   LTCL, ARCM, FTCL
 Newman College, Genners La, Bartley Grn, Birmingham
   B32 3NT t 021-476 1181
 Westhill College of Education, Selly Oak, Birmingham
   B29 6LL t 021-472 1563/4
BISHOPS STORTFORD.   Hockerill College, Bishops
   Stortford, Herts CM23 5HG t Bishops Stortford 53475.
   R. E. Slee MA, ARCM, ARCO
*BLACKPOOL.   Preston Polytechnic School of Education,
   Poulton-le-Fylde Campus, 75 Breck Rd, Poulton-le-
   Fylde, nr Blackpool, Lancs FY6 7AW t Poulton-le-
   Fylde 884651. Denis T. Brooks BA, LRAM, ARCM, LTCL,
   Cert Ed
BOGNOR REGIS.   Bognor Regis College of Education,

Upper Bognor Rd, Bognor Regis, Sussex PO21 1HR t
Bognor Regis 5581.   Outpost at Gales Pl, Three
Bridges, Crawley, Sussex RH10 1QG t Crawley 28284.
C. Humphreys M Mus, FRCO, GRSM, LRAM, ARCM
BRADFORD.   Margaret McMillan College of Education,
Trinity Rd, Bradford BD5 OJE t Bradford 33291.
Miss M. Atkin ARCM, GRSM, B Mus
BRENTWOOD.   Brentwood College of Education, Sawyers
Hall La, Brentwood, Essex CM15 9BT t Brentwood
216971.   Outpost at Colman Ho, Victoria Av, South-
end-on-Sea SS2 6DT t Southend-on-Sea 41621.   Neville
Osborne FRCO, GRSM, ARCM, LRAM
BRIGHTON.   Brighton College of Education, Falmer,
Brighton, Sussex BN1 9PH t Brighton 66622.
I. A. Copley B Mus, PhD, GRSM, ARCM
BRISTOL
Redland College, Redland Hill, Bristol BS6 6UZ t
Bristol 311251.   A. L. Smith B Mus, ARCM
St Matthias (College of) Fishponds, Bristol BS16 2JJ
t Bristol 655384/5.   Kenneth D. Smith MA, LRAM
BROMSGROVE.   Shenstone New College, Burcot La, Broms-
grove, Worcs B60 1PQ t Bromsgrove 74151.   John C.
Phillips B Mus, LRAM, ARCM
CAMBRIDGE
Cambridge University Department of Education, 17
Brookside, Cambridge CB2 1JG t Cambridge 55271
*Homerton College, Cambridge CB2 2PH t Cambridge
45931 (normally women only)
* CANTERBURY.   Christ Church College, North Holmes Rd,
Canterbury, Kent CT1 1QU t Canterbury 65548
CARDIFF
†City of Cardiff College of Education, Cyncoed, Cardiff
CF2 6XD t Cardiff 751345.   D. W. Elias MA, LRAM
University College of Wales Department of Education,
Senghennydd Rd, Cardiff CF2 4AG t Cardiff 44211
CARMARTHEN.   Trinity College, College Rd, Carmarthen
SA31 3EP t Carmarthen 7971/3.   John F. Williams
B Mus, ARCO
CHELTENHAM
*St Mary's College, The Park, Cheltenham, Glos GL50
2RH t Cheltenham 53836 (women only)
St Paul's College, Cheltenham, Glos GL50 4AZ t
Cheltenham 28111 (men only)
CHESTER.   Chester College, Cheyney Rd, Chester CH1
4BJ t Chester 28401.   Colin Jones MA, Mus B, FRCO,
GTCL, FTCL.   Chor schol £100 p.a.
CHICHESTER.   Bishop Otter College of Education,
College La, Chichester, Sussex PO19 4PE t
Chichester 87911
CHORLEY.   Chorley College of Education, Union St,
Chorley, Lancs PR7 1ED t Chorley 5811

CLACTON. St Osyth's College, Marine Parade East,
    Clacton-on-Sea, Essex CO15 6JQ t Clacton-on-Sea
    22324/7.   D. C. Glass B Mus, GTCL, LTCL
COVENTRY.   Coventry College of Education, Canley,
    Coventry CV4 8EE t Coventry 462531. V. S. Garrison
    B Mus, Dip Ed
CREWE
Crewe and Alsager College of Higher Education, Crewe
    Rd, Crewe, Ches CW1 1DU t Crewe 583661.   Mrs Greta
    M. Fleetwood Mus B, LRAM
Madeley College of Education, Madeley, Crewe CW3 9HY
    t Stoke on Trent 750356.   Annexe at Nelson Hall,
    Standon Rock, nr Stafford t Standon Rock 270283.
    J. G. Pattinson Mus B, ARCO, GRSM, ARMCM
DARLINGTON
Darlington College of Education, Vane Ter, Darlington,
    Co Durham DL3 7AX t Darlington 3553
Middleton St George College of Education, Middleton
    St George, nr Darlington, Co Durham DL2 1RQ t
    Darlington 732661.   Alan Oyston TD, MA, LTCL
DARTFORD.   Dartford College of Education, Oakfield
    La, Dartford, Kent DA1 2SZ t Dartford 21328.
    Miss J. F. E. Lang GRSM, ARCM
DERBY.   Bishop Lonsdale College of Education, Western
    Rd, Mickleover, Derby DE3 5GX t Derby 54911
DONCASTER
Doncaster College of Education, High Melton Hall,
    Doncaster DN5 7SZ t Mexborough 2427.   Alan Cowell
    GRSM, LRAM
Scawsby College of Education, Barnsley Rd, Scawsby,
    Doncaster DN5 7UD t Doncaster 67421
DUDLEY.   Dudley College of Education, Castle View,
    Dudley, Worcs DY1 3HR t Dudley 59741
DUNDEE.   Dundee College of Education, Park Pl, Dundee
    DD1 4HP t Dundee 2584/6
DURHAM
*Durham University Department of Education, 48 Old
    Elvet, Durham DH1 3JH t Durham 64466.   Ernest
    Bowcott MA, M Ed
 Neville's Cross College, Durham DH1 4SY t Durham
    2325/7
 St Hild and St Bede (College of), Durham DH1 1SZ t
    Durham 63741
EASTBOURNE.   Eastbourne College of Education, Darley
    Rd, Eastbourne, Sussex BN20 7UN t Eastbourne 27633.
    Robert E. Jones B Mus, LRAM
EDINBURGH
Craiglockhart College of Education, 219 Colinton Rd,
    Edinburgh EH14 1DJ t 031-443 9961.   Miss Margaret
    McDonald LRAM
Moray House College of Education, 37-9 Holyrood Rd,

Edinburgh EH8 8AQ t 031-556 4415/8.   Alexander R.
C. Scott B Mus
EGHAM.   Shoreditch College, Cooper's Hill, Englefield
Grn, Egham, Surrey TW20 OJZ t 01-389 3981
EXETER.   St Luke's College, Exeter EX1 2LU t Exeter
52221.   Victor D. Whitburn LLCM.   Day outpost at
Redruth Technical College, Redruth, Cornwall t
Camborne 2076
†*EXMOUTH.   Rolle College, Exmouth, Devon EX8 2AT t
Exmouth 5344.   Reginald Pocock B Mus
GLASGOW
Jordanhill College of Education, Southbrae Dr, Glasgow
G13 1PP t 041-959 1232
Notre Dame College of Education, Bearsden, Glasgow
G61 4QA t 041-942 2363.   Also at 74 Victoria Cres
Rd, Glasgow G12 9JH t 041-334 9651
GLOUCESTER.   Gloucestershire College of Education,
Oxstalls La, Gloucester GL2 9HW t Gloucester 26321.
D. Hutchin Mus B, LRAM, ARCM, LTCL
GRANTHAM.   Kesteven College of Education, Stoke Roch-
ford, Grantham, Lincs NG33 5EJ t Grantham 83337/8.
Annexe at Cottesmore Clo, Peterborough PE3 6PT t
Peterborough 264330.   Eric S. Bennett, LRAM, LTCL
HEREFORD.   Hereford College of Education, College Rd,
Hereford HR1 1EB t Hereford 65725/7
HERTFORD.   Balls Park College of Education, Hertford,
Herts SG13 8QF t Hertford 57474.   H. C. Kelynack
MA, Mus B, FRCO, Hon FTCL
†HUDDERSFIELD.   Department of Education, The Polytech-
nic, Queensgate, Huddersfield HD1 3DH t Huddersfield
30501 (peripatetic training at School of Music,
see p. 112).   Derek Ramsbottom ARCO, LTCL, Cert Ed
HULL
Endsleigh College of Education, Inglemire Av, Hull
HU6 7LJ t Hull 42157.   A. R. A. Walker B Mus, FLCM,
ARCO, ARCM
Hull University Department of Educational Studies,
173 Cottingham Rd, Hull HU5 2EH t Hull 46311
Kingston-upon-Hull College of Education, Cottingham
Rd, Hull HU6 7RT t Hull 41451
ILKLEY.   Ilkley College of Education, Wells Rd, Ilkley,
Yorks LS29 9RD t Ilkley 2892
*LANCASTER.   S Martin's College of Education, Bower-
ham, Lancaster LA1 3JD t Lancaster 63446.   Peter
J. Moore MA, B Phil, FRCO, LRAM
LEEDS
City of Leeds and Carnegie College, Beckett Pk,
Leeds LS6 3QS t Leeds 759061.   John C. Pitts M Mus,
B Mus, LTCL, ARCM, Cert Ed
James Graham College, Lawns Ho, Chapel La, Farnley,
Leeds LS12 5ET t Leeds 630505/7;   Leeds 636691/2

Leeds Polytechnic Department of Educational Studies,
    Calverley St, Leeds LS1 3HE t Leeds 41101
*Leeds University Department of Education, Leeds LS2
    9JT t Leeds 31751. Jack Pilgrim BA, B Mus
 Trinity and All Saints' Colleges, Brownberrie La,
    Horsforth, Leeds LS18 5HD t Horsforth 4341/4
 LEICESTER. City of Leicester College of Education,
    Scraptoft, Leicester LE7 9SU t Thurnby 4101.
    B. B. Daubney BA, ARCM, LRAM
 LINCOLN. Bishop Grosseteste College, Lincoln LN1
    3DY t Lincoln 27347. Day outpost at Armstrong
    St, Grimsby, Lincs t Grimsby 57966
 LIVERPOOL
*C. F. Mott College of Education, The Hazels, Prescot,
    Merseyside L34 1NP t 051-489 6201. C. H. Willis
    BA, ARCO, LRAM
*Christ's College, Woolton Rd, Liverpool L16 8ND t
    051-772 7331
 Ethel Wormald College, Mount Pleasant, Liverpool
    L3 5SN t 051-709 6342/4
 Notre Dame College of Education, Mount Pleasant,
    Liverpool L3 5SP t 051-709 7454/8. P. E. Clark
    M Mus, Cert Ed
*St Katharine's College, Stand Pk Rd, Liverpool L16
    9JD t 051-722 2361/3
 LOUGHBOROUGH. Loughborough College of Education,
    Ashby Rd, Loughborough, Leics LE11 3TN t Lough-
    borough 5751. J. V. Crowther MA
 LUTON. Putteridge Bury College of Education,
    Putteridge Bury, Luton, Beds LU2 8LE t Luton
    20457. Miss G. F. A. Lewis GRSM, LRAM
 MANCHESTER
*De La Salle College of Education, Hopwood Hall,
    Middleton, Manchester M24 3XH t 061-643 5331
*Didsbury College of Education, Wilmslow Rd, Man-
    chester M20 8RR t 061-445 7871/4. L. Manion BA,
    B Mus, M Sc, Ph D, LRAM
†Manchester College of Education, Long Millgate,
    Manchester M3 1SD t 061-832 7555
*Manchester University Department of Education,
    Manchester M13 9PL t 061-273 3333
 Mather College, Whitworth St, Manchester M1 3HA t
    061-236 9872
 Sedgley Park College of Education, Prestwich,
    Manchester M25 8JT t 061-773 4001/4. E. C. Holman
    B Mus, ARCO, ARMCM
 MATLOCK. Matlock College of Education, Matlock,
    Derbys DE4 3FW t Matlock 238314/5. John Clements
    FRCO
 MIDDLESBROUGH. Teesside College of Education, Flatts
    La, Middlesbrough TS6 0QS t Middlesbrough 47033.

Dorothy Armstrong-Wilson LRAM, ARCM, LTCL, BA (Ed)
MILTON KEYNES. Milton Keynes College of Education,
Stratford Rd, Wolverton Mill, Milton Keynes MK12
5NS t Wolverton 314840. A. D. Harris
NEWCASTLE UPON TYNE
*Newcastle upon Tyne Polytechnic Faculty of Education
and Humanities, Lipman Bldg, Sandyford Rd,
Newcastle upon Tyne t Newcastle upon Tyne 612181
*Newcastle upon Tyne University School of Education,
St Thomas' St, Newcastle upon Tyne NE1 7RU t
Newcastle upon Tyne 28511
Northern Counties College of Education, Coach La,
Newcastle upon Tyne NE7 7XA t Newcastle upon Tyne
666241. Mrs G. M. Polwarth LRAM. Annexe at
Ridley Hall, Bardon Mill, Hexham, Northumb NE47
7BP t Bardon Mill 282
Northumberland College of Education, Ponteland,
Newcastle upon Tyne NE20 OAB t Ponteland 3391.
A. J. G. McDonald B Mus, Cert Ed, LRAM, ARCM, LGSM.
Annexe at Allendale Rd, Hexham, Northumb NE46 2ND
t Hexham 3651
*St Mary's College of the Sacred Heart, Fenham,
Newcastle upon Tyne NE4 9YD t Newcastle upon Tyne
30151
NEWPORT. Gwent College of Higher Education, Caer-
leon, Newport, Gwent NP6 1XJ t Caerleon 421292.
P. Sidaway BA, M Ed
NEWTOWNABBEY. Ulster College, Northern Ireland
Polytechnic, Jordanstown, Newtownabbey, Co.
Antrim BT37 OQB t Whiteabbey 65131
NORTHAMPTON. Nene College of Education, Moulton Pk,
Northampton NN2 7AL t Northampton 22321. R.Davies
B Mus, FRCO, LRAM
*NORWICH. Keswick Hall Church of England College of
Education, Norwich, Norfolk NR4 6TL t Norwich
56841. Geoffrey N. S. Laycock GRSM, ARCM, LRAM,
LTCL, ARCO
NOTTINGHAM. Nottingham College of Education, Clifton,
Nottingham NG11 8NS t Nottingham 211181/4.
David Renouf MA, B Mus, FTCL, FTSC, LRAM, ARCM,
ARCO
ORMSKIRK. Edge Hill College of Education, Ormskirk,
Lancs K39 4QP t Ormskirk 75171. A. T. Crimlisk
B Ed, LTCL, ALCM, Cert Ed
OXFORD
Lady Spencer-Churchill College of Education,
Wheatley, Oxford OX9 1HX t Wheatley 2691
Westminster College, North Hinksey, Oxford OX2 9AT
t Oxford 47644. John V. Cockshoot B Litt, B Mus,
MA, D Phil, LRAM

PLYMOUTH.   College of St Mark and St John, Derriford
   Rd, Plymouth PL6 8BH t Plymouth 51591.   K. G. Jones
   B Mus (Wales), Dip Ed (Wales)
PORTSMOUTH.   Portsmouth Polytechnic Faculty of
   Educational Studies, Locksway Rd, Milton, Ports-
   mouth PO4 8JF t Portsmouth 35241.   H. S. Davis MA,
   Mus B, ARCM, ARCO
READING
†*Berkshire College of Education, Bulmershe Ct, Wood-
   lands Av, Earley, Reading RG6 1HY t Reading 663387.
   Gwyn Arch MA, FTCL, LRAM
 *Reading University School of Education, London Rd,
   Reading RG1 5AQ t Reading 85234
RETFORD.   Eaton Hall College of Education, Retford,
   Notts DN22 OPR t Retford 6441.   Miss D. Willoughby
   GRSM, LRAM, ARCM
RIPON.   Ripon College of Education, Ripon, Yorks
   HG4 2QX t Ripon 2691
ROTHERHAM.   Lady Mabel College of Education, Went-
   worth Woodhouse, Rotherham, Yorks S62 7TJ t
   Barnsley 742161
RUGBY.   St Paul's College, Newbold Revel, Rugby,
   Warks CV23 OJS t Rugby 832561.   J. J. Watkins B Mus,
   ARCO, ARMCM
SAFFRON WALDEN.   Saffron Walden College, Saffron
   Walden, Essex CB11 3DP t Saffron Walden 22119
SALISBURY.   College of Sarum St Michael, 65 The
   Close, Salisbury, Wilts SP1 2EW t Salisbury 28241.
   Miss R. A. Bryant LRAM
SCARBOROUGH.   North Riding College of Education,
   Filey Rd, Scarborough, Yorks YO11 3AZ t Scarborough
   62392/4.   Leslie J. Burtonshaw B Mus, LRAM, ARCM
SHEFFIELD
*Sheffield City College of Education, 36 Collegiate
   Cres, Sheffield S10 2BP t Sheffield 665274.
   A. G. Kimberley M Mus
 Totley-Thornbridge College of Education, Totley Hall
   La, Sheffield S17 4AB t Sheffield 368116
SITTINGBOURNE.   Sittingbourne College of Education,
   Sittingbourne, Kent ME10 1LF t Sittingbourne 23141
   Annexe at 370 High St, Chatham, Kent ME4 4NP t
   Medway 47371
SOUTHAMPTON.   La Sainte Union College of Education,
   The Avenue, Southampton SO9 5HB t Southampton
   28761/4
SUNDERLAND
Sunderland College of Education, Langham Tower, Ry-
   hope Rd, Sunderland, Co Durham SR2 7EE t Sunderland
   71217
Sunderland Polytechnic Education Department, Sunder-
   land SR1 3SD t Sunderland 76191

SWANSEA. Swansea College of Education, Townhill Rd,
 Swansea SA2 OUT t Swansea 23482/4
TOTNES. Dartington College of Arts, Totnes, Devon
 TQ9 6EJ t Totnes 862224. Jack P. B. Dobbs BA,
 M Ed, M Phil, LRAM, LTCL
†*WAKEFIELD. Bretton Hall College of Education, West
 Bretton, Wakefield, Yorks WF4 4LG t Bretton 261.
 Miss D. M. Bird M Litt, Mus B, LRAM
WALSALL. West Midlands College of Education, Gorway,
 Walsall, Staffs WS1 3BD t Walsall 29141. Gerald
 A. C. Eades MA, ARCO, ARCM
*WARRINGTON. Padgate College of Education, Fearnhead,
 Warrington, Lancs WA2 ODB t Warrington 33571/4.
 D. S. Blott MA, FRCO, LRAM
WATFORD. Wall Hall College, Aldenham, Watford, Herts
 WD2 8AT t Radlett 4961/3
WEYMOUTH. Weymouth College of Education, Cranford
 Av, Weymouth, Dorset DT4 7LQ t Weymouth 72311.
 Annexe at Shaftesbury Ho, Constitution Hill Rd,
 Parkstone, Poole BH14 OQA t Parkstone 742041.
 George Sutton GRSM, LRAM
*WINCHESTER. King Alfred's College of Education,
 Sparkford Rd, Winchester, Hants SO22 4NR t Win-
 chester 62281. Outpost at Bramblys Clo, Basing-
 stoke RG21 1UP t Basingstoke 3676. B. Longthorne
 FRCO, LRAM, ARCM, ATCL
WOLVERHAMPTON. Wolverhampton Teachers' College for
 Day Students, Walsall St, Wolverhampton WV1 3LE t
 Wolverhampton 51941. Day outpost at Oakengates,
 Hartsbridge, Telford, Salop TF2 6BA t Telford 62505
WORCESTER. Worcester College of Education, Henwick
 Gro, Worcester WR2 6AJ t Worcester 422131.
 G. B. Stanley B Mus, ARCM, ARCO
WREXHAM. Cartrefle College of Education, Wrexham,
 Clwyd LL13 9NL t Wrexham 51782. J. R. Williams
 M Mus, FRCO
*YORK. St John's College, York YO3 7EX t York 56771

9   In-service Courses for Teachers

The following long in-service music courses are
arranged on a regular basis. Diplomas or other
awards (if any) granted on passing the courses are
shown in italic. Further information can be obtained
from the institutions where the courses are held or
from the Department of Education and Science, Higher
and Further Education Branch I (c), Elizabeth Ho,
York Rd, London SE1 7PH t 01-928 9222 ext 3385.

Information about *shorter* in-service courses is available from the Department of Education and Science, Teachers' Short Courses, Elizabeth Ho, York Rd, London SE1 7PH t 01-928 9222 ext 3185.

ONE-YEAR COURSES

LONDON. Music with special reference to children up to the age of 13. Froebel Institute College of Education, Grove Ho, Roehampton La, London SW15 5PJ t 01-876 2242. For teachers in primary and middle schools. Qualifications required: initial training, 5 years' teaching experience. Enrol by 31 Jan. *Dip in the Teaching of Mus*

LONDON. Refresher course for teachers with musical skills. Trinity College of Music, 11 Mandeville Pl, London W1M 6AQ t 01-935 5773. Qualifications required: 5 years' teaching experience, successful completion of entrance examination

BIRMINGHAM. Refresher course for teachers with musical skills. Birmingham School of Music, City of Birmingham Polytechnic, Paradise Circus, Birmingham B3 3HG t 021-235 4355. Qualifications required: 5 years' teaching experience

EXETER. Music for adolescents. School of Education, University of Exeter, Gandy St, Exeter EX4 3LZ t Exeter 77911. For graduate and non-graduate teachers responsible for music in primary and secondary schools, colleges of further education, youth clubs. Qualifications required: initial training, 3 years' teaching experience. Enrol by 31 Jan. *Dip Ed*

KEELE. Music in education. Institute of Education, University of Keele, Keele, Newcastle, Staffs ST5 5BG t Keele Park 371. For primary and secondary teachers. Qualifications required: initial training, 3 years' teaching experience *or* degree, postgraduate certificate in education, 3 years' teaching experience. May be taken part time over 2 years. Enrol by 28 Feb. *Dip of Advanced Study in Ed*

ONE-TERM COURSES

BRENTWOOD. Brentwood College of Education, Sawyers Hall La, Brentwood, Essex CM15 9BT t Brentwood 216971. For primary and middle school teachers

EXETER. Music for slow learners. Dartington College of Arts, Totnes, Devon TQ9 6EJ t Totnes 862224.

For teachers of slow learners in special or ordinary schools. Qualifications required: some music
teaching experience. Enrol by 30 Jun
EXMOUTH. Rolle College, Exmouth, Devon EX8 2AT t
Exmouth 5344. For primary and middle school
teachers
OXFORD. Presenting music to children. Westminster
College of Education, North Hinksey, Oxford OX2
9AT t Oxford 47644. For primary and middle school
teachers

10 Colleges of Further and Higher Education

These are local authority institutions, providing
full- and part-time courses for those over 16 to GCE
'O' and 'A' (and equivalent) levels, diploma, and
occasionally degree standard. Application should be
made to the individual colleges.

There is no central clearing house for applications,
but information and guidance can be obtained from
the local advisory officer of the Department of
Education and Science's Further Education Information
Service (address from Room 2/6T, DES - see p. 75 -
or from local education offices). Comprehensive
details of available courses are provided annually,
during the summer vacation, by the Higher Education
Advisory Centre, Middlesex Polytechnic, Church St,
London N9 9PD t 01-807 1060.

*

The name, address and telephone number of the
college is followed by the name of the senior person
in charge of music, to whom further inquiries should
be addressed. Institutions in London are listed
first, then others in alphabetical order by towns.

LONDON
Barking College of Technology, Dagenham Rd, Romford
RM7 0XU t Romford 66841
Barnet College of Further Education, Wood St, Barnet,
Herts EN5 4AZ t 01-449 9191. Miss E. J. M. Gilmore
LRAM
Chiswick Music Centre, Chiswick Polytechnic, Bath
Rd, London W4 1LW t 01-994 3454. Brian Richardson
Ealing Music Centre, Ealing Technical College, St
Mary's Rd, London W5 5RF t 01-579 4111. Donald
Cashmore B Mus, B Sc, FRCO

Hackney College, Stoke Newington Centre, Ayrsome Rd,
London N16 ORH t 01-254 2768
Havering Technical College, Ardleigh Green Rd, Horn-
church, Essex RM11 2LL t Hornchurch 55011
Kennington College, Riley Rd, London SE1 3DP t
01-237 8178
Kingsway-Princeton College of Further Education,
Sidmouth St, Gray's Inn Rd, London WC1H 8JB t
01-837 8185. George Biddlecombe MA, GRSM, LRAM,
ARCM
Middlesex Polytechnic, Trent Park, Cockfosters,
Barnet, Herts EN4 OPT t 01-449 9691. Marjorie L.
Glynne-Jones MFF, LRAM, ARCM
Redbridge Technical College, Little Heath, Romford
RM6 4XT t 01-599 5231
Southgate Technical College, High St, London N14 6BS
t 01-886 6521. Terence Hawes MA, ARCM
Southwark College for Further Education, The Cut,
London SE1 8LE t 01-928 6561

ABERDEEN. Aberdeen College of Commerce, Holburn St,
Aberdeen AB9 2YT t Aberdeen 52528
ACCRINGTON. Accrington and Rossendale College, Sandy
La, Accrington, Lancs BB5 2AW t Accrington 35334
ASHINGTON. Northumberland County Technical College,
Ashington, Northumb NE63 9RG t Ashington 3248/3240
ASHTON-UNDER-LYNE. Tameside College of Technology,
Beaufort Rd, Ashton-under-Lyne, Lancs O26 6NX t
061-330 6911. Mrs M. de Mierre Mus B
BATHGATE. West Lothian College of Further Education,
Marjoribanks St, Bathgate, West Lothian EH48 1QJ
t 031-515 5801
BOSTON. Boston College of Further Education, Rowley
Rd, Boston, Lincs PE21 6JF t Boston 5701.
W. B. Moore MA, B Mus, LRAM
BRACKNELL. South-East Berkshire College of Further
Education, Church Rd, Bracknell, Berks RG12 1DJ t
Bracknell 20411. Miss Audrey Jones MA, M Litt,
GRSM
BRADFORD. Bradford College of Art and Technology,
Gt Horton Rd, Bradford BD7 1AY t Bradford 28837.
Mrs M. E. Grimley A Mus TCL, Cert Ed
BRIDGNORTH. Bridgnorth College of Further Education,
Stourbridge Rd, Bridgnorth WV15 6AL t Bridgnorth
4431
BRIGHTON. Brighton Technical College, Pelham St,
Brighton BN1 4FA t Brighton 685971
BRISTOL. Filton Technical College, Gloucester Rd
North, Filton, Bristol BS12 7AT t Bristol 694217.
B. R. Snary GTCL, Dip Ed, MTC
BROMSGROVE. Bromsgrove College of Further Education,

School Dr, Stratford Rd, Bromsgrove, Worcs B60 1BB
t Bromsgrove 74402. H. J. Taylor ARMCM
BROXBOURNE. East Herts College of Further Education,
Turnford, Broxbourne, Herts t Hoddesdon 66451
CAMBRIDGE. Cambridgeshire College of Arts and Tech-
nology, Collier Rd, Cambridge CB1 2AJ t Cambridge
63271. Norman Hearn MA, FRCO, ARCM
CHELMSFORD. Mid-Essex Technical College and School
of Art, Victoria Rd South, Chelmsford, Essex CM1
1LL t Chelmsford 54491
CHICHESTER. Chichester College of Further Education,
Westgate Fields, Chichester, Sussex PO19 1SB t
Chichester 86321. Miss A. D. Lawrence Dip Mus Ed
(RSAM), LRAM
CLYDEBANK. Clydebank Technical College, Kilbowie Rd,
Clydebank, Dunbartonshire G81 2AA t 041-952 7771
COLCHESTER. North-East Essex Technical College,
Sheepen Rd, Colchester, Essex CO3 3LL t Colchester
70271. Donald Hughes D Mus, B Sc, FRCO
COVENTRY. Coventry School of Music, Percy St,
Coventry CV1 3BY t Coventry 23803. P. L. Isher-
wood MA
DARLINGTON. Darlington College of Technology,
Cleveland Av, Darlington, Co Durham DL3 7BB t
Darlington 67651
DUDLEY. Dudley Technical College, The Broadway,
Dudley, Worcs DY1 4AS t Dudley 53585
DUNDEE. Dundee College of Commerce, 30 Constitution
Rd, Dundee DD3 6TB t Dundee 27651
DURHAM. Durham Technical College, Framwellgate Moor,
Durham DH1 5ES t Durham 62421
EDINBURGH
Napier College of Commerce and Technology, Sighthill
Ct, Edinburgh EH11 4BN t 031-443 6061. Neil
Butterworth MA
Stevenson College of Further Education, Bankhead Av,
Edinburgh EH11 4DE t 031-443 7111
Telford College of Further Education, Crewe Toll,
Edinburgh EH4 2NZ t 031-332 7631
EXETER. Exeter College, Hele Rd, Exeter EX4 4JS t
Exeter 76381. A. Robinson
GLASGOW
Cardonald College of Further Education, 720 Mospark
Dr, Glasgow G52 3AY t 041-883 6151
Langside College of Further Education, 50 Prospect-
hill Rd, Glasgow G42 9LB t 041-649 4991
GRAY'S THURROCK. Thurrock Technical College, Wood-
view, Grays, Essex RM16 4YR t Gráy's Thurrock
71621. J. F. Hanchet BA
GUILDFORD. Guildford County College of Technology,
Stoke Pk, Guildford, Surrey GU1 1EZ t Guildford
73201

HALIFAX. Percival Whitley College of Further Education, Francis St, Halifax, Yorks HX1 3UZ t Halifax
54764

HARROGATE. Harrogate College of Art and Adult
Studies, 2 Victoria Av, Harrogate HG1 1EL t Harrogate 62446

HEMEL HEMPSTEAD. Dacorum College of Further Education, Marlowes, Hemel Hempstead, Herts HP1 1HD t
Hemel Hempstead 63771. T. P. Loten B Mus

HITCHIN. Music School, Dept of Adult Education,
Hitchin College of Further Education, Cambridge Rd,
Hitchin, Herts SG4 OJD t Hitchin 2351. John
Railton FRAM, GRSM

HUDDERSFIELD. Huddersfield School of Music, The
Polytechnic, Queensgate, Huddersfield HD1 3DH t
Huddersfield 30501. P. G. Forbes MA, ARCO

LANCASTER. Lancaster Adult Centre, St Leonard's Ho,
St Leonardgate, Lancaster LA1 1NN t Lancaster
60141. David T. Jackson B Mus

LIVERPOOL. Mabel Fletcher Technical College, Sandown
Rd, Liverpool L15 4JB t 051-733 7211. Peter B.
Cooper MA, B Mus, ARCM

NEWARK. Newark Technical College, Chauntrey Pk,
Newark, Notts NG24 1PB t Newark (Notts) 5921

NEWCASTLE UPON TYNE. School of Music, Newcastle
College of Arts and Technology, Rye Hill, Newcastle
upon Tyne NE4 5TQ t Newcastle upon Tyne 22752.
P. J. Abbot MA, ARCO

NEWTOWNABBEY. School of Music and Drama, Ulster
College, N Ireland Polytechnic, Shore Rd, Newtownabbey, Co Antrim BT37 OQB t Antrim 65131

NORTHWICH. Mid-Cheshire Central College of Further
Education, Chester Rd, Hartford, Northwich,
Cheshire CW8 1LJ t Northwich 75281. B. W. Howitt
MA, ARCM, Cert Ed

NORWICH. Norwich City College, Ipswich Rd, Norwich
NR2 2LJ t Norwich 60011

NOTTINGHAM. Clarendon College of Further Education,
Pelham Av, Nottingham NG5 1AL t Nottingham 607201.
A. D. Cator GRSM, LRAM, ARCM

OSWESTRY. Oswestry College of Further Education,
College Rd, Oswestry, Salop SY11 2SA t Oswestry
3067

OXFORD. Oxford Polytechnic, Headington, Oxford OX3
OBP t Oxford 64777. T. E. Chatburn B Mus, M Mus

PETERBOROUGH. Peterborough Technical College, Park
Cres, Peterborough PE1 4DZ t Peterborough 67366.
T Keates ARCM

POOLE. Poole Technical College, North Rd, Poole,
Dorset BH14 OLS t Parkstone 747600. D. Riddell BA,
B Mus, LRAM, L Mus TCL

PRESTON. Preston Polytechnic, Corporation St, Preston,
Lancs PR1 2TQ t Preston 51831
REDRUTH. Cornwall Technical College, Redruth, Corn-
wall TR15 3RD t Redruth 2911
SALFORD. Salford Music Centre, Salford College of
Technology, Frederick Rd, Salford M6 6PU t
061-736 2983
SCUNTHORPE. North Lindsey College of Technology,
Kingsway, Scunthorpe, Lincs DN17 1AJ t Scunthorpe
4738
SHEFFIELD. Stannington College of Further Education,
Myers Grove La, Sheffield S6 5JL t Sheffield 341691.
B. W. N. Cooper BA, Dip Ed
SLOUGH. Slough College of Technology, Wellington St,
Slough SL1 1YG t Slough 34585
SOUTHEND. Southend College of Technology, Carnarvon
Rd, Southend-on-Sea SS2 6LS t Southend-on-Sea
49606. M. Bailey Mus B, FTCL, LRAM, ARCM
STAFFORD. Stafford College of Further Education,
Earl St, Stafford ST16 2QR t Stafford 2361.
R. A. L. Roper MA, B Mus, ARCM, Cert Ed
STOKE-ON-TRENT. Elms Technical College, College Rd,
Stoke-on-Trent ST4 2DQ t Stoke-on-Trent 22107
STRATFORD-UPON-AVON. South Warwickshire College of
Further Education, The Willows, Stratford-upon-
Avon, Warks CV37 9QR t Stratford-upon-Avon 66245
TONBRIDGE. West Kent College of Further Education,
Brook St, Tonbridge, Kent TN9 2PW t Tonbridge
63101/2
TOTNES. Dartington College of Arts, Totnes, Devon
TQ9 6EJ t Totnes 862224. Jack P. B. Dobbs BA,
M Ed, M Phil, LRAM, LTCL
WESTON-SUPER-MARE. Weston-super-Mare Technical
College, Knightstone Rd, Weston-super-Mare, Somer-
set BS23 2AL t Weston-super-Mare 21301
WEYBRIDGE. Brooklands Technical College, Heath Rd,
Weybridge, Surrey KT13 8TT t Weybridge 53300.
Frank R. Heald GTCL, LTCL
WINCHESTER. Winchester School of Art, Park Av, Win-
chester, Hants SO23 8DL t Winchester 61891
WISBECH. Isle of Ely College of Further Education,
Ramnoth Rd, Wisbech, Cambs PE13 2JE t Wisbech 2561.
G. W. R. Stevens Cert Ed
WREXHAM. Denbighshire Technical College, Mold Rd,
Wrexham, Clwyd LL11 2AW t Wrexham 3551
YEOVIL. Yeovil Technical College, Ilchester Rd,
Yeovil, Somerset BA21 3BA t Yeovil 3921

11 Instrument-making and Technology

Full-time professional training is offered at the
institutions listed below. Piano technology, tuning
and repair are also taught at the Royal Normal
College for the Blind in Shrewsbury (see p. 146).
Certain manufacturers and retailers with their own
repair workshops will also give apprenticeship
training. Evening classes are available at some
Colleges of Further Education (see p. 158).

*

The name, address and telephone number of the
institutions is followed by the name of the senior
person in charge of musical instrument technology,
to whom further inquiries should be addressed.

London College of Furniture, Department of Musical
    Instrument Technology, 41-71 Commercial Rd, London
    El 1LA t 01-247 1953. Three year course includes
    early keyboard instrument making; fretted instru-
    ment, violin and early woodwind making; piano
    construction, tuning, maintenance; electronics.
    Two-year course in piano tuning and maintenance.
    Three-year course in stringed keyboard instrument
    design and repair. Various part-time courses.
    P. L. Shirtcliff
Newark Technical College, Chauntry Pk, Newark, Notts
    NG24 1PB t Newark 5921/2/3. Full-time courses in
    music, piano tuning, piano, violin and woodwind
    making and repair. A. S. Fawcett B Mus, Cert Ed

12 Arts Administration Courses

Further details of the following courses, and a list
of long and short courses in related fields, are
available from the Arts Council of Great Britain,
105 Piccadilly, London W1V OAU t 01-629 9495.

Diploma Course in Arts Administration.   Room A241B,
  City University, St John St, London EC1V 4PB t
  01-253 4399 ext 533.   One-year full-time course
  arranged in conjunction with the Arts Council of
  Great Britain.   Open to applicants aged 21 and
  over in possession of a degree or equivalent
  qualification, with significant experience in one
  or more artistic fields.
Practical Training Course in Arts Administration.
  The Training Officer, Arts Council of Great Britain,
  105 Piccadilly, London W1V OAU t 01-629 9495.
  3-9 months practical secondment to arts organizations, including a 6-week business course at the
  Polytechnic of Central London.   Open to applicants
  aged 21 and over with previous experience in
  administration.

13   Part-time Adult Tuition

Among institutions providing part-time adult education in music are the Open University, the extra-
mural departments of other universities, the Workers'
Educational Association, and various residential or
non-residential adult education centres which may be
independent or under the control of university extra-
mural departments or of local education authorities.
  Most local authorities are members of the National
Institute of Adult Education (England and Wales), 35
Queen Anne St, London W1M OBL t 01-637 4241, which
has a selection of prospectuses available for
perusal, including those of both independent and LEA
adult centres.   It also publishes a yearbook. (£1.25).
A similar function is fulfilled in Scotland by the
Scottish Institute of Adult Education, 57 Melville
St, Edinburgh EH3 7HL t 031-226 7200.
  Most education centres are members of the Educa-
tional Centres Association, Friends' Hall, Greenleaf
Rd, London E17 6QP t 01-520 2867.   Adult education
also comes within the scope of the Rural Music
Schools Association (see p. 168), and of certain
recreational courses (see p. 209).

THE OPEN UNIVERSITY

Walton Hall, Milton Keynes, Bucks MK7 6AA t Milton
Keynes 74066. *Professor of Music* Gerald Hendrie MA,
Mus B, PhD, FRCO, ARCM.

The University provides part-time higher education
throughout the British Isles for adults (usually over
21), largely by home-study methods, in courses leading to the award of a BA or BA (Hons) degree. A
minimum of 3 years is normally needed. Music is
studied conjointly with other subjects, and in specific aspects rather than comprehensively; it is hoped
to extend the number of available aspects over the
next few years. Higher degrees are offered for
research only.

A *Guide for Applicants for Undergraduate Courses*
is obtainable free from the Admissions Office, PO
Box 48, The Open University, and a *Postgraduate Prospectus* from the Higher Degrees Office, PO Box 49.

UNIVERSITY EXTRA-MURAL EDUCATION

Working within defined geographical areas, the
universities offer part-time courses which vary
considerably in length, are based largely on the
tutorial class, and may lead to the award of diplomas
or certificates. Summer schools for students from
home and overseas are also arranged. Information
can be obtained from the Head of the Extra-Mural
Department (EMD) or Department of Adult Education
(DAE), or as otherwise indicated.

LONDON. University of London (EMD), 7 Ridgmount St,
London WC1E 7AD t 01-636 8000

ABERDEEN (EMD). Kings College, Old Aberdeen AB9
1AS t Aberdeen·40241
BATH (DAE). University of Bath, Northgate Ho, Bath
BA1 5AL t Bath 4276
BELFAST (EMD). Queen's University of Belfast, BT7
1NN t Belfast 45133
BIRMINGHAM (EMD). The University, PO Box 363,
Birmingham B15 2TT t 021-472 1301 ext 2149
BRISTOL (EMD). The University, 32 Tyndall's Pk Rd,
Bristol BS8 1HR t Bristol 24161 ext 684
CAMBRIDGE (EMD). Stuart Ho, Mill La, Cambridge CB2
1RY t Cambridge 56275/6
DUNDEE (EMD). The University, Nethergate, Dundee
DD1 4HN t Dundee 23181
DURHAM (EMD). 32 Old Elvet, Durham DH1 3JB t Durham
64466
EDINBURGH (DAE). 11 Buccleuch Pl, Edinburgh EH8 9JT
t 031-667 1011
EXETER (EMD). Gandy St, Exeter EX4 3QN t Exeter
77911

GLASGOW (EMD).   57-9 Oakfield Av, Glasgow G12 8LW t
   041-339 8855 ext 392-7
HULL (DAE).   195 Cottingham Rd, Hull HU5 2EQ t Hull
   497411
KEELE (DAE).   The University, Keele, Newcastle,
   Staffs ST5 5BG t Keele Park 313
LEEDS (DAE).   The University, University Rd, Leeds
   LS2 9JT t Leeds 31751
LEICESTER (DAE).   The University, University Rd,
   Leicester LE1 7RH t Leicester 50000
LIVERPOOL (EXTENSION STUDIES).   Abercromby Sq,
   Liverpool L69 3BX t 051-709 6022 ext 420
LONDONDERRY.   The New University of Ulster Institute
   of Continuing Education, Magee University College,
   Londonderry BT48 7JL t Londonderry 65621
MANCHESTER (EMD).   The University, Oxford Rd, Man-
   chester M13 9PL t 061-273 3333
NEWCASTLE UPON TYNE (DAE).   The University, Newcastle
   upon Tyne NE1 7RU t Newcastle upon Tyne 28511
NOTTINGHAM (DAE).   14-22 Shakespeare St, Nottingham
   NG1 4FJ t Nottingham 43022/3
OXFORD (EXTERNAL STUDIES).   Rewley Ho, Wellington Sq,
   Oxford OX1 2JA t Oxford 52901
READING.   Senior Assistant Registrar, The University,
   Reading RG26 2AH t Reading 85123 ext 250
ST ANDREWS (EMD).   3 St Mary's Pl, St Andrews, Fife
   KY16 9UZ t St Andrews 3429
SHEFFIELD (EMD).   Broomspring Ho, 85 Wilkinson St,
   Sheffield S10 2GJ t Sheffield 77758/9
SOUTHAMPTON (EMD).   The University, Southampton SO9
   5NH t Southampton 559122
SURREY (DAE).   The University, Stag Hill, Guildford
   GU2 5XH t Guildford 71281
SUSSEX (CENTRE FOR CONTINUING EDUCATION).   The
   University, Falmer, Brighton BN1 9QN t Brighton
   66755
WALES.   Secretary of the Extension Board, University
   Registry, Cathays Pk, Cardiff CF1 3NS t Cardiff
   22656
   ABERYSTWYTH (EMD).   9 Marine Terr, Aberystwyth SY23
      2AZ t Aberystwyth 7616
   BANGOR (EMD).   University College of North Wales,
      College Rd, Bangor, Gwynedd LL57 2DG t Bangor
      51151 ext 494
   CARDIFF (EMD).   University College, Cardiff, 38-40
      Park Pl, Cardiff CF1 3BB t Cardiff 44211
   SWANSEA (EMD).   6 Uplands Terr, Swansea SA2 0GU t
      Swansea 57168

WORKERS' EDUCATIONAL ASSOCIATION
9 Upper Berkeley St, London WClH 8BY t Ol-402 5608/9

The Association is recognized by the Department of
Education and Science as a responsible body in providing educational facilities; branches and districts
have the support of their local authorities, and
organize their own classes in subjects chosen by the
students themselves. Information can be obtained
from the Secretary of the relevant district:

LONDON.   32 Tavistock Sq, London WClH 9EZ t Ol-387
   8966

BERKS, BUCKS AND OXON.   3 Cornmarket, Oxford OXl 3EX
   t Oxford 46270
EASTERN.   17 Botolph La, Cambridge CB2 3RE t Cam-
   bridge 50978
EAST MIDLAND.   16 Shakespeare St, Nottingham NGl 4GF
   t Nottingham 45162
NORTHERN.   51 Grainger St, Newcastle upon Tyne NEl
   5JE t Newcastle upon Tyne 23957
NORTHERN IRELAND.   56 Dublin Rd, Belfast BT2 7HP t
   Belfast 29718
NORTH OF SCOTLAND.   Kittybrewster, Aberdeen AB2 3RZ
   t Aberdeen 494016
NORTH STAFFS.   Cartwright Ho, Broad St, Stoke-on-
   Trent STl 4EU t Stoke-on-Trent 24187
NORTH WALES.   33 College Rd, Bangor, Gwynedd LL57
   2AP t Bangor 3254
NORTH-WESTERN.   c/o W. Long, College of Further
   Education, Cavendish St, All Saints, Manchester
   Ml5 9DG t 061-273 5944/5086
SOUTH-EASTERN.   4 Castle Hill, Rochester, Kent MEl
   lQQ t Medway 42140
SOUTH-EAST SCOTLAND.   Riddle's Ct, Edinburgh EHl 2PG
   t 031-226 3456
SOUTHERN.   4 Carlton Cres, Southampton SO9 5UG t
   Southampton 29810
SOUTH WALES.   49 Charles St, Cardiff CFl 4EB t
   Cardiff 31176
SOUTH-WESTERN.   Martin's Gate Annexe, Bretonside,
   Plymouth PL4 OAT t Plymouth 64989
WESTERN.   7 St Nicholas St, Bristol BSl lUE t Bristol
   28322
WEST LANCS AND CHESHIRE.   39 Bluecoat Chambers,
   School La, Liverpool Ll 3BX t 051-709 8023
WEST MIDLAND.   9-ll Digbeth, Birmingham B5 6BH t
   021-643 0717/8
WEST OF SCOTLAND.   212 Bath St, Glasgow G2 4HW t
   041-332 3609

YORKSHIRE NORTH. 7 Woodhouse Sq, Leeds LS3 1AD t
   Leeds 453304/455944
YORKSHIRE SOUTH. St Paul's Chambers, St Paul's Pde,
   Sheffield S1 2JL t Sheffield 22641

OTHER EDUCATION CENTRES

LONDON
City Literary Institute, Stukeley St, **Drury** La,
   London WC2B 5LJ t 01-242 6971 *head of mus* Kenneth
   van Barthold, Laur du Cons Nat de Mus de Paris,
   LRAM
Morley College, 61 Westminster Bridge Rd, London SE1
   7HT t 01-928 8501 *mus dir* Michael Graubart
University of London - Goldsmiths' College, Dept of
   Adult Studies, Lewisham Way, London SE14 6NW t
   01-692 0211/4398 *mus dir* Malcolm Barry M Mus

ALFRETON. Alfreton Hall Adult Education Centre,
   Alfreton, Derby DE5 7AH t Alfreton 2201
CAMBRIDGE. Swavesey Village College, Swavesey,
   Cambridge CB4 5RS t Swavesey 30373 *mus dir*
   R. W. F. Brett Dip Ed, LRAM
CRAYFORD. Crayford Manor House Centre, Crayford,
   Kent DA1 4HB t Crayford 21463
LEEDS. Swarthmore Education Centre, 3-7 Woodhouse
   Sq, Leeds LS3 1AD t Leeds 32210
LEICESTER. Vaughan College, St Nicholas Circle,
   Leicester LE1 4LB t Leicester 57368 *mus organizer*
   Trevor J. Hold B Mus, MA
MANCHESTER. Whitefield Centre and Club, Higher La,
   Whitefield, nr Manchester M25 7FX t 061-766 5118
WEYBRIDGE. Walton and Weybridge Institute of Further
   Education, Churchfield Rd, Weybridge, Surrey KT13
   8DB t Weybridge 47029

14   Rural Music Schools Association

The headquarters (residential music centre, library,
practice rooms, etc) are at Little Benslow Hills,
Benslow La, Hitchin, Herts SG4 9RD t Hitchin 3446
director of music Bernard Shore CBE, FRCM, FTCL, Hon
RAM, ARCM. The Association publishes the quarterly
Making Music (see p. 232), lists of recommended music,
etc. Teaching and courses take place at headquarters
and at the following centres (the person in charge of
music is named):

Cornwall Rural Music School, 85 Truro Rd, St Austell,
Cornwall PL6 7BN t St Austell 2939.   Leslie
Russell MA, D Mus, ARCO
Doncaster Schools' Music Centre, St Sepulchre Gate
West, Doncaster DN4 0AA t Doncaster 23556.
Peter Bear
Dorset Rural Music School, Music Centre, The Close,
Blandford Forum, Dorset DT11 7HA t Blandford 2511.
Belinda Gooch GRSM, ARCM
East Kent, Westgate Towers, Pound La, Canterbury CT1
2BZ t Canterbury 64320. Ivan Phillips ARCM
Hampshire Council for Amateur Music, Park Av, Win-
chester, Hants t Winchester 63738. Dudley Mendham
GTCL, LTCL, MTC (Lond)
Hertfordshire County Music School, Westfield Ho, West
St, Hertford SG13 8HA t Hertford 54619. John
Westcombe MA
Holland Rural Music School, Music Centre, Shodfriars
La, Boston, Lincs PE21 6HJ t Boston 62438. Derek
Shepherd LRAM. (Also at High School, London Rd,
Spalding, Lincs PE11 2TE t Spalding 5527)
Kent Music School, Master's Ho, Old College, Maid-
stone, Kent ME15 6YQ t Maidstone 50885. Rosalind
Borland ARCM
Norfolk Association for Amateur Music, County
Council, County Hall, Norwich NR1 2DL t Norwich
22288 ext 391. Sidney Twemlow B Mus, LRAM
North and West Kent, St Stephen's Centre, Penbury
Rd, Tonbridge TN9 2AE t Tonbridge 3390. Patrick
Strevens LRAM
North Bucks Music Centre, The Pavilion, Sherwood Dr,
Bletchley, Milton Keynes MK3 6DR t Milton Keynes
73786. David Stevenson GTCL, LTCL, LRAM, LLCM
Suffolk Rural Music School, 253 Ranelagh Rd, Ipswich
IP2 0AP t Ipswich 53426. Brian Lincoln GRSM, LRAM,
ARCM, ARCO
West Suffolk, Education Offices, St Mary's Sq, Bury
St Edmunds, Suffolk IP33 2AN t Bury St Edmunds 2281
ext 368. Keith Shaw LTCL, ARCO
Wiltshire Rural Music School, 113 Gloucester Rd,
Trowbridge, Wilts BA14 0AE t Trowbridge 3175.
David Morris LTCL, LRAM

15   General Schools with Special Music Curricula

Specialist advice for parents of gifted children is
given by the National Association for Gifted Children
Ltd, 27 John Adam St, London WC2N 6HX t 01-839 1861.
In the following list, all schools are privately run
except where marked LEA or ILEA (Inner London Education Authority).

LONDON
Pimlico Comprehensive School (ILEA). Lupus St,
   London SWlV 3AT t 01-828 0774
Purcell School, Oakhurst, Mount Park Rd, Harrow on
   the Hill, Middx HAl 3JS t 01-422 1284.   Lenore
   Reynell LRAM, MA (Oxon), *mus dir*

MANCHESTER
Chetham's Hospital School of Music, Manchester M3 lSB
   t 061-834 7509
Manchester High School of Art (LEA), Southall St,
   Manchester M3 lHQ t 061-834 7417;   061-834 9015
SOUTHWELL. Minster Grammar School, Church St, South-
   well, Notts NG25 OHN t Southwell 813228
STOKE D'ABERNON. Yehudi Menuhin School, Cobham Rd,
   Stoke d'Abernon, Cobham, Surrey KTll 3QQ t Cobham
   4739 (strings and piano). Robert H. Masters FRAM,
   mus dir
WELLS. Wells Cathedral Music School, Cathedral Green,
   Wells, Somerset BA5 2SX t Wells 72970

16   Choir Schools

The following schools (which are preparatory, unless
otherwise stated) maintain special provision for the
education of cathedral or collegiate church choir-
boys. Further information is available from the
Choir Schools Association, Cathedral Choir School,
Whitcliffe La, Ripon, Yorks HG4 2LA t Ripon 2134.
Announcements of the holding of voice trials are
often to be found in the *Musical Times* (see p. 233).

(see p. 233)

*

The name of the director of music (or equivalent) is
given. Institutions in London are listed first, then
others in alphabetical order by towns.

LONDON
City of London School, Victoria Embankment, EC4Y 0DL
  t 01-353 0046. 1 inst schol of 2/3 cost of school
  fees or 2 exhibs of 1/3 cost of school fees;
  choristers of the Temple Church receive £265 towards fees; choristers of the Chapel Royal have
  full fees paid. Anthony Gould MA, Mus B, FRCO
St Paul's Cathedral Choir School, New Change, London
  EC4M 9AD t 01-248 5156. Choristers and probation-
  ers of St Paul's Cathedral have full fees paid.
Westminster Abbey Choir School, Dean's Yard, London
  SW1P 3NY t 01-222 6151

CAMBRIDGE
King's College School, West Rd, Cambridge CB3 9DN t
  Cambridge 65814/5. Chorister schols. C. A.
  Farmer LRAM, GRSM, Dip Ed
St John's College School, Grange Rd, Cambridge CB3
  9AB t Cambridge 53532. Chorister schols of £480
  p.a. C. Walker Cert Ed
CHESTER. Cathedral Choir School, 1 Abbey Sq, Chester
  CH1 2HU t Chester 25068
CHICHESTER. Prebendal School, Chichester, Sussex PO19
  1RT t Chichester 82026. Choral and leaving schols.
  I. R. Fox MA, FRCO
DURHAM. Chorister School, The College, Durham DH1
  3EL t Durham 2935
EDINBURGH. St Mary's Junior Music School (incorporat-
  ing Cathedral Choir School), Manor Pl, Edinburgh
  EH3 7EB t 031-225 1831. Primary and secondary.
  Dennis Townhill Mus B, FRCO
ELY. King's School, 1 The Gallery, Ely, Cambs CB7
  4DJ t Ely 2824
EXETER. Cathedral School, Palace Gate, Exeter EX1
  1HX t Exeter 55298. Choral schols of £350 p.a.
  Additional bursaries. Paul Morgan MA, B Mus, FRCO
GLOUCESTER. The King's School, Gloucester GL1 2BG
  t Gloucester 21251/2. Cathedral schol gives free
  tuition to chorister. School mus schols. Andrew
  H. Auster BA, Dip Ed
GRIMSBY. St James' Choir School, Bargate, Grimsby
  DN34 5AA t Grimsby 2958
HEREFORD. Cathedral School, 1 Castle St, Hereford
  HR1 2NN t Hereford 3575
LICHFIELD. St Chad's Cathedral School, The Close,
  Lichfield WS13 7LH t Lichfield 23326

LINCOLN. Cathedral School, Eastgate, Lincoln LN2
  1QG t Lincoln 23769
LLANDAFF. Cathedral School, Cardiff Rd, Llandaff,
  Cardiff CF5 2YH t Cardiff 563179
MANCHESTER. Chetham's Hospital School of Music (see
  p. 170); provides places for choristers from
  Manchester Cathedral.
NEWCASTLE. Cathedral School, 35 Grainger Pk Rd,
  Newcastle upon Tyne NE4 8SA t Newcastle upon Tyne
  33426
OXFORD
Christ Church Cathedral School, 3 Brewer St, Oxford
  OX1 1QW t Oxford 42561
Magdalen College School, Oxford OX4 1DZ t Oxford
  42191. Direct grant; choristership for half of
  fees; voice trial Feb. Bernard Rose MA, PhD
New College School, Oxford OX1 3UA t Oxford 43657
PETERBOROUGH. King's School, Peterborough PE1 2UE
  t Peterborough 64938/9. Grammar (cathedral).
  Paul White MA
REIGATE. St Mary's Choir School, Chart La, Reigate,
  Surrey RH2 7RN t Reigate 44880
RIPON. Cathedral Choir School, Whitcliffe La, Ripon,
  Yorks HG4 2LA t Ripon 2134. 18 chor schols of
  £225. Mrs S. C. Thomson MA
ROCHESTER. King's School, The Precincts, Rochester,
  Kent ME1 1TA t Rochester 43913
SALISBURY. Cathedral School, The Close, Salisbury,
  Wilts SP1 2EQ t Salisbury 22652
SOUTHWELL. Minster Grammar School, Church St, South-
  well, Notts NG25 0HN t Southwell 813228
TENBURY WELLS. St Michael's College, Tenbury Wells,
  Worcs WR15 8PH t Tenbury Wells 810282. Chor schols
  remit 1/3 of fees for boys aged 8-9½. Roger Judd
  MA, FRCO
TRURO. Cathedral School, Kenwyn, Truro, Cornwall TR1
  3DS t Truro 2735. Independent. J. C. Winter FTCL,
  ARCM
WELLS. Cathedral School, Cathedral Green, Wells,
  Somerset BA5 2ST t Wells 72117; mus school Wells
  72970. Special scheme for str players. Assistance
  on basis of means test. William Whittle FRCO, LRAM
WINCHESTER. Pilgrims' School, 3 The Close, Winchest-
  er, Hants SO23 9LT t Winchester 4189. Chorister-
  ships in Cathedral choir, quiristerships in college
  chapel choir; half boarder fees paid.
  C. C. McWilliam FRCO, ARCM, B Mus
WINDSOR. St George's School, Windsor Castle, Berks
  SL4 1QF t Windsor 65553
WORCESTER. King's School, Worcester WR1 2LP t
  Worcester 23016

YORK. Minster Song School, Deangate, York YO1 2JA
    t York 25217

17 Fee-paying Schools Offering Music Scholarships

Further information may be obtained from *The Public
and Preparatory Schools' Yearbook* and *The Girls
Schools' Yearbook* (A. & C. Black), and *Schools*
(Truman & Knightley Educational Trust).

*

These schools offer special scholarships on the basis
of musical ability. Details of scholarships are
given where known (sums mentioned are annual), and
are followed by name of school's music director. The
schools are for boys only unless otherwise stated.
Listing is alphabetically by names of schools.

Abbotsholme School (co-ed), Rochester, Uttoxeter,
    Staffs ST14 5BS t Rochester 217. Awards up to
    £840. R. G. Clark ARCM
Aldenham School, Elstree, Herts WD6 3AJ t Radlett
    6131. Schols up to £540. A. P. Vening MA, Mus B,
    FRCO
Abbey School (girls), Malvern Wells, Hereford and
    Worcester WR14 4HG t Malvern 3441. Schols up to
    £300. Mrs P. Reuby GRSM, LRAM
Allhallows School, Rousdon, nr Lyme Regis, Dorset
    DT7 3RA t Seaton (Devon) 20444. At least 1 schol
    £760; exhibs £380; bursaries £190. Adrian
    Carpenter MA, B Mus, FTCL
Ampleforth College, York YO6 4ER t Ampleforth 224.
    2 schols £100 each. D. S. Bowman Mus B, FRCO,
    ARMCM
Ardingly College, Haywards Heath, Sussex RH17 6SQ t
    Ardingly 557. Inst, chor schols and exhibs totall-
    ing £800. Alan Angus B Mus, FRCO, ARCM
Badminton School (girls), Westbury Rd, Bristol BS9 3BA
    t Bristol 626033. Webb-Johnson Music Schol £150;
    3 schols up to £400 open to music candidates and
    others. Richard Thorn ARCM, LTCL
Bearwood College, Bear Wood, Wokingham, Berks RG11
    5BG t Wokingham 786915. Inst, org, chor schols up
    to £250; exhibs for tuition on 1 inst. S. Marston
    Smith ARCO, LTCL
Bedales School (co-ed), Church Rd, Steep, Petersfield,

Hants GU32 2DG t Petersfield 2970.   Schol up to
£600.   W. A. T. Agnew ARCM, ARCO
Bedford School, Burnaby Rd, Bedford MK40 2TU t Bed-
ford 53436.   Inst schol £150 with free mus tuition.
E. J. Amos MA, B Mus, ARAM, ARCM
Bembridge School, Isle of Wight PO35 5PH t Bembridge
2101.   Schols and exhibs £50-£250 based on entrance
exam with credit for music
Bethany School, Curtisden Grn, Goudhurst, Cranbrook,
Kent TN17 1LB t Goudhurst 273
Bishop's Stortford College, Hadham Rd, Bishop's
Stortford, Herts CM23 2QZ t Bishop's Stortford
54055.   Schols up to £200 with free mus tuition.
D. B. Fielder ARCM
Bloxham School, Banbury, Oxon OX15 4PE t Banbury
720206;   mus school Banbury 720736.   Schols up to
£500;   exhibs.   Martin Roberts MA, B Mus, ARCO (CHM)
Blundell's School, Blundell's Rd, Tiverton, Devon
EX16 4DT t Tiverton 2543.   Schols totalling at
least £400;   exhib £30.   P. H. Matthews MA, B Mus,
ARCO
Bradfield College, Bradfield, Reading, Berks RG7 6BH
t Bradfield (Berks) 207.   Schol £350 with free mus
tuition.   F. N. Reed BA, GRSM, ARCO, LRAM, ARCM
Brighton College, Brighton BN2 2AL t Brighton 65788.
2 chor or inst schols up to £180 each with free
tuition in 2 insts.   G. B. G. Lawson MA, B Mus, ARCM
Bromsgrove School, 17 New Rd, Bromsgrove, Worcs B60
2JE t Bromsgrove 72774.   Schol £200.   R. S. Hewitt
MA, LRSM
Bryanston School, Blandford Forum, Dorset DT11 OPX t
Blandford 2411.   4 schols £300-£500.   Peter A.
Lattimer MA, FRCO
Campbell College, Belfast BT4 2ND t Belfast 63076/9.
Schol £100 with free mus tuition.   D. A. Leggat
Hon RSCM, ARCM, LRAM
Canford School, Wimborne, Dorset BH21 3AD t Wimborne
2411;   mus school Wimborne 3944.   2 schols up to
£500 with free tuition in 2 insts;   4 exhibs £75.
B. E. R. Manning MA, Mus B, FRCO
Canonesses of St Augustine (girls), Convent of Our
Lady, 116 Filsham Rd, St Leonards-on-Sea, Sussex
TN38 OPF t Hastings 470.   Schol £100.   Jonathan
Martin FTCL, ARCM, LTCL, ATCL
Charterhouse, Godalming, Surrey GU7 2DN t Godalming
6226.   3 schols £600, £420, £240 with free mus
tuition.   William Llewellyn B Mus, FRAM, ARCO
Cheltenham College, Bath Rd, Cheltenham, Glos GL53
7LD t Cheltenham 24841.   2 schols £240.   R. J. F.
Proctor MA, Mus B, FRCO
Christ College, Brecon LD3 8AG t Brecon 3359.   Awards
£100-£450.   C. R. Burn MA, ARCO

City of London School, Victoria Embankment, EC4Y ODL
t 01-353 0046. Inst schol 2/3 of school fees; 2
exhibs 1/3 of school fees; choristers of Temple
Royal receive £265 towards fees; choristers of
Chapel Royal have full fees paid. Anthony Gould
MA, Mus B, FRCO

Clayesmore School, Iwerne Minster, Blandford Forum,
Dorset DT11 8LL t Fontmell Magna 217. Inst schols
£150-£395 with free tuition; org schol £495; chor
schol £200. N. J. Zelle GRSM

Clifton College, Bristol BS8 3JH t Bristol 35945. 2
schols £700, £350; exhib £125; free mus tuition.
David R. Pettit MA, B Mus, FRCO, LGSM

Clifton High School for Girls, Bristol BS8 3JD t
Bristol 30201. Schols up to 3/4 of fees. Mrs
Sheila M. Mathew Forster B Mus, LRAM

Cranbrook School (co-ed), Cranbrook, Kent TN17 3JD

Cranleigh School, Horseshoe La, Cranleigh, Surrey GU6
8QQ t Cranleigh (Surrey) 3666. 2 schols £800, £600.
Other minor awards. J. Polglase MA

Croft House School (girls), Shillingstone, Blandford
Forum, Dorset DT11 0QS t Child Okeford 295.
Bursary £30. H. C. Easton MA, ARCM

Dean Close School (co-ed), Cheltenham, Glos GL51 6HE
t Cheltenham 22640; mus school t Cheltenham 55741.
Schols up to 40% of fees; exhib 20% of fees; free
tuition in any number of insts. G. H. S. Howarth
MA, FRCO, ARCM

Denstone College, Uttoxeter, Staffs ST14 5HN t
Rochester 484. 3 or 4 schols £100-£400.
P. J. Macken MA

Dover College, Dover, Kent CT17 9RX t Dover 205969.
At least 1 schol £100-£300 with free mus tuition.
L. G. Forsdyke FRCO (CHM), LRAM, ARCM, LTCL

Downe House (girls), Hermitage Rd, Cold Ash, Newbury,
Berks RG16 9JJ t Hermitage 286. Schol or exhibs up
to £150. A. W. Sidebottom BSc, LRAM

Dulwich College, London SE21 7LD t 01-693 3601.
Inst schol £250 increased to £500 in cases of need;
free inst tuition. Alan R. Morgan BA, LRAM, ARCO

Durham School, Quarryheads La, Durham City, Co
Durham DH1 4SZ t Durham 64783. Schols to the
value of £450. Music can be offered as subject
for Kings Scholarship (£1000) for all-round
academic ability. Edward J. Kay BA, LTCL

Eastbourne College, Eastbourne, Sussex BN21 4JX t
Eastbourne 37655. Awards up to £500. J. C. C.
Walker MA

Ellesmere College, Ellesmere, Salop SY12 9AB t Ellesmere (Salop) 2321. 2 awards £300, £400; chor
awards £175 increased in cases of need. Anthony
E. D. Dowlen BA, Cert Ed.

Epsom College, Surrey KT17 4JQ t Epsom 23273.   Schol
£300 with free tuition in 1 inst.   D. J. De Ville
MA, FRCO, ARCM
Eton College, Windsor, Berks SL4 6DL t Windsor
68418.   3 schols at least £640;   exhibs at least
£320;   preference str players, choristers.   All
awards made up to full fees in cases of need.
Graham Smallbone MA, ARCM, ARCO
Felixstowe College (girls), Felixstowe, Suffolk IP11
7NQ t Felixstowe 4269.   Schol, preference str player
Felsted School, Dunmow, Essex CM6 3LL t Gt Dunmow
820258.   Schols up to £300 altogether
Forest School, nr Snaresbrook, London E17 3PY t
01-520 1744.   2 schols £125.   R. C. Godel MA (Hons),
ARCO
Framlingham College, Framlingham, Woodbridge, Suffolk
IP13 9EY t Framlingham 723789.   Entrance schols
may be awarded for mus.   J. P. Willmett BA, FRCO,
ARCM
Giggleswick School, Settle, Yorks BD24 ODE t Settle
3545.   Inst schols up to £500.   Peter Read MA,
FRCO, ARCM
Gordonstoun School, Duffus, Elgin, Morayshire IV30
2RF t Hopeman 445.   Schol £500.   J. R. Nicholson
GRSM, ARMCM
Goudhurst College (girls), Doddington Hall, Nantwich,
Ches CW5 7NL t Bridgemere 238.   Schols for girls
15 and over.
Great Walstead School, Lindfield, Sussex RH16 2QL t
Lindfield 2142.   Schol £50.   T. M. Buzzard GRSM,
LRAM, Dip Ed
Gresham's School, Holt, Norfolk NR25 6EA t Holt 3271.
Schol £300;   mus can be offered as subject for
other awards.   M. H. Allard MA, B Mus, FRCO
Haileybury, Hertford SG13 7NU t Hoddesdon 62352.
At least 2 awards £200.   J. Hindmarsh FRCO
Highgate School, Bishopswood Rd, London N6 4PP t
01-340 1524.   Schol £180
Hollington Park School (girls), St Leonards-on-Sea,
E. Sussex TN38 OSR t Hastings 436606.   2 schols
£100, £80.   Miss M. G. Pearse GRSM, LRAM
Howell's School (girls), Denbigh LL16 3EN t Denbigh
2121.   Musical ability may be taken into considera-
tion for Foundation Awards.   Bridget McNeile GRSM,
ARCM
Hurstpierpoint College, Hassocks, Sussex BN6 9JS t
Hassocks 3636.   Exhibs £60-£200.   N. J. W. Page BA,
FTCL, LRAM, ARCO
Ipswich School, Henley Rd, Ipswich, Suffolk IP1 3SG
t Ipswich 55313.   2 awards;   exhibs;   remission of
up to full tuition fees for promising instrumenta-

lists. K. C. Griffiths MA, B Mus, FRCO
Kelly College, Tavistock, Devon PL19 OHZ t Tavistock
   3005. At least 1 schol £125-£600. Raymond Reynolds
Kingham Hill School, Kingham, Oxford OX7 6TH t King-
   ham 218. 2 inst schols £210 or more, with free
   tuition in 1 or more insts. Wadham Francis Sutton
   B Mus, ARCM, ARCO
King's College, Taunton, Somerset TA1 3DX t Taunton
   2708. Inst schols up to £500 with free mus tuition.
   T. D. Harrison MA, FRCO
King's School, Plox, Bruton, Somerset BA10 OED t
   Bruton 3326. Schols up to £402. R. W. Slogrove
   LRAM, LTCL
King's School, The Precincts, Canterbury, Kent CT1
   2ES t Canterbury 62963. 8 inst schols up to £550;
   other discretionary awards. Edred Wright ARSCM,
   Mus Bac
King's School, Ely, Cambs CB7 4DB t Ely (Cambs) 2824.
   Schols up to 3/4 of fees. Gerald Michael Gifford
   B Mus, GRSM (Hons), FRCO, ARCM
King's School, The Precincts, Rochester, Kent ME1
   1TA t Medway 43913. Schols up to £402; organ
   schol £402; free tuition in any number of insts.
   Gavin Williams GRSM, FRCO, ARCM, LRAM
King's School, Worcester WR1 21H t Worcester 23016.
   Schol up to £350. H. W. Bramma MA, FRCO
King William's College, Isle of Man t Castletown
   2551. Schols £60 (boarders), £30 (day boys)
   augmented, up to full fees, in cases of need.
   C. Crabe GRSM, FRCO
Lancing College, Lancing, Sussex BN15 ORW t Shoreham
   2213. 2 or 3 schols up to £500; 6 junior awards
   £75. Robin Sheldon MA, FRCO, ARCM
Leeds Grammar School, Moorland Rd, Leeds LS6 1AN t
   Leeds 33417. A. J. Cooke MA, Mus B, LRAM, FRCO
   (CHM), ADCM
Leighton Park School, Reading, Berks RG2 7DH t
   Reading 82065. David Hughes FTCL
Leys School, Cambridge CB2 2AD t Cambridge 55327.
   Awards up to £300 with free tuition on 2 insts.
   K. N. Naylor MA, Mus B, FRCO
Lord Wandsworth College, Long Sutton, Basingstoke,
   Hants RG25 1TG t Long Sutton (Hants) 482. 2
   schols £150 with free tuition in all mus subjects.
   Philip Hildesley LTCL
Loretto School, Millhill, Musselburgh, Midlothian
   EH21 7RE t 031-665 2567
Malvern College, Malvern, Worcs t Malvern 3497.
   Schols up to £500; exhibs; free tuition.
   C. M. Brett MA
Malvern Girls' College, Malvern, Worcs WR14 3BA t

Malvern 3405. Schols for girls entering middle
school and sixth form. Mrs P. Mullin LRAM
Marlborough College, Wilts SN8 1PA t Marlborough
2882. Awards totalling £1000 may be made; any
schol may be awarded for mus alone or mus may be
offered as supporting subject in academic schol
exam. Roy Wilkinson MA, GRSM, ARCM
Merchant Taylors' School, Sandy Lodge, Northwood,
Middx HA6 2HT t Northwood 23857. 2 schols £250,
£125. K. C. Griffiths MA, Mus B, FRCO (CHM), ARCM
Millfield School, Street, Somerset BA16 0YD t Street
(Somerset) 2295. 4 schols up to £1500 each.
G. M. Keating MA, ARCM
Mill Hill School, London NW7 1QS t 01-959 4207.
Schols up to £500. Alfred Champniss MA, FRCO, ARCM
Milton Abbey School, Blandford Forum, Dorset DT11
0BZ t Milton Abbas 484. Schol up to £300 with
additional bursary up to £300 in case of need.
W. T. Doar MA (Cantab), Mus B (Cantab)
Monkton Combe School, nr Bath, Somerset BA2 7HG t
Limpley Stoke 3523. Up to 2 inst schols £250 (up
to £375 for sons of clergy and missionaries), with
free tuition in 1 inst. H. W. E. Jones MA, Hon
FTCL
Oakham School, Oakham, Rutland LE15 6DT t Oakham 2850.
Inst and chor schols up to £600. Peter William
Dains FTCL, GTCL, LRAM, ARCM
Oratory School, Woodcote, nr Reading, Berks RG8 0PJ
t Woodcote 207. Various schols; free mus tuition.
M. J. Crump B Mus
Oundle School, Peterborough, Northants PE8 4EJ t
Oundle 3536; mus school Oundle 2227. Up to 3
schols maximum value £690; preference str players.
T. C. Brown MA
Pangbourne College, Pangbourne, Berks RG8 8LA t
Pangbourne 2101. Schol up to £400
Pocklington School, Pocklington, York YO4 2NJ t
Pocklington 3125. Schols and exhibs up to £75;
free tuition in 1 inst. F. A. Sefton Cottom
B Mus (Dunelm), FRCO, FTCL, ARCM
Queen Ethelburga's School (girls), Penny Pot La,
Harrogate, N. Yorks HG3 1RH t Harrogate 64125.
Schol £150. Miss R. B. Baines GRSM, ARCM
Queenswood (girls), Shepherds Way, Brookmans Pk,
Hatfield, Herts AL9 6NS t Potters Bar 52262.
Special mus award on exam results. Myers Foggin
CBE, FTCL, FRAM, Hon RCM
Radley College, Abingdon, Oxon OX14 2HR t Abingdon
294. 3 inst schols £500, £300, £100; further
awards may be made. D. W. M. Paine MA, B Mus,
FRCO

Redrice School, nr Andover, Hants SP11 7PE t Abbotts
Ann 258.   Schol £50-£250

Rendcomb College, nr Cirencester, Glos GL7 7HA t
North Cerney 213.   Schol up to £240

Repton School, Derby DE6 6FH t Repton 2375.   Awards
£120-£360 with free tuition.   E. M. Salter BA,
A Mus TCL, ALCM

Ringwood Grammar School, West Hill Rd, Bournemouth t
Bournemouth 24352.   Inst schol £150

Rossall School, Fleetwood, Lancs FY7 8JW t Fleetwood
3849.   4 senior schols £189-£516;   2 junior schols
£75-£165.   J. A. Aveyard MA, Mus B, FRCO

Rugby School, Lawrence Sheriff St, Rugby, Warks CV22
5EH t Rugby 3465.   Schols up to £1000 increased to
full fees in cases of need.   D. A. H Youngman MA,
B Mus, ARCM, ARCO

Rydal School, Colwyn Bay, Clwyd LL29 7BT t Colwyn Bay
30155.   Exhibs totalling £350 with free tuition in
1 inst.   R. O. Smith GRSM

St Audrie's School (girls), West Quantoxhead, nr
Taunton, Somerset TA4 4DS t Williton 426.   Schol
£100 with free tuition in 2 insts.   Miss B. M.
Knight GRSM, ARCO, ARCM, LRAM

St Bees School, St Bees, Cwmbria CA27 ODU t St Bees
263.   B. S. Howard MA, FRCO

St Brandon's School (girls), Clevedon, Avon BS21 7SD
t Clevedon 2825.   Schol pays full board.
Miss N. Colbourne LRAM

St Edmund's College, Old Hall Grn, Ware, Herts SG11
1DS t Ware 821504.   Schols £60-£300.   N. D. Howard
BA, FRCO, LTCL

St Edmund's School, St Thomas Hill, Canterbury, Kent
CT2 8HU t Canterbury 63922.   P. A. S. Cameron BA,
FRCO, LRAM, ARCM

St Edward's College, Sandfield Pk, Liverpool L12 2AR
t 051-228 3376.   Schols available to choristers at
Liverpool Metropolitan Cathedral.   C. Lyons

St Edward's School, Oxford OX2 7NN t Oxford 54411;
mus school Oxford 54871.   Schols totalling £1000.
Preference str players and boys with Cathedral-type
singing experience.   D. P. Pritchard BA, FRCO, LTCL

St John's School, Epsom Rd, Leatherhead, Surrey KT22
8SP t Leatherhead 72016.   Schol £350;   exhibs.
Geoffrey P. Harvey BA, ARCO

St Lawrence College, Ramsgate, Kent CT11 7AE t
Thanet 52699.   2 schols £450, £200 with free mus
tuition, preference sgrs (especially treble).
E. A. Perkins B Mus, FRCO (CHM)

St Leonard's School (girls), St Andrews, Fife KY16
9QX t St Andrews 2126.   Exhib;   schol £20.
G. M. W. McIntosh Dip Mus Ed, RSAM

St Paul's Girls' School, Brook Grn, London W6 7BS t
01-603 2288. Nicola LeFanu MA
St Paul's School, Lonsdale Rd, London SW13 9JT t
01-748 9162. Dennis Brain Schol; 2 foundation
schols (value according to means). Jonathan P.
Varcoe MA, ARCO
Scarborough College, Filey Rd, Scarborough, Yorks
YO11 3BA t Scarborough 60620. Free mus tuition.
M. A. H. Fletcher BA, FRCO
Seaford College, Petworth, W. Sussex GU28 ONB t
Seaford 893556. Inst, chor schols. Philip Hill
M Mus
Sedbergh School, Sedbergh, Cumbria LA10 5RY t Sed-
bergh 20535. Schols up to £300. D. H. Cox FTCL,
ARCO, LRAM, ARCM, AGSM
Sherborne School, Abbey Rd, Sherborne, Dorset DT9 3AP
t Sherborne 2646; mus school Sherborne 2559. 3
schols £200, £350, £600 with free mus tuition.
Brian R. Judge MA, ARCO
Sherborne School for Girls, Bradford Rd, Sherborne,
Dorset DT9 3QN t Sherborne 2245. Miss R. Augusta
Miller AGSM, ARCM
Shrewsbury School, Shrewsbury, Shropshire SY3 7BB t
Shrewsbury 4537. 2 awards up to £600 and £450.
Lester Standish MA, FRCO
Solihull School, Warks B91 3DJ t 021-705 0958.
Schol pays full fees
Stonyhurst College, nr Blackburn, Lancs BB6 9PZ t
Stonyhurst 345. Schols £200 or more with possible
extra bursaries. A. John GRSM, ARCO, LRAM, ARCM
Stowe School, Stowe, Buckingham, Bucks MK18 5EH t
Buckingham 3165. 2 schols, 2 exhibs up to 1/3 of
fees; another occasional schol
Strathallan School, Fordagenny, Perth PH2 9EG t
Bridge-of-Earn 232. Schol £100. G. West BA,
LRAM, AGSM
Sutton Valence School, North St, Sutton Valence,
Maidstone, Kent ME17 3HN t Sutton Valence 2281.
Inst schols, exhibs. A. G. Foulkes MA
Taunton School, Staplegrove Rd, Taunton, Somerset
TA2 6AD t Taunton 84596
Tettenhall College, Wolverhampton WV6 8QX t Wolver-
hampton 751119. 2 or 3 awards up to £300 with
free mus tuition. M. R. H. Davey FRCO, FTCL
Tonbridge School (The Music School), Kent TN9 1JP t
Tonbridge 63211. Schols totalling £1300.
John G. Cullen MA, Mus B, FRCO, ARCM
Trent College, Long Eaton, Nottingham NG10 4AD t
Long Eaton 5789. 3 schols, totalling £900;
exhibs; free mus tuition; minimum standard, Grade
5. Michael Barlow BA, ARCO, MTC (London)

Trinity College, Glenalmond, Perthshire PH1 3RY t
    Glenalmond 205; mus dir Glenalmond 300. 2 schols
    £250 each (increased in cases of need), with free
    mus tuition. N. H. C. de Jongh MA, ARCM, ARCO
Trinity School of John Whitgift, Shirley Pk, Croydon
    CR9 7AT t 01-656 9541. Inst schol pays full fees.
    David Squibb ARAM
Truro School, Trennick La, Truro, Cornwall TR1 1TH t
    Truro 2763. Organ schol. Henry Doughty GRSM, ARAM,
    ARCO
Uppingham School, Rutland, Leics LE15 9QE t Uppingham
    205. 2 schols at least £650 each with free mus
    tuition; exhibs with free mus tuition. James
    Peschek MA, Mus B, ARAM, ARCO
Wellingborough School, Northants NN8 2BX t Welling-
    borough 2427. Schols up to £400 with free tuition
    in at least 1 inst. S. F. Ostler GRSM, LRAM, ARCM
Wellington College, Crowthorne, Berks RG11 7PU t
    Crowthorne 2261; mus school Crowthorne 2639. 2
    open awards £275, £75; 3 closed awards for
    candidates from choir schools. J. G. Armstrong
    MA, B Mus, ARCO
Westminster School, Little Deans Yard, London SW1P
    3PF t 01-222 5516. Adrian Boult Schol; Arnold
    Foster Bursaries give free mus tuition. D. O.
    Byrt GRSM, ARCM
Westonbirt School (girls), Tetbury, Glos GL8 8QG t
    Tetbury 333. M. Naylor LRAM, ARCM
Whitgift School, Haling Pk, South Croydon CR2 6YT t
    01-688 9222. Schol pays full tuition. John S.
    Odom Mus B, ARCM
Winchester College, College St, Winchester, Hants
    SO23 9NA t Winchester 64951; mus school Winchester
    62769. Schols pay half fees, or more in cases of
    need, with free tuition on 1 inst; quiristerships
    pay half fees, or more in cases of need, with free
    tuition on 1 inst.
Worksop College, Welbeck, Worksop, Notts S80 3LN t
    Worksop 2286
Wrekin College, Wellington, Telford, Salop TF1 3BG t
    Wellington 44963. 2 inst or chor schols totalling
    £300 with free mus tuition. M. M. Davey MA, FRCO,
    LRAM, ARCM
Wycliffe College, Stonehouse, Glos GL10 2JQ t Stone-
    house (Glos) 2452. Inst schols, exhibs totalling
    £500 (maximum award £300), with free mus tuition
    (supplemented in cases of need). Bernard Williams
    MA, FRCO, LRAM, ARCM
Wycombe Abbey (girls), High Wycombe, Bucks HP11 1PE
    t High Wycombe 20381. Whitelaw Schol £150.
    Miss M. McKendrick LRAM, ARCM

18   Local Music Education Advisers

Extensive reorganization in the work of Local Education Authorities, consequent on the re-drawing of
boundaries, has taken place in the last few years.
Not all authorities deal with music, and with music
staff, in the same way. In addition to their responsibility for schools, most LEAs operate their own
music centres giving instrumental tuition to children
during or after school hours.
   For assistance in compiling this list of music
advisers to LEAs, the Editor is greatly indebted to
the Music Advisers' National Association (membership
secretary: Miss M. Blackwell, London Borough of
Brent, 9 Park La, Wembley, Middx HA9 7RW t 01-903
1400 **ext** 578). Where no appointment is listed,
inquiries should be directed to the Chief Executive
Officer at the address given.

*

Order of listing: London;   County Council Education
Committees (England, then Wales);   Metropolitan
Districts Education Committees (England);   Scotland;
Northern Ireland;   Isle of Man.

INNER LONDON AND GREATER LONDON

INNER LONDON EDUCATION AUTHORITY
Senior Inspector of Music   ILEA Music Centre
John Hosier MA   Ebury Bridge
                                         London SW1V 4LH
Inspector of Music   01-828 4906
G. H. H. Preston MA, ARCM

Inspector of Music
Miss A. Dennett GGSM, AGSM, LRAM

BARKING   Education Offices
Music Adviser   Town Hall
W. A. Newell B Mus, FRCO (CHM),   Barking
ARCM   01-594 3880

BARNET
Music Adviser
J. Maxwell Pryce BA (Hons), ARCM

Education Offices
Town Hall
Friern Barnet
London N11 3DL
01-368 1255

BEXLEY
Music Adviser
R. Sabor BA (Hons), LRAM

Bexley Music Centre
27 Station Rd
Sidcup DA15 7EB
01-302 1456

BRENT
Music Adviser
Miss M. Blackwell GRSM, LRAM

Education Office
Chesterfield Ho
9 Park La
Wembley
Middlesex HA9 7RW
01-903 1400 ext 531

BROMLEY
Music Adviser
L. R. Smith ARCM

Education Office
Sunnymead
Bromley La
Chislehurst BR7 6CH
01-467 5561

CROYDON
Inspector of Schools
B. E. Knight ARCM

Education Offices
Taberner Ho
Park La
Croydon CR9 1TP
01-686 4433

EALING
Music Adviser
A. Bohman ARCM, GRSM (Lond)

79-81 Uxbridge Rd
London W5 5SU
01-579 2424

ENFIELD
Music Adviser
R. Friar GRSM, ARMCM

Education Offices
Church St
Edmonton
London N9 9PD
01-807 1060

HARINGEY
Music Adviser
Miss C. Clarke B Mus, LRAM

Education Offices
Somerset Rd
Tottenham
London N17 9EH
01-808 3251

HARROW
Music Adviser
P. J. Hinkley BA Mus, L Mus,
LTCL (TTD), LGSM, ARCM

Education Offices
The Civic Centre
PO Box 22
Station Rd
Harrow HA1 2UW
01-863 5611

HAVERING
Music Adviser
Norman Dannatt FTCL, LTCL

Teachers' Centre
Annexe
Tring Gdns
Romford
Essex RM14 9QR
Ingrebourne 71481

HILLINGDON
Music Adviser
E. W. Stephenson LRAM, ARCM,
FTCL

Education Offices
38 Market Sq
High St
Uxbridge
Middlesex UB8 1AA
Uxbridge 38232

HOUNSLOW
Music Adviser
J. E. Griffiths BA, LRAM, LGSM

Education Offices
88 Lampton Rd
Hounslow
Middlesex TW3 4DW
01-570 7728

KINGSTON-UPON-THAMES
Music Adviser
A. Calvert

Kingston Teachers'
Centre
Hollyfield Rd
Surbiton
01-390 1081

MERTON
Music Adviser
Miss A. Clifford GRSM

Education Offices
Station Ho
London Rd
Morden
Surrey
01-542 8101

NEWHAM
Music Organizer
M. Toll ABSM, LRAM, ARCO

Newham Academy of
Music
Wakefield St
London E6
01-472 9895

REDBRIDGE
Music Adviser
M. J. Bidgood

Education Office
Lynton Ho
259 High Rd
Ilford
Essex IG1 1NN
01-478 3020

RICHMOND-UPON-THAMES
Music Adviser
J. W. Hugill B Mus, LRAM, ARCO

Education Offices
Regal Ho
London Rd
Twickenham
Middlesex TW1 3QB
01-892 4466

SUTTON

The Grove
High St
Carshalton
Surrey SM5 3AL
01-669 4499

WALTHAM FOREST
Music Adviser
C. Rouse

Music Centre
Teachers' Centre
Queen's Rd
London E17 8QS
01-521 2021

COUNTY COUNCIL EDUCATION COMMITTEES - ENGLAND

AVON
Senior Music Adviser
R. A. Smith FRAM, FTCL

Music Adviser
F. S. Robinson B Mus

Education Dept
Avon House North
St James Barton
Bristol BS99 7EB
Bristol 290777

BEDFORDSHIRE
General Music Adviser
M. E. Rose ARAM, FTCL, GRSM,
LRAM, ARCM

Education Offices
County Hall
Bedford
Beds MK42 9AP
Bedford 63222

BERKSHIRE
County Music Adviser
R. Noble MA, ARCM

Music Adviser
Bryn Williams B Mus, FTCL,
LRAM, LTCL

Education Offices
Shire Hall
Reading RG1 3EZ
Reading 55981

BUCKINGHAMSHIRE
Senior Music Adviser
K. R. V. Collingham ARAM, ARCM

Music Adviser
P. Smith GRSM

Education Offices
County Offices
Aylesbury HP20 1OZ
Aylesbury 5000

CAMBRIDGESHIRE
Senior Music Adviser
D. L. Young ARCM, LRAM

Music Adviser
G. N. Ratcliffe GNSM, LRAM

Education Offices
Shire Hall
Castle Hill
Cambridge CB3 OAP
Cambridge 58811

CHESHIRE
Senior Music Adviser
R. T. Mallaband FRCO

Education Offices
County Hall
Chester
Chester 603351

Music Adviser
P. Room LTCL

CLEVELAND
Music Adviser
E. M. Raymond B Mus, LRAM, ARCM

Education Offices
Woodlands Rd
Middlesborough
Teesside TS1 3BN
Middlesborough 48155

Music Adviser
P. J. Haughton B Mus, ARMCM

CORNWALL
Senior Music Adviser
H. G. Mills LRAM

Education Offices
County Hall
Truro
Cornwall
Truro 4282

Assistant Music Adviser
J. Ayerst GGSM, AGSM

CUMBRIA
Educational Music Adviser
J. Hutchings LRAM, ARCM

Education Offices
County Offices
Kendal
Cumbria LA9 4RQ
Kendal 21000

Educational Music Adviser
D. N. Parkinson GRSM, ARMCM

Education Offices
5 Portland Sq
Carlisle CA1 1PU
Carlisle 23456 ext 305

Educational Music Adviser
G. Uren BA

Education Offices
John Whinnerah
Institute
Barrow-in-Furness
LA14 1XN
Barrow-in-Furness
25500

DERBYSHIRE
Senior Music Adviser
J. A. Hudson

Education Offices
County Offices
Matlock
Derbyshire DE4 3AG
Derby 31111

Music Adviser
vacancy

DEVON
Music Adviser
J. R. Bolsover LRAM, ARCM

Education Offices
County Hall
Exeter EX2 4QG
Exeter 77977

DORSET
Senior Music Adviser
H. J. Sargent LRAM

Music Adviser
J. G. Staff GTCL

Education Offices
County Hall
Dorchester
Dorset DT1 1XJ
Dorchester 3131

DURHAM
Music Adviser
G. M. L. Hutchinson BA (Mus)

Music Adviser
T. M. Pratt B Mus

Education Offices
County Hall
Durham
Durham 4411

EAST SUSSEX
County Music Adviser
Miss N. Plummer ARCM

County Music Centre
Watergate La
Lewes BN7 1UQ
Lewes 2336/7

Assistant Area Music Advisers
(Central Area)
M. Ades, Mus B. Miss V. L. Davies

Area Music Adviser (Western
Area)
D. Gray B Mus, Dip Ed.

Assistant Area Music Adviser
(Western Area)
Miss M. M. Hart

Area Education
Offices
Royal York Bldgs
Old Steine
Brighton BN1 1NP
Brighton 29801

Area Music Adviser (Eastern
Area)
J. M. Simpson GTCL, LTCL

Assistant Area Music Adviser
(Eastern Area)
Mrs M. Spreadbury BA, LRAM

Area Education
Offices
20 Wellington Sq
Hastings TN34 1PJ
Hastings 425780

ESSEX
Senior Inspector for Music
E. W. Y. Stapleton MA, B Mus,
LRAM

Assistant County Inspector for
Music
G. Usher B Mus (Dunelm)

Education Offices
PO Box 47
Threadneedle Ho
Market Rd
Chelmsford CM1 1LD
Chelmsford 67222

GLOUCESTERSHIRE
County Music Adviser
R. W. Clifford FTCL, GTCL

Education Offices
Shire Hall
Gloucester
Gloucester 21444

Assistant Music Adviser
T. Hewitt-Jones MA (Oxon), ARCO

Gloucestershire
Community Council
College Grn
Gloucester
Gloucester 28491

HAMPSHIRE
Senior County Music Adviser
J. D. Lovelock MA

Education Offices
The Castle
Winchester SO23 8UG
Winchester 69611

County Music Adviser
R. D. Fletcher GRSM (M/C), ARMCM,
LTCL

County Music Adviser
W. B. Johnstone B Mus (Lond),
FTCL

Education Offices
6 Portland Terr
Southsea
Hants
Portsmouth 23844

HEREFORD AND WORCESTER
County Music Adviser
A. W. Benoy MA

Education Offices
County Education
Dept
Castle St
Worcester WR1 3AJ
Worcester 27131

Assistant County Music Adviser
M. F. Baker B Mus (Dunelm),
LRAM, ARCM

HERTFORDSHIRE
County Music Adviser
P. Fowler FTCL, LRAM, LLCM (T.D)

Education Offices
County Hall
Hertford
Hertford 54242

HUMBERSIDE
Music Adviser (North)
D. A. Wigley

Divisional Education
Office
Manor Rd
Beverley
N. Humberside HU17 7BH
Beverley 887251
ext 218

Music Adviser (Hull)
G. Heald-Smith GRSM, LRAM, ARCM

Teachers' Centre
Park Avenue
Hull
Hull 492899

Music Adviser (South Hull)
C. Edmondson Mus B (Dublin),
FRCO, (CHM), ARCM, LRAM

Education Dept
Cole Street Annexe
Scunthorpe
South Humberside
Scunthorpe 3563

ISLE OF WIGHT
County Music Adviser
D. J. Wickens B Mus, A Mus, TCL

County Hall
Newport
Isle of Wight PO30
1UD
Newport 4031

KENT
Inspector of Music Education
Dr Bela de Csillery

Assistant Inspector
L. R. Harverson LRAM, ARCM

Education Offices
Springfield
Maidstone
Kent ME14 2LJ
Maidstone 54371

Assistant Inspector
J. V. Martin BA

LANCASHIRE
Senior Music Adviser
B. M. Doley FTCL

Education Offices
County Hall
Preston PR1 8RJ
Preston 54868

Area Advisory Music Officer
M. Armsby MA (Hons), Music ARCO,
A Mus, TCL

Education Office
Lancaster District
Office
High St Ho
Lancaster LA1 1LB
Lancaster 63243

Area Advisory Music Officer
Miss D. Griffiths ARCM, FRCO

Area Advisory Office
121 Hornby Rd
Blackpool
Blackpool 28640

Area Advisory Music Officer
S. D. Sidgreaves B (Hons), Music
ARCM

The Area Advisory
Offices
The Lodge Edgehill
College of Education
St Helens Rd
Ormskirk
Ormskirk 76317

Area Advisory Music Officer
Miss M. Tomlinson LRAM

The County Advisory
Services
103 Preston New Rd
Blackburn
Blackburn 60877

Area Advisory Music Officer
G. Balson ARCM

Area Advisory Offices
Springfield
Todmorden Rd
Burnley
Burnley 38593

LEICESTERSHIRE   Education Offices
County Music Adviser   County Hall
A. E. Pinkett OBE, LRAM   Glenfield
                                      Leicester LE3 8RF
County Music Adviser   Leicester 871313
D. G. Davies BA, B Mus, FRCO,
LRAM

County Music Adviser
J. A. Whitworth MA (Cantab), ARCM

LINCOLNSHIRE   Education Offices
Senior Music Adviser   County Offices
G. J. Timmins BA   Newland
                                      Lincoln LN1 1YO
County Music Adviser   Lincoln 29931
R. Friar GRSM, ARMCM

County Music Adviser
Miss C. M. Watson MA, B Mus, FRCO,
ARCM

NORFOLK   Education Offices
Senior Music Adviser   County Hall
F. J. Firth B Mus (Lond), ARCM   Martineau La
                                      Norwich NOR 49A
Senior Music Adviser   Norwich 22288
S. T. Twemlow B Mus

Music Adviser
E. L. Evans GNSM, LRAM, ARCM

NORTH YORKSHIRE   Education Offices
Senior Music Adviser   County Hall
E. B. Griffiths ARCO, ARMCM,   Northallerton DL7 8AE
ARCM   Northallerton 3123

Music Adviser
R. L. Black GRSM

NORTHAMPTONSHIRE   Education Offices
Music Adviser   Northampton Ho
J. M. Tyler FRCO, LRAM   Northampton
                                      Northampton 34833
Music Adviser
G. Heard B Mus

NORTHUMBERLAND   Education Offices
General Music Adviser   Eldon Ho, Regent
J. M. Hollingworth   Centre, Newcastle
                                      upon Tyne NE3 3HZ
                                      Newcastle 850181

NOTTINGHAMSHIRE
Music Adviser
K. J. Eade B Mus, FTCL, ARCM,
LRAM

Music Adviser
D. C. McIntosh MA, B Mus

Music Adviser
vacancy

Education Offices
County Hall
West Bridgford
Nottingham NG2 7QP
Nottingham 863366

OXFORDSHIRE
Senior Music Adviser
M. Sheldon LRAM, ARCM

Music Adviser
M. Evans GRSM

Music Section
39 Park End St
Oxford
Oxford 44298

SALOP
County Music Adviser
R. N. White B Mus, LTCL

Education Offices
Shirehall
Abbey Foregate
Shrewsbury SY2 6NF
Shrewsbury 52211

SOMERSET
County Director of Music
M. Stocks BA

Education Offices
County Hall
Taunton TA1 4DY
Taunton 3451 ext 754

STAFFORDSHIRE
County Music Adviser
J. W. R. Taylor ARCM, LRAM

Music Adviser
Alex Fawcett ARCO, A Mus, TCL

Assistant Music Adviser
E. Bennett FRSM, LRAM, LTCL

Education Offices
Tipping St
Stafford
Stafford 51715

SUFFOLK
Senior Music Adviser
K. L. Shaw LTCL, ARCO

Education Offices
Shire Hall
Bury St Edmunds
Bury St Edmunds 63141

Music Adviser
D. W. Ingate B Mus, FRCO, ARCM,
LTCL

Education Offices
County Hall
Ipswich IP4 2JS
Ipswich 55801

SURREY
Inspector
E. A. Mongor ARCM

Education Dept
County Hall
Kingston-upon-Thames
Surrey KT1 2DJ
01-549 3315

Assistant Music Inspector
V. H. Briggs BA, ARCM

Education Dept
South East Area
Education Office
123 Blackborough Rd
Reigate
Surrey
Redhill 66441

Assistant Music Inspector
Mrs J. Scowen-King GRSM, ARCM

Education Dept
Central Area
Education Office
Bridge Ho
Bridge St
Leatherhead KT22 8HW
Leatherhead 77901

WARWICKSHIRE
Ccunty Music Adviser
D. H. Jones Mus B

Education Offices
22 Northgate St
Warwick CV34 4SR
Warwick 43431

WEST SUSSEX
Ccunty Music Adviser
J. G. Atkins LRAM, LTCL (CMT)

Education Offices
County Hall
West St
Chichester PO19 1RE
Chichester 85100

WILTSHIRE
County Music Adviser
vacancy

County Hall
By the Sea Rd
Trowbridge BA14 8YA
Trowbridge 3541

Music Adviser
D. H. Morris LRAM, L Mus, TCL

Wiltshire Rural Music
School
113 Gloucester Rd
Trowbridge
Wilts
Trowbridge 3175

Music Adviser
W. I. Davies B Mus

Education Sub-Office
Wyvern Ho
Theatre Sq
Swindon
Wilts
Swindon 26161

COUNTY COUNCIL EDUCATION COMMITTEES - WALES

CLWYD
Senior Music Adviser
D. Roland Morris BA, B Mus, LRAM

County Music Adviser
R. Williams Mus B, BA, FRCO

Education Offices
Education Dept
Shire Hall
Mold CH7 6ND
Mold 2121

DYFED
County Music Adviser
Alan W. Jones BA

County Education
Office
Swyddfa'r Sir
Aberystwyth

County Music Adviser
Elwyn Jones ARMCM, ARCO

County Music Adviser
Gethin Jones LRAM

Education Offices
County Hall
Carmarthen SA31 1JP
Carmarthen 4251/4261

GWENT
County Music Adviser
Glynne Jones BA

Assistant Music Adviser
A. Barton

Education Dept
County Hall
Cwmbran
Gwent NP4 2XE
Cwmbran 67711

GWYNEDD
County Music Adviser
J. Arwyn Jones

Education Offices
County Hall
Llangefni Ynys Mon
Gwynedd

County Music Adviser
Hywel Williams

County Education
Offices
Dolgellau
Gwynedd

MID GLAMORGAN
County Music Adviser
D. G. Francis BA, LRAM

County Offices
Cathays Pk
Cardiff CF1 3NF
Cardiff 28033

POWYS
County Music Adviser
Eric Jones FTCL, ARCM, LTCL

Education Offices
County Hall
Llandrindod Wells
LD1 5LE
Llandrindod Wells 2816

Music Adviser
Mrs E. Ogwen Thomas Mus Bac

Education Office
6 Glamorgan St
Brecon, Powys
Brecon 2206/8

SOUTH GLAMORGAN
County Music Adviser
D. Arwyn Jones BA, LRAM

Education Office
South Glamorgan
Municipal Offices
Kingsway
Cardiff CF1 4JG
Cardiff 31033

WEST GLAMORGAN
County Music Adviser
J. Jenkins

Education Offices
Princess Ho
Princess Way
Swansea SA1 4PD
Swansea 42024

METROPOLITAN DISTRICTS EDUCATION COMMITTEES

BARNSLEY, *S. Yorks*
Music Adviser
Miss V. Potter GTCL

Education Offices
50 Huddersfield Rd
Barnsley S75 1DP
Barnsley 87621

BIRMINGHAM, *W. Midlands*
Music Adviser
P. N. Davies B Mus

225 Bristol Rd
Birmingham B5 7UB
021-440 4111

Assistant Music Adviser
A. le Fleming

BOLTON, *Gtr Manchester*
Music Adviser
R. G. Carter BA

Education Offices
PO Box 53
Victoria Ho
Civic Centre
Bolton BL1 1JW
Bolton 22311

BRADFORD, *W. Yorks*
General and Music Adviser
A. R. Knight BA

Education Offices
31-39 Piccadilly
Bradford BD1 3TA
Bradford 34866
ext 259

General and Music Adviser
B. Cryer GRSM (Lond), LRAM, ARCM

BURY, *Gtr Manchester*
Music Adviser
R. J. Wynn Davies LRAM, ARCM

Education Offices
Athenaeum Ho
Market St
Bury
Lancs BL9 0SW
061-761 5121 ext 829

CALDERDALE, *W. Yorks*
Music Adviser
D. Maxwell-Timmins LRAM, ARCM

Education Offices
Alexandra Bldgs
King Edward St

Halifax
Halifax 57133

COVENTRY, *W. Midlands*
Music Adviser
P. L. Isherwood MA

Coventry School of
Music
Percy St
Coventry CV1 3BY
Coventry 23803

DONCASTER, *S. Yorks*
Music Organizer
G. F. Gentry AGSM

Education Offices
Princegate
Doncaster DN1 3EP
Yorks
Doncaster 49211

DUDLEY, *W. Midlands*
Music Adviser
D. I. Lewis LRAM, LTCL

Education Offices
23 St James's Rd
Dudley
Worcestershire DY1 3JQ
Dudley 55271/55433

GATESHEAD, *Tyne & Wear*
Music Organizer
C. L. W. Barratt BA, GRSM (Lond)
LRAM, ARCM, LTCL, FRSA

Education Offices
Prince Consort Rd S.
Gateshead NE8 4LP
Co Durham
Gateshead 783031/40

KIRKLEES, *W. Yorks*
Music Adviser
C. A. Browning BA

Music Adviser
Miss E. M. Gill

Education Offices
Civic Centre
High St
Huddersfield
Yorks HD1 2NE
Huddersfield 22133

KNOWSLEY, *Merseyside*
Adviser Music/Drama
P. Morris Dip Mus

Education Offices
Council Offices
Archway Rd
Huyton L36 9UX
051-486 8711

LEEDS, *W. Yorks*
Music/Senior Adviser
R. E. Rimmer GRSM, ARCM, ARMCM

Music/General Adviser
W. C. Hart BA, B Mus

Music/General Adviser
P. V. Greenwood B Mus, LRAM

Education Offices
Calverley St
Leeds LS1 3AE
Leeds 446231

LIVERPOOL, *Merseyside*   Education Offices
Adviser for Music   14 Sir Thomas St
K. Miles B Mus, LRAM   Liverpool L1 6BJ
                                   051-236 5480

Assistant Adviser for Music
M. G. Bush

Organizer, Youth Music   42 Bluecoat Chambers
Committee   School La
R. Mulholland   Liverpool L1 3BX

MANCHESTER, *Gtr Manchester*   Education Offices
Senior District Inspector -   Crown Sq
Music   Manchester M60 3BB
J. V. Fox MA, LRAM, ARCM, LGSM   061-228 2191 ext 7254

NEWCASTLE UPON TYNE, *Tyne & Wear* Teachers' Centre
Music Adviser   Pendower Hall
D. P. Marshall FTCL, LTCL (CMT),   West Rd
LRAM, ARCM   Newcastle upon Tyne
                                   NE15 6PP
                                   Newcastle upon Tyne
                                   30811

NORTH TYNESIDE, *Tyne & Wear*   Education Offices
Music Adviser   The Chase
N. A. Bonfield LRAM, LTCL (CMT)   North Shields NE29 OHW
                                   North Shields 76621

OLDHAM, *Gtr Manchester*   Education Offices
Music Adviser   Old Town Hall
J. B. Boyce   Chadderton
                                   Oldham
                                   Lancs
                                   061-633 2181

ROCHDALE, *Gtr Manchester*   Education Offices
Music Adviser   Municipal Offices
G. K. Millington B Mus, LRAM   Manchester Old Rd
                                   Middleton M24 4EA
Assistant Music Adviser   Lancs
vacancy   061-643 5541

ROTHERHAM, *S. Yorks*   Education Offices
General Music Adviser   Municipal Offices
D. Ragsdale LRAM, ARCM, FTCL   Howard St
                                   Rotherham
                                   Yorks S60 1QR
                                   Rotherham 2121

ST HELENS, *Merseyside*
Music Adviser
R. K. Tindley LTCL

Education Offices
Century Ho
Hardshaw St
St Helens
Lancs
St Helens 24061

SALFORD, *Gtr Manchester*
Senior Adviser
J. Fryer BA

Education Offices
Chapel St
Salford
Lancs M3 5LT
061-832 9751

SANDWELL, *W. Midlands*
Music Adviser
W. S. Johnson A Mus, LCM, LTCL,
LGSM

Education Offices
Highfields
West Bromwich
Staffs
021-569 2547

SEFTON, *Merseyside*
General Music Adviser
M. A. E. Burton FRCO, ARCM

Local Education
Office
46 Hoghton St
Southport
Merseyside
Southport 33133
ext 125/178

SHEFFIELD, *S. Yorks*
Music Adviser
D. A. Clover D Mus, LRAM, GTCL

Education Offices
PO Box 67
Leopold St
Sheffield S1 1PJ
Sheffield 26341

SOLIHULL, *W. Midlands*
General Inspector with respon-
sibility for Music
S. J. Gill LRAM, LTCL

Education Offices
The Council Ho
PO Box 20
Solihull
Warwickshire
021-705 6789

SOUTH TYNESIDE, *Tyne & Wear*
General Adviser with respon-
sibility for Music
L. T. Whaley LTCL

Education Offices
Town Hall
Jarrow
South Tyneside
Jarrow 898271

STOCKPORT, *Gtr Manchester*
Education Music Adviser
P. Harle LTCL

Education Offices
Town Hall
Stockport
061-480 4949

SUNDERLAND, *Tyne & Wear*   Education Offices
Music Adviser   Town Hall
H. A. Tye LTCL   Civic Centre
                                         Sunderland SR2 7DN
                                         Sunderland 76161

TAMESIDE, *Gtr Manchester*   Education Offices
General Music Adviser   Town Hall
P. M. Tweddell BA (Dunelm),   Dukinfield
ARCM   Cheshire SK16 4LA
                                         061-330 8300

TRAFFORD, *Gtr Manchester*   Education Offices
Music Adviser   Town Hall
M. J. Farrington LRAM, ARCM   Sale
                                         Cheshire M33 1XF
                                         061-973 2253

WAKEFIELD, *W. Yorks*   Education Offices
Music Adviser   8 Bond St
C. Matthews BA, ARMCM, LRAM,   Wakefield
ARCM   Yorks WF1 2GL
                                         Wakefield 75234

WALSALL, *W. Midlands*   Education Development
Adviser   Centre
J. Jethro Ingram M Mus   Aldridge Ct
                                         Little Aston Rd
                                         Aldridge W59 ONN
                                         Aldridge 54728

WIGAN, *Gtr Manchester*   Education Offices
Music Adviser   Civic Centre
E. G. Newton   Millgate
                                         Wigan WN1 1YD
                                         Wigan 44991

WIRRAL, *Merseyside*   Education Offices
Senior Music Adviser   Municipal Offices
N. Lythgoe ARMCM   Cleveland St
                                         Birkenhead L41 6NH
                                         051-647 7000

WOLVERHAMPTON, *W. Midlands*   Education Offices
Inspector of Schools - Music   St John Sq
J. S. Barker ARCM, LTCL, (CMT)   Wolverhampton WV2 4DB
                                         Wolverhampton 27811

SCOTLAND

ABERDEEN, *City*
Organizer of Music
T. F. Devine Dip Mus Ed, RSAM

Adviser in Music
D. Hawksworth

Education Offices
St Nicholas Ho
Broad St
Aberdeen AB9 1AG
Aberdeen 23456

ABERDEEN, *County*
County Music Supervisor
J. L. Wilson MA, LRAM, ARCM,
LTCL

Education Offices
County Bldgs
22 Union Terr
Aberdeen AB9 1HJ
Aberdeen 23444

County Music Adviser
vacancy

Education Offices
Woodhill Ho
Ash Grove Rd West
Aberdeen
Aberdeen 23401

ANGUS
County Music Organizer
R. Evans MA, Dip Ed (Oxon),
ARCM

Education Offices
County Bldgs
Forfar
Angus DD8 3LF
Forfar 3661

ARGYLL, *County*
County Music Adviser
R. C. Cowieson

Advisory Centre
Hillfoot St
Dunoon
Argyll
Dunoon 4418

AYRSHIRE
County Music Adviser
W. T. Berry, Dip Mus Ed, RSAM,
LRAM

Adviser in Music
J. Clark

Education Offices
Newton Centre
Green St La
Ayr RA8 8BH
Ayr 60325

BANFF, *County*
County Music Organizer
H. Edwards BA (Hons), Dip Ed,
LRAM

Education Offices
Keith
Banffshire AB5 3EJ
Keith 2281

County Music Adviser
B. Anderson

BERWICK, *County*

Education offices
Southfield
Duns TD11 3EN

BUTE, *County*   County Offices
                                      Mount Pleasant Rd
                                      Rothesay PA20 9AH

CAITHNESS   Education Office
                                      Rhind Ho
                                      Wick KW1 5LZ

CLACKMANNAN   County Offices
County Music Adviser   Viewforth
E. J. B. Catto LRAM, ARCM   Stirling
                                      Stirling 3111

DUMFRIES AND GALLOWAY   Education Offices
Adviser in Music   27 Moffat Rd
R. K. Brown B Mus, ARCO   Dumfries
                                      Dumfries 4222
Adviser in Music
C. Fox Dip Mus Ed, RSAM

Adviser in Music (Stranraer   Education Offices
Division)   Market St
A. Leiper   Stranraer DG9 7RG
                                      Stranraer 2151

DUMBARTONSHIRE   Education Offices
County Supervisor of Music   County Council Offices
J. Pickup   Dumbarton
                                      Dumbarton 5151

DUNDEE   Teachers' Centre
Adviser in Music   Seymour Lodges
A. A. Souter LRAM   Perth Rd
                                      Dundee
Assistant Adviser in Music   Dundee 69371
T. Devine Dip Mus Ed, RSAM

EAST LOTHIAN   Education Office
                                      County Bldgs
                                      Haddington EH41 3HQ

EDINBURGH   Dean Education Centre
Adviser in Music   Belford Rd
J. B. Watson LRAM, ARCM   Edinburgh EH4 3DS
                                      031-332 7947

FIFE   County Offices
County Organizer of Music   Wemyssfield
D. L. Merchant B Mus   Kirkcaldy
                                      Fife KY1 1XS
Assistant County Organizer of   Kirkcaldy 62351
Music
R. Galloway

GLASGOW   Education Offices
Adviser in Music   129 Bath St
I. Barrie MA, B Mus, FRCO, LRAM   Glasgow G2 2SY
                                        041-221 9600
Assistant Adviser in Music
J. McAdam B Mus, FRCO

INVERNESS   Education Offices
County Music Organizer   County Bldgs
A. Curtis Craig MA, LTCL   Ardross St
                                        Inverness
                                        Inverness 34121

KINCARDINESHIRE   Education Offices
                                        Stonehaven AB3 2DQ

KINROSS (see Perthshire)

KIRKCUDBRIGHT   Education Offices
County Music Organizer   Castle Douglas
C. Fox Dip Mus Ed, RSAM   Kirkcudbright
                                        Castle Douglas 2351

LANARK, *County*   Education Offices
Organizer in Music   County Bldgs
vacancy   Hamilton
                                        Lanark ML3 QAE
                                        Hamilton 21100

MIDLOTHIAN   Education Offices
Organizer of Music   New County Bldgs
A. R. Kerr Dip Mus Ed, RSAM   George IV Bridge
                                        Edinburgh EH1 1HQ
                                        031-225 2562

MORAY AND NAIRN   Education Offices
County Music Organizer   County Bldgs
G. R. Wiseman MA (Hons)   Elgin
                                        Elgin 3451

ORKNEY   Education Office
County Music Adviser   Kirkwall KW15 1HH
E. Holt FTCL, ARCM   Kirkwall 3141

PEEBLESHIRE   County Bldgs
                                        Peebles EH45 8HG

PERTHSHIRE AND KINROSS   Perth & Kinross Joint
Supervisor of Music   County Council Offices
D. Eoin Bennett Dip Mus Ed,   York Pl
RSAM, LRAM, ARCM   Perth
                                        Perth 21222

RENFREWSHIRE
County Music Organizer
F. W. Ladds LRAM, ARCM, LTCL

County Education
Office
16 Glasgow Rd
Paisley PA1 1LE
041-889 5454

ROSS AND CROMARTY
County Music Adviser
A. Brocklebank LRAM, LTCL

Education Offices
County Bldgs
Dingwall
Ross-shire IV15 9HU
Dingwall 3444

ROXBURGH, *County*
County Music Organizer
J. Brian Bonsor LRAM

Education Offices
Newtown St Boswells
Newtown St Boswells
3301

SELKIRK
County Music Organizer
J. Brian Bonsor LRAM

Education Offices
Thorniedean
Melrose Rd
Galashiels
Selkirkshire
Galashiels 2888

SHETLAND (see Zetland)

STIRLINGSHIRE
Adviser in Music
G. C. McVicar Dip Mus Ed, RSAM,
FTSC

County Offices
Viewforth
Stirling
Stirling 3111

SUTHERLAND
County Music Organizer
F. P. Miller LRAM, ALCM

Education Offices
Brora
Brora 382

WEST LOTHIAN
County Organizer of Music
R. S. Weir Dip Mus Ed, RSAM

Education Offices
County Bldgs
Linlithgow EH49 7HB
Linlithgow 3121

WIGTOWN, *County*
County Music Organizer
A. Leiper

Education Offices
Market St
Stranraer DG9 7RG
Stranraer 2151

ZETLAND, *County*
County Music Organizer
H. McB. Stevenson Dip Mus Ed,
RSAM, LGSM, LTCL

Education Office
Brentham Pl
Lerwick
Shetland AB3 OLS
Lerwick 822

NORTHERN IRELAND

BELFAST
Music Adviser
vacancy

Belfast Education and
Library Board
40 Academy St
Belfast BT1 2NQ
Belfast 2911

NORTH-EASTERN EDUCATION AND
LIBRARY BOARD
Music Adviser
J. M. Fletcher FLCM, LLCM

Deputy Music Adviser
D. Liddle ARMCM, GRMCM

N. E. Education &
Library Board
County Hall
182 Galgorm Rd
Ballymena
Co Antrim BT42 1HN
Ballymena 3333

SOUTHERN EDUCATION AND LIBRARY
BOARD
Music Adviser
R. E. Blake

Deputy Music Adviser
R. Jarvis

S. Education and
Library Board
Charlemont Pl
The Hall
Armagh
Armagh 2441

SOUTH EASTERN EDUCATION AND
LIBRARY BOARD
Music Adviser
D. A. Newham LRAM

S. E. Education and
Library Board
18 Windsor Av
Belfast BT9 6EF
Belfast 2911

WESTERN EDUCATION AND LIBRARY
BOARD
Music Adviser
A. Bell LRAM

Deputy Music Adviser
D. Asater

W. Education and
Library Board
Campsie Rd
Omagh

ISLE OF MAN

DOUGLAS
Instrumental Co-ordinator
B. G. F. Osborne ARCM

Isle of Man Board of
Education
Strand St
Douglas
Isle of Man
Douglas 3406

19   Youth Orchestras and Bands

The following list shows *national* youth orchestras and bands only. Most local education authorities have established local youth orchestras; inquiries can be made either to the local education offices (see p. 182), or to the National Association of Youth Orchestras (secretary J. W. Babb, 30 Park Dr, Grimsby, Lincs DN32 OEG t South Humberside 78002). Various courses for young orchestral players are sponsored by the Schools Music Association (see p. 81) and the Rural Music Schools Association (see p. 168).

Inquiries for school brass bands may be made to Charles Sweby, National School Brass Band Association, 2 Gray's Clo, Barton-le-Clay, Bedford MK45 4PH t Luton 881560.

British Youth Symphony Orchestra. S. A. Andrews, *dir*. 17 Eight Bells Clo, Buxted, Sussex TN22 4JT t Buxted 2369; K. Brown, *dir*. 6 Tennis Ct Av, Huntingdon PE18 6RW t Huntingdon 54727

British Youth Wind Orchestra. Michael Toll, *hon course dir*. 6 Woodpond Av, Hockley, Essex SS5 4PX t Hockley 4565

National Youth Brass Band of Great Britain. D. S. Reakes, *sec*. 67 Yarningale Rd, Birmingham B14 6LT t 021-444 1164

National Youth Brass Band of Scotland. James Easson MBE, *sec*. Scottish Amateur Music Association, 7 Randolph Cres, Edinburgh EH3 7TE t 031-225 7592

National Youth Jazz Orchestra of Great Britain. Bill Ashton, *sec*. 11 Victor Rd, Harrow, Middx HA2 6PT t 01-863 2717

National Youth Orchestra of Great Britain. Simon E. Allfree, *admintr*. 94 Park La, Croydon, Surrey CRO 1JB t 01-686 6237

National Youth Orchestra of Wales. D. Andrew Davies, *sec*. 245 Western Av, Cardiff CF5 2YX t Cardiff 561231

National Youth String Orchestra of Scotland. James Easson MBE, *sec*. Scottish Amateur Music Association, 7 Randolph Cres, Edinburgh EH3 7TE t 031-225 7592

National Youth Wind Band of Scotland. James Easson MBE, *sec*. Scottish Amateur Music Association, 7 Randolph Cres, Edinburgh EH3 7TE t 031-225 7592

20 Youth Concession Schemes

City of Birmingham Symphony Orchestra, 60 Newhall St, Birmingham B3 3RP t 021-236 1556: those under 18 and all full-time students may join the junior CBSO for £1 pa and buy concert tickets with up to 25p reduction

Ernest Read Music Association (ERMA), 143 King Henry's Rd, London NW3 3RD t 01-722 3020. Children's concerts at the Royal Festival Hall and Purcell Room; Saturdays

Friends of the SNO, c/o Scottish National Orchestra Society Ltd, 150 Hope St, Glasgow G2 2TH t 041-332 7244

Hallé Concerts Soc, 30 Cross St, Manchester M2 7BA t 061-834 8363: 50% transport subsidy scheme for parties (min 10), for those living in North West Arts Association area, to attend Hallé concerts in Manchester. Also special concessions for school parties

Haslemere Festival, Jesses, Grayswood Rd, Haslemere, Surrey GU27 2BS t Haslemere 3818: concerts for schools and young people, tickets 35p

Junior Western Orchestral Soc, Westover Mansions, Gervis Pl, Bournemouth BH1 2AW t Bournemouth 20363: half-price admission to any concert for £1.50 pa if living within a 15-mile radius of Bournemouth and for £1 if living outside this radius. Tickets at half-price for Society-promoted events. School parties (min 10 pupils) can obtain tickets at half-price

Kaleidoscope Music for Children, 52 King Henry's Rd, London NW3 3RP t 01-722 0945: family concerts, with short programmes specially designed for 4-11 year-olds, given by top professional ensembles. Reasonable prices for children

Liverpool Philharmonic Club, Philharmonic Hall, Hope St, Liverpool L1 9BP t 051-709 2895 (sec David Davies): subscription £1.50, persons under 18 £1

London Philharmonic Soc, 53 Welbeck St, London W1M 7HE t 01-486 9771 (membership sec Mrs Anne H. Neill): has a junior section for those under 18

London Union of Youth Clubs, St Anne's Ho, Venn St, London SW4 0BW t 01-622 4347 (sec Miss Virginia Blackmore-Reed): the Greater London Arts Association is subsidizing schemes by which live professional music and theatre are made available to young people at greatly reduced cost

Morley College, 61 Westminster Bridge Rd, London SE1 7HT t 01-928 8501: 'family concerts' at reduced prices for family parties

Northern Arts, 31 New Bridge St, Newcastle upon Tyne NE1 8JY: under-21 ticket voucher scheme. 15p off seats at over 25p

Northern Sinfonia Orchestra, Osborne Ho, 28 Osborne Rd, Newcastle upon Tyne NE2 2BS t Newcastle upon Tyne 811366/815500: Saturday morning children's concerts, seats 25p, 30p

Robert Mayer Concerts, c/o BBC, 156 Gt Portland St, London W1N 6AJ t 01-580 4468 ext 4522. 6 Royal Festival Hall concerts designed for children aged 8-12; season tickets, £3, £2.50

Sadler's Wells Theatre, Promotions Dept, Rosebery Av, London EC1R 4TN t 01-278 6563: cheap admission to most productions one hour before curtain, for children and students

Ulster Orchestra, 26 Antrim Rd, Belfast BT15 2AA t Belfast 749201/2: vouchers for those under 25 to obtain certain tickets at 50% reduction

Wavendon Allmusic Plan, Junior Section (Junior WAP), The Stables, Wavendon, Milton Keynes MK17 8LT t Milton Keynes 582522: for 5-15 yr olds; cheaper tickets for many concerts and prior booking facilities

Young Friends of Covent Garden, Royal Opera House, London WC2E 7QA t 01-240 1200: those under 26 may join for £2.50 instead of £7 pa and obtain tickets at reduced prices

Youth and Music, 22 Blomfield St, London EC2M 7AP t 01-588 4714 (founded by Sir Robert Mayer): events for members (aged 14-25) at concessionary prices; grants to enable outstanding young performers to participate in international competitions, and youth orchestras and choirs to perform abroad. Affiliated to International Federation of Jeunesses Musicales. Other centres to be established in Manchester, Liverpool, Birmingham, Sheffield, Newcastle upon Tyne

21 Individual Tuition

There is no official or recognized register of individual music teachers in Britain. Many of the better teachers, however, are members of the Incor-

porated Society of Musicians (see p. 80). The
honorary local secretaries, listed below, will be
pleased to give advice.

LONDON
Bromley. C. I. W. Fackrell, 81 Riefield Rd, London
    SE9 2RB t 01-850 6588
Croydon. D. Pearn, 78 Mount Pk Av, South Croydon CR2
    6DJ t 01-660 5960
London. L. H. F. Smith, 24 Tilsworth Rd, Wattleton
    Pk, Beaconsfield, Bucks HP9 1TR t Beaconsfield 4412

ABERDEEN. Miss Madge Lamont, 62a Hamilton Pl,
    Aberdeen AB2 4BA t Aberdeen 26407
BIRMINGHAM. Miss Margery Elliott, 58 Oakham Rd,
    Harborne, Birmingham B17 9DG t 021-427 1020
BOURNEMOUTH. Mrs Joyce Pearce, 75 Keith Rd, Bourne-
    mouth BH3 7DT t Bournemouth 58110
BRIGHTON. Miss Mary Cadogan, Flat 2, 9 Royal Cres,
    Brighton BN2 1AL
BRISTOL. Miss Enid Hunt LRAM, LTCL, ARCO, 13 Clare
    Rd, Bristol BS6 5TB t Bristol 45676
CAMBRIDGE. Miss Jean Robson, 10 Park Terr, Cambridge
    CB1 1JH t Cambridge (Cambs) 52181
CARDIFF. Roy Bohana MBE, Welsh Arts Council, 9
    Museum Pl, Cardiff CF1 3NX t Cardiff 394711
CHELTENHAM. Miss Edwina Hart, 48 Albemarle Gate,
    Cheltenham GL50 4PJ t Cheltenham 29454
CORNWALL. Alan Hall, Melody Ho, Baldhu, Truro,
    Cornwall TR3 6EG t Three Waters 605
COVENTRY. Alexander Youngman, School House Stables,
    Dunchurch Rd, Rugby, Warks CV22 6AQ t Rugby 72553
DARLINGTON. T. I. Phizacklea, 130 Grange Rd, Hartle-
    pool, Co Durham TS26 8JJ t Hartlepool 3850
DERBY. Wallace Ross, 46 Park Gro, Derby DE3 1HF t
    Derby 47251
DEVON. Miss Margaret Rawlings, 3 Trunfield Av,
    Exmouth, Devon EX8 3JU t Exmouth 72754
DUNDEE. Mrs H. M. Brown, 23 Renny Cres, Montrose,
    Angus DD10 9EW
EAST KENT. Colin Samuel, 11 Whitstable Rd, Faversham,
    Kent ME13 8BE t Faversham 3305
EDINBURGH. Colin Tipple, Fettes College, Edinburgh
    EH4 1QX t 031-332 2281
GLASGOW AND WEST OF SCOTLAND. Miss Ellinor Culbert,
    5a Central Av, Cambuslang, Glasgow G72 8AX t
    041-641 3708
HASTINGS. Miss Marjorie Isaac, 271 London Rd, St
    Leonard's-on-Sea, Sussex TN37 6NB
HUDDERSFIELD. Miss Dorothy Bergan, 4 Jackroyd La,

Huddersfield HD4 6QU t Huddersfield 31794
HULL. Mrs Doreen Stephenson, Old Forge Ho, 14 Main
St, Hutton Cranswick, Driffield, N Humberside
IPSWICH. K. C. Griffiths, Ipswich School, 25 Henley
Rd, Ipswich IP1 35G t Ipswich 55313
KENDAL. J. P. Dowell LRAM, ARCM, 58 Croft Av, Penrith,
Cumbria CA11 7RL
LEEDS. Miss Christine Brown, 10a Chandos Gdns, Leeds
LS8 1LW t Leeds 664043
LEICESTER. Miss Kathleen Warner, Holmwood, College
Av, Leicester LE2 OJF t Leicester 59461
LINCOLN. Miss Cynthia Watson MA, B Mus, FRCO, ARCM,
2 Field Cl, Nettleham, Lincoln LN2 2RX t Nettleham
640
LIVERPOOL. Albert Griffiths, 117 Childwall Rd,
Liverpool L15 6UR t 051-722 6288
MANCHESTER. Miss Vera Waterhouse, The Grange, Stock-
port Rd, Lydgate, Oldham, Lancs OL4 4JJ t Saddle-
worth 2693
MID-LANCS. Mrs Irene Westmoreland, 9 Inglewood Clo,
Warton, Preston t Freckleton 633846
NEWCASTLE. Hermann McLeod, 66 Queen's Rd, Newcastle
upon Tyne NE2 2PR t Newcastle upon Tyne 811906
NORTHERN IRELAND. Frederick Haughton FTSC, LTCL, MRST,
39 South Pde, Ormeau Rd, Belfast BT7 2GL t Belfast
641086
NORTH WALES. Mrs Peggy Williams, Orchard End,
Meliden Rd, Prestatyn, Clwyd LL19 8RL t Prestatyn
3658
NORWICH. Miss Gwendoline Lee ARCM, LRAM, 161 Earlham
Rd, Norwich NA2 3RG t Norwich 53438
NOTTINGHAM. Mrs Shirley Bexon, 10 The Lawns, Wood-
hill Rd, Collingham nr Newark, Notts NG23 7NR t
Newark 892576
OXFORD. Hugo Langrish, Radley College, Abingdon,
Oxon OX14 2HR t Abingdon 20294
PORTSMOUTH. Mrs E. M. Wood, 4 Bury Cres, Gosport,
Hants PO12 3TZ t Gosport 83579
READING. Stuart Marston Smith, Bearwood Coll, 1
Orchard View, Sindlesham, Wokingham RG11 5BG t
Brookside 8317
SHEFFIELD. Miss Margaret Long LRAM, ARCM, 52 Whirlow-
dale Rd, Sheffield S7 2NH t Sheffield 362973
SOUTHAMPTON. Miss Freda Ferguson, 20 Atherley Rd,
Southampton SO1 5DQ t Southampton 22305
SOUTHEND. Mrs Olive Redfarn, 15 Warwick Rd, Southend-
on-Sea SS1 3BN t Thorpe Bay 588772
STOKE-ON-TRENT. Mrs Margaret Howle, Westwood, Palmers
Grn, Hartshill, Stoke-on-Trent t Stoke-on-Trent
63375
SWANSEA. Miss Megan Jones, 34 Brynmead Cl, Tycoch,
Swansea SA2 9EY t Swansea 26702

TORQUAY. Mrs Wanda Radford, 58 Milton St, Brixham,
   Devon TQ5 OAR
WORCESTER. Geoffrey B. Stanley, 2 Penmanor Cl,
   Worcester WR2 5QA t Worcester 21827

22 Recreational Courses

Non-academic courses held in holidays, at weekends,
in the evenings, etc, are listed here in alphabetical
order of the organizing body, followed by the address
for applications, the venue (if different from the
first address), the nature of the course (if specific),
and the approximate dates. Indications of time of
year are subject to variation. Music may also be
included in summer schools offered by university
music departments (p. 86) or extra-mural departments
(p. 165), and by the University of London Institute
of Education, Malet St, London WC1 7HS t 01-636 1500.
The central office of the Workers' Educational Association (p. 167) provides on request a list of
summer schools run by its local branches on various
subjects including music.
   Music courses lasting less than four weeks for
teachers, held in vacation and in term, are organized
by the Department of Education and Science (Short
Courses for Teachers, DES, Elizabeth Ho, York Rd,
London SE1 7PH t 01-928 9222 ext 3185) and the Educational Development Association (Arnold W. Zimmermann,
sec., 8 Windmill Gdns, Enfield, Middx EN2 7DU).
   Announcements of programmes, etc., for major annual
courses are to be found in the issues of the *Musical
Times* and *Music and Musicians* from January each
year; weekend and similar courses are often advert-
ised in the *New Statesman*. For a comprehensive list
of summer schools, see the February issue of *Music
Teacher*. The National Institute of Adult Education
publishes information about residential short courses,
including music courses.

Airedale and Wharfedale College of Further Education,
   Calverley La, Horsforth, Leeds LS18 4RQ t Horsforth
   87234. 'Music at Ilkley': str and wind; Jul
Alston Hall, Longridge, Preston, Lancs PR3 3BP t
   Longridge 3589. Appreciation, chmbr mus; Jul-Aug.
   Also redrs; Apr. Sgrs; Jul
Annual Holiday for String Players, 82 Brightfield Rd,
   London SE12 8QF t 01-852 7962. Springfield Ct, Rye,
   Sussex; Mar-Apr

Arvon Foundation, Totleigh Barton, Sheepwash, Bea-
worthy, Devon EX21 5NS t Black Torrington 338.
Sheepwash, Devon and Hebden Bridge, W. Yorks.
Courses in composition etc. organized through
schools, colleges; open jazz courses
Attingham Park, Shrewsbury, Salop SY4 4TN t Shrewsbury
77255. Mar-Apr
Beamish Hall, Stanley, Co Durham DH9 0RG t Stanley
3147. History, performance
Belstead House, Ipswich, Suffolk IP8 3NA t Ipswich
56321. Orch, inst, appreciation; Feb, May, Jun
Brant Broughton Residential Centre, Brant Broughton,
Lincs LN5 0SL t Fulbeck 200. Gtr and other; Aug,
Dec
British Federation of Music Festivals, 106 Gloucester
Pl, London W1H 3DB t 01-935 6371. Downe House,
Newbury, Berks and elsewhere; school mus, school
orch, pno, chmbr mus, gtr, sgrs; Jul, Aug
Burton Manor, Burton, Neston, Ches L64 5SJ t 051-336
2262. Jun, Sep
Butlin's Adventure in Education Weeks, 21 Southern-
hay West, Exeter EX1 1PR t Exeter 59619. Barry,
Minehead and other centres available for off-season
hire by children's groups with adult leader's assist-
ed by Butlin's staff and specialist instructors;
choice of activities includes music; Mar-May
Cambridge Ward Method Centre Vacation Music Courses,
Newnham College, Cambridge CB3 9DF t Cambridge
62273. Primary school class music; Aug
Cambridgeshire Education Committee, Gazeley Ho,
Huntingdon PE18 6NS t Huntingdon 52181. Orton
Hall, nr Peterborough; Jul
Canford Summer School of Music, 250 Purley Way,
Croydon CR9 4QD t 01-681 0855. Hurstpierpoint
College, Sussex; Aug
Canterbury Cathedral, Chapter Office, 8 The Pre-
cincts, Canterbury, Kent CT1 2EE t Canterbury
63135. Brass and choral; Aug
Caversham Adult Education Centre, Mansbridge Ho,
College Rd, Reading, Berks RG6 1QB t Reading
477646. Missenden Abbey, Bucks; orch playing;
Easter
Choir Courses, 96 Bustlehome La, West Bromwich, Staffs
B71 3AW t 021-588 2822. Various courses for
choristers and choirmasters
Cleveland Technical College, Corporation Rd, Redcar
TS10 1EZ t Redcar 2518. Orch; Easter
Coleg Harlech, Merioneth LL46 2UA t Harlech 363/561.
Aug
Concordia Enterprises, 52 Ravensdale Av, London N12
9HT t 01-445 7891. Musical wknds at Middle Aston

House, Oxon; May, Oct

Consort of Musicke Summer School, Flat B, 6 Harvist Rd, London NW6 6SD t 01-969 0474. Halsway Manor; Jul

Country-wide Holidays Association, Birch Heys, Cromwell Range, Manchester M14 6HU t 061-224 2887/8; choir, orch, chmbr mus; Jul, Sep

Dalcroze Society Inc, 16 Heathcroft, Hampstead Way, London NW11 7HH t 01-455 1268. Dalcroze eurhythmics wknd; Apr

Darlington College of Technology, Cleveland Av, Darlington, Co Durham DL3 7BB t Darlington 67651. Operatic and other; Mar, Apr, Jul-Aug

Debden House, Debden Grn, Loughton, Essex IG10 2NZ t 01-508 3008

Dillington House, Ilminster, Somerset TA19 9DZ t Ilminster 2427. Orch wknd

Dolmetsch Summer School, Marley Copse, Marley Common, Haslemere, Surrey GU27 3PU t Haslemere 3619. Aug

Earnley Concourse, Earnley nr Chichester, Sussex t Bracklesham Bay 392. Non-playing study wks

Education at the Maltings, Dr W. H. Swinburne, Education Adviser, Aldeburgh Festival Office, Aldeburgh, Suffolk IP15 5AX t Aldeburgh 2935. Opera, solo singing, str mus; Jul-Aug

Emscote Lawn Music School, c/o M. G. Jones, Emscote Lawn, Warwick CV34 5QD. Orch, chmbr mus for 8-14 yr olds; Easter

English Folk Dance and Song Society, 2 Regent's Pk Rd, London NW1 7AY t 01-485 2206. Blackpool; Easter

Ernest Read Music Association (ERMA), 143 King Henry's Rd, London NW3 3RD t 01-722 3020. Roedean School, Brighton; adults (over 17), 3 sym orchs, str and wind ensembles, choir cond course; Aug. Also Junior Orchestral Summer Course, 39 Cassiobury Pk Av, Watford, Herts WD1 7LA; Bradfield College, Berks; children 12-17. 3 sym orchs, str and wind chmbr mus; Aug

Folk for Youth, Miss E. J. Wood, 19 Malpas Dr, Duston, Northampton NN5 6XL t Northampton 57991. Windmill Ho, Alvechurch; Apr

Gloucestershire Community Council County Music Committee, Community Ho, College Grn, Gloucester GL1 2LZ t Gloucester 28491. Choral and orch; Apr, Aug

Grantley Hall, Ripon, Yorks HG4 3ET t Sawley 259. Orch, chmbr mus; Mar, Apr

Halsway Manor Society, Crowcombe, Taunton, Somerset TA4 4BD t Crowcombe 274. Folk mus wknds

Hawkwood College, Wick St, Stroud, Glos GL6 7QW t Stroud 4607. Str wknd; Feb. Cheltenham Festival

Highlights, str, wnd orch; Jul. Various wknd
courses throughout yr
Helen Just Chamber Music Summer School, c/o 7 Bagg-
allay St, Hereford HR4 ODZ t Hereford 6011. St
Paul's Coll, Cheltenham
Hilderstone, 14-16a St Peter's Rd, Broadstairs, Kent
CT10 2AQ t Thanet 61380. 'Opera for Pleasure'
wknd; May
Hill Residential College, Pen-y-Pound, Abergavenny,
Gwent NP7 7RP t Abergavenny 2551. Jul, Oct, Dec
Holiday Course for Organists, c/o Dr D. Hopkins,
Royal Academy of Music, Marylebone Rd, London NW1
5HT t 01-935 5461. Royal Academy of Mus; Jul-Aug
Holiday Fun with Music, 2 Queensmead, St John's Wood
Park, London NW8 6RE t 01-722 9828. London:
'Story and Music' activities for children; Easter,
Aug, Christmas. Also regular after-school 'Tea-
and-Story' and 'On-Location' sessions for children
aged 3-11
Horncastle Residential College, Horncastle, Lincs N9
6BW t Horncastle 2449
International Music Weeks, c/o Cambridgeshire College
of Arts and Technology, Collier Rd, Cambridge CB1
2AJ t Cambridge 63271. Choral, orch, chmbr mus;
in Britain and abroad
International Musicians Seminar, c/o Anna Maggio, 76
Lonsdale Rd, London SW13 9JS t 01-741 0596.
Prussia Cove, Cornwall; str chmbr mus; Apr
International Summer School, 4 Abbots Barton Walk,
Canterbury, Kent CT1 3AX t Canterbury 65548 ext 57.
St Augustine's and Christ Church Colleges, Canter-
bury; woodwnd, str, chor mus; Jul-Sep
Islington Training-Course for Church Organists, c/o
Bryan J. Gipps, 126F Rotherfield St, London N1 3DA.
St Stephen's Church, London N1, wknd in Aug;
various wknds throughout yr
Kato Havas Spring Violin School, 37 Frenchfield Gdns,
Penrith, Cumbria CA11 8TX t Penrith 3538. Highham
Hall, Lake District; vln, vla, vcl; May-Jun
Kato Havas Summer Violin School, 15 Rocks La, London
SW13 ODB t 01-876 7012. St George's School
Langton Matravers, Swanage; vlnsts and cellists;
Jul-Aug
Kent County Music Committee, Music Centre, Master's
Ho, Old College, Maidstone, Kent ME15 6YQ t
Maidstone 51327. Benenden School, Cranbrook, Kent;
choral, orch, chmbr mus, pno master class; Aug
Knuston Hall, Irchester, Wellingborough, Northants
NN9 7EU t Wellingborough 2104. Various wknd
courses throughout yr
London Repertoire Orchestra, c/o Jack Graty, All-
farthings, Hermitage Rd, Kenley, Surrey CR2 5EB t

01-660 6278. Spring wknd
London Saxophone Quartet, c/o C. Gradwell, 32 Maxwell
Rd, Welling, Kent DA16 2ES t 01-303 0908. Stock-
well College, Bromley; woodwind workshop; Aug
Lute Society Summer School, 71 Priory Rd, Kew Gdns,
Richmond, Surrey TW9 3DH t 01-940 7086. St Paul's
Coll, Cheltenham; for players and interested non-
players; Aug
Mid-Glamorgan Education Committee, County Further
Education Officer, Cathays Pk, Cardiff CF1 3NF t
Cardiff 28033. Barry; summer
Missenden Abbey, Gt Missenden, Bucks HP16 OBD t Gt
Missenden 2328. Chmbr mus; May. Choral; Jun
Monastic Music Panel, c/o Anthony J. Greening, 22
Archery Clo, London W2 2BE t 01-262 8478. Stan-
brook Abbey, Callow End nr Worcester; choir, organ
training for monastic musicians; after Christmas,
Easter, summer
Moor Park College, Farnham, Surrey GU10 1QR t Farnham
6401
Music Teachers' Association, 106 Gloucester Pl,
London W1H 3DB t 01-935 6371. Downe House, New-
bury, Berks; school orch (ages 12-19); Aug. Also
York Univ; school mus and pno (min age 16); Aug
Musical Holidays in the Lake District for Young
Musicians, c/o Lady Moon, 19 Northmoor Rd, Oxford
OX2 6UW t Oxford 59442. Apr, Jul-Aug
National Operatic and Dramatic Association (NODA),
1 Crestfield St, London WC1H 8AU t 01-837 5655.
Ripon College; opera; Aug
Newbattle Abbey College, Dalkeith, Midlothian EH22
3LL t 031-663 1921. Rcdr
Northern Recorder Course, 41 Grosvenor Rd, Sale,
Ches M33 1WL t 061-973 2050. St John's Coll, York;
Apr
Northumbrian Recorder and Viol School, Mrs M. Binns,
Randalholme, Claremont Av, Newcastle upon Tyne
NE15 7LE t Newcastle upon Tyne 674573. Durham;
Aug
Orff-Schulwerk Courses, c/o 31 Roedean Cres, London
SW15 5JX t 01-876 1944. Lady Mabel Coll, nr
Rotherham; Apr, Aug
Pendley Manor (c/o Warden), Tring, Herts HP23 5QZ t
Tring 2481. Folk; Feb
Pendrell Hall College, Codsall Wood, Wolverhampton,
Staffs WV8 1PQ t Codsall 2398. Brass band: Feb.
Rcdr; Mar
Pipers' Guild, 15 Wyke Av, Worthing, Sussex BN11 1PB
t Worthing 34835. Various centres
Project Muse, 2 Queensmead, St Johns Wood Pk,
London NW8 6RE t 01-722 9828. Holiday Inn, Swiss

Cottage, London: music enjoyment seminars for
adults; 10-weekly evening sessions starting Oct,
Jan, May
Recorder in Education Summer School, 2 Meadowhead
Clo, Sheffield S8 7TX t Sheffield 747316. Mary
Ward Coll, Keyworth, Notts; Jul-Aug
Rehearsal Orchestra, 29 Exhibition Rd, London SW7
2AS t 01-589 1525. Edinburgh (3 one-week courses,
during Festival); Aug-Sep. Also various 1 and 2-
day courses throughout country during yr
Royal School of Church Music, Addington Palace,
Croydon, Surrey CR9 5AD t 01-654 7676. 2-4 day
residential courses; 1-day non-residential
courses; 3-month intensive summer course for
special needs of overseas students
Rural Music Schools Association, Little Benslow Hills,
Hitchin, Herts SG4 9RD t Hitchin 3446. Offley
Place, Hitchin; insts; Aug. Also various wknds
throughout yr. (For regional centres, see p. 168)
Schools Music Association, The, 4 Newman Rd, Bromley,
Kent BR1 1RJ t 01-460 4043. Various centres
Scottish Amateur Music Association, 7 Randolph Cres,
Edinburgh EH3 7TE. St Andrews; chmbr mus, choral
singing, opera; Jul
Sing for Pleasure Summer School, 26 Bedford Sq, Lon-
don WC1B 3HU t 01-636 4066. Easenhall, Warks;
conductors, sgrs, age 15+; Aug
Society for the Promotion of New Music, 29 Exhibition
Rd, London SW7 2AS t 01-584 6716. Goldsmiths'
Coll, London; composers; Jul
Southend-on-Sea Summer School of Music, c/o Chief
Education Officer, Education Dept, PO Box 6, Civic
Centre, Southend-on-Sea SS2 6ER t Southend-on-Sea
49451. Aug-Sep
Spode House, Hawkesyard Priory, Rugeley, Staffs WS15
1PT t Armitage 490112. Folk mus; wknds. Also
mus wk; Easter
Stonyhurst Summer School of Music, 9 Bay View, Over
Kellet, nr Carnforth, Lancs LA6 1DR. Master
classes; Aug-Sep
Stowe Summer School of Music, Willowdown, Megg La,
Chipperfield, Herts t Kings Langley 63715. Wood-
wnd, brass; Jul-Aug
Summer Holiday Course for Flute and Recorder Players,
15 Castlenau, London SW13 9RP t 01-748 6991.
Moulsford Preparatory School, nr Wallingford, Oxon;
Aug
Summer Music, 22 Gresley Rd, London N19 3JZ t 01-272
5664. Hurstpierpoint College, Sussex; str players,
sgrs, pnsts, choir, gtrsts, early mus; Feb, Mar,
May, Aug. Also wknd courses at Haywards Heath,

Hitchin, Lewes, Salisbury
Summer School in String Orchestral Playing, Mans-
bridge Ho, 28 College Rd, Reading, Berks RG6 1QB
t Reading 62575. Missenden Abbey, Bucks; Jul
Summer School of Music Ltd, 48 Ridgway, London SW19
4QP t 01-947 2244. Dartington Hall, Totnes, Devon;
Jul-Aug
Sussex Opera and Ballet Society, Wych Cross Ho, South-
over High St, Lewes, Sussex BN7 1H4 t Lewes 3601.
Wknd course on Glyndebourne Festival operas; May.
Wknd course on ballet, drama and opera; Sep
Talbot Lampson School for Conductors and Accompanists,
c/o Joan Derriman, 45 Beaufort Mans, Beaufort St,
London SW3 5AG t 01-352 6265. Trinity College of
Music, 11 Mandeville Pl, London; Sep
Urchfont Manor (c/o Warden), Devizes, Wilts SN10 4RG
t Chirton 610. 2 mus wknds; Jun, Dec
Viola da Gamba Summer School, 26 Derwent Dr, Tun-
bridge Wells, Kent TN4 9TB. St Paul's Coll,
Cheltenham; Aug
Warwickshire Education Committee, County Education
Officer, 22 Northgate St, Warwick CV34 4SR t
Warwick 43431. Moreton Morrell; 'Music in Educa-
tion' for teachers; Jul
Wavendon Allmusic Plan, The Stables, Wavendon, Milton
Keynes MK17 8LT t Milton Keynes 582522. Advanced
students and amateurs, composition, improvisation,
ens playing, etc; Easter. Camps for children (8-
18); summer
Wedgwood Memorial College, Barlaston, Stoke-on-Trent
ST12 9DG t Barlaston 2105. Art and mus; Aug
West Dean College, West Dean, Chichester, Sussex
PO18 OQZ t Singleton 301. Inst making; Feb, Sep
Westham Adult College, Barford, Warks CV35 8DP t
Barford 206. Madrigal wknds; Jan & Mar. Rcdr
playing; Mar. Folk dance and song; Aug. Carol
wknd; Dec
Winchester Summer Music Course, 52 Ravensdale Av,
London N12 6HT t 01-445 7891. King Alfred's Coll,
Winchester; Aug
Workers' Music Association Summer School, 71 Green-
field Gdns, London NW2 1HU t 01-458 2321. Wortley,
Yorks; Aug. See also p. 167
York University Music Department, Heslington, York
YO1 5DD t York 59861 (in association with Universal
Edition). New music for teachers of music, drama,
dance; May-Jun
Youth Music Centre, c/o Mrs Elizabeth Kingsley, 132
Wemborough Rd, Stanmore, Middx HA7 2EG t 01-907
8018. Hampstead Garden Suburb, London NW11 7BN;
10-day orch course for children, young people;
summer

Ystym Colwyn Summer School of Opera, Director,
   Frederick Sharp Hon ARCM, Royal Coll of Music,
   Prince Consort Rd, London SW7 2BS t 01-589 3643.
   Meifod, Powys

23   Scholarships and Grants for Study

The Department of Education and Science (p. 75)
publishes leaflets on state scholarships. Local
education authorities (p. 182) will normally support
students only up to the stage of a first university
degree or equivalent, but the Department of Education and Science offers studentships on a competitive
basis for full-time postgraduate study in the UK
(and exceptionally elsewhere).
   A list of *Competitions, Awards and Scholarships
for Music Students* is available free from the Arts
Council; requests, enclosing a large stamped
addressed envelope, should be addressed to The Arts
Council of Great Britain, 105 Piccadilly, London W1V
0AU. The National Union of Students (p. 81) can
supply a list of general and regional *Educational
Charities* (price 25p plus 11p postage), including
those concerned with music. Reference may also be
made to *The Directory of Grant-Making Trusts* (price
£10 from the Charities Aid Foundation, 48 Pembury
Rd, Tonbridge, Kent TN9 2JD t Tonbridge 62323) and
The Grants Register (£6 from St James Press, London).
   Grants and scholarships for Commonwealth students,
tenable in Commonwealth universities outside their
own country, are listed in the *Scholarships Guide
for Commonwealth Postgraduate Students* (£2.50 from
the Association of Commonwealth Universities, 36
Gordon Sq, London WC1H OPF t 01-387 8572).
   Enquiries about the scholarships listed below
should be sent to the Secretary (or as otherwise
indicated) at the addresses given. Unless otherwise
stated, scholarships are available to British and
Commonwealth students only.

Arlen (Stephen) Memorial Fund. Coliseum, St Martin's
   La, London WC2N 4ES. Biennial bursaries to persons
   aged 20-30 following careers in opera, music,
   drama, ballet
Barbirolli (Sir John) Memorial Foundation. 11 Blen-
   heim St, London W1Y OLJ. Young conds and other
   musicians

Best (W. T.) Memorial Scholarship (administered by the Worshipful Company of Musicians). Orgsts to be nominated by certain profs of mus or prins of mus colls; application through nominators only (next 1977)

Boise Foundation Scholarships. Hon Sec, 14 Bedford Sq, London WC1B 3JG. Performers, max age 30, to be nominated by heads of mus colls, etc.; auditions April

Bonwick Bequest. Clerk, Royal College of Organists, Kensington Gore, London SW7 2QS. Orgsts max age 19; closing date May 1

British Academy. Burlington Ho, Piccadilly, London W1V ONS. Research awards at post-doctoral or equivalent level (funds not available for work toward higher degree); closing date Nov 30

Butterworth (George) Memorial Trust. Dr A. J. Croft, Clarendon Laboratory, Oxford OX1 3PU. Grants towards cost of copying mus, provided a performance has been arranged

Caird's (Sir James) Travelling Scholarship Trust. 136 Nethergate, Dundee DD1 4PA. Scottish students; Wiseman Prize £100 for Scottish national; closing date Feb 28

Chown Music Scholarship Fund. Warden, Toynbee Hall, 28 Commercial St, London E1 6LS. Residents of E London, over 17

Clements Memorial Prize. St Margarets, Broomfield Av, London N13 4JJ. £200 biennial award for chamber mus composers; closing date Oct 1 (next 1977)

Collard (John Clementi) Fellowship (administered by the Worshipful Company of Musicians). Professional musicians engaged in composition, research or performance, nominated by certain profs and heads of mus colls; application through nominators only (next 1977)

Craxton (Harold) Memorial Trust. c/o Antony Craxton MVO, 39a Portsmouth Rd, Cobham, Surrey KT11 1JQ. Grants for outstanding young performers and composers beginning a career

Cunningham (G. D.) Scholarship in Music. Barber Institute of Fine Arts, The University, Birmingham B15 2TS. Postgraduate study in music

Davis (Henry and Lily) Fund. Deputy Music Director, Arts Council of Great Britain, 105 Piccadilly, London W1V OAU. Performers (not conductors or composers) aged 21-30, for short-term postgraduate study projects; auditions spring and autumn

Dio Fund. Deputy Music Director, Arts Council of Great Britain, 105 Piccadilly, London W1V OAU.

Young composers offered commission fee for instrumental or vocal work; closing date Dec 31
Drapers' Company. Clerk, Drapers' Hall, Throgmorton St, London EC2N 2DQ. Grants to students in need, max age 20, where LEA help not available
Ferrier (Kathleen) Memorial Scholarship Fund. Administrative Sec, Royal Philharmonic Society, 29 Exhibition Rd, London SW7 2AS. Sgrs aged 21-5
Gottlieb (Fritz) Memorial Scholarship for Piano. 39 Wood Vale, London N10 3DJ. Max age 25: 2 yrs tuition by Vera Yelverton, Purcell Room recital; closing date Mar 21
Gulbenkian (Calouste) Foundation Music Fellowships. 98 Portland Pl, London W1N 4ET. Performers; nomination only by prominent musicians etc
James (Catherine and Lady Grace) Foundation. 9 Market St, Aberystwyth, Dyfed SY23 1DL. Welsh male students requiring further training
Lander (Mabel) Memorial Scholarships. 46 Clarendon Rd, London W11 2HH. Pnsts aged 8-23, comprehensive training in Russian and Viennese traditions; by competition, Mar (offered by Tanya Polunin School of Pianoforte Playing)
Martin Musical Scholarship Fund. 61 Carey St, London WC2A 2JG. UK musicians max age 30, awards inc tuition fees, subsistence grants, professional recitals, etc; closing date Oct 1
Mendelssohn Scholarship Foundation. 14 Bedford Sq, London WC1B 3JG. Composers of any nationality resident UK or Ireland, max age 30; biennial
Munster (Countess of) Musical Trust. Wormley Hill, Godalming, Surrey GU8 5SG. British and Commonwealth students, max age 30: tuition and maintenance grants, tenable at home and abroad; closing date Mar 31
Noble (John) Bursary for Singers. Scottish Opera, 39 Elmbank Cres, Glasgow G2 4PT. £400 bursary awarded annually to singer(s) born or trained in Scotland; final auditions Mar
Pocklington Apprenticeship Trust. Town Clerk, Royal Borough of Kensington and Chelsea, Town Hall, London W8 4SQ. Children born and/or living in the borough for 10 years
Rupert Foundation. 27 Baker St, London W1M 2AE. Conds, aged 22-30
Rushworth (William) Memorial Trust. Liverpool Council of Social Service, 14 Castle St, Liverpool L2 0NJ. Socs and individuals within 60-mile radius of Liverpool
Stapley (Sir Richard) Educational Trust. 121 Gloucester Pl, Portman Sq, London W1H 3PJ. Supple-

mentary grants to univ mus students (not to those
at mus colls)

Suggia (Guilhermina) Gift for the Cello. Deputy
Music Director, Arts Council of Great Britain, 105
Piccadilly, London W1V OAU. Cellists of soloist
potential, any nationality, max age 21; auditions
summer

Taylor (Muriel) Scholarship. Mrs Faith Deller OBE,
Copsley Ct, Outwood, Redhill, Surrey RH1 5PP.
Cellists; awarded annually for a year's advanced
study

Thew (H. A.) Fund. Deputy Music Director, Arts
Council of Great Britain, 105 Piccadilly, London
W1V OAU. Mus students and organizations in Mersey-
side

Tillett Trust. Ibbs & Tillett, 124 Wigmore St,
London W1H OAX. Occasional assistance for advanced
study, normally by nomination only

Wall (Thomas) Trust. 1 York St, London W1H 1PZ.
Supplementary grants for students who have not
already gained a first qualification

White's (Sir Thomas) Educational Foundation Music
Scholarship. Clerk to the Trustees, Old Bablake,
Hill St, Coventry CV1 4AN. Tenable in a higher
education institution approved by Trustees;
students with local connection only

24 Study Abroad

Students wishing to enter a conservatory or university music department abroad should first inquire of
the Cultural Department of the embassy concerned for
a list of such institutions, terms of admission, etc.
For universities see also *The World of Learning* (**£18**
from Europa Publications, London). Certain specialist institutions abroad advertise in British
specialist journals listed in this book - e.g. the
International Opera Centre, Zurich (Zurich Opera,
CH-8001 Zurich, Switzerland) in the journal *Opera*
(see p. 234).

SCHOLARSHIPS

The British Council assists a number of foreign
governments in administering scholarships and
bursaries for British students. Among countries
offering scholarships to musicians are Austria,

Belgium, Bulgaria, Czechoslovakia, Denmark, Finland,
France, Germany (Federal Republic), Greece, Hungary,
Italy, Japan, Netherlands, Poland, Romania, Sweden,
USSR. Details are in *Scholarships Abroad*, available
from Higher Education Dept, British Council, 10
Spring Gdns, London SW1A 2BN t 01-930 8466. The
Italian Institute provides information on advanced
training and scholarships in Italy (including study
at some opera centres attached to principal opera
houses). Inquiries to Bursary Dept, 39 Belgrave Sq,
London SW1X 8NX t 01-235 1461.

Grants and scholarships for Commonwealth students,
tenable in Commonwealth universities outside their
own country, are listed in the *Scholarships Guide for
Commonwealth Postgraduate Students* (£2.50 from the
Association of Commonwealth Universities, 36 Gordon
Sq, London WC1H OPF t 01-387 8572).

*

Some principal British scholarships for study abroad
are listed below. In addition, certain other British
educational trusts (see p. 77) provide scholarships
for those wishing to study abroad.

Beecham (Sir Thomas) Scholarship. Leche Trust, c/o
    Gartmore Investment, Cayzer Ho, St Mary Axe, London
    EC3A 8BP. For young opera singers
Churchill (Winston) Memorial Trust. Director-General,
    15 Queen's Gate Terr, London SW7 5PR. Travelling
    Fellowships in arts subjects, not necessarily
    music; applications Sep-Oct
Drogheda-Mayer Fellowship. Royal Opera Ho, Covent
    Gdn, London WC2E 7QA. For young opera singers
Licette (Miriam) Scholarship. Arts Council, 105
    Piccadilly, London W1V OAU. For female singers to
    study in Paris, max age 30; annual
Stratton (John) and RCA Scholarships. Royal Society
    of Arts, 8 John Adam St, London WC2N 6EZ. For post-
    graduate British or Commonwealth musicians
Tauber (Richard) Memorial Prize. Anglo-Austrian
    Music Society, 139 Kensington High St, London W8
    6SX. Travel bursary; study grant and public
    recital in London open to British or Austrian
    singers.

SUMMER COURSES

Some *summer music courses* (at various times between

June and September) in continental Europe which invite
international participation are listed below: at
many, instruction in English is available. The
fields offered (instruments etc) may vary from year
to year. Financial grants and/or free accommodation
may be offered on scholarship terms: inquire of the
institution or (for foreign government grants) of the
cultural office of the appropriate embassy or lega-
tion in London. The addresses given here are those
of the organizing bodies, and are not necessarily the
.same as the address of the course itself.

AUSTRIA
Berwang: Holiday Music Course. Willowdown, Megg La,
  Chipperfield, Herts WD4 9JN t Kings Langley 63715;
  01-624 5705
Breiteneich: wind inst courses. Walter Hermann
  Sallagar, Neulinggasse 42/10, A-1030 Vienna
Ossiach: Opera Seminar. Carinthischer Sommer, A-
  9570 Ossiach
Retz: Baroque Ensemble-Playing. 111 Fernside Rd,
  London SW12 8LH t 01-673 0367
Salzburg: International Summer Academy Mozarteum.
  Schwarzstrasse 26, A-5020 Salzburg
Salzburg: Opera Workshop. Barbara Owens, Hans
  Wartenberg, Reidenburgerstrasse 2, A-5020 Salzburg
Salzburg: Orff-Schulwerk Course. 31 Roedean Cres,
  London SW15 5JX t 01-876 1944
Vienna: Master courses in chor, chmbr, opera
  conducting and singing. Council on Intercultural
  Relations, Bindergasse 5-9, A-1090 Vienna 9

BELGIUM
Antwerp: Harpsichord Summer Course. Ruckers-Genoot-
  sch v.z.w., Vleeshouwersstraat 38-40, B-2000
  Antwerp
Antwerp: Piano Summer Course. Koninklijk Vlaams
  Muziekconservatorium, Desguinlei 25, B-2000 Antwerp
Louvain: Study Week for Singers. Festival of
  Flanders, BRT-Omroepcentrum, August Reyerslaan 52,
  B-1040 Brussels
Marche-les-Dames: Early Music on Historical Instru-
  ments (at L'Abbaye Notre-Dame-du-Vivier). Studium
  Musicae, 5a av du Furet, 1180 Brussels

CZECHOSLOVAKIA
Bad Luhacovice: International Interpretation Course.
  Janacek Academy of Music and Dramatic Art, 6
  Komenskeho nam, Brno
Prague: International Interpretation Course (key-

boards). Academy of Music, Dum umelcu, Prague 1
Prague: International Summer Master Courses. Dum
umelcu, Prague 1

FINLAND
Jyvaskyla: chmbr mus summer academy. Jyvaskyla Arts
Festival, Kauppakatu 9 C 36, 40100 Jyvaskyla 10
Kaustinen: folk mus courses. Folk Music Festival
Office, 69600 Kaustinen
Kuopio: seminar for brass band conductors. Kuopio
Dance and Music Festival, Kuopion Yhteisteatteri,
Niiralankatu 2, Kuopio
Pori: jazz lectures and seminars. Pori Jazz 66 ry,
Luvianpuistokatu 2 D, 28100 Pori
Savonlinna: lieder and opera course. City Tourist
Office, Olavinkatu 35, SF57 130 Savonlinna 13
Savonlinna: youth inst course. City Tourist Office,
Olavinkatu 35, SF57 130 Savonlinna 13

FRANCE
Arles: International Guitar Interpretation Meeting.
Rencontres Internationales de la Guitare, Stage
d'interprétation, 4 rue Demarquay, 75010 Paris
Crupies/Richerenches: choral, orch, inst course.
Fédération des Centres Musicaux Ruraux de France,
34 rue d'Hauteville, 75-Paris 10e
Lyons: choral and inst courses. Fédération des
Centres Musicaux Ruraux de France, 34 rue d'Haute-
ville, 75-Paris 10e
Montry: various courses. Fédération des Centres
Musicaux Ruraux de France, 34 rue d'Hauteville,
75-Paris 10e
Moulins: early mus course. Ligue Française de
l'Enseignement et de l'Education Permanente, 3 rue
Récamier, 75-Paris 7e
Paris: International Guitar Course. Festival
Estival, 5 place des Ternes, Paris 17e
Paris: International Harpsichord Course. Festival
Estival, 5 place des Ternes, Paris 17e
Paris: mus, choral, orch course. Fédération des
Centres Musicaux Ruraux de France, 34 rue d'Haute-
ville, 75-Paris 10e
Paris: rcdr course. Fédération des Centres Musicaux
Ruraux de France, 34 rue d'Hauteville, 75-Paris 10e
Saint-Maximin: Summer School of French Music.
Couvent Royal, 83470 Saint-Maximin en Provence
Thiviers/Osseja: choral, orch, inst course. Federa-
tion des Centres Musicaux Ruraux de France, 34 rue
d'Hauteville, 75-Paris 10e
Tours: European Summer School for Young Musicians.
11 Bruton Way, London W13 OBY t 01-997 8165
Vallorcine: mus workshop. Camps de Lycéens, 3

avenue Barral, Seynod, 74000 Annecy
Vesc: choral, orch, inst course. Fédération des
Centres Musicaux Ruraux de France, 34 rue d'Hauteville, 75-Paris 10e
various: musical holidays. Fédération Nationale
d'Associations Culturelles d'Expansion Musicale,
23 rue Asseline, 75-Paris 14e

GERMANY (DEMOCRATIC REPUBLIC, 'EAST GERMANY')
Weimar: International Music Seminar. Hochschule
für Musik 'Franz Liszt', 53 Weimar, Platz der
Demokratie 2/3

GERMANY (FEDERAL REPUBLIC)
Bayreuth: choral, orch, perc, chmbr mus course.
International Youth Festival Meeting, D-858 Bay-
reuth
Darmstadt: comp and interpretation of modern mus.
Internationales Musikinstitut, Nieder-Ramstadter
Strasse 190, D-6100 Darmstadt
Freiburg: International Master Courses. Freiburg,
7801 Horben
Weikersheim (near Würzburg): chmbr mus, orch, opera
courses. Musikalische Jugend Deutschlands eV,
Hirschgartenallee 19, D-8 Munich 19

HUNGARY
Budapest: Bartók Seminar, Vorosmarty ter 1, Budapest
5
Budapest: International Bartók Seminar; pno, vln,
str quartet courses. Budapest Office of Music
Competitions, POB 80, Vorosmarty ter 1, Budapest 5
Esztergom: Kodály seminar; Music Education in
Hungary. Danube Bend Summer University Course on
Arts, 16 Beke ter, Esztergom
Pecs: International Music Course. Youth and Music
of Hungary, Vorosmarty ter 1, Budapest 5

IRELAND (REPUBLIC OF)
Dublin: Irish mus and various courses. Royal Irish
Academy of Music, 36-8 Westland Row, Dublin 2

ITALY
Barga: young opera sgrs. Teatro dei Differenti,
Barga, Lucca
Florence: Tito Gobbi Opera Workshop. Villa
Schifanoia, Via Boccaccio 123, 50133 Florence
Monterosso: Aeolian Summer Music Course for str
players. Jocelyn Selson, 55 Denman Dr, London
NW11 6RA t 01-455 4518
Rome: inst, opera, chmbr mus courses. Centro Inter-

nazionale Studi Musicali, Palazzo del Bufalo, Largo
del Nazareno 8, 00187 Rome
Siena: inst, vocal, cond, chmbr mus master classes;
seminars and special courses in opera, pno, chmbr
mus, comp. Accademia Musicale Chigiana, via de'
Città 89, 53100 Siena
Taormina: inst, opera, chmbr mus courses. Centro
Internazionale Studi Musicali, Palazzo del Bufalo,
Largo del Nazareno 8, 00187 Rome
Venice: musical holidays. Conservatorio Benedetto
Marcello, Campo S Stefano 2809, Venice

NETHERLANDS
Breukelen: harp study conference. Eduard van Beinum
Stichting, Huize 'Queekhoven', Breukelen
Breukelen: Music of the Middle Ages, Eduard van
Beinum Stichting, Huize 'Queekhoven', Breukelen
Breukelen: Musicultura (oriental mus). Eduard van
Beinum Stichting, Huize 'Queekhoven', Breukelen
Haarlem: summer academy for orgsts. Stichting Inter-
nationaal Orgelconcours, Zomeracademie voor
Organisten, Stadhuis, Haarlem
Hilversum: International Opera Course for Conductors
and Directors. Nederlandse Omroep Stichting,
Information Service, PO Box 10, Hilversum
's-Hertogenbosch: sgrs course. Stadhuis; 's-Hertogenbosch
various: inst and vocal courses; inst-making
courses. Vereniging voor Huismuziek, Begijnehof
7, Utrecht

PORTUGAL
Estoril: International Summer Music Courses of the
Costa do Sol. Junta de Turismo da Costa do Sol,
Estoril

SWEDEN
Ingesund: International Music Workshop. Musik for
Ungdom, Rikskonserter Box 1225, S-111 82 Stockholm
Ransater: International Choral and Instrumental
Week. Ingvar Sahlin, Geijerskolan, S-68400
Ransater, Munkfors 1

SWITZERLAND
Berne: Max Rostal Master Course for Violin (Viola)
Playing. Weststrasse 12, CH-3005 Berne
Geneva: pno, vln, sgrs master classes. Conservatory
of Music of Geneva, place Neuve, CH-1204, Geneva
Lucerne: master courses at Lucerne Conservatoire.
International Festival of Music, Dreilindenstrasse
93, CH-6006 Lucerne

Montreux-Vévey: International Flute Course. 27 bis
    avenue des Alpes, 1820 Montreux
Zurich: keyboard, sgrs master classes. Foundation
    for International Master-classes in Music, PO Box
    647, 8022 Zurich

25 Examination Boards

PRACTICAL EXAMINATIONS IN MUSIC

Practical examinations in music are available under
the following auspices, whether or not the student
is enrolled at the college mentioned.

Associated Board of the Royal Schools of Music (Royal
    Academy of Music, Royal College of Music, Royal
    Northern College of Music, Royal Scottish Academy
    of Music and Drama). Philip Cranmer MA, B Mus
    (Oxon), Hon RAM, FRCO, *sec.* 14 Bedford Sq, London
    WC1B 3JG t 01-636 4478 tg musexam London WC1
Guildhall School of Music and Drama. Charles Henden,
    examinations dir. Victoria Embankment, London
    EC4Y OAR t 01-353 7774
London College of Music Examinations. Kenwyn R.
    Beard Hon FLCM, *sec.* 47 Gt Marlborough St, London
    W1V 2AS t 01-437 6120 tg supertonic
Trinity College of Music. Ernest Heberden MA, Hon
    FTCL, *dir of examinations.* 11 Mandeville Pl,
    London W1M 6AQ t 01-935 5773

SECONDARY EDUCATION

England and Wales

THE GENERAL CERTIFICATE OF EDUCATION ('O' and 'A'
levels) is awarded by the following independent
examination boards. The Joint Matriculation Board
and the Welsh Joint Education Committee serve limited
areas but otherwise candidates may take the examinations of any Board regardless of the area in which
they live or where their school is situated.

Associated Examining Board. H. O. Childs BSc, *sec.* Wellington Ho, Aldershot, Hants GU11 1BQ t Aldershot 25551

Joint Matriculation Board. R. Christopher MA, M Ed, *sec.* Manchester M15 6EU t 061-273 2565

Oxford and Cambridge Schools Examination Board. H. F. King, A. R. Davis, *secs.* 10 Trumpington St, Cambridge CB2 1QB t Cambridge 64326; Elsfield Way, Oxford OX2 8EP t Oxford 54421

Oxford Delegacy of Local Examinations. R. J. Rayson, *sec.* Ewert Pl, Summertown, Oxford OX2 7BZ t Oxford 54291

Southern Universities' Joint Board for School Examinations. Cotham Rd, Bristol BS6 6DD t Bristol 36042

University of Cambridge Local Examinations Syndicate. F. Wild, *sec.* Syndicate Buildings, 17 Harvey Rd, Cambridge CB1 2EU t Cambridge 61111

University of London University Entrance and Schools Examination Council. A. R. Stephenson MA, *sec.* 66-72 Gower St, London WC1E 6EE t 01-636 8000

Welsh Joint Education Committee. D. Andrew Davies BA, *sec.* 245 Western Av, Cardiff CF5 2YX t Cardiff 561231

THE CERTIFICATE OF SECONDARY EDUCATION (CSE) is awarded by the following regional examination boards. In addition to setting external examinations based on syllabuses prepared by teachers serving on subject panels, the boards also examine externally on the basis of syllabuses prepared by individual schools or groups of schools. The boards moderate examinations prepared and marked by schools themselves to ensure reasonably comparable standards.

Associated Lancashire Schools Examining Board. P. Lawrence BA, MA, *sec.* 77 Whitworth St, Manchester M1 6HA t 061-236 6020/6521. Metropolitan districts of Bolton, Manchester, Oldham, Rochdale, Salford; parts of Derbyshire

East Anglian Examinations Board. A. Johnson, MSc, *sec.* The Lindens, Lexden Rd, Colchester, Essex CO3 3RL t Colchester 71244. Cambridgeshire, Essex, Hertfordshire, Norfolk, Suffolk; and London boroughs of Barking, Barnet, Havering, Redbridge, Waltham Forest

East Midland Regional Examinations Board. D. J. Ramsden BA, *sec.* Robins Wood Ho, Robins Wood Rd, Aspley, Nottingham NG8 3NH t Nottingham 295367. Derbyshire, Leicestershire, Lincolnshire, North-

amptonshire, Nottinghamshire, Humberside
Metropolitan Regional Examinations Board. D. H.
   Board MA, *sec.* 104 Wandsworth High St, London
   SW18 4LF t 01-870 2144. Inner London, Newham,
   Croydon
Middlesex Regional Examining Board. W. J. Leake BA,
   sec. 53-63 Wembley Hill Rd, Wembley, Middx HA9
   8BH t 01-903 3961. London boroughs of Brent,
   Ealing, Enfield, Haringey, Harrow, Hillingdon,
   Hounslow, Barnet (part), Richmond upon Thames (part)
North Regional Examinations Board. J. A. Winter-
   bottom BA, *sec.* Wheatfield Rd, Westerhope, Newcastle
   upon Tyne NE5 5JZ t Newcastle upon Tyne 862711.
   Cleveland, Cumbria, Durham, Northumberland; Gates-
   head, Newcastle upon Tyne, North Tyneside, South
   Tyneside, Sunderland
North-Western Secondary School Examinations Board.
   J. E. Tipping BA, *sec.* Orbit Ho, Albert St, Eccles,
   Manchester M30 0WL t 061-788 9521. Lancashire
   (except former county borough of Preston), Cheshire,
   Greater Manchester (part), Merseyside (part); the
   former county borough of Barrow-in-Furness; Isle
   of Man
South-East Regional Examinations Board. P. N.
   Anderson VRD, BA, *sec.* 2-4 Mt Ephraim Rd, Tun-
   bridge Wells, Kent TN1 1EU t Tunbridge Wells 20913-5.
   East Sussex, Kent Surrey; London boroughs of
   Bexley, Bromley, Kingston-upon-Thames, Sutton
Southern Regional Examinations Board. H. G. Macin-
   tosh MA, *sec.* 53 London Rd, Southampton SO9 4YL t
   Southampton 27061. Dorset, Hampshire, West Sussex,
   Isle of Wight, Berkshire, Oxfordshire, Bucking-
   hamshire, Channel Islands and for the schools over-
   seas of the Service Children's Education Authority
South Western Examinations Board. H. L. M. Household
   BSc, *sec.* 23-9 Marsh St, Bristol BS1 4BP t Bristol
   23434. Avon, Cornwall, Devon, Gloucestershire,
   Somerset, Wiltshire
West Midlands Examinations Board. G. Flack BA, PhD,
   sec. Norfolk Ho, Smallbrook Queensway, Birmingham
   B5 4NJ t 021-643 2081. Hereford and Worcester,
   Salop, Staffordshire, Warwickshire, West Midlands
West Yorkshire and Lindsey Regional Examining Board.
   R. G. Capes MA, LLB, *sec.* 136 Derbyshire La,
   Sheffield S8 8SE t Sheffield 53538. Parts of
   Humberside, Lincolnshire, North Yorkshire; parts
   of Barnsley, Doncaster, Rotherham, Sheffield,
   Bradford, Calderdale, Kirklees, Leeds, Wakefield
Yorkshire Regional Examinations Board. P. E. Roe BSc,
   sec. 31-3 Springfield Av, Harrogate, North Yorks
   HG1 2HW t Harrogate 3959. The former counties of

North and East Riding and the former county
boroughs of York, Hull, Leeds, Bradford, Halifax,
Huddersfield, Dewsbury, Wakefield

Scotland

Examinations at secondary school level (Ordinary,
Higher and the Certificate of Sixth Form Studies)
are administered by the following Board. The examinations may be taken by external candidates including those outside Scotland.

Scottish Certificate of Education Examination Board.
    J. H. Walker MA, M Ed, PhD, *dir*. Ironmills Rd,
    Dalkeith, Midlothian EH22 1BR

Northern Ireland

Examinations are administered by the following
Council.

Northern Ireland Schools Examinations Council.
    J. McGilton BA, M Ed, PhD, *chief officer*. 42 Bee-
    chill Rd, Belfast BT8 4RS t Belfast 647261

26 Music Periodicals

Principal field or proprietary organization is
indicated where title is insufficient, followed by
the number of issues per annum. The name of the
editor (or, if unavailable, director or publisher)
follows with address. Price quoted is price per
issue unless otherwise stated. Reduced yearly rates,
and sometimes special professional or student rates,
may be available.

Accordion Times (incorp Harmonica News) (4-6).
    J. J. Black (Publishers) Ltd, Somerset Ho,
    Cranleigh, Surrey t Cranleigh 3554. *10p*
Angel, The (choir schools, church mus) (2). Rev
    Desmond Morse-Boycott, 79 Ashacre La, Offington,
    Worthing, Sussex BN13 2DE t Worthing 60927. *12½p*
Audio (12). Peter Herring, ed. Fleetway Ho,
    Farringdon St, London EC4A 4AD t 01-634 4344. *25p*
Beat Instrumental and International Recording Studio

(12).   Ray Hammond, ed.   Beat Publications Ltd,
58 Parker St, London WC2 t 01-242 1961.   *25p*
Black Music (soul music, blues, reggae) (12).   Alan
Lewis, ed.   IPC Specialist and Professional Press
Ltd, Dorset Ho, Stamford St, London SE1 9LU;
sales from Surrey Ho, Throwley Way, Sutton, Surrey
SM1 4QQ.   *30p*
Blues and Soul Music Review (26).   John E. Abbey, ed.
Contempo International Ltd, 42 Hanway St, London W1
t 01-636 2283.   *15p*
BMG (for players of banjo, mandolin, guitar etc)
(12).   J. McNaghten, ed.   BMG Publications Ltd,
20 Earlham St, London WC2H 9LR t 01-836 2810.   *25p*
Braille Musical Magazine (12).   John Busbridge, ed.
Royal National Institute for the Blind, 224-228
Gt Portland St, London W1N 6AA t 01-388 1266.   *60p*
annually
Brass Band News (12).   Brass Band News Co, Parlia-
ment St, Gloucester t Gloucester 23438/21254.   *7½p*
Brio (International Association of Music Libraries,
UK branch) (2).   Clifford Bartlett, ed.   156 Gt
Portland St, London W1N 6AJ t 01-580 4468 ext
2414 & Malcolm Jones, ed.   73 Redwood Rd, Birming-
ham B30 1AE t 021-458 7879
British Bandsman (52).   Geoffrey Brand, ed.   Bands-
man's Press Ltd, 210 Strand, London WC2R 1AP t
01-353 1166/3618.   *7p*
British Catalogue of Music (twice yearly and
annually).   British Library (Bibliographic Services
Division), Store St, London WC1E 7DG t 01-636 0755.
£6 annually
British Mouthpiece (brass and military bands) (52).
E. C. Buttress, ed.   Mechanics' Institute, Spring
St, Shuttleworth, Ramsbottom, Lancs t Ramsbottom
2385.   *9p*
British Music Yearbook (1).   Arthur Jacobs, ed.
Bowker Publishing Co Ltd, 58-62 High St, Epping,
Essex CM16 4BU t Epping 77333
Budget Price Records (4).   Francis Antony Ltd,
Trenance Mill, Blowinghouse Hill, St Austell,
Cornwall PL25 5AH t St Austell 3476.   *30p. £1.60*
annually
Buzz (religious pop) (12).   Peter Meadows, ed.   MGO
Ltd, 10 Seaforth Av, New Malden, Surrey KT3 6JP t
01-942 8847.   *15p*
Church Music (Royal School of Church Music) (4).
Robert McDowall, ed.   Addington Palace, Croydon
CR9 5AD t 01-654 7676.   *35p*
Collectors' Catalogue (1).   Harold S. Moores,
Richard J. Potts, eds.   Henry Stave & Co, 9 Dean St,
Oxford St, London W1E 6QZ t 01-437 2757/4153.   *30p*

Composer (Composers' Guild of Gt Britain) (3).
Richard Stoker, ed. 10 Stratford Pl, London W1N
9AE t 01-499 8567; advts Arthur Boyars, 4 Holly-
wood Mews, London SW10 t 01-352 6400. *30p*
Contact (3). Keith Potter, ed. 17 Turners Croft,
Heslington, York YO1 5EL t York 51372. *25p*
Country (12). Bryan Chalker, ed. Hanover Books, 61
Berners St, London W1D 3AE t 01-637 0507. *20p*
Country Music People (12). Bob Powel, ed. Country
Music Press Ltd, Powerscroft Rd, Footscray, Sidcup,
Kent DA14 5DT t 01-300 7535. *22p*
Crescendo International (jazz, etc) (12). Denis
Matthews CBE, ed. Crescendo Publications Ltd, 122
Wardour St, London W1V 5LA t 01-437 8892. *45p*
Disc and Music Echo (52). Gavin Petrie, ed. Disc
Echo Ltd, 161-6 Fleet St, London EC4P 4AA t
01-353 5011. *6p*
Discotheque and Dance (12). George Bennett, ed.
Ridley's Ltd, Wheatsheaf Ho, Carmelite St, London
EC4 t 01-353 1141. *£2.10 annually*
Drums and Percussion (4). 20 Denmark St, London
WC2H 8NA t 01-836 2325. *40p*
Early Music (4). J. M. Thomson, ed. Oxford
University Press Music Dept, 44 Conduit St, London
W1R ODE t 01-734 0504; sales through Journals
Manager, Oxford University Press, Press Rd,
London NW10 ODD t 01-450 7205. *£1.20, £4.50
annually*
Elvis Monthly (12). Printhouse Ltd, Industrial
Estate, Cromford Rd, Langley Mill, Nottingham t
Langley Mill 2466. *20p*
English Church Music (1). Royal School of Church
Music, Addington Palace, Croydon CR9 5AD t
01-654 7676. *£1*
English Dance and Song (4). Tony Wales, ed.
English Folk Dance and Song Society, 2 Regent's
Pk Rd, London NW1 7AY t 01-485 2206. *40p plus
postage*
English Harpsichord Magazine (2). Edgar Hunt, ed.
Rose Cottage, Bois La, Chesham Bois, Amersham,
Bucks HP6 6BP t Amersham 7580. *75p*
Fabulous 208 (pop) (52). Betty Hale, ed. IPC
Magazines Ltd, PO Box 21, Tower Ho, Southampton
St, London WC2E 9QX t 01-836 4363. *8p*
Fabulous 208 Annual (1). IPC Magazines Ltd, PO Box
21, Tower Ho, Southampton St, London WC2E 9QX t
01-836 4363. *90p*
Folk Directory (1). Mira Curtis, ed. English Folk
Dance & Song Society, 2 Regent's Park Rd, London
NW1 7AY t 01-485 2206.
Folk Review (12). Fred Woods, ed. Austin Ho,

Hospital St, Nantwich, Cheshire t Nantwich 65542.
25p
Gilbert and Sullivan Journal (Gilbert & Sullivan
Society) (3). Colin Prestige, ed. J. Antony
Gower, hon business mgr, 23 Burnside, Sawbridge-
worth, Herts. *20p*
Gramophone (12). Malcolm Walker, ed. General
Gramophone Publications Ltd, 177-9 Kenton Rd,
Harrow, Middx HA3 OHA t 01-907 4476. *40p*
Guitar (12). 20 Denmark St, London WC2H 8NA t
01-836 2325. *30p*
Hallé (4). Clive Smart, ed. 30 Cross St, Manchester
M2 7BA t 061-834 8363. *25p*
Hi-Fi Answers (12). R. Chapman, ed. Haymarket
Publishing Ltd, 34 Fouberts Pl, London W1A 2HG t
01-439 4242. *30p*
Hi-Fi for Pleasure (12). Trevor Preece, ed. Blake-
ham Publications Ltd, 1 Benwell Rd, London N7 7AX
t 01-607 6411. *30p*
Hi-Fi News & Record Review (12). John Crabbe, ed.
Link House Publications Ltd, Link Ho, Dingwall Av,
Croydon CR9 2TA t 01-686 2599. *30p*
Hi-Fi Sound (12). Clement Brown, ed. Haymarket
Publishing Group, 54-62 Regent St, London W1A 4YJ
t 01-439 4242. *30p*
Hi-Fi Sound Annual (1). Haymarket Publishing Group,
54-62 Regent St, London W1A 4YJ t 01-439 4242
Hi-Fi Trade Journal (4). Denys G. Killick, ed.
6 Disraeli Gdns, Fawe Park Rd, London SW15 2QB t
01-874 6640
Hi-Fi Year Book (1). IPC Electrical-Electronic
Press Ltd, Dorset Ho, Stamford St, London SE1 9LU
t 01-261 8043
Hot Dinners. John Varnom, ed. 10 South Warf Rd,
London W2 t 01-402 5231
International Musician and Recording World (12).
Ray Hammond, ed. Cover Publications Ltd, 17 Tavi-
stock St, London WC2E 7PA t 01-836 5061. *25p*
Jazz Catalogue (1). Jazz Journal Ltd, 27 Willow
Vale, London W12 OPA t 01-743 2372. *£1.25*
Jazz Journal & Jazz and Blues (12). Sinclair Traill
& Burnett James, eds. Novello & Co Ltd, 1-3 Upper
James St, London W1R 4BP t 01-734 8080. *30p*
Jazz Times (British Jazz Society) (12). John G.
Boddy, ed. 10 Southfield Gdns, Twickenham, Middx
TW1 4SZ t 01-892 0133. *4p*
Jazznocracy (irreg). Sheila Watson, ed. 7 Rockside
Rd, Liverpool L18 4PL t 051-724 5309. *12p*
Journal of Incorporated Society of Organ Builders
(irreg). Herbert Norman, ed. Incorporated
Society of Organ Builders, 120 Moorgate, London E2

t 01-606 6651. *Price varies*
Kemp's Music and Recording Industry Year Book (1).
F. J. Goodliffe, exec ed. The Kemp's Group
(Printers & Publishers) Ltd, 1-5 Bath St, London
EC1V 9QA t 01-253 5314. *£3.75*
Let It Rock (12). Dave Laing, ed. Hanover Books
Ltd, 61 Berners St, London W1D 3AE t 01-492 3936.
20p
Living Music (4). R. Sadleir, ed. 44 Berners St,
London W1P 3AB t 01-580 7811. *£1 annually*
Making Music. (Rural Music Schools Association;
Standing Conference for Amateur Music) (3).
Lionel Nutley, ed. Little Benslow Hills, Hitchin,
Herts SG4 9RD t Hitchin 3446; advts JEP &
Associates Ltd, 107-11 Fleet St, London EC4A 2AB
t 01-353 3712. *25p*
Matrix jazz record research magazine (4). G. W. G.
Hulme, ed. Matrix Publications, 30 Hughes Rd,
Hayes, Middx UB3 3AW t 01-573 0331. *£1.50 annually*
Melody Maker (52). Ray Coleman, ed. IPC Specialist
and Professional Press Ltd, 23-34 Meymott St,
London SE1 9LU t 01-261 8000. *12p*
Melody Maker Year Book (1). Ray Coleman, ed. IPC
Specialist and Professional Press Ltd, 23-34 Mey-
mott St, London SE1 9LU t 01-261 8000
Music Accord (12). Francis Wright, ed. 5 Univer-
sity Rd, Leicester LE1 7RA. *10p*
Music and Letters (4). Denis Arnold and Edward
Olleson, eds. 32 Holywell St, Oxford OX1 3SL;
advts Oxford University Press, 44 Conduit St,
London W1R ODE; subs Oxford University Press,
Sub dept, Press Rd, London NW10 t 01-450 8080. *60p*
Music and Life (4). (Music Group of Communist Party).
16 King St, London WC2 t 01-836 2151. *5p*
Music and Liturgy (Society of St Gregory) (4). Paul
Inwood, ed. 102 Palace Gates Rd, London N22 4BL
t 01-802 1485. *£3 annually*
Music and Musicians (12). Michael Reynolds, ed.
Hansom Books, Artillery Mansions, 75 Victoria St,
London SW1 OHZ t 01-799 4452. *50p*
Music in Education (6). Gordon Reynolds, ed.
Novello & Co Ltd, 1-3 Upper James St, London W1R
4BP t 01-734 8080 ext 7160. *15p*
Music Journal (Incorporated Society of Musicians)
(3). Brian Newbould, ed. 48 Gloucester Pl,
London W1H 3HJ t 01-935 9791
Music Review (4). A. F. Leighton Thomas, ed.
Heffers Printers Ltd, King's Hedges Rd, Cambridge
CB4 2PQ t Cambridge (Cambs) 51571. *£9 annually*
Music Stand (music in the classroom) (3). Rex

Billingham, ed. J. & W. Chester Ltd, Eagle Ct, London EC1M 5QD t 01-253 6947. *40p*

Music Stand (5). Beresford King-Smith, ed. City of Birmingham Symphony Orchestra, 60 Newhall St, Birmingham B3 3RP t 021-236 1555. *15p*

Music Teacher (12). David Renouf, ed. Evans Bros Ltd, Montague Ho, Russell Sq, London WC1B 5BX t 01-636 8521. *35p*

Music Trade Directory (biennial). Music Industry Publications, 351 Cheriton Rd, Folkestone, Kent t Folkestone 75222. *£1.80*

Music Trades International (12). Philip Absalom, ed. Trade Papers (London) Ltd, 46-7 Chancery La, London WC2A 1JB t 01-405 5334. *£5.45 annually*

Music Trades International Directory (1). Philip Absalom, ed. 46-7 Chancery La, London WC2H 1JB t 01-405 5334

Music Week (52). Brian Mulligan, ed. Billboard Ltd, 7 Carnaby St, London W1V 1PG t 01-437 8090. *55p*

Music Week Year Book (1). Billboard Ltd, 7 Carnaby St, London W1V 1PG t 01-437 8090. *£2.50*

Musical Opinion (12). Laurence Swinyard, ed. Musical Opinion Ltd, 87 Wellington St, Luton, Beds LU1 5AF t Luton 30963. *25p*

Musical Salvationist (4). 117 Judd St, London WC1H 9NN t 01-387 1656. *12p*

Musical Times, The (12). Stanley Sadie, ed. Novello & Co Ltd, 1-3 Upper James St, London W1R 4BP t 01-734 8080. *35p*

Musician, The (52). 101 Queen Victoria St, London EC4P 4EP t 01-236 5222; Salvationist Publishing and Supplies Ltd, 117-121 Judd St, London WC1H 9NN t 01-387 1656. *5p*

NAO Yearbook (1). J. J. Black (Publishers) Ltd, Somerset Ho, Cranleigh, Surrey t Cranleigh 3554

New Cassettes and Cartridges (12). Francis Antony Ltd, Trenance Mill, Blowinghouse Hill, St Austell, Cornwall PL25 5AH t St Austell 3476. *6p, £1.60 annually*

New Musical Express (52). Nick Logan, ed. 128 Long Acre, London WC2E 9QH t 01-240 2266. *12p*

New Records (12). Francis Antony Ltd, Trenance Mill, Blowinghouse Hill, St Austell, Cornwall PL25 5AH t St Austell 3476. *6p, £1.60 annually*

New Singles (50). Francis Antony Ltd, Trenance Mill, Blowinghouse Hill, St Austell, Cornwall PL25 5AH t St Austell 3476. *£4.75 annually*

NODA Bulletin (3). National Operatic and Dramatic Association, 1 Crestfield St, London WC1H 8AU t 01-837 5655

Okie (12). Norah Swallow, ed. 43 Thirlmere Av,
   Westfield, Wyke, Bradford BD12 9DS t Bradford
   674848. *5p*
Opera (13). Harold Rosenthal, ed. 6 Woodland Rise,
   London N10 3UH t 01-883 4415; advts John Heller,
   Cheiron Press Ltd, 8-10 Parkway, London NW1 7AD;
   publishers: Seymour Press Ltd, 334 Brixton Rd,
   London SW9 t 01-733 4444. *40p*
Opry (country and western mus) (12). Brian A.
   Chalker, ed. Country Music Enterprises, 2 Beech-
   brook Ho, Lubbock Rd, Chislehurst, Kent t 01-467
   6181; advts Country Music Enterprises, 98 Count-
   ford Av, Walderslade, nr Chatham, Kent t Medway
   62123. *17½p*
Organ (4). Laurence Swinyard, ed. Musical Opinion
   Ltd, 87 Wellington St, Luton, Beds LU1 5AF t Luton
   30963. *60p*
Organists' Review (4). Basil Ramsey, ed. 604 Ray-
   leigh Rd, Eastwood, Leigh-on-Sea, Essex SS9 5HU t
   Southend-on-Sea 524305; advts Trevor Tildsley, 9
   Hill View, Milton, Stoke-on-Trent ST2 7AR
Piano Tuners' Quarterly (Braille) (4). A. J. Le-
   Feuvre, ed. Royal National Institute for the
   Blind, 224 Gt Portland St, London W1N 6AA t 01-388
   1266. *25p annually*
Popular Hi-Fi (12). Hugh Johnstone, ed. Haymarket
   Publishing Ltd, Gillow Ho, Winsley St, London W1N
   7AQ t 01-636 3600. *25p*
Proceedings of the Royal Musical Association (1).
   Edward Olleson, ed. Cambridge Music Shop, 1 All
   Saints' Passage, Cambridge CB2 3LT
Record and Radio Mirror (52). Peter Jones, ed.
   Billboard Publications, 7 Carnaby St, London W1V
   1PG t 01-437 8090. *7p*
Recorded Sound (4). (British Institute of Recorded
   Sound), 29 Exhibition Rd, London SW7 t 01-589
   6603/4. *£1.25*
Recorder and Music (4). Edgar Hunt, ed. 48 Gt
   Marlborough St, London W1V 2BN t 01-437 1246. *25p*
Records and Recording (12). Trevor Richardson, ed.
   Hansom Books, Artillery Mansions, 75 Victoria St,
   London SW1H OHZ t. 01-799 4452. *40p*
Rolling Stone (pop) (26). Andrew Bailey, ed.
   Straight Arrow Publishers Ltd, 25 Newman St, London
   W1P 3HA t 01-637 4038. *20p*
Sounding Brass (4). (National Association of Brass
   Band Conductors). Bram Gay, Edward Gregson, eds.
   Novello & Co Ltd, 1-3 Upper James St, London W1R
   4BP t 01-734 8080. *15p*
Sounds (52). W. Walker, ed. Spotlight Publications
   Ltd, 1-11 Benwell Rd, London N7 t 01-607 6411. *6p*

Sound Verdict (1). The Director of Libraries & Arts,
   London Borough of Camden, St Pancras Library, 100
   Euston Rd, London NW1 2AJ t 01-278 4444. *50p*
Stage (52). Peter Hepple, ed. 19 Tavistock St,
   London WC2E 7PA t 01-836 5213. *8p*
Strad (12). Novello & Co Ltd, 1-3 Upper James St,
   London W1R 4BP t 01-734 8080. *10p*
Studio Sound (12). Michael Thorne, ed. Link House
   Publications Ltd, Link Ho, Dingwall Av, Croydon
   CR9 2TA t 01-686 2599. *35p*
Tape Guide, The (3). Richard Robson, ed. Cardfont
   Publishers Ltd, 7 Carnaby St, London W1V 1PG t
   01-437 8090. *60p*
Tempo (4). David Drew, ed. Boosey & Hawkes Ltd,
   295 Regent St, London W1A 1BR t 01-580 2060. *40p*

27 Youth Festivals

Competitive festivals on a local basis are listed in
the *British Music Yearbook*. There is customarily
provision for entry on the basis of age. The
following festivals are national or international in
scope.

International Festival of Youth Brass and Symphonic
   Bands. Annual (Aug). Inquiries: 24 Cadogan Sq,
   London SW1X OJP t 01-235 6641
International Festival of Youth Orchestras and
   Performing Arts. In London and Aberdeen. Annual
   (Aug). Inquiries: 24 Cadogan Sq, London SW1X OJP
   t 01-235 6641
National Festival of Music for Youth. At Fairfield
   Halls, Croydon, Surrey. Annual (July). Inquiries:
   Festival Director, 23a Kings Rd, London SW3 4RP t
   01-730 2628

Section Six

QUICK-REFERENCE GUIDE

to Universities
and Principal Colleges of Music

Universities: Courses and Facilities

See p. 86 for addresses, staff lists, etc. The
table on the following pages represents the answers
supplied in summer 1975 by the institutions to a
questionnaire. The answers should be regarded as
minimal, based on the necessity for drawing border-
lines of information: e.g. an institution which is
entered as *not* having an electronic music studio may
have a portable synthesizer available; accommodation listed as available for first-year students
may also be available for second-year, etc. The
student-staff ratio (in certain cases not available)
should be treated as an approximation and does not
necessarily account for part-time teachers.

Universities are listed alphabetically by name,
except that the Queen's University, Belfast, is listed
under 'Belfast'.

		ABERDEEN	BELFAST	BIRMINGHAM
A.	**ENTRANCE.** Is A-level music (or equivalent) normally required?	Yes	Yes	Yes
B. ⑴	**FIRST DEGREE.** 1) Name of music-only degree course, with length in years.	B Mus 3 or 4	B Mus 4	B Mus 3 or 4
	2) Name of course combining music with other subject(s) with length in years.	MA 3 or 4	BA 3 or 4	BA 3
	3) Is performance, apart from keyboard harmony, optional (O) or compulsory (C) in first-degree course?	O	O	C
C.	**HIGHER DEGREES.** 1) Name of higher degree(s) in music.	M Mus M Litt D Mus Ph D	MA Ph D	MA Ph D
	2) Can composition be offered for higher degree?	Yes	Yes	No
D.	**SPECIAL FACILITIES.** Are the following available under the guidance of university teaching staff? 1) Choral chapel services	Yes	No	No
	2) Orchestra	Yes	Yes	Yes
	3) Chorus	Yes	Yes	Yes
	4) Early music (pre-1700) group	Yes	Yes	Yes
	5) Electronic music studio	Yes	No	No
	Is opera mounted 6) officially by music department	Yes	No	Yes
	7) by a university society?	Yes	Yes	Yes
E.	**PERFORMANCE TEACHING.** Is instrumental/vocal tuition provided 1) by staff lecturers?	Yes	No	No
	2) by visiting teachers?	Yes	No	No
	3) at a near-by college of music?	No	Yes	Yes
F.	**STUDENT-STAFF RATIO.**	7:1	7:1	—
G.	**ACCOMMODATION.** 1) Is residential accommodation on or near campus available for 1st-year students?	Yes	Yes	Yes
	2) Are practice-rooms available on university premises?	Yes	Yes	Yes

	BRISTOL	CAMBRIDGE	CITY UNIVERSITY	DURHAM	EAST ANGLIA	EDINBURGH	EXETER	GLASGOW	HULL	KEELE
	Yes	Yes	No	Yes	Yes	Yes	Yes	Yes	Yes	Yes
	BA 3	BA 3	BSc 3 or 4	BA 3	BA 3	B Mus 3 or 4	BA 3 B Mus 3	B Mus 3 or 4	BA 3 B Mus 3	–
	BA 3 or 4	–	–	BA 3	–	BA 3 BSc 3	BA 3	MA 3 or 4	BA 3	BA3 or 4 BSc 3
	O	C	C	O	C	C	C	C	O	O
	MA M Mus M Litt Ph D D Mus	B Mus M Litt Ph D Mus D	–	MA M Mus Ph D	M Mus M Phil Ph D	M Mus Ph D D Mus	M Mus MA Ph D	Ph D D Mus	MA M Mus Ph D	MA Ph D
	Yes	Yes	No	Yes	Yes	Yes	Yes	Yes	Yes	Yes
	No	Yes	No	No	Yes	No	No	Yes	Yes	Yes
	Yes	Yes	Yes	No	Yes	Yes	Yes	Yes	Yes	Yes
	Yes	Yes	Yes	No	Yes	Yes	Yes	Yes	Yes	Yes
	Yes	Yes	Yes	Yes	Yes	Yes	Yes	Yes	Yes	Yes
	No	No	Yes	Yes	Yes	No	No	Yes	No	Yes
	No	No	No	No	No	No	No	No	No	No
	Yes	Yes	No	Yes	Yes	Yes	Yes	Yes	Yes	No
	No	No	No	Yes	No	No	No	No	No	No
	No	Yes	No	Yes	Yes	Yes	Yes	No	Yes	Yes
	No	No	Yes	No	Yes	No	No	No	No	Yes
	7:1	15:1	–	–	8:1	7:1	9:1	8.5:1	10.3:1	6:1
	Yes	Yes	Yes	Yes	Yes	Yes	Yes	Yes	Yes	Yes
	Yes	Yes	Yes	Yes	Yes	Yes	Yes	Yes	Yes	Yes

		LANCASTER	LEEDS	LEICESTER
A.	**ENTRANCE.** Is A-level music (or equivalent) normally required?	Yes	Yes	No
B.	**FIRST DEGREE.** 1) Name of music-only degree course, with length in years.	BA 3	BA 3	–
	2) Name of course combining music with other subject(s) with length in years.	BA 3 B Sc 3	BA 3 B Sc 3	BA 3
	3) Is performance, apart from keyboard harmony, optional (O) or compulsory (C) in first-degree course?	O	C	O
C.	**HIGHER DEGREES.** 1) Name of higher degree(s) in music.	M Litt Ph D	B Mus M Phil Ph D	MA M Phil Ph D
	2) Can composition be offered for higher degree?	Yes	Yes	No
D.	**SPECIAL FACILITIES.** Are the following available under the guidance of university teaching staff? 1) Choral chapel services	Yes	No	No
	2) Orchestra	Yes	Yes	Yes
	3) Chorus	Yes	Yes	Yes
	4) Early music (pre-1700) group	Yes	Yes	Yes
	5) Electronic music studio	Yes	No	No
	Is opera mounted 6) officially by music department?	Yes	No	Yes
	7) by a university society?	Yes	Yes	Yes
E.	**PERFORMANCE TEACHING.** Is instrumental/vocal tuition provided 1) by staff lecturers?	Yes	No	Yes
	2) by visiting teachers?	Yes	Yes	Yes
	3) at a near-by college of music?	No	No	No
F.	**STUDENT-STAFF RATIO.**	6:1	10:1	–
G.	**ACCOMMODATION.** 1) Is residential accommodation on or near campus available for 1st-year students?	Yes	Yes	Yes
	2) Are practice-rooms available on university premises?	Yes	Yes	Yes

LIVERPOOL	LONDON GOLDSMITHS	KINGS	ROYAL HOLLOWAY	SCHOOL OF ORIENTAL AND AFRICAN STUDIES	MANCHESTER	NEWCASTLE UPON TYNE	NOTTINGHAM	OXFORD
Yes	Yes	Yes	Yes	Yes	Yes	Yes	Yes	Yes
BA 3	B Mus 3	B Mus 3	B Mus 3	–	B Mus 3 or 4	BA 3	B Mus 3	BA 3
BA 3	–	B Sc 3 BA 3	BA 3 or 4	BA 3	–	BA 3	BA 3	–
C	O	O	O	O	O	C	C	O
B Mus MA Ph D	M Mus	M Mus M Phil Ph D	M Phil M Mus Ph D	MA Ph D	Mus M Ph D Mus D	MA M Litt M Mus Ph D	MA M Phil Ph D	B Litt B Mus B Phil D Phil
Yes	No	Yes	No	No	Yes	Yes	Yes	Yes
No	No	No	Yes	No	No	No	Yes	Yes
Yes	Yes	Yes	Yes	No	Yes	Yes	Yes	Yes
Yes	Yes	Yes	Yes	No	Yes	Yes	Yes	Yes
Yes	No	Yes	Yes	No	Yes	Yes	Yes	Yes
No	Yes	No	Yes	No	No	No	No	Yes
Yes	Yes	Yes	No	No	No	No	No	No
Yes	Yes	Yes	Yes	No	No	Yes	Yes	Yes
No	Yes	Yes	No	Yes	Yes	No	No	No
Yes	Yes	Yes	Yes	No	No	No	Yes	Yes
No	Yes	Yes	No	No	Yes	No	No	No
8:1	–	7:1	–	–	8:1	7:1	–	13:1
Yes	Yes	Yes	Yes	Yes	Yes	Yes	Yes	Yes
Yes	Yes	Yes	Yes	Yes	Yes	Yes	Yes	Yes

		READING	ST ANDREWS	SALFORD
A.	**ENTRANCE.** Is A-level music (or equivalent) normally required?	Yes	Yes	No
B.	**FIRST DEGREE.** 1) Name of music-only degree course, with length in years.	BA 3	–	–
	2) Name of course combining music with other subject(s) with length in years.	BA 3 or 4 B Sc 3	MA 3 or 4	B Sc 3
	3) Is performance, apart from keyboard harmony, optional (O) or compulsory (C) in first-degree courses?	C	O	O
C.	**HIGHER DEGREES.** 1) Name of higher degree(s) in music.	B Mus M Phil Ph D	B Phil Ph D	–
	2) Can composition be offered for higher degree?	Yes	No	No
D.	**SPECIAL FACILITIES.** Are the following available under the guidance of university teaching staff? 1) Choral chapel services	No	Yes	No
	2) Orchestra	Yes	Yes	Yes
	3) Chorus	Yes	Yes	Yes
	4) Early music (pre-1700) group	No	Yes	No
	5) Electronic music studio	Yes	No	No
	Is opera mounted 6) officially by music department?	No	No	No
	7) by a university society?	Yes	Yes	No
E.	**PERFORMANCE TEACHING.** Is instrumental/vocal tuition provided 1) by staff lecturers?	Yes	No	Yes
	2) by visiting teachers?	Yes	Yes	Yes
	3) at a near-by college of music?	No	No	No
F.	**STUDENT-STAFF RATIO.**	7.5:1	–	–
G.	**ACCOMMODATION.** 1) Is residential accommodation on or near campus available for 1st-year students?	Yes	Yes	Yes
	2) Are practice-rooms available on university premises?	Yes	Yes	Yes

SHEFFIELD	SOUTHAMPTON	SURREY	SUSSEX	*WALES* ABERYSTWYTH	BANGOR	CARDIFF	YORK
Yes	Yes	Yes	Yes	Yes	Yes	Yes	Yes
B Mus 3	BA 3	B Mus 3 or 4	–	B Mus 3	B Mus 3	B Mus 3	BA 3
BA 3	BA 3	–	BA 3	BA 3	BA 3	BA 3	BA 3
O	O	C	C	O	O	O	C
MA D Mus Ph D	M Mus M Phil Ph D	M Mus M Phil Ph D	MA M Phil D Phil	MA M Mus Ph D	M Mus MA Ph D	MA M Mus Ph D	B Phil M Phil D Phil
No	Yes	Yes	Yes	Yes	Yes	Yes	Yes
No	No	No	Yes	No	No	No	No
Yes	Yes	Yes	Yes	Yes	Yes	Yes	Yes
Yes	Yes	Yes	Yes	Yes	Yes	Yes	Yes
Yes	Yes	Yes	Yes	No	No	Yes	Yes
Yes	Yes	Yes	Yes	No	Yes	Yes	Yes
Yes	Yes	No	No	Yes	No	Yes	Yes
Yes	No	Yes	No	Yes	No	No	No
No	Yes	No	Yes	Yes	Yes	Yes	No
Yes	Yes	Yes	No	Yes	Yes	Yes	Yes
No	No	No	Yes	No	Yes	No	No
12:1	8:1	8.5:1	11:1	–	6.9:1	15.5:1	12:1
Yes	Yes	Yes	Yes	Yes	Yes	No	Yes
Yes	Yes	Yes	Yes	Yes	Yes	Yes	Yes

Principal Colleges of Music: Courses and Facilities

See p. 103 for addresses, staffs, etc. The table on
the following pages represents the answers supplied
in summer 1975 by the institutions to a questionnaire.
The answers should be regarded as *minimal*, based on
the necessity for drawing border-lines of information:
e.g. an institution which is entered as *not* keeping
its practice-rooms open 'at least six hours on
Sunday' may have *some* Sunday opening; an institution
which lists only one *orchestra* may nevertheless have
other almost comparable ensembles, such as a wind
band.

Note: the questions are numbered A to G and are
spread over *two* double-pages.

		BIRMINGHAM	DARTINGTON	GUILDHALL
A.	**ENTRANCE.** 1) Minimum number of A-levels required for 'diploma' or 'performers' (non-graduate-equivalent) courses.	0	0	0
	2) Minimum number of A-levels required for degree or graduate-equivalent course (eg GRSM)	0	2	1
	3) Minimum Associated Board (or equivalent) grade required for performers	8	8	8
	4) Is an audition compulsory for students from UK?	Yes	Yes	Yes
	5) Certified tape-recording (without audition) accepted from overseas students?	Yes	Yes	Yes
B.	**STANDARD COURSE.** 1) Name of first-degree, graduate-equivalent and diploma course(s) with normal length in years	GBSM 3 ABSM 3	BA (CNAA) 3	GGSM 3 AGSM 3 or 4
	2) In the course directed to performance, how many hours' weekly instruction is provided in the first year on the student's 'first-study' instrument (or voice)?	1	1	1
	3) In the course directed to performance, is a student invariably required to take a second instrument (or voice)?	Yes	Yes	No
	Are non-musical class subjects — eg languages, general history — available to 4) singers?	Yes	Yes	Yes
	5) others?	No	Yes	Yes
C.	**NON-STANDARD COURSES.** 1) Name of higher degree or diploma, with minimum length in years.	–	–	Cert Adv Studies 1 LGSMT (Mus Therapy)
	2) Are students of postgraduate or post-diploma status accepted for further studies without aiming at a fixed higher qualification?	Yes	Yes	Yes

HUDDERSFIELD	LONDON	NEWTON PARK	N E ESSEX	ROYAL ACADEMY	ROYAL COLLEGE	ROYAL NORTHERN	ROYAL SCOTTISH	TRINITY	WELSH COLLEGE
1	0	2	1	0	0	0	0	0	0
2	0	2	2	2	2	0	1	Deg:2 GTCL:0	1
8	7	7	8	0	0	8	8	8	8
Yes	Yes	Yes	Yes	Yes	Yes	Yes	Yes	Yes	Yes
No	Yes	No	No	No	Yes	Yes	Yes	Yes	Yes
BA (CNAA) 3. Dip 2 or 3	GLCM 3 LLCM 3 LLCM	BA (Hons)3 Dip HE 3 (Mus)2	BA (CNAA) 3	B Mus 3 GRSM 3 Perf 3	B Mus				
1	1	2	1½	1	1	2	1½	1	1
Yes	Yes	Yes	Yes	Yes	No	No	Yes	No	Yes
Yes	Yes	Yes	Yes	Yes	Yes	Yes	Yes	Yes	Yes
Yes	No	Yes	Yes	No	No	Yes	Yes	No	Yes
M Phil (CNAA) 2	–	–	–	–	Opera 2 Cert Adv Studies	–	–	–	Adv Cert 1
No	Yes	No	No	Yes	Yes	Yes	Yes	Yes	Yes

		BIRMINGHAM	DARTINGTON	GUILDHALL
D.	**SPECIAL FACILITIES.** 1) Number of college orchestras officially provided (including chamber orchestras).	4	2	2
	2) Number of college choruses officially provided (including chamber choruses).	2	2	2
	3) Is there special tuition in the ensemble performance of avantgarde music?	Yes	Yes	Yes
	4) Is there special tuition in the ensemble performance of early (pre-1700) music?	Yes	Yes	Yes
	5) Is there an electronic music studio in which instruction is provided?	No	Yes	Yes
	6) Is opera regularly performed with orchestra and in public?	Yes	No	Yes
E.	**PRACTICE.** Are practice rooms open during term-time 1) on weekday evenings till at least 9 pm?	Yes	Yes	Yes
	2) at least six hours on Saturday?	Yes	Yes	Yes
	3) at least six hours on Sunday?	Yes	Yes	No
	4) Are practice rooms open during (most of) vacations?	Yes	Yes	No
F.	**ACCOMMODATION.** Is accommodation in a hostel (or in similar centralized conditions) available for first-year students?	Yes	Yes	No
G.	**SUPPLEMENTARY.** 1) Is adult part-time study offered?	Yes	Yes	Yes
	2) Is there a junior department?	No	Yes	Yes
	3) Is the institution part of a bigger school (eg polytechnic, music-plus-drama school)?	Yes	Yes	Yes

HUDDERSFIELD	LONDON	NEWTON PARK	N E ESSEX	ROYAL ACADEMY	ROYAL COLLEGE	ROYAL NORTHERN	ROYAL SCOTTISH	TRINITY	WELSH COLLEGE
3	3	2	3	4	5	3	2	3	3
2	2	1	2	1	2	2	4	3	2
Yes	Yes	Yes	Yes	Yes	Yes	Yes	No	No	Yes
Yes	Yes	Yes	Yes	Yes	Yes	Yes	No	Yes	Yes
No	No	Yes	No	Yes	Yes	Yes	Yes	No	Yes
No	No	Yes	Yes	Yes	Yes	Yes	Yes	No	Yes
Yes	No	Yes	Yes	Yes	No	Yes	Yes	No	Yes
No	No	Yes	Yes	No	No	Yes	Yes	No	Yes
No	No	Yes	No	No	No	Yes	No	No	No
Yes	No	Yes	Yes	Yes	No	Yes	Yes	Yes	No
Yes	No	Yes	No	Yes	Yes	Yes	Yes (women)	Yes	No
No	No	No	Yes	No	No	No	Yes	Yes	Yes
Yes	Yes	No	Yes	Yes	Yes	Yes	Yes	Yes	Yes
Yes	No	Yes	Yes	No	No	No	Yes	No	Yes

INDEX

1 Persons

The following list is confined to living persons mentioned in the book. 'Miss' and 'Mrs' are specified where the name is otherwise identified only by initials.

Jones, Megan   208
Jones, M.G.   211
Jones, M.L. Glynne   70
Jones, Peter   234
Jones, Philip (oboe)   131
Jones, Philip (trumpet)
                           64,132
Jones, Richard D.P.   102
Jones, Richard Elfyn   101
Jones, Robert E.   151
Jones, Roderick   100
Jones, Rowland   102,108
Jonson, Guy   121
Jordan, David   129
Jorysz, Walter   131
Joseph, Vivian   122,138
Josephs, N.A.   91
Joubert, John   87
Joyce, Robert   142
Judd, Anthony   123
Judd, Roger   172
Judge, Brian R.   180
Just, Helen   126

Kaletsky, Jacob   138
Kallenberg, Gladys   98
Kantrovitch, Vera   138
Katona, Béla   138
Kautsch, Friederike   137
Kay, Constance   130
Kay, Edward J.   175
Kealey, Wilfrid   107,
                          109,115
Keaney, Jack   134,136
Keates, T.   161
Keating, G.M.   178
Keeffe, Bernard   137
Keeler, Ellis   108,129
Keetman, G.   70
Kellaway, Renna   104
Kelleher, Frank   141,142
Kelly, Alexander   121
Kelly, Bryan   68,124
Kelly, David   134
Kelynack, H.C.   152
Kemp, I.M.   88
Kemp-Potter, Joan   116
Kenny, Yvonne   64
Kent, Philip   141
Kerr, A.R.   201

Kershaw, D.   102
Keys, Ivor   23,87
Kidd, Cecil   132
Killick, Denys G.   231
Kimbell, David   89
Kimber, Anne   106
Kimberley, A.G.   155
Kinder, Geoffrey   106
King, A.V.   94
King, H.F.   225
King, Thea   127
Kingsley, Colin   90
Kingsley, Elizabeth   215
King-Smith, Beresford   233
Kingswood, Peter   100
Kinnear, George   93,138,140
Kitchin, Alfred   138
Kitching, Gerald   107
Kite, Christopher   109
Kliewer, V.L.   70
Kneale, H.P.   149
Knight, A.R.   194
Knight, Miss B.M.   179
Knight, B.E.   183
Knight, Norman   123
Knowles, Clifford   131
Kohler, Irene   138
Kok, Alexander   144
Kok, Felix   126
Kruszynski, Michael   112,114
Kutcher, Samuel   138

Ladds, F.W.   202
Laine, Cleo   64
Laing, Dave   232
Lake, Ian   125
Lambert, Catherine   125
Lambert, John   124,128
Laming, S. Metheringham   96
Lamont, Madge   207
Lampard, Ann   64
Landon, H.C. Robbins   101
Lane, B.M.   76
Lane, Michael   70,106
Lang, Miss J.F.E.   151
Langdon, John   134,136
Lange, Hans Jung   110
Langford, Audrey   143
Langford, William   64
Langley, Enid   140

2 Towns and Institutions

The following list refers to institutions mentioned in the Directory (i.e. between pp. 75 and 235), plus towns or cities (excluding London) principally as specified in the addresses of these institutions.
  Where an institution's title begins with 'Association...', 'Society...' or 'National Association...', it is indexed under its subsequent specialist name: e.g. the Association for Adult Education is indexed as *Adult Education, Association for*.

ADVERTISEMENT INDEX

Patron: Her Majesty The Queen / President: Her Royal Highness The Duchess of Kent
Principal: John Manduell, FRAM, FRNCM, Hon FTCL

Graduate and Postgraduate Courses

conducted by distinguished staff in the College's
six academic departments headed by
**Cecil Aronowitz, Terence Greaves, Clifton Helliwell,
Philip Jones, John Wray** and **Alexander Young**
and in the opera unit by **Joseph Ward**

RESIDENTIAL ACCOMMODATION
in **Hartley Hall,** the College's extensively modernised residence,
which also possesses recreational and sporting facilities

CONCERTS, OPERA, DRAMA, DANCE, RECITALS, TALKS and EXHIBITIONS
held regularly in the College's Concert Hall, Opera Theatre
Recital Room and Public Concourse

LIBRARY FACILITIES
with fast growing audio, performance and reference sections

ENTRANCE and SCHOLARSHIPS
obtainable by competitive examination

PREPARATORY STUDY
in the Junior School at the College

CONFERENCE FACILITIES

The Prospectus may be obtained by application to
The Secretary for Admissions and Examinations
Information about Public Events at the College
may be obtained from The Events Co-ordinator
Enquires about Conference Facilities or Hire of Halls
should be addressed to The Accommodation Officer

Royal Northern College of Music
124 Oxford Road
Manchester M13 9RD
Telephone: 061-273-6283

Kingsway Princeton College

Principal F.D. Flower
MBE, BA, BSc (Econ)
Sidmouth Street
Tel: 01-837 8185

Full-time Course for the Young Musician

This two-year course is designed to meet the educational requirements of gifted young musicians between 16 and 18 years old looking towards the possibility of a career in music either as performers or teachers. Students are prepared for college entrance auditions and examinations and for A levels.

For further details write to:
Head of Arts and Languages Dept
Kingsway-Princeton College
Sidmouth Street
LONDON WC1H 8JB

SUMMER SCHOOLS
In August annually at Downe House, Berkshire

SINGERS AND PIANISTS WEEK
Solo and choral singing; Madrigals and Motets; Conducting and Training Choirs. Lectures on aspects of piano teaching and performance, including preparation for Associated Board examinations; Piano Accompanists Course. Evening recitals by distinguished artists, and concerts by students.

CHAMBER MUSIC
Wind and String Ensembles; Chamber Orchestra; Young Pianists Course; Evening Concerts by the Medici Quartet, and concerts by students.

MUSIC IN SCHOOL
Classroom Ensembles; Kodaly Method; Instrumental Conducting; Contemporary Music in the School; Choral Singing and Repertoire; CSE and GCE Preparation; Chamber Orchestra; Evening Concerts.

SCHOOL ORCHESTRA COURSE (12-19 years)
Daily rehearsals and sectional coaching for final concerts open to the public.
Talks, films, swimming, folk dance parties.
Colour brochures available from: Summer Schools, 106 Gloucester Place, London W1H 3DB. Please enclose 6½p stamp, and specify your particular interest.

These Summer Schools are organised by The British Federation of Music Festivals (incorporating The Music Teachers Association).

Now available

BRITISH MUSIC YEARBOOK 1976

Approximately 800 pages, £10.50

An Abbreviated Table of Contents

MUSICIAN OF THE YEAR:
Benjamin Britten as Conductor and Performer — An appreciation by John Culshaw, with complete discography

SURVEY AND STATISTICS
Musical Britain: Report; awards; appointments; obituary
London Concerts: Report; first performances; débuts
London Opera: Report; first night cast lists
Concerts Outside London: Report; first performances
Opera Outside London: Report; major new productions
Pop: Report; awards
On Stage and Screen: Report
New on Record: Report
Radio: Report; broadcast premières
Television: Report
Dance: First performances
Books on Music

REFERENCE ARTICLES

The Musician and the Law
The Musician and Insurance
The Musician and Income Tax
The Musician, Business and
  VAT
Copyright in Music
Copyright: Some Practical
  Obligations
Beginning a Performer's Career
The Young Composer's Path

Publicity for Music
Guiding the Musical Child
Higher Education in Music
The BBC and Music
Postage of Musical Material
Public Transport of Instruments
Standard Contracts and
  Agreements
Standards of Musical
  Measurement

DIRECTORY

Government offices; Radio and television; Trade and professional associations; Amateur organizations, etc.

Halls, theatres; Agents and promoters; Orchestras, opera companies, ensembles; Opera producers; Pop soloists and groups; Composers, librettists, translators

Festivals; Competitions (UK and abroad); Young performers' concert schemes

Record Companies; Music Publishers; Book Publishers; Music Criticism; Music Periodicals

Education, Libraries, Museums

Music in Places of Worship

Military and Brass Bands; Folk Music; Music and the Disabled

*   *   *

Some extracts from reviews of the 1975 edition:

I would recommend anyone working in the professional music world as agent, concert promoter, educationalist or performer to have a copy.   *— Music and Musicians*

The British Music Yearbook has quickly established itself as an indispensable reference work covering every aspect of British musical life.   *— Daily Telegraph*

Whatever did we do before this publication first appeared? No matter what one wants to look up — it's all there.   *— The Gramophone*

No practising musician, classical or pop, no professional musician or agent or teacher or journalist, should be without it.   *— Music Week*

Anybody whose business is music should not be without this book.   *— The Stage*

A necessity in our musical life as an essential handbook and guide to just about everything, brilliantly edited.   *— Yorkshire Post*

BRITISH MUSIC YEARBOOK 1976
Bowker Publishing Co. Ltd.

**MABEL FLETCHER
TECHNICAL COLLEGE**
Sandown Road, Liverpool, L15 4JB
Tel: 051-733 7211

Department of Music

HEAD OF DEPARTMENT: P. B. COOPER, M.A., B.Mus., A.R.C.M.

18 full-time staff (September 1975).
28 part-time staff including P.L.P.O. principals.
Full-time Courses:
    General Music
    Diploma in Music
    Diploma in Speech and Drama

The Diploma Courses include preparation for recognised external diplomas, and may be followed by a College of Education short course to complete teacher qualification.

Write for information to the Head of the Department of Music at the College.

Musical Instrument Technology Courses

This department offers full-time courses in the Design, Construction and Maintenance of Violins, Fretted instruments, Harpsichords, Early Woodwind instruments, Pianos and a course in Electronics as related to music and musical instruments.

There are also part-time courses in the Construction and Maintenance of Violins, Fretted instruments, Early Woodwind, Piano Tuning and Maintenance and Modern Woodwind Repair and Maintenance.

For details apply to:
**Department of Musical Instrument Technology,
London College of Furniture,
41-71 Commercial Road,
London E1 1LA**